Set in Africa and England, these nineteen stories offer a variety of background and mood, but certain themes suggest themselves again and again:

"One Off the Short List" is a scarifying story of a calculated seduction that lays bare the weakness and egotism of a professional philanderer.

"The New Man" tells of the brief, intensely felt encounter of a middle-aged man and a nymphet—from Lolita's viewpoint.

In "Each Other," a young woman sees her husband off to work, then receives into her marriage bed a clandestine lover—her own brother.

Not for the timid or conventional reader, these are stories of unflinching candor, written with artistry, power, and extraordinary passion by one of the most important English writers of our day.

A
MAN
AND
TWO WOMEN

. .
.

Stories by Doris Lessing

BALLANTINE BOOKS • NEW YORK

With acknowledgments to
the *New Reasoner,* the *New Statesman,*
Encounter, Partisan Review,
Kenyon Review, London Magazine

This edition published by arrangement with Simon and
Schuster, Inc.

First Printing: October, 1965

Library of Congress Catalog Card Number: 63-19277
Manufactured in the United States of America

BALLANTINE BOOKS, INC.,
101 Fifth Avenue, New York, N. Y. 10003

For Clancy

Contents

One off the Short List

•

•   •

WHEN he had first seen Barbara Coles, some years before, he only noticed her because someone said: "That's Johnson's new girl." He certainly had not used of her the private erotic formula: *Yes, that one.* He even wondered what Johnson saw in her. "She won't last long," he remembered thinking, as he watched Johnson, a handsome man, but rather flushed with drink, flirting with some unknown girl while Barbara stood by a wall looking on. He thought she had a sullen expression.

She was a pale girl, not slim, for her frame was generous, but her figure could pass as good. Her straight yellow hair was parted on one side in a way that struck him as gauche. He did not notice what she wore. But her eyes were all right, he remembered: large, and solidly green, square-looking because of some trick of the flesh at their corners. Emeraldlike eyes in the face of a schoolgirl, or young schoolmistress who was watching her lover flirt and would later sulk about it.

Her name sometimes cropped up in the papers. She was a stage decorator, a designer, something on those lines.

Then a Sunday newspaper had a competition for stage design and she won it. Barbara Coles was one of the "names" in the theatre, and her photograph was seen about. It was always serious. He remembered having thought her sullen.

One night he saw her across the room at a party. She was talking with a well-known actor. Her yellow hair was still done on one side, but now it looked sophisticated. She wore an emerald ring on her right hand that seemed deliberately to invite comparison with her eyes. He walked over and said: "We have met before, Graham Spence." He noted, with discomfort, that he sounded abrupt. "I'm sorry, I don't remem-

9

ber, but how do you do?" she said, smiling. And continued her conversation.

He hung around a bit, but soon she went off with a group of people she was inviting to her home for a drink. She did not invite Graham. There was about her an assurance, a carelessness, that he recognised as the signature of success. It was then, watching her laugh as she went off with her friends, that he used the formula: *"Yes, that one."* And he went home to his wife with enjoyable expectation, as if his date with Barbara Coles were already arranged.

His marriage was twenty years old. At first it had been stormy, painful, tragic—full of partings, betrayals and sweet reconciliations. It had taken him at least a decade to realise that there was nothing remarkable about this marriage that he had lived through with such surprise of the mind and the senses. On the contrary, the marriages of most of the people he knew, whether they were first, second or third attempts, were just the same. His had run true to form even to the serious love affair with the young girl for whose sake he had *almost* divorced his wife—yet at the last moment had changed his mind, letting the girl down so that he must have her for always (not unpleasurably) on his conscience. It was with humiliation that he had understood that this drama was not at all the unique thing he had imagined. It was nothing more than the experience of everyone in his circle. And presumably in everybody else's circle too?

Anyway, round about the tenth year of his marriage he had seen a good many things clearly, a certain kind of emotional adventure went from his life, and the marriage itself changed.

His wife had married a poor youth with a great future as a writer. Sacrifices had been made, chiefly by her, for that future. He was neither unaware of them, nor ungrateful; in fact he felt permanently guilty about it. He at last published a decently successful book, then a second which now, thank God, no one remembered. He had drifted into radio, television, book reviewing.

He understood he was not going to make it; that he had become—not a hack, no one could call him that—but a member of that army of people who live by their wits on the fringes of the arts. The moment of realisation was when he was in a pub one lunchtime near the B.B.C. where he often dropped in to meet others like himself: he understood that was why he went there—they *were* like him. Just as that melodramatic marriage had turned out to be like everyone else's—except that it had been shared with one woman instead of with two or three—so it had turned out that his unique talent, his struggles as a writer had led him here, to this pub and the half dozen pubs like it, where all the men in sight had the same history. They all had their novel, their play, their book of poems, a moment of fame, to their credit. Yet here they were, running television programmes about which they were cynical (to each other or to their wives) or writing reviews about other people's books. Yes, that's what he had become, an impresario of other people's talent. These two moments of clarity, about his marriage and about his talent, had roughly coincided; and (perhaps not by chance) had coincided with his wife's decision to leave him for a man younger than himself who had a future, she said, as a playwright. Well, he had talked her out of it. For her part she had to understand he was not going to be the T. S. Eliot or Graham Greene of our time—but after all, how many were? She must finally understand this, for he could no longer bear her awful bitterness. For his part he must stop coming home drunk at five in the morning, and starting a new romantic affair every six months which he took so seriously that he made her miserable because of her implied deficiencies. In short he was to be a good husband. (He had always been a dutiful father.) And she a good wife. And so it was: the marriage became stable, as they say.

The formula: *Yes, that one* no longer implied a necessarily sexual relationship. In its more mature form, it was far from being something he was ashamed of. On the contrary, it expressed a humorous respect for what he was, for his real talents and flair, which had turned out to be not artistic after all, but to do with emotional life, hard-earned experience. It expressed an ironical dignity, a proving to himself not only: I can be honest about myself, but also: I have earned the best in *that* field whenever I want it.

He watched the field for the women who were well known in the arts, or in politics; looked out for photographs, listened for bits of gossip. He made a point of going to see them act, or dance, or orate. He built up a not unshrewd picture of them. He would either quietly pull strings to meet her or—more often, for there was a gambler's pleasure in waiting—bide his time until he met her in the natural course of events, which was bound to happen sooner or later. He would be seen out with her a few times in public, which was in order, since his work meant he had to entertain well-known people, male and female. His wife always knew, he told her. He might have a brief affair with this woman, but more often than not it was the appearance of an affair. Not that he didn't get pleasure from other people envying him—he would make a point, for instance, of taking this woman into the pubs where his male colleagues went. It was that his real pleasure came when he saw her surprise at how well she was understood by him. He enjoyed the atmosphere he was able to set up between an intelligent woman and himself: a humorous complicity which had in it much that was unspoken, and which almost made sex irrelevant.

Onto the list of women with whom he planned to have this relationship went Barbara Coles. There was no hurry. Next week, next month, next year, they would meet at a party. The world of well-known people in London is a small one. Big and little fishes, they drift around, nose each other, flirt their fins, wriggle off again. When he bumped into Barbara Coles, it would be time to decide whether or not to sleep with her.

Meanwhile he listened. But he didn't discover much. She had a husband and children, but the husband seemed to be in the background. The children were charming and well brought up, like everyone else's children. She had affairs, they said; but while several men he met sounded familiar with her, it was hard to determine whether they had slept with her, because none directly boasted of her. She was spoken of in terms of her friends, her work, her house, a party she had given, a job she had found someone. She was liked, she was respected, and Graham Spence's self-esteem was flattered because he had chosen her. He looked forward to saying in just the same tone: "Barbara Coles asked me what I thought about the set and I told her quite frankly. . . ."

Then by chance he met a young man who did boast about Barbara Coles; he claimed to have had the great love affair with her, and recently at that; and he spoke of it as something generally known. Graham realised how much he had already become involved with her in his imagination because of how perturbed he was now, on account of the character of this youth, Jack Kennaway. He had recently become successful as a magazine editor—one of those young men who, not as rare as one might suppose in the big cities, are successful from sheer impertinence, effrontery. Without much talent or taste, yet he had the charm of his effrontery. "Yes, I'm going to succeed, because I've decided to; yes, I may be stupid, but not so stupid that I don't know my deficiencies. Yes, I'm going to be successful because you people with integrity, etc., etc., simply don't believe in the possibility of people like me. You are too cowardly to stop me. Yes, I've taken your measure and I'm going to succeed because I've got the courage, not only to be unscrupulous, but to be quite frank about it. And besides, you admire me, you must, or otherwise you'd stop me. . . ." Well, that was young Jack Kennaway, and he shocked Graham. He was a tall, languishing young man, handsome in a dark melting way, and, it was quite clear, he was either asexual or homosexual. And this youth boasted of the favours of Barbara Coles; boasted, indeed, of her love. Either she was a raving neurotic with a taste for neurotics; or Jack Kennaway was a most accomplished liar; or she slept with anyone. Graham was intrigued. He took Jack Kennaway out to dinner in order to hear him talk about Barbara Coles. There was no doubt the two were pretty close—all those dinners, theatres, weekends in the country—Graham Spence felt he had put his finger on the secret pulse of Barbara Coles; and it was intolerable that he must wait to meet her; he decided to arrange it.

It became unnecessary. She was in the news again, with a run of luck. She had done a successful historical play, and immediately afterwards a modern play, and then a hit musical. In all three, the sets were remarked on. Graham saw some interviews in newspapers and on television. These all centered around the theme of her being able to deal easily with so many different styles of theatre; but the real point was, of course, that she was a woman, which naturally added piquancy to the thing. And now Graham Spence was asked to do a half-hour radio interview with her. He planned the questions he would ask her with care, drawing on what people had said of her, but above all on his instinct and experience with women. The interview was to be at nine-thirty at night; he was to pick her up at six from the theatre where she was currently at work, so that there would be time, as the letter from the B.B.C. had put it, "for you and Miss Coles to get to know each other."

At six he was at the stage door, but a message from Miss Coles said she was not quite ready, could he wait a little. He hung about, then went to the pub opposite for a quick one, but still no Miss Coles. So he made his way backstage, directed by voices, hammering, laughter. It was badly lit, and the group of people at work did not see him. The director, James Poynter, had his arm around Barbara's shoulders. He was newly well-known, a carelessly good-looking young man reputed to be intelligent. Barbara Coles wore a dark blue overall, and her flat hair fell over her face so that she kept pushing it back with the hand that had the emerald on it. These two stood close, side by side. Three young men, stage-hands, were on the other side of a trestle which had sketches and drawings on it. They were studying some sketches. Barbara said, in a voice warm with energy: "Well, so I thought if we did *this*—do you see, James? What do you think, Steven?" "Well, love," said the young man she called Steven, "I see your idea, but I wonder if . . ." "I think you're right, Babs," said the director. "Look," said Barbara, holding one of the sketches towards Steven, "look, let me show you." They all leaned forward, the five of them, absorbed in the business.

Suddenly Graham couldn't stand it. He understood he was shaken to his depths. He went off stage, and stood with his back against a wall in the dingy passage that led to the dressing rooms. His eyes were filled with tears. He was seeing what a long way he had come from the crude, uncompromising, admirable young egomaniac he had been when he was twenty. That group of people there—working, joking, arguing, yes, that's what he hadn't known for years. What bound them was the democracy of respect for each other's work, a confidence in themselves and in each other. They looked like people banded together against a world which they—no, not despised, but which they measured, understood, would fight to the death, out of respect for what *they* stood for, for what *it* stood for. It was a long time since he felt part of that balance. And he understood that he had seen Barbara Coles when she was most herself, at ease with a group of people she worked with. It was then, with the tears drying on his eyelids, which felt old and ironic, that he decided he would sleep with Barbara Coles. It was a necessity for him. He went back through the door onto the stage, burning with this single determination.

The five were still together. Barbara had a length of blue gleaming stuff which she was draping over the shoulder of Steven, the stagehand. He was showing it off, and the others watched. "What do you think, James?" she asked the director. "We've got that sort of dirty green, and I thought . . ." "Well," said James, not sure at all, "well, Babs, well . . ."

Now Graham went forward so that he stood beside Barbara, and said: "I'm Graham Spence, we've met before." For the second time she smiled socially and said: "Oh I'm sorry, I don't remember." Graham nodded at James, whom he had known, or at least had met off and on, for years. But it was obvious James didn't remember him either.

"From the B.B.C.," said Graham to Barbara, again sounding abrupt, against his will. "Oh I'm sorry, I'm so sorry, I forgot all about it. I've got to be interviewed," she said to the group. "Mr. Spence is a journalist." Graham allowed himself a small smile ironical of the word journalist, but she was not looking at him. She was going on with her work. "We should decide tonight," she said. "Steven's right." "Yes, I am right," said the stagehand. "She's right, James, we need that blue with that sludge-green everywhere." "James," said Barbara, "James, what's wrong with it? You haven't said." She moved forward to James, passing Graham. Remembering him again, she became contrite. "I'm sorry," she said, "we can none of us agree. Well, look"—she turned to Graham—"you advise us, we've got so involved with it that . . ." At which James laughed, and so did the stagehands. "No, Babs," said James, "of course Mr. Spence can't advise. He's just this moment come in. We've got to decide. Well I'll give you till tomorrow morning. Time to go home, it must be six by now."

"It's nearly seven," said Graham, taking command.

"It isn't!" said Barbara, dramatic. "My God, how terrible, how appalling, how could I have done such a thing. . . ." She was laughing at herself. "Well, you'll have to forgive me, Mr. Spence, because you haven't got any alternative."

They began laughing again: this was clearly a group joke. And now Graham took his chance. He said firmly, as if he were her director, in fact copying James Poynter's manner with her: "No, Miss Coles, I won't forgive you, I've been kicking my heels for nearly an hour." She grimaced, then laughed and accepted it. James said: "There, Babs, that's how you ought to be treated. We spoil you." He kissed her on the cheek, she kissed him on both his, the stagehands moved off. "Have a good evening, Babs," said James, going, and nodding to Graham, who stood concealing his pleasure with difficulty. He knew, because he had had the courage to be firm, indeed, peremptory, with Barbara, that he had saved himself hours of maneuvering. Several drinks, a dinner—perhaps two or three evenings of drinks and dinners—had been saved because he was now on this footing with Barbara Coles, a man who could say: "No, I won't forgive you, you've kept me waiting."

She said: "I've just got to . . ." and went ahead of him. In the passage she hung her overall on a peg. She was thinking, it seemed, of something else, but seeing him watching her, she smiled at him, companionably: he realised with triumph it was the sort of smile she would offer one of the stagehands, or even James. She said again: "Just one second . . ." and went to the stage-door office. She and the stage doorman conferred. There was some problem. Graham said, taking another chance: "What's the trouble, can I help?"—as if he could help, as if he expected to be able to. "Well . . ." she said, frowning. Then, to the man: "No, it'll be all right. Goodnight." She came to Graham. "We've got ourselves into a bit of a fuss because half the set's in Liverpool and half's here and—but it will sort itself out." She stood, at ease, chatting to him, one colleague to another. All this was admirable, he felt; but there would be a bad moment when they emerged from the special atmosphere of the theatre into the street. He took another decision, grasped her arm firmly, and said: "We're going to have a drink before we do anything at all, it's a terrible evening out." Her arm felt resistant, but remained within his. It was raining outside, luckily. He directed her, authoritative: "No, not that pub, there's a nicer one around the corner." "Oh, but I like this pub," said Barbara, "we always use it."

"Of course you do," he said to himself. But in that pub there would be the stagehands, and probably James, and he'd lose contact with her. He'd become a *journalist* again. He took her firmly out of danger around two corners, into a pub he picked at random. A quick look around—no, they weren't there. At least, if there were people from the theatre, she showed no sign. She asked for a beer. He ordered her a double Scotch, which she accepted. Then, having won a dozen preliminary rounds already, he took time to think. Something was bothering him—what? Yes, it was what he had observed backstage, Barbara and James Poynter. Was she having an affair with him? Because if so, it would all be much more difficult. He made himself see the two of them together, and thought with a jealousy surprisingly strong: *Yes, that's it.* Meantime he sat looking at her, seeing himself look at her, *a man gazing in calm appreciation at a woman:* waiting for her to feel it and respond. She was examining the pub. Her white woollen suit was belted, and had a not unprovocative suggestion of being a uniform. Her flat yellow hair, hastily pushed back after work, was untidy. Her clear white skin, without any colour, made her look tired. Not very exciting, at the moment, thought Graham, but maintaining his appreciative pose for when she would turn and see it. He knew what she would see: he was relying not only on the "warm kindly" beam of his gaze, for this was merely a reinforcement of the impression he knew he made. He had black hair, a little greyed. His clothes were loose and bulky—masculine. His eyes were humorous and appreciative. He was not, never had been, concerned to lessen the impression of being settled, dependable: the husband and father. On the contrary, he knew women found it reassuring.

When she at last turned she said, almost apologetic: "Would you mind if we sat down? I've been lugging great things around all day." She had spotted two empty chairs in a corner. So had he, but rejected them, because there were other people at the table. "But my dear, of course!" They took the chairs, and then Barbara said: "If you'll excuse me a moment." She had remembered she needed make-up. He watched her go off, annoyed with himself. She was tired; and he could have understood, protected, sheltered. He realised that in the other pub, with the people she had worked with all day, she would not have thought: "I must make myself up, I must be on show." That was for outsiders. She had not, until now, considered Graham an outsider, because of his taking his chance to seem one of the working group in the theatre; but now he had thrown his opportunity away. She returned armoured. Her hair was sleek, no longer defenceless. And she had made up her eyes. Her eyebrows were untouched, pale gold streaks above the brilliant green eyes whose lashes were blackened. Rather good, he thought, the contrast. Yes, but the moment had gone when he could say: Did you know you had a smudge on your cheek? Or— my dear girl!—pushing her hair back with the edge of a brotherly hand. In fact, unless he was careful, he'd be back at starting point.

He remarked: "That emerald is very cunning"—smiling into her eyes.

She smiled politely, and said: "It's not cunning, it's an accident, it was my grandmother's." She flirted her hand lightly by her face, though, smiling. But that was something she had done before, to a compliment she had had before, and often. It was all social, she had become social entirely. She remarked: "Didn't you say it was half past nine we had to record?"

"My dear Barbara, we've got two hours. We'll have another drink or two, then I'll ask you a couple of questions, then we'll drop down to the studio and get it over, and then we'll have a comfortable supper."

"I'd rather eat now, if you don't mind. I had no lunch, and I'm really hungry."

"But my dear, of course." He was angry. Just as he had been surprised by his real jealousy over James, so now he was thrown off balance by his anger: he had been counting on the long quiet dinner afterwards to establish intimacy. "Finish your drink and I'll take you to Nott's." Nott's was expensive. He glanced at her assessingly as he mentioned it. She said: "I wonder if you know Butler's? It's good and it's rather close." Butler's was good, and it was cheap, and he gave her a good mark for liking it. But Nott's it was going to be. "My dear, we'll get into a taxi and be at Nott's in a moment, don't worry."

She obediently got to her feet: the way she did it made him understand how badly he had slipped. She was saying to herself: Very well, he's like that, then all right, I'll do what he wants and get it over with. . . .

Swallowing his own drink he followed her, and took her arm in the pub doorway. It was polite within his. Outside it drizzled. No taxi. He was having bad luck now. They walked in silence to the end of the street. There Barbara glanced into a side street where a sign said: BUTLER'S. Not to remind him of it, on the contrary, she concealed the glance. And here she was, entirely at his disposal, they might never have shared the comradely moment in the theatre.

They walked half a mile to Nott's. No taxis. She made conversation: this was, he saw, to cover any embarrassment he might feel because of a half-mile walk through rain when she was tired. She was talking about some theory to do with the theatre, with designs for theatre building. He heard himself saying, and repeatedly: Yes, yes, yes. He thought about Nott's, how to get things right when they reached Nott's. There he took the headwaiter aside, gave him a pound, and instructions. They were put in a corner. Large Scotches appeared. The menus were spread. "And now, my dear," he said, "I apologise for dragging you here, but I hope you'll think it's worth it."

"Oh, it's charming, I've always liked it. It's just that . . ." She stopped herself saying: it's such a long way. She smiled at him, raising her glass, and said: "It's one of my very favourite places, and I'm glad you dragged me here." Her voice was flat with tiredness. All this was appalling; he knew it; and he sat thinking how to retrieve his position. Meanwhile she fingered the menu. The headwaiter took the order, but Graham made a gesture which said: Wait a moment. He wanted the Scotch to take effect before she ate. But she saw his silent order; and, without annoyance or reproach, leaned forward to say, sounding patient: "Graham, please, I've got to eat, you don't want me drunk when you interview me, do you?"

"They are bringing it as fast as they can," he said, making

it sound as if she were greedy. He looked neither at the headwaiter nor at Barbara. He noted in himself, as he slipped further and further away from contact with her, a cold determination growing in him; one apart from, apparently, any conscious act of will, that come what may, if it took all night, he'd be in her bed before morning. And now, seeing the small pale face, with the enormous green eyes, it was for the first time that he imagined her in his arms. Although he had said: *Yes, that one,* weeks ago, it was only now that he imagined her as a sensual experience. Now he did, so strongly that he could only glance at her, and then away towards the waiters who were bringing food.

"Thank the Lord," said Barbara, and all at once her voice was gay and intimate. "Thank heavens. Thank every power that is. . . ." She was making fun of her own exaggeration; and, as he saw, because she wanted to put him at his ease after his boorishness over delaying the food. (She hadn't been taken in, he saw, humiliated, disliking her.) "Thank all the gods of Nott's," she went on, "because if I hadn't eaten inside five minutes I'd have died, I tell you." With which she picked up her knife and fork and began on her steak. He poured wine, smiling with her, thinking that *this* moment of closeness he would not throw away. He watched her frank hunger as she ate, and thought: Sensual—it's strange I hadn't wondered whether she would be or not.

"Now," she said, sitting back, having taken the edge off her hunger: "Let's get to work."

He said: "I've thought it over very carefully—how to present you. The first thing seems to me, we must get away from that old chestnut: Miss Coles, how extraordinary for a woman to be so versatile in her work . . . I hope you agree?" This was his trump card. He had noted, when he had seen her on television, her polite smile when this note was struck. (The smile he had seen so often tonight.) This smile said: All right, if you *have* to be stupid, what can I do?

Now she laughed and said: "What a relief. I was afraid you were going to do the same thing."

"Good, now you eat and I'll talk."

In his carefully prepared monologue he spoke of the different styles of theatre she had shown herself mistress of, but not directly: he was flattering her on the breadth of her experience; the complexity of her character, as shown in her work. She ate, steadily, her face showing nothing. At last she asked: "And how did you plan to introduce this?"

He had meant to spring that on her as a surprise, something like: Miss Coles, a surprisingly young woman for what she has accomplished (she was thirty? thirty-two?) and a very attractive one. . . . "Perhaps I can give you an idea of what she's like if I say she could be taken for the film star Marie Carletta. . . ." The Carletta was a strong earthy blonde, known to be intellectual. He now saw he could not possibly say this: he could imagine her cool look if he did. She said: "Do you mind if we get away from all that—my manifold talents, et cetera. . . ." He felt himself stiffen with annoyance; particularly because this was not an accusation, he saw she did not think him worth one. She had assessed him: This is the kind of man who uses this kind of flattery and therefore. . . . It made him angrier that she did not even trouble to say: Why did you do exactly what you promised you wouldn't? She was being invincibly polite, trying to conceal her patience with his stupidity.

"After all," she was saying, "it is a stage designer's job to design what comes up. Would anyone take, let's say Johnnie Cranmore" (another stage designer) "onto the air or television and say: How very versatile you are because you did that musical about Java last month and a modern play about Irish labourers this?"

He battened down his anger. "My dear Barbara, I'm sorry. I didn't realise that what I said would sound just like the mixture as before. So what shall we talk about?"

"What I was saying as we walked to the restaurant: can we get away from the personal stuff?"

Now he almost panicked. Then, thank God, he laughed from nervousness, for she laughed and said: "You didn't hear one word I said."

"No, I didn't. I was frightened you were going to be furious because I made you walk so far when you were tired."

They laughed together, back to where they had been in the theatre. He leaned over, took her hand, kissed it. He said: "Tell me again." He thought: Damn, now she's going to be earnest and intellectual.

But he understood he had been stupid. He had forgotten

himself at twenty—or, for that matter, at thirty; forgotten one could live inside an idea, a set of ideas, with enthusiasm. For in talking about her ideas (also the ideas of the people she worked with) for a new theatre, a new style of theatre, she was as she had been with her colleagues over the sketches or the blue material. She was easy, informal, almost chattering. This was how, he remembered, one talked about ideas that were a breath of life. The ideas, he thought, were intelligent enough; and he would agree with them, with her, if he believed it mattered a damn one way or another, if any of these enthusiasms mattered a damn. But at least he now had the key, he knew what to do. At the end of not more than half an hour, they were again two professionals, talking about ideas they shared, for he remembered caring about all this himself once. *When? How many years ago was it that he had been able to care?*

At last he said: "My dear Barbara, do you realise the impossible position you're putting me in? Margaret Ruyen who runs this programme is determined to do you personally, the poor woman hasn't got a serious thought in her head."

Barbara frowned. He put his hand on hers, teasing her for the frown: "No, wait, trust me, we'll circumvent her." She smiled. In fact Margaret Ruyen had left it all to him, had said nothing about Miss Coles.

"They aren't very bright—the brass," he said. "Well, never mind: we'll work out what we want, do it, and it'll be a *fait accompli.*"

"Thank you, what a relief. How lucky I was to be given you to interview me." She was relaxed now, because of the whisky, the food, the wine, above all because of this new complicity against Margaret Ruyen. It would all be easy. They worked out five or six questions, over coffee, and took a taxi through rain to the studios. He noted that the cold necessity to have her, to make her, to beat her down, had left him. He was even seeing himself, as the evening ended, kissing her on the cheek and going home to his wife. This comradeship was extraordinarily pleasant. It was balm to the wound he had not known he carried until that evening, when he had had to accept the justice of the word *journalist.* He felt he could talk forever about the state of the theatre, its finances, the stupidity of the government, the philistinism of . . .

At the studios he was careful to make a joke so that they walked in on the laugh. He was careful that the interview began at once, without conversation with Margaret Ruyen; and that from the moment the green light went on, his voice lost its easy familiarity. He made sure that not one personal note was struck during the interview. Afterwards, Margaret Ruyen, who was pleased, came forward to say so; but he took her aside to say that Miss Coles was tired and needed to be taken home at once: for he knew this must look to Barbara as if he were squaring a producer who had been expecting a different interview. He led Barbara off, her hand held tight in his against his side. "Well," he said, "we've done it, and I don't think she knows what hit her."

"Thank you," she said, "it really was pleasant to talk about something sensible for once."

He kissed her lightly on the mouth. She returned it, smiling. By now he felt sure that the mood need not slip again, he could hold it.

"There are two things we can do," he said. "You can come to my club and have a drink. Or I can drive you home and you can give me a drink. I have to go past you."

"Where do you live?"

"Wimbledon." He lived, in fact, at Highgate; but she lived in Fulham. He was taking another chance, but by the time she found out, they would be in a position to laugh over his ruse.

"Good," she said. "You can drop me home then. I have to get up early." He made no comment. In the taxi he took her hand; it was heavy in his, and he asked: "Does James slave-drive you?"

"I didn't realize you knew him—no,, he doesn't."

"Well I don't know him intimately. What's he like to work with?"

"Wonderful," she said at once. "There's no one I enjoy working with more."

Jealousy spurted in him. He could not help himself: "Are you having an affair with him?"

She looked: what's it to do with you? but said: "No, I'm not."

"He's very attractive," he said, with a chuckle of worldly complicity. She said nothing, and he insisted: "If I were a woman I'd have an affair with James."

It seemed she might very well say nothing. But she remarked: "He's married."

His spirits rose in a swoop. It was the first stupid remark she had made. It was a remark of such staggering stupidity that . . . he let out a humoring snort of laughter, put his arm around her, kissed her, said: "My dear little Babs."

She said: "Why Babs?"

"Is that the prerogative of James. And of the stagehands?" he could not prevent himself adding.

"I'm only called that at work." She was stiff inside his arm.

"My dear Barbara, then . . ." He waited for her to enlighten and explain, but she said nothing. Soon she moved out of his arm, on the pretext of lighting a cigarette. He lit it for her. He noted that his determination to lay her, and at all costs, had come back. They were outside her house. He said quickly: "And now, Barbara, you can make me a cup of coffee and give me a brandy." She hesitated; but he was out of the taxi, paying, opening the door for her. The house had no lights on, he noted. He said: "We'll be very quiet so as not to wake the children."

She turned her head slowly to look at him. She said, flat, replying to his real question: "My husband is away. As for the children, they are visiting friends tonight." She now went ahead of him to the door of the house. It was a small house, in a terrace of small and not very pretty houses. Inside a little, bright, intimate hall, she said: "I'll go and make some coffee. Then, my friend, you must go home because I'm very tired."

The *my friend* struck him deep, because he had become vulnerable during their comradeship. He said gabbling: "You're annoyed with me—oh, please don't, I'm sorry."

She smiled, from a cool distance. He saw, in the small light from the ceiling, her extraordinary eyes. "Green" eyes are hazel, are brown with green flecks, are even blue. Eyes are chequered, flawed, changing. Hers were solid green, but really, he had never seen anything like them before. They were like very deep water. They were like—well, emeralds;

or the absolute clarity of green in the depths of a tree in summer. And now, as she smiled almost perpendicularly up at him, he saw a darkness come over them. Darkness swallowed the clear green. She said: "I'm not in the least annoyed." It was as if she had yawned with boredom. "And now I'll get the things . . . in there." She nodded at a white door and left him. He went into a long, very tidy white room, that had a narrow bed in one corner, a table covered with drawings, sketches, pencils. Tacked to the walls with drawing pins were swatches of coloured stuffs. Two small chairs stood near a low round table: an area of comfort in the working room. He was thinking: I wouldn't like it if my wife had a room like this. I wonder what Barbara's husband . . .? He had not thought of her till now in relation to her husband, or to her children. Hard to imagine her with a frying pan in her hand, or for that matter, cosy in the double bed.

A noise outside: he hastily arranged himself, leaning with one arm on the mantelpiece. She came in with a small tray that had cups, glasses, brandy, coffeepot. She looked abstracted. Graham was on the whole flattered by this: it probably meant she was at ease in his presence. He realised he was a little tight and rather tired. Of course, she was tired too, that was why she was vague. He remembered that earlier that evening he had lost a chance by not using her tiredness. Well now, if he were intelligent . . . She was about to pour coffee. He firmly took the coffeepot out of her hand, and nodded at a chair. Smiling, she obeyed him. "That's better," he said. He poured coffee, poured brandy, and pulled the table towards her. She watched him. Then he took her hand, kissed it, patted it, laid it down gently. Yes, he thought, I did that well.

Now, a problem. He wanted to be closer to her, but she was fitted into a damned silly little chair that had arms. If he were to sit by her on the floor . . . ? But no, for him, the big bulky reassuring man, there could be no casual gestures, no informal postures. Suppose I scoop her out of the chair onto the bed? He drank his coffee as he plotted. Yes, he'd carry her to the bed, but not yet.

"Graham," she said, setting down her cup. She was, he

saw with annoyance, looking tolerant. "Graham, in about half an hour I want to be in bed and asleep."

As she said this, she offered him a smile of amusement at this situation—man and woman maneuvering, the great comic situation. And with part of himself he could have shared it. Almost, he smiled with her, laughed. (Not till days later he exclaimed to himself: Lord what a mistake I made, not to share the joke with her then: that was where I went seriously wrong.) But he could not smile. His face was frozen, with a stiff pride. Not because she had been watching him plot; the amusement she now offered him took the sting out of that; but because of his revived determination that he was going to have his own way, he was going to have her. He was not going home. But he felt that he held a bunch of keys, and did not know which one to choose.

He lifted the second small chair opposite to Barbara, moving aside the coffee table for this purpose. He sat in this chair, leaned forward, took her two hands, and said: "My dear, don't make me go home yet, don't, I beg you." The trouble was, nothing had happened all evening that could be felt to lead up to these words and his tone—simple, dignified, human being pleading with human being for surcease. He saw himself leaning forward, his big hands swallowing her small ones; he saw his face, warm with the appeal. And he realised he had meant the words he used. They were nothing more than what he felt. He wanted to stay with her because she wanted him to, because he was her colleague, a fellow worker in the arts. He needed this desperately. But she was examining him, curious rather than surprised, and from a critical distance. He heard himself saying: "If James were here, I wonder what you'd do?" His voice was aggrieved; he saw the sudden dark descend over her eyes, and she said: "Graham, would you like some more coffee before you go?"

He said: "I've been wanting to meet you for years. I know a good many people who know you."

She leaned forward, poured herself a little more brandy, sat back, holding the glass between her two palms on her chest. An odd gesture: Graham felt that this vessel she was cherishing between her hands was herself. A patient, long-suffering gesture. He thought of various men who had mentioned her. He thought of Jack Kennaway, wavered, panicked, said: "For instance, Jack Kennaway."

And now, at the name, an emotion lit her eyes—what was it? He went on, deliberately testing this emotion, adding to it: "I had dinner with him last week—oh, quite by chance!— and he was talking about you."

"Was he?"

He remembered he had thought her sullen, all those years ago. Now she seemed defensive, and she frowned. He said: "In fact he spent most of the evening talking about you."

She said in short, breathless sentences, which he realised were due to anger: "I can very well imagine what he says. But surely you can't think I enjoy being reminded that . . ." She broke off, resenting him, he saw, because he forced her down onto a level she despised. But it was not his level either: it was all her fault, all hers! He couldn't remember not being in control of a situation with a woman for years. Again he felt like a man teetering on a tightrope. He said, trying to make good use of Jack Kennaway, even at this late hour: "Of course, he's a charming boy, but not a man at all."

She looked at him, silent, guarding her brandy glass against her breasts.

"Unless appearances are totally deceptive, of course." He could not resist probing, even though he knew it was fatal.

She said nothing.

"Do you know you are supposed to have had the great affair with Jack Kennaway?" he exclaimed, making this an amused expostulation against the fools who could believe it.

"So I am told." She set down her glass. "And now," she said, standing up, dismissing him. He lost his head, took a step forward, grabbed her in his arms, and groaned: "Barbara!"

She turned her face this way and that under his kisses. He snatched a diagnostic look at her expression—it was still patient. He placed his lips against her neck, groaned "Barbara" again, and waited. She would have to do something. Fight free, respond, something. She did nothing at all. At last she said: "For the Lord's sake, Graham!" She sounded amused: he was again being offered amusement. But if he shared it with her, it would be the end of this chance to have her. He clamped his mouth over hers, silencing her. She did not fight him off so much as blow him off. Her mouth treated his attacking mouth as a woman blows and laughs in water, puffing off waves or spray with a laugh, turning aside her head. It was a gesture half annoyance, half humour. He continued to kiss her while she moved her head and face about under the kisses as if they were small attacking waves.

And so began what, when he looked back on it afterwards, was the most embarrassing experience of his life. Even at the time he hated her for his ineptitude. For he held her there for what must have been nearly half an hour. She was much shorter than he, he had to bend, and his neck ached. He held her rigid, his thighs on either side of hers, her arms clamped to her side in a bear's hug. She was unable to move, except for her head. When his mouth ground hers open and his tongue moved and writhed inside it, she still remained passive. And he could not stop himself. While with his intelligence he watched this ridiculous scene, he was determined to go on, because sooner or later her body must soften in wanting his. And he could not stop because he could not face the horror of the moment when he set her free and she looked at him. And he hated her more, every moment. Catching glimpses of her great green eyes, open and dismal beneath his, he knew he had never disliked anything more than those "jewelled" eyes. They were repulsive to him. It occurred to him at last that even if by now she wanted him, he wouldn't know it, because she was not able to move at all. He cautiously loosened his hold so that she had an inch or so leeway. She remained quite passive. As if, he thought derisively, she had read or been told that the way to incite men maddened by lust was to fight them. He found he was thinking: Stupid cow, so you imagine I find you attractive, do you? You've got the conceit to think that!

The sheer, raving insanity of this thought hit him, opened his arms, his thighs, and lifted his tongue out of her mouth. She stepped back, wiping her mouth with the back of her hand, and stood dazed with incredulity. The embarrassment that lay in wait for him nearly engulfed him, but he let anger postpone it. She said positively apologetic, even, at this moment, humorous: "You're crazy, Graham. What's the matter, are you drunk? You don't seem drunk. You don't even find me attractive."

The blood of hatred went to his head and he gripped her again. Now she had got her face firmly twisted away so that he could not reach her mouth, and she repeated steadily as he kissed the parts of her cheeks and neck that were available to him: "Graham, let me go, do let me go, Graham." She went on saying this; he went on squeezing, grinding, kissing and licking. It might go on all night: it was a sheer contest of wills, nothing else. He thought: It's only a really masculine woman who wouldn't have given in by now out of sheer decency of the flesh! One thing he knew, however: that she would be in that bed, in his arms, and very soon. He let her go, but said: "I'm going to sleep with you tonight, you know that, don't you?"

She leaned with hand on the mantelpiece to steady herself. Her face was colourless, since he had licked all the makeup off. She seemed quite different: small and defenceless with her large mouth pale now, her smudged green eyes fringed with gold. And now, for the first time, he felt what it might have been supposed (certainly by her) he felt hours ago. Seeing the small damp flesh of her face, he felt kinship, intimacy with her, he felt intimacy of the flesh, the affection and good humour of sensuality. He felt she was flesh of his flesh, his sister in the flesh. He felt desire for her, instead of the will to have her; and because of this, was ashamed of the farce he had been playing. Now he desired simply to take her into bed in the affection of his senses.

She said: "What on earth am I supposed to do? Telephone for the police, or what?" He was hurt that she still addressed the man who had ground her into sulky apathy; she was not addressing *him* at all.

She said: "Or scream for the neighbours, is that what you want?"

The gold-fringed eyes were almost black, because of the depth of the shadow of boredom over them. She was bored and weary to the point of falling to the floor, he could see that.

He said: "I'm going to sleep with you."

"But how can you possibly want to?"—a reasonable, a civilised demand addressed to a man who (he could see) she believed would respond to it. She said: "You know I don't want to, and I know you don't really give a damn one way or the other."

He was stung back into being the boor because she had not the intelligence to see that the boor no longer existed; because she could not see that this was a man who wanted her in a way which she must respond to.

There she stood, supporting herself with one hand, looking small and white and exhausted, and utterly incredulous. She was going to turn and walk off out of simple incredulity, he could see that. "Do you think I don't mean it?" he demanded, grinding this out between his teeth. She made a movement—she was on the point of going away. His hand shot out on its own volition and grasped her wrist. She frowned. His other hand grasped her other wrist. His body hove up against hers to start the pressure of a new embrace. Before it could, she said: "Oh Lord, no, I'm not going through all that again. Right, then."

"What do you mean—right, then?" he demanded.

She said: "You're going to sleep with me. O.K. Anything rather than go through that again. Shall we get it over with?"

He grinned, saying in silence: "No darling, oh no you don't, I don't care what words you use, I'm going to have you now and that's all there is to it."

She shrugged. The contempt, the weariness of it, had no effect on him, because he was now again hating her so much that wanting her was like needing to kill something or someone.

She took her clothes off, as if she were going to bed by herself: her jacket, skirt, petticoat. She stood in white bra and panties, a rather solid girl, brown-skinned still from the summer. He felt a flash of affection for the brown girl with her loose yellow hair as she stood naked. She got into bed and lay there, while the green eyes looked at him in civilised appeal: Are you really going through with this? Do you have to? Yes, his eyes said back: I do have to. She shifted her gaze aside, to the wall, saying silently: Well, if you want to take me without any desire at all on my part, then go ahead, if you're not ashamed. He was not ashamed, because he was maintaining the flame of hate for her which he knew quite well was all that stood between him and shame. He took off his clothes, and got into bed beside her. As he did so, knowing he was putting himself in the position of raping a woman who was making it elaborately clear he bored her, his flesh subsided completely, sad, and full of reproach because a few moments ago it was reaching out for his sister whom he could have made happy. He lay on his side by her, secretly at work on himself, while he supported himself across her body on his elbow, using the free hand to manipulate her breasts. He saw that she gritted her teeth against his touch. At least she could not know that after all this fuss he was not potent.

In order to incite himself, he clasped her again. She felt his smallness, writhed free of him, sat up and said: "Lie down."

While she had been lying there, she had been thinking: The only way to get this over with is to make him big again, otherwise I've got to put up with him all night. His hatred of her was giving him a clairvoyance: he knew very well what went on through her mind. She had switched on, with the determination to *get it all over with,* a sensual good humour, a patience. He lay down. She squatted beside him, the light from the ceiling blooming on her brown shoulders, her flat fair hair falling over her face. But she would not look at his face. Like a bored, skilled wife, she was; or like a prostitute. She administered to him, she was setting herself to please him. Yes, he thought, she's sensual, or she could be. Meanwhile she was succeeding in defeating the reluctance of his flesh, which was the tender token of a possible desire for her, by using a cold skill that was the result of her contempt for him. Just as he decided: Right, it's enough, now I shall have her properly, she made him come. It was not a trick, to hurry or cheat him, what defeated him was her transparent thought: Yes, that's what he's worth.

Then, having succeeded, and waited for a moment or two, she stood up, naked, the fringes of gold at her loins and in her armpits speaking to him a language quite different from that of her green, bored eyes. She looked at him and thought, showing it plainly: What sort of man is it who . . . ? He watched the slight movement of her shoulders: a just-checked shrug. She went out of the room: then the sound of running water. Soon she came back in a white dressing gown, carrying a yellow towel. She handed him the towel, looking away in politeness as he used it. "Are you going home now?" she enquired hopefully, at this point.

"No, I'm not." He believed that now he would have to start fighting her again, but she lay down beside him, not touching him (he could feel the distaste of her flesh for his) and he thought: Very well, my dear, but there's a lot of the night left yet. He said aloud: "I'm going to have you properly tonight." She said nothing, lay silent, yawned. Then she remarked consolingly, and he could have laughed outright from sheer surprise: "Those were hardly conducive circumstances for making love." She was *consoling* him. He hated her for it. A proper little slut: I force her into bed, she doesn't want me, but she still has to make me feel good, like a prostitute. But even while he hated her he responded in kind, from the habit of sexual generosity. "It's because of my admiration for you, because . . . after all, I was holding in my arms one of the thousand women."

A pause. "The thousand?" she enquired, carefully.

"The thousand especial women."

"In Britain or in the world? You choose them for their brains, their beauty—what?"

"Whatever it is that makes them outstanding," he said, offering her a compliment.

"Well," she remarked at last, inciting him to be amused again: "I hope that at least there's a short list you can say I am on, for politeness' sake."

He did not reply for he understood he was sleepy. He was still telling himself that he must stay awake when he was slowly waking and it was morning. It was about eight. Barbara was not there. He thought: My God! What on earth shall I tell my wife? Where was Barbara? He remembered the ridiculous scenes of last night and nearly succumbed to shame. Then he thought, reviving anger: If she didn't sleep beside me here I'll never forgive her. . . . He sat up, quietly, determined to go through the house until he found her and, having found her, to possess her, when the door opened and she came in. She was fully dressed in a green suit, her hair done, her eyes made up. She carried a tray of coffee, which she set down beside the bed. He was conscious of his big loose hairy body, half uncovered. He said to himself that he was not going to lie in bed, naked, while she was dressed. He said: "Have you got a gown of some kind?" She handed him, without speaking, a towel, and said: "The bathroom's second on the left." She went out. He followed, the towel around him. Everything in this house was gay, intimate— not at all like her efficient working room. He wanted to find out where she had slept, and opened the first door. It was the kitchen, and she was in it, putting a brown earthen-ware dish into the oven. "The next door," said Barbara. He went hastily past the second door, and opened (he hoped quietly) the third. It was a cupboard full of linen. "This door," said Barbara, behind him.

"So all right then, where did you sleep?"

"What's it to do with you? Upstairs, in my own bed. Now, if you have everything, I'll say goodbye, I want to get to the theatre."

"I'll take you," he said at once.

He saw again the movement of her eyes, the dark swallowing the light in deadly boredom. "I'll take you," he insisted.

"I'd prefer to go by myself," she remarked. Then she smiled: "However, you'll take me. Then you'll make a point of coming right in, so that James and everyone can see— that's what you want to take me for, isn't it?"

He hated her, finally, and quite simply, for her intelligence; that not once had he got away with anything, that she had been watching, since they had met yesterday, every movement of his campaign for her. However, some fate or inner urge over which he had no control made him say sentimentally: "My dear, you must see that I'd like at least to take you to your work."

"Not at all, have it on me," she said, giving him the lie direct. She went past him to the room he had slept in. "I shall be leaving in ten minutes," she said.

He took a shower, fast. When he returned, the workroom was already tidied, the bed made, all signs of the night gone. Also, there were no signs of the coffee she had brought in for him. He did not like to ask for it, for fear of an out-right refusal. Besides, she was ready, her coat on, her hand-bag under her arm. He went, without a word, to the front door, and she came after him, silent.

He could see that every fibre of her body signalled a simple message: Oh God, for the moment when I can be rid of this boor! She was nothing but a slut, he thought.

A taxi came. In it she sat as far away from him as she could. He thought of what he should say to his wife.

Outside the theatre she remarked: "You could drop me here, if you liked." It was not a plea, she was too proud for that. "I'll take you in," he said, and saw her thinking: Very well, I'll go through with it to shame him. He was determined to take her in and hand her over to her colleagues, he was afraid she would give him the slip. But far from playing it down, she seemed determined to play it his way. At the stage door, she said to the doorman: "This is Mr. Spence, Tom—do you remember, Mr. Spence from last night?" "Good morning, Babs," said the man, examining Graham, politely, as he had been ordered to do.

Barbara went to the door to the stage, opened it, held it open for him. He went in first, then held it open for her. Together they walked into the cavernous, littered, badly lit place and she called out: "James, James!" A man's voice called out from the front of the house: "Here, Babs, why are you so late?"

The auditorium opened before them, darkish, silent, save for an early-morning busyness of charwomen. A vacuum cleaner roared, smally, somewhere close. A couple of stagehands stood looking up at a drop which had a design of blue and green spirals. James stood with his back to the auditorium, smoking. "You're late, Babs," he said again. He saw Graham behind her, and nodded. Barbara and James kissed. Barbara said, giving allowance to every syllable: "You remember Mr. Spence from last night?" James nodded: How do you do? Barbara stood beside him, and they looked together up at the blue-and-green backdrop. Then Barbara looked again at Graham, asking silently: All right now, isn't that enough? He could see her eyes, sullen with boredom.

He said: "Bye, Babs. Bye, James. I'll ring you, Babs." No response, she ignored him. He walked off slowly, listening for what might be said. For instance: "Babs, for God's sake, what are you doing with him?" Or she might say: "Are you wondering about Graham Spence? Let me explain."

Graham passed the stagehands who, he could have sworn,

didn't recognise him. Then at last he heard James's voice to Barbara: "It's no good, Babs, I know you're enamoured of that particular shade of blue, but do have another look at it, there's a good girl. . . ." Graham left the stage, went past the office where the stage doorman sat reading a newspaper. He looked up, nodded, went back to his paper. Graham went to find a taxi, thinking: I'd better think up something convincing, then I'll telephone my wife.

Luckily he had an excuse not to be at home that day, for this evening he had to interview a young man (for television) about his new novel.

The Story of Two Dogs

GETTING a new dog turned out to be more difficult than we thought, and for reasons rooted deep in the nature of our family. For what, on the face of it, could have been easier to find than a puppy once it had been decided: "Jock needs a companion, otherwise he'll spend his time with those dirty Kaffir dogs in the compound"? All the farms in the district had dogs who bred puppies of the most desirable sort. All the farm compounds owned miserable beasts kept hungry so that they would be good hunters for their meat-starved masters; though often enough puppies born to the cage-ribbed bitches from this world of mud huts were reared in white houses and turned out well. Jacob our builder heard we wanted another dog, and came up with a lively puppy on the end of a bit of rope. But we tactfully refused. The thin flea-bitten little object was not good enough for Jock, my mother said; though we children were only too ready to take it in.

Jock was a mongrel himself, a mixture of Alsatian, Rhodesian ridgeback, and some other breed—terrier?—that gave him ears too cocky and small above a long melancholy face. In short, he was nothing to boast of, outwardly: his qualities were all intrinsic or bestowed on him by my mother who had given this animal her heart when my brother went off to boarding school.

In theory Jock was my brother's dog. Yet why give a dog to a boy at that moment when he departs for school and will be away from home two-thirds of the year? In fact my brother's dog was his substitute; and my poor mother, whose children were always away being educated, because we were farmers, and farmers' children had no choice but to go to the cities for their schooling—my poor mother caressed Jock's too-small intelligent ears and crooned: "There, Jock! There, old boy! There, good dog, yes, you're a *good* dog, Jock, you're such a *good* dog. . . ." While my father said, uncomfortably: "For goodness sake, old girl, you'll ruin him, that isn't a house pet, he's not a lapdog, he's a farm dog." To which my mother said nothing, but her face put on a most familiar look of misunderstood suffering, and she bent it down close so that the flickering red tongue just touched her cheeks, and sang to him: "Poor old Jock then, yes, you're a poor old dog, you're not a rough farm dog, you're a good dog, and you're not strong, no you're delicate."

At this last word my brother protested; my father protested; and so did I. All of us, in our different ways, had refused to be "delicate"—had escaped from being "delicate"—and we wished to rescue a perfectly strong and healthy young dog from being forced into invalidism, as we all, at different times, had been. Also of course we all (and we knew it and felt guilty about it) were secretly pleased that Jock was now absorbing the force of my mother's pathetic need for something "delicate" to nurse and protect.

Yet there was something in the whole business that was a reproach to us. When my mother bent her sad face over the animal, stroking him with her beautiful white hands on which the rings had grown too large, and said: "There, good dog, yes Jock, you're such a gentleman—" well, there was something in all this that made us, my father, my brother and myself, need to explode with fury, or to take Jock away and make him run over the farm like the tough young brute he was, or go away ourselves forever so that we didn't have to hear the awful yearning intensity in her voice. Because it was entirely our fault that note was in her voice at all; if we had allowed ourselves to be delicate, and good, or even gentlemen or ladies, there would have been no need for Jock to sit between my mother's knees, his loyal noble head on her lap, while she caressed and yearned and suffered.

It was my father who decided there must be another dog, and for the expressed reason that otherwise Jock would be turned into a "sissy." (At this word, reminder of a hundred earlier battles, my brother flushed, looked sulky, and went right out of the room.) My mother would not hear of another dog until her Jock took to sneaking off to the farm compound to play with the Kaffir dogs. "Oh you bad dog, Jock," she said sorrowfully, "playing with those nasty dirty dogs, how could you, Jock!" And he would playfully, but in an agony of remorse, snap and lick at her face, while she bent the whole force of her inevitably betrayed self over him, crooning: "How could you, oh how could you, Jock?"

So there must be a new puppy. And since Jock was (at heart, despite his temporary lapse) noble and generous and above all well-bred, his companion must also possess these qualities. And which dog, where in the world, could possibly be good enough? My mother turned down a dozen puppies; but Jock was still going off to the compound, slinking back to gaze soulfully into my mother's eyes. This new puppy was to be my dog. I decided this: if my brother owned a dog, then it was only fair that I should. But my lack of force in claiming this puppy was because I was in the grip of abstract justice only. The fact was I didn't want a good noble and well-bred dog. I didn't know what I did want, but the idea of such a dog bored me. So I was content to let my mother turn down puppies, provided she kept her terrible maternal energy on Jock, and away from me.

Then the family went off for one of our long visits in another part of the country, driving from farm to farm to stop a night, or a day, or a meal, with friends. To the last place we were invited for the weekend. A distant cousin of my father, "a Norfolk man" (my father was from Essex), had married a woman who had nursed in the war (First World War) with my mother. They now lived in a small brick and iron house surrounded by granite *kopjes* that erupted everywhere from thick bush. They were as isolated as any people I've known, eighty miles from the nearest railway station. As my father said, they were "not suited," for they quarrelled or sent each other to Coventry all the weekend. However, it was not until much later that I thought about the pathos of these two people, living alone on a minute pension in the middle of the bush, and "not suited"; for that weekend I was in love.

It was night when we arrived, about eight in the evening, and an almost full moon floated heavy and yellow above a

stark granite-bouldered *kopje*. The bush around was black
and low and silent, except that the crickets made a small
incessant din. The car drew up outside a small boxlike structure whose iron roof glinted off moonlight. As the engine
stopped, the sound of crickets swelled up, the moonlight's
cold came in a breath of fragrance to our faces; and there
was the sound of a mad wild yapping. Behold, around the
corner of the house came a small black wriggling object that
hurled itself towards the car, changed course almost on
touching it, and hurtled off again, yapping in a high delirious
yammering which, while it faded behind the house, continued faintly, our ears, or at least mine, straining after it.

"Take no notice of that puppy," said our host, the man
from Norfolk. "It's been stark staring mad with the moon
every night this last week."

We went into the house, were fed, were looked after; I
was put to bed so that the grownups could talk freely. All
the time came the mad high yapping. In my tiny bedroom
I looked out onto a space of flat white sand that reflected
the moon between the house and the farm buildings, and
there hurtled a mad wild puppy, crazy with joy of life, or
moonlight, weaving back and forth, round and round, snapping at its own black shadow and tripping over its own clumsy feet—like a drunken moth around a candle flame, or like
. . . like nothing I've ever seen or heard of since.

The moon, large and remote and soft, stood up over the
trees, the empty white sand, the house which had unhappy
human beings in it; and a mad little dog yapping and beating its course of drunken joyous delirium. That, of course,
was my puppy; and when Mr. Barnes came out from the
house saying: "Now, now, come now, you lunatic animal . . ." finally almost throwing himself on the crazy
creature, to lift it in his arms still yapping and wriggling
and flapping around like a fish, so that he could carry it to
the packing case that was its kennel, I was already saying,
as anguished as a mother watching a stranger handle her
child: Careful now, careful, that's my dog.

Next day, after breakfast, I visited the packing case. Its
white wood oozed out resin that smelled tangy in hot sunlight, and its front was open and spilling out soft yellow
straw. On the straw a large beautiful black dog lay with her

head on outstretched forepaws. Beside her a brindled pup
lay on its fat back, its four paws sprawled every which way,
its eyes rolled up, as ecstatic with heat and food and laziness
as it had been the night before from the joy of movement. A
crust of mealie porridge was drying on its shining black lips
that were drawn slightly back to show perfect milk teeth. His
mother kept her eyes on him, but her pride was dimmed with
sleep and heat.

I went inside to announce my spiritual ownership of the
puppy. They were all around the breakfast table. The man
from Norfolk was swapping boyhood reminiscences (shared
in space, not time) with my father. His wife, her eyes still
red from the weeping that had followed a night quarrel, was
gossiping with my mother about the various London hos-
pitals where they had ministered to the wounded of the War
they had (apparently so enjoyably) shared.

My mother at once said: "Oh my dear, no, not that puppy,
didn't you see him last night? We'll never train him."

The man from Norfolk said I could have him with pleasure.

My father said he didn't see what was wrong with the
dog, if a dog was healthy that was all that mattered: my
mother dropped her eyes forlornly, and sat silent.

The man from Norfolk's wife said she couldn't bear to
part with the silly little thing, goodness knows there was little enough pleasure in her life.

The atmosphere of people at loggerheads being familiar to
me, it was not necessary for me to know *why* they disagreed,
or in what ways, or what criticisms they were going to make
about my puppy. I only knew that inner logics would in due
course work themselves out and the puppy would be mine.
I left the four people to talk about their differences through
a small puppy, and went to worship the animal, who was
now sitting in a patch of shade beside the sweet-wood-smell-
ing packing case, its dark brindled coat glistening, with dark
wet patches on it from its mother's ministering tongue. His
own pink tongue absurdly stuck out between white teeth,
as if he had been too careless or lazy to withdraw it into its
proper place under his equally pink wet palate. His brown
buttony beautiful eyes . . . but enough, he was an ordinary
mongrelly puppy.

Later I went back to the house to find out how the battle balanced: my mother had obviously won my father over, for he said he thought it was wiser not to have that puppy: "Bad blood tells, you know."

The bad blood was from the father, whose history delighted my fourteen-year-old imagination. This district being wild, scarcely populated, full of wild animals, even leopards and lions, the four policemen at the police station had a tougher task than in places nearer town; and they had bought half a dozen large dogs to (a) terrorise possible burglars around the police station itself and (b) surround themselves with an aura of controlled animal savagery. For the dogs were trained to kill if necessary. One of these dogs, a big ridgeback, had "gone wild." He had slipped his tether at the station and taken to the bush, living by himself on small buck, hares, birds, even stealing farmers' chickens. This dog, whose proud lonely shape had been a familiar one to farmers for years, on moonlit nights, or in grey dawns and dusks, standing aloof from human warmth and friendship, had taken Stella, my puppy's mother, off with him for a week of sport and hunting. She simply went away with him one morning; the Barneses had seen her go; had called after her; she had not even looked back. A week later she returned home at dawn and gave a low whine outside their bedroom window, saying: I'm home; and they woke to see their errant Stella standing erect in the paling moonlight, her nose pointed outwards and away from them towards a great powerful dog who seemed to signal to her with his slightly moving tail before fading into the bush. Mr. Barnes fired some futile shots into the bush after him. Then they both scolded Stella who in due time produced seven puppies, in all combinations of black, brown and gold. She was no pure-bred herself, though of course her owners thought she was, or ought to be, being their dog. The night the puppies were born, the man from Norfolk and his wife heard a sad wail or cry, and arose from their beds to see the wild police dog bending his head in at the packing-case door. All the bush was flooded with a pinkish-gold dawn light, and the dog looked as if he had an aureole of gold around him. Stella was half wailing, half growling her welcome, or protest, or fear at his great powerful reappearance and his thrusting muzzle so close to her seven helpless pups. They called out, and he turned his outlaw's head to the window where they stood side by side in striped pyjamas and embroidered pink silk. He put back his head and howled, he howled, a mad wild sound that gave them gooseflesh, so they said; but I did not understand that until years later when Bill the puppy "went wild" and I saw him that day on the antheap howling his pain of longing to an empty listening world.

The father of her puppies did not come near Stella again; but a month later he was shot dead at another farm, fifty miles away, coming out of a chicken run with a fine white Leghorn in his mouth; and by that time she had only one pup left, they had drowned the rest. It was bad blood, they said, no point in preserving it, they had only left her that one pup out of pity.

I said not a word as they told this cautionary tale, merely preserved the obstinate calm of someone who knows she will get her own way. Was right on my side? It was. Was I owed a dog? I was. Should anybody but myself choose my dog? No, but . . . very well then, I had chosen. I chose this dog. I chose it. Too late, I *had* chosen it.

Three days and three nights we spent at the Barneses' place. The days were hot and slow and full of sluggish emotions; and the two dogs slept in the packing case. At night, the four people stayed in the living room, a small brick place heated unendurably by the paraffin lamp whose oily yellow glow attracted moths and beetles in a perpetual whirling halo of small moving bodies. They talked, and I listened for the mad far yapping, and then I crept out into the cold moonlight. On the last night of our stay the moon was full, a great perfect white ball, its history marked on a face that seemed close enough to touch as it floated over the dark cricket-singing bush. And there on the white sand yapped and danced the crazy puppy, while his mother, the big beautiful animal, sat and watched, her intelligent yellow eyes slightly anxious as her muzzle followed the erratic movements of her child, the child of her dead mate from the bush. I crept up beside Stella, sat on the still-warm cement beside her, put my arm around her soft furry neck, and my head beside her alert moving head. I adjusted my breathing so that my rib cage moved up and down beside her, so as to be closer to the warmth of her barrelly furry chest, and together we turned our eyes from the great staring floating moon to the tiny black hurtling puppy who shot in circles from near us, so near he all but crashed into us, to two hundred yards away where he just missed the wheels of the farm waggon. We watched, and I felt the chill of moonlight deepen on Stella's fur, and on my own silk skin, while our ribs moved gently up and down together, and we waited until the man from Norfolk came to first shout, then yell, then fling himself on the mad little dog and shut him up in the wooden box where yellow bars of moonlight fell into black dog-smelling shadow. "There now, Stella girl, you go in with your puppy," said the man, bending to pat her head as she obediently went inside. She used her soft nose to push her puppy over. He was so exhausted that he fell and lay, his four legs stretched out and quivering like a shot dog, his breath squeezed in and out of him in small regular wheezy pants like whines, and so I left them, Stella and her puppy, to go to my bed in the little brick house which seemed literally crammed with hateful emotions. I went to sleep, thinking of the hurtling little dog, now at last asleep with exhaustion, his nose pushed against his mother's breathing black side, the slits of yellow moonlight moving over him through the boards of fragrant wood.

We took him away next morning, having first locked Stella in a room so that she could not see us go.

It was a three-hundred-mile drive, and all the way Bill yapped and panted and yawned and wriggled idiotically on his back on the lap of whoever held him, his eyes rolled up, his big paws lolling. He was a full-time charge for myself and my mother, and, after the city, my brother, whose holidays were starting. He, at first sight of the second dog, reverted to the role of Jock's master, and dismissed my animal as altogether less valuable material. My mother, by now Bill's slave, agreed with him, but invited him to admire the adorable wrinkles on the puppy's forehead. My father demanded irritably that both dogs should be "thoroughly trained."

Meanwhile, as the nightmare journey proceeded, it was noticeable that my mother talked more and more about Jock, guiltily, as if she had betrayed him. "Poor little Jock, what will he say?"

Jock was in fact a handsome young dog. More Alsatian than anything, he was a low-standing, thick-coated animal of a warm gold colour, with a vestigial "ridge" along his spine, rather wolflike, or foxlike, if one looked at him frontways, with his sharp cocked ears. And he was definitely not "little." There was something dignified about him from the moment he was out of puppyhood, even when he was being scolded by my mother for his visits to the compound.

The meeting, prepared for by us all with trepidation, went off in a way which was a credit to everyone, but particularly Jock, who regained my mother's heart at a stroke. The puppy was released from the car and carried to where Jock sat, noble and restrained as usual, waiting for us to greet him. Bill at once began weaving and yapping around the rocky space in front of the house. Then he saw Jock, bounded up to him, stopped a couple of feet away, sat down on his fat backside and yelped excitedly. Jock began a yawning, snapping movement of his head, making it go from side to side in half-snarling, half-laughing protest, while the puppy crept closer, right up, jumping at the older dog's lifted wrinkling muzzle. Jock did not move away; he forced himself to remain still, because he could see us all watching. At last he lifted up his paw, pushed Bill over with it, pinned him down, examined him, then sniffed and licked him. He had accepted him, and Bill had found a substitute for his mother who was presumably mourning his loss. We were able to leave the child (as my mother kept calling him) in Jock's infinitely patient care. "You are such a good dog, Jock," she said, overcome by this scene, and the other touching scenes that followed, all marked by Jock's extraordinary forbearance for what was, and even I had to admit it, an intolerably destructive little dog.

Training became urgent. But this was not at all easy, due, like the business of getting a new puppy, to the inner nature of the family.

To take only one difficulty: dogs must be trained by their masters, they must owe allegiance to one person. And who was Jock to obey? And Bill: I was his master, in theory. In practice, Jock was. Was I to take over from Jock? But even to state it is to expose its absurdity: what I adored was the graceless puppy, and what did I want with a well-trained dog? Trained for *what*?

A watchdog? But all our dogs were watchdogs. "Natives" —such was the article of faith—were by nature scared of dogs. Yet everyone repeated stories about thieves poisoning fierce dogs, or making friends with them. So apparently no one really believed that watchdogs were any use. Yet every farm had its watchdog.

Throughout my childhood I used to lie in bed, the bush not fifty yards away all around the house, listening to the cry of the nightjar, the owls, the frogs and the crickets; to the tom-toms from the compound; to the mysterious rustling in the thatch over my head, or the long grass it had been cut from down the hill; to all the thousand noises of the night on the veld; and every one of these noises was marked also by the house dogs, who would bark and sniff and investigate and growl at all these; and also at starlight on the polished surface of a leaf, at the moon lifting itself over the mountains, at a branch cracking behind the house, at the first rim of hot red showing above the horizon—in short at anything and everything. Watchdogs, in my experience, were never asleep; but they were not so much a guard against thieves (we never had any thieves that I can remember) as a kind of instrument designed to measure or record the rustlings and movements of the African night that seemed to have an enormous life of its own, but a collective life, so that the falling of a stone, or a star shooting through the Milky Way, the grunt of a wild pig, and the wind rustling in the mealie field were all evidences and aspects of the same truth.

How did one "train" a watchdog? Presumably to respond only to the slinking approach of a human, black or white. What use is a watchdog otherwise? But even now, the most powerful memory of my childhood is of lying awake listening to the sobbing howl of a dog at the inexplicable appearance of the yellow face of the moon; of creeping to the window to see the long muzzle of a dog pointed black against a great bowl of stars. We needed no moon calendar with those dogs, who were like traffic in London: to sleep at all, one had to learn not to hear them. And if one did not hear them, one would not hear the stiff warning growl that (presumably) would greet a marauder.

At first Jock and Bill were locked up in the dining room at night. But there were so many stirrings and yappings and rushings from window to window after the rising sun or moon, or the black shadows which moved across whitewashed walls from the branches of the trees in the garden, that soon we could no longer stand the lack of sleep, and they were turned out on to the verandah. With many hopeful injunctions from my mother that they were to be "good dogs": which meant that they should ignore their real natures and sleep from sundown to sunup. Even then, when Bill was just out of puppyhood, they might be missing altogether in the early mornings. They would come guiltily up the road from the lands at breakfasttime, their coats full of grass seeds, and we knew they had rushed down into the bush after an owl, or a grazing animal, and, finding themselves farther from home than they had expected in a strange nocturnal world, had begun nosing and sniffing and exploring in practice for their days of wildness soon to come.

So they weren't watchdogs. Hunting dogs perhaps? My brother undertook to train them, and we went through a long and absurd period of "Down, Jock," "To heel, Bill," while sticks of barley sugar balanced on noses, and paws were offered to be shaken by human hands, etc., etc. Through all this Jock suffered, bravely, but saying so clearly with every part of him that he would do anything to please my mother—he would send her glances half proud and half apologetic all the time my brother drilled him, that after an hour of training my brother would retreat, muttering that it was too hot, and Jock bounded off to lay his head on my mother's lap. As for Bill he never achieved anything. Never did he sit still with the golden lumps on his nose, he ate them at once. Never did he stay to heel. Never did he remember what he was supposed to do with his paw when one of us offered him a hand. The truth was, I understood then, watching the training sessions, that Bill was stupid. I pretended of course that he despised being trained, he found it humiliating; and that Jock's readiness to go through with the silly business showed his lack of spirit. But alas, there was no getting around it, Bill simply wasn't very bright.

Meanwhile he had ceased to be a fat charmer; he had become a lean young dog, good-looking, with his dark brindled coat, and his big head that had a touch of Newfoundland. He had a look of puppy about him still. For just as Jock seemed born elderly, had respectable white hairs on his chin from the start; so Bill kept something young in him; he was a young dog until he died.

The training sessions did not last long. Now my brother said the dogs would be trained on the job: this to pacify my father, who kept saying that they were a disgrace and "not worth their salt."

There began a new regime, my brother, myself, and the two dogs. We set forth each morning, first, my brother, earnest with responsibility, his rifle swinging in his hand, at his heels the two dogs. Behind this time-honoured unit, myself, the girl, with no useful part to play in the serious masculine business, but necessary to provide admiration. This was a very old role for me indeed: to walk away on one side of the scene, a small fierce girl, hungry to be part of it, but knowing she never would be, above all because the heart that had been put to pump away all her life under her ribs was not only critical and intransigent, but one which longed so bitterly to melt into loving acceptance. An uncomfortable combination, as she knew even then—yet I could not remove the sulky smile from my face. And it *was* absurd: there was my brother, so intent and serious, with Jock the good dog just behind him; and there was Bill the bad dog intermittently behind him, but more often than not sneaking off to enjoy some side path. And there was myself, unwillingly following, my weight shifting from hip to hip, bored and showing it.

I knew the route too well. Before we reached the sullen thickets of the bush where game and birds were to be found, there was a long walk up the back of the *kopje* through a luxuriant pawpaw grove, then through sweet potato vines that tangled our ankles, and tripped us, then past a rubbish heap whose sweet rotten smell was expressed in a heave of glittering black flies, then the bush itself. Here it was all dull green stunted trees, miles and miles of the smallish, flattish, msasa trees in their second growth: they had all been cut for mine furnaces at some time. And over the flat ugly bush a large overbearing blue sky.

We were on our way to get food. So we kept saying. Whatever we shot would be eaten by "the house," or by the house's servants, or by "the compound." But we were hunting according to a newer law than the need for food, and we knew it and that was why we were always a bit apologetic about these expeditions, and why we so often chose to return empty-handed. We were hunting because my brother had been given a new and efficient rifle that would bring down (infallibly, if my brother shot) birds, large and small; and small animals, and very often large game like koodoo and sable. We were hunting because we owned a gun. And because we owned a gun, we should have hunting dogs, it made the business less ugly for some reason.

We were on our way to the Great Vlei, as distinct from the Big Vlei, which was five miles in the other direction. The Big Vlei was burnt out and eroded, and the waterholes usually dried up early. We did not like going there. But to reach the Great Vlei, which was beautiful, we had to go through the ugly bush "at the back of the *kopje*." These ritual names for parts of the farm seemed rather to be names for regions in our minds. "Going to the Great Vlei" had a fairy-tale quality about it, because of having to pass through the region of sour ugly frightening bush first. For it did frighten us, always, and without reason: we felt it was hostile to us and we walked through it quickly, knowing that we were earning by this danger the water-running peace of the Great Vlei. It was only partly on our farm; the boundary between it and the next farm ran invisibly down its centre, drawn by the eye from this outcrop to that big tree to that pothole to that antheap. It was a grassy valley with trees standing tall and spreading on either side of the watercourse which was a half-mile width of intense greenness broken by sky-reflecting brown pools. This was old bush, these trees had never been cut: the Great Vlei had the inevitable look of natural bush—that no branch, no shrub, no patch of thorn, no outcrop, could have been in any other place or stood at any other angle.

The potholes here were always full. The water was stained clear brown, and the mud bottom had a small movement of creatures, while over the brown ripples skimmed blue jays and hummingbirds and all kinds of vivid flashing birds we did not know the names of. Along the lush verges lolled pink and white water lilies on their water-gemmed leaves.

This paradise was where the dogs were to be trained.

During the first holidays, long ones of six weeks, my brother was indefatigable, and we set off every morning after breakfast. In the Great Vlei I sat on a pool's edge under a thorn tree, and daydreamed to the tune of the ripples my swinging feet set moving across the water, while my brother, armed with the rifle, various sizes of stick, and lumps of sugar and biltong, put the two dogs through their paces. Sometimes, roused perhaps because the sun that fell through the green lace of the thorn was burning my shoulders, I turned to watch the three creatures, hard at work a hundred yards off on an empty patch of sand. Jock, more often than not, would be a dead dog, or his nose would be on his paws while his attentive eyes were on my brother's face. Or he would be sitting up, a dog statue, a golden dog, admirably obedient. Bill, on the other hand, was probably balancing on his spine, all four paws in the air, his throat back so that he was flat from nose to tailtip, receiving the hot sun equally over his brindled fur. I would hear, through my own lazy thoughts: "Good dog, Jock, yes good dog. Idiot Bill, fool dog, why don't you work like Jock?" And my brother, his face reddened and sweaty, would come over to flop beside me, saying: "It's all Bill's fault, he's a bad example. And of course Jock doesn't see why he should work hard when Bill just plays all the time." Well, it probably was my fault that the training failed. If my earnest and undivided attention had been given, as I knew quite well was being demanded of me, to this business of the boy and the two dogs, perhaps we would have ended up with a brace of efficient and obedient animals, ever ready to die, to go to heel, and to fetch it. Perhaps.

By next holidays, moral disintegration had set in. My father complained the dogs obeyed nobody, and demanded training, serious and unremitting. My brother and I watched our mother petting Jock and scolding Bill, and came to an unspoken agreement. We set off for the Great Vlei but once there we loafed up and down the waterholes, while the dogs did as they liked, learning the joys of freedom.

The uses of water, for instance. Jock, cautious as usual, would test a pool with his paw, before moving in to stand chest deep, his muzzle just above the ripples, licking at them with small yaps of greeting or excitement. Then he walked gently in and swam up and down and around the brown pool in the green shade of the thorn trees. Meanwhile Bill would have found a shallow pool and be at his favourite game. Starting twenty yards from the rim of a pool he would hurl himself, barking shrilly, across the grass, then across the pool, not so much swimming across it as bouncing across it. Out the other side, up the side of the vlei, around in a big loop, then back, and around again . . . and again and again and again. Great sheets of brown water went up into the sky above him, crashing back into the pool while he barked his exultation.

That was one game. Or they chased each other up and down the four-mile-long valley like enemies, and when one caught the other there was a growling and a snarling and a fighting that sounded genuine enough. Sometimes we went to separate them, an interference they suffered; and the moment we let them go one or another would be off, his hind quarters pistoning, with the other in pursuit, fierce and silent. They might race a mile, two miles, before one leaped at the other's throat and brought him down. This game too, over and over again, so that when they did go wild, we knew how they killed the wild pig and the buck they lived on.

On frivolous mornings they chased butterflies, while my brother and I dangled our feet in a pool and watched. Once, very solemnly, as if it were in parody of the ridiculous business (now over, thank goodness) of "fetch it" and "to heel," Jock brought us in his jaws a big orange and black butterfly, the delicate wings all broken, and the orange bloom smearing his furry lips. He laid it in front of us, held the still fluttering creature flat with a paw, then lay down, his nose pointing at it. His brown eyes rolled up, wickedly hypocritical, as if to say: "Look, a butterfly, I'm a *good* dog." Meanwhile, Bill leaped and barked, a small brown dog hurling himself up into the great blue sky after floating coloured wings. He had taken no notice at all of Jock's captive. But we both felt that Bill was much more likely than Jock to make such a seditious comment, and in fact my brother said: "Bill's corrupted Jock. I'm sure Jock would never go wild like this unless Bill was showing him. It's the blood coming out." But alas, we had no idea yet of what "going wild" could mean. For a couple of years yet it still meant small indisciplines, and mostly Bill's.

For instance, there was the time Bill forced himself through a loose plank in the door of the store hut, and there ate and ate, eggs, cake, bread, a joint of beef, a ripening guineafowl, half a ham. Then he couldn't get out. In the morning he was a swollen dog, rolling on the floor and whining with the agony of his overindulgence. "Stupid dog, Bill, Jock would never do a thing like that, he'd be too intelligent not to know he'd swell up if he ate so much."

Then he ate eggs out of the nest, a crime for which on a farm a dog gets shot. Very close was Bill to this fate. He had actually been seen sneaking out of the chicken run, feathers on his nose, egg smear on his muzzle. And there was a mess of oozing yellow and white slime over the straw of the nests. The fowls cackled and raised their feathers whenever Bill came near. First, he was beaten, by the cook, until his howls shook the farm. Then my mother blew eggs and filled them with a solution of mustard and left them in the nests. Sure enough, next morning, a hell of wild howls and shrieks: the beatings had taught him nothing. We went out to see a brown dog running and racing in agonised circles with his tongue hanging out, while the sun came up red over black mountains—a splendid backdrop to a disgraceful scene. My mother took the poor inflamed jaws and washed them in warm water and said: "Well now Bill, you'd better learn, or it's the firing squad for you."

He learned, but not easily. More than once my brother and I, having arisen early for the hunt, stood in front of the house in the dawn hush, the sky a high far grey above us, the edge of the mountains just reddening, the great spaces of silent bush full of the dark of the night. We sniffed at the small sharpness of the dew, and the heavy somnolent night-smell off the bush, felt the cold heavy air on our cheeks. We stood, whistling very low, so that the dogs would come from wherever they had chosen to sleep. Soon Jock would appear, yawning and sweeping his tail back and forth. No Bill—then we saw him, sitting on his haunches just outside the chicken run, his nose resting in a loop of the wire, his eyes closed in yearning for the warm delicious ooze of fresh egg. And we would clap our hands over our mouths and double up with heartless laughter that had to be muffled so as not to disturb our parents.

On the mornings when we went hunting, and took the dogs, we knew that before we'd gone half a mile either Jock or Bill would dash off barking into the bush; the one left would look up from his own nosing and sniffing and rush away too. We would hear the wild double barking fade away with the crash and the rush of the two bodies, and, often enough, the subsidiary rushings away of other animals who had been asleep or resting and just waiting until we had gone away. Now we could look for something to shoot which probably we would never have seen at all had the dogs been there. We could settle down for long patient stalks, circling around a grazing koodoo, or a couple of duikers. Often enough we would lie watching them for hours, afraid only that Jock and Bill would come back, putting an end to this particular pleasure. I remember once we caught a glimpse of a duiker grazing on the edge of a farmland that was still half dark. We got onto our stomachs and wriggled through the long grass, not able to see if the duiker was still there. Slowly the field opened up in front of us, a heaving mass of big black clods. We carefully raised our heads, and there, at the edge of the clod sea, a couple of arm's lengths away, were three little duikers, their heads turned away from us to where the sun was about to rise. They were three black, quite motionless silhouettes. Away over the other side of the field, big clods became tinged with reddish gold. The earth turned so fast towards the sun that the light came running from the tip of one clod to the next across the field like flames leaping along the tops of long grasses in front of a strong wind. The light reached the duikers and outlined them with warm gold. They were three glittering little beasts on the edge of an imminent sunlight. They then began to butt each other, lifting their hind quarters and bringing down their hind feet in clicking leaps like dancers. They tossed their sharp little horns and made short half-angry rushes at each other. The sun was up. Three little buck danced on the edge of the deep green bush where we lay hidden, and there was a weak sunlight warming their gold hides. The sun separated itself from the line of the hills, and became calm and big and yellow; a warm yellow colour filled the world, the little buck stopped dancing, and walked slowly off, frisking their white tails and tossing their pretty heads, into the bush.

We would never have seen them at all, if the dogs hadn't been miles away.

In fact, all they were good for was their indiscipline. If we wanted to be sure of something to eat, we tied ropes to the dogs' collars until we actually heard the small clink-clink-clink of guineafowl running through the bush. Then we untied them. The dogs were at once off after the birds who rose clumsily into the air, looking like flying shawls that sailed along, just above grass level, with the dogs' jaws snapping underneath them. All they wanted was to land unobserved in the long grass, but they were always forced to rise painfully into the trees, on their weak wings. Sometimes, if it was a large flock, a dozen trees might be dotted with the small black shapes of guineafowl outlined against dawn or evening skies. They watched the barking dogs, took no notice of us. My brother or I—for even I could hardly miss in such conditions—planted our feet wide for balance, took aim at a chosen bird and shot. The carcase fell into the worrying jaws beneath. Meanwhile a second bird would be chosen and shot. With the two birds tied together by their feet, the rifle, justified by utility, proudly swinging, we would saunter back to the house through the sun-scented bush of our enchanted childhood. The dogs, for politeness' sake, escorted us part of the way home, then went off hunting on their own. Guineafowl were very tame sport for them, by then.

It had come to this, that if we actually wished to shoot something, or to watch animals, or even to take a walk through bush where every animal for miles had not been scared away, we had to lock up the dogs before we left, ignoring their whines and their howls. Even so, if let out too soon, they would follow. Once, after we had walked six miles or so, a leisurely morning's trek towards the mountains, the dogs arrived, panting, happy, their pink wet tongues hot on our knees and forearms, saying how delighted they were to have found us. They licked and wagged for a few moments—then off they went, they vanished, and did not come home until evening. We were worried. We had not known that they went so far from the farm by themselves. We spoke of how bad it would be if they took to frequenting other farms—perhaps other chicken runs? But it was all too late. They were too old to train. Either they had to be kept permanently on leashes, tied to trees outside the house, and for dogs like these it was not much better than being dead—either that, or they must run free and take their chances.

We got news of the dogs in letters from home and it was increasingly bad. My brother and I, at our respective boarding schools where we were supposed to be learning discipline, order, and sound characters, read: "The dogs went away a whole night, they only came back at lunch time." "Jock and Bill have been three days and nights in the bush. They've just come home, worn out." "The dogs must have made a kill this time and stayed beside it like wild animals, because they came home too gorged to eat, they just drank a lot of water and fell off to sleep like babies. . . ." "Mr. Daly rang up yesterday to say he saw Jock and Bill hunting along the hill behind his house. They've been chasing his oxen. We've got to beat them when they get home because if they don't learn they'll get themselves shot one of these dark nights. . . ."

They weren't there at all when we went home for the holidays. They had already been gone for nearly a week. But, or so we flattered ourselves, they sensed our return, for back they came, trotting gently side by side up the hill in the moonlight, two low black shapes moving above the accompanying black shapes of their shadows, their eyes gleaming red as the shafts of lamplight struck them. They greeted us, my brother and me, affectionately enough, but at once went off to sleep. We told ourselves that they saw us as creatures like them, who went off on long exciting hunts: but we knew it was sentimental nonsense, designed to take the edge off the hurt we felt because our animals, *our* dogs, cared so little about us. They went away again that night, or rather, in the first dawnlight. A week later they came home. They smelled foul, they must have been chasing a skunk or a wildcat. Their fur was matted with grass seeds and their skin lumpy with ticks. They drank water heavily, but refused food: their breath was foetid with the smell of meat.

They lay down to sleep and remained limp while we, each taking an animal, its sleeping head heavy in our laps, removed ticks, grass seeds, blackjacks. On Bill's forepaw was a hard ridge which I thought was an old scar. He sleep-whimpered when I touched it. It was a noose of plaited grass, used by Africans to snare birds. Luckily it had snapped off. "Yes," said my father, "that's how they'll end, both of them, they'll die in a trap, and serve them both right, they won't get any sympathy from me!"

We were frightened into locking them up for a day; but we could not stand their misery, and let them out again.

We were always springing gametraps of all kinds. For the big buck, the sable, the eland, the koodoo, the Africans bent a sapling across a path, held it by light string, and fixed on it a noose of heavy wire cut from a fence. For the smaller buck there were low traps with nooses of fine baling wire or plaited tree fibre. And at the corners of the cultivated fields or at the edges of waterholes, where the birds and hares came down to feed, were always myriad tiny tracks under the grass, and often across every track hung a small noose of plaited grass. Sometimes we spent whole days destroying these snares.

In order to keep the dogs amused, we took to walking miles every day. We were exhausted, but they were not, and simply went off at night as well. Then we rode bicycles as fast as we could along the rough farm tracks, with the dogs bounding easily beside us. We wore ourselves out, trying to please Jock and Bill, who, we imagined, knew what we were doing and were trying to humour us. But we stuck at it. Once, at the end of a glade, we saw the skeleton of a large animal hanging from a noose. Some African had forgotten to visit his traps. We showed the skeleton to Jock and Bill, and talked and warned and threatened, almost in tears, because human speech was not dogs' speech. They sniffed around the bones, yapped a few times up into our faces—out of politeness, we felt; and were off again into the bush.

At school we heard that they were almost completely wild. Sometimes they came home for a meal, or a day's sleep, "treating the house," my mother complained, "like a hotel."

Then fate struck, in the shape of a bucktrap.

One night, very late, we heard whining, and went out to greet them. They were crawling towards the front door, almost on their bellies. Their ribs stuck out, their coats stared, their eyes shone unhealthily. They fell on the food we gave them; they were starved. Then on Jock's neck, which was bent over the food bowl, showed the explanation: a thick strand of wire. It was not solid wire, but made of a dozen twisted strands, and had been chewed through, near the collar. We examined Bill's mouth: chewing the wire through must have taken a long time, days perhaps: his gums and lips were scarred and bleeding, and his teeth were worn down to stumps, like an old dog's teeth. If the wire had not been stranded, Jock would have died in the trap. As it was, he fell ill, his lungs were strained, since he had been half strangled with the wire. And Bill could no longer chew properly, he ate uncomfortably, like an old person. They stayed at home for weeks, reformed dogs, barked around the house at night, and ate regular meals.

Then they went off again, but came home more often than they had. Jock's lungs weren't right: he would lie out in the sun, gasping and wheezing, as if trying to rest them. As for Bill, he could only eat soft food. How, then, did they manage when they were hunting?

One afternoon we were shooting, miles from home, and we saw them. First we heard the familiar excited yapping coming towards us, about two miles off. We were in a large vlei, full of tall whitish grass which swayed and bent along a fast regular line: a shape showed, it was a duiker, hard to see until it was close because it was reddish brown in colour, and the vlei had plenty of the pinkish feathery grass that turns a soft intense red in strong light. Being near sunset, the pale grass was on the verge of being invisible, like wires of white light; and the pink grass flamed and glowed; and the fur of the little buck shone red. It swerved suddenly. Had it seen us? No, it was because of Jock who had made a quick maneuvering turn from where he had been lying in the pink grass, to watch the buck, and behind it, Bill, pistoning along like a machine. Jock, who could no longer run fast, had turned the buck into Bill's jaws. We saw Bill bound at the little creature's throat, bring it down and hold it until Jock came in to kill it: his own teeth were useless now.

We walked over to greet them, but with restraint, for these two growling snarling creatures seemed not to know us, they raised eyes glazed with savagery, as they tore at the dead buck. Or rather, as Jock tore at it. Before we went away we saw Jock pushing over lumps of hot steaming meat towards Bill, who otherwise would have gone hungry.

They were really a team now; neither could function without the other. So we thought.

But soon Jock took to coming home from the hunting trips early, after one or two days, and Bill might stay out for a week or more. Jock lay watching the bush, and when Bill came, he licked his ears and face as if he had reverted to the role of Bill's mother.

Once I heard Bill barking and went to see. The telephone line ran through a vlei near the house to the farm over the hill. The wires hummed and sang and twanged. Bill was underneath the wires, which were a good fifteen feet over his head, jumping and barking at them: he was playing, out of exuberance, as he had done when a small puppy. But now it made me sad, seeing the strong dog playing all alone, while his friend lay quiet in the sun, wheezing from damaged lungs.

And what did Bill live on, in the bush? Rats, birds' eggs, lizards, anything *soft* enough? That was painful too, thinking of the powerful hunters in the days of their glory.

Soon we got telephone calls from neighbours: Bill dropped in, he finished off the food in our dog's bowl. . . . Bill seemed hungry, so we fed him. . . . Your dog Bill is looking very thin, isn't he? . . . Bill was around our chicken run—I'm sorry, but if he goes for the eggs, then . . .

Bill had puppies with a pedigreed bitch fifteen miles off: her owners were annoyed: Bill was not good enough for them, and besides there was the question of his "bad blood." All the puppies were destroyed. He was hanging around the house all the time, although he had been beaten, and they had even fired shots into the air to scare him off. Was there anything we could do to keep him at home? they asked; for they were tired of having to keep their bitch tied up.

No, there was nothing we could do. Rather, there was nothing we *would* do; for when Bill came trotting up from the bush to drink deeply out of Jock's bowl, and to lie for a while nose to nose with Jock, well, we could have caught him and tied him up, but we did not. "He won't last long anyway," said my father. And my mother told Jock that he was a sensible and intelligent dog; for she again sang praises of his nature and character just as if he had never spent so many glorious years in the bush.

I went to visit the neighbour who owned Bill's mate. She was tied to a post on the verandah. All night we were disturbed by a wild sad howling from the bush, and she whimpered and strained at her rope. In the morning I walked out into the hot silence of the bush, and called to him: Bill, Bill, it's me. Nothing, no sound. I sat on the slope of an antheap in the shade, and waited. Soon Bill came into view, trotting between the trees. He was very thin. He looked gaunt, stiff, wary—an old outlaw, afraid of traps. He saw me, but stopped about twenty yards off. He climbed halfway up another anthill and sat there in full sunlight, so I could see the harsh patches on his coat. We sat in silence, looking at each other. Then he lifted his head and howled, like the howl dogs give to the full moon, long, terrible, lonely. But it was morning, the sun calm and clear, and the bush without mystery. He sat and howled his heart out, his muzzle pointed away towards where his mate was chained. We could hear the faint whimperings she made, and the clink of her metal dish as she moved about. I couldn't stand it. It made my flesh cold, and I could see the hairs standing up on my forearm. I went over to him and sat by him and put my arm around his neck as once, so many years ago, I had put my arm around his mother that moonlit night before I stole her puppy away from her. He put his muzzle on my forearm and whimpered, or rather cried. Then he lifted it and howled. . . . "Oh, my God, Bill, don't do that, please don't, it's not the slightest use, please, dear Bill. . . ." But he went on, until suddenly he leaped up in the middle of a howl, as if his pain were too strong to contain in sitting, and he sniffed at me, as if to say: That's you, is it, well, goodbye—then he turned his wild head to the bush and trotted away.

Very soon he was shot, coming out of a chicken run early one morning with an egg in his mouth.

Jock was quite alone now. He spent his old age lying in the sun, his nose pointed out over the miles and miles of bush between our house and the mountains where he had hunted all those years with Bill. He was really an old dog, his legs were stiff, and his coat was rough, and he wheezed and gasped. Sometimes, at night, when the moon was up, he went out to howl at it, and we would say: He's missing Bill. He would come back to sit at my mother's knee, resting his head so that she could stroke it. She would say: "Poor old Jock, poor old boy, are you missing that bad dog Bill?"

Sometimes, when he lay dozing, he started up and went trotting on his stiff old legs through the house and the outhouses, sniffing everywhere and anxiously whining. Then he stood, upright, one paw raised, as he used to do when he was young, and gazed over the bush and softly whined. And we would say: "He must have been dreaming he was out hunting with Bill."

He got ill. He could hardly breathe. We carried him in our arms down the hill into the bush, and my mother stroked and patted him while my father put the gun barrel to the back of his head and shot him.

The Sun Between Their Feet

THE road from the back of the station went to the Roman Catholic Mission, which was a dead end, being in the middle of a Native Reserve. It was a poor mission, with only one lorry, so the road was always deserted, a track of sand between long or short grasses. The station itself was busy with trains and people, and the good country in front was settled thick with white farmers, but all the country behind the station was unused because it was granite boulders, outcrops, and sand. The scrub cattle from the Reserve strayed there. There were no human beings. From the track it seemed the hills of boulders were so steep and laced with vines and weed there would be no place to go between them. But you could force your way in, and there it became clear that in the past people had made use of this wilderness. For one thing there were the remains of earth and rock defences built by the Mashona against the Matabele when they came raiding after cattle and women before Rhodes put an end to all that. For another, the undersurfaces of the great boulders were covered with Bushman paintings. After a hundred yards or so of clambering and squeezing there came a flattish sandy stretch before the boulders erupted again. In this space, at the time of the raiding, the women and the cattle would have been kept while the men held the surrounding defences. From this space, at the time of the Bushmen, small hunting men took coloured clays, and earths, and plant juices for their pictures.

It had rained last night and the low grass was still wet around my ankles and the early sun had not dried the sand. There was a sharp upjut of rock in the middle of the space.

The rock was damp, and I could feel the wet heat being dragged up past my bare legs.

Sitting low here, the encircling piles of boulders seemed like mountains, heightening the sky on tall horizons. The rocks were dark grey, but stained with lichens. The trees between the boulders were meagre, and several were lightning-struck, no more than black skeletons. This was hungry country, growing sand and thin grass and rocks and heat. The sun came down hard between heat-conserving rocks. After an hour of sun the sand between the grasses showed a clean dry glistening surface, and a dark wet underneath.

The Reserve cattle must have moved here since the rains last night, for there were a score of fresh cow pats laid on the grass. Big flies swore and tumbled over them, breaking the crust the sun had baked. The air was heavy and sweet. The buzzing of the flies, the tiny sucking sound of the heat, the cooing of the pigeons, made a morning silence.

Hot, and silent; and save for the flies, no movement anywhere, for what winds there were blew outside this sheltered space.

But soon there was new movement. Where the flies had broken the crust of the nearest dung clot, two beetles were at work. They were small, dusty, black, round-bodied beetles. One had set his back legs over a bit of dung and was heaving and levering at it. The other, with a fast rolling movement, the same that a hen makes settling roused feathers over eggs, was using his body to form the ball even before it was heaved clear of the main lump of matter. As soon as the piece was freed, both beetles assaulted it with legs and bodies, modelling fast, frantic with creation, seizing it between their back legs, spinning it, rolling it under them, both tugging and pushing it through the thick encumbering grass stems that rose over them like forest trees until at last the ball rolled away from them into a plain, or glade, or inch-wide space of sand. The two beetles scuttled about among the stems, looking for their property. They were on the point of starting again on the mother-pile of muck, when one of them saw the ball lying free in the open, and both ran after it.

All over the grassy space, around the cow pats, dung beetles were at work, the blowflies hustled and buzzed, and by night all the new cow-stomach-worked grass would be lifted away, rolled away, to feed flies, beetles and new earth. That is, unless it rained hard again, when everything would be scattered by rods of rain.

But there was no sign of rain yet. The sky was the clear slow blue of African mornings after night storms. My two beetles had the sky on their side. They had all day.

The book says that dung beetles form a ball of dung, lay their eggs in it, search for a gentle slope, roll the ball up it, and then allow it to roll down again so that in the process of rolling "the pellet becomes compacted."

Why must the pellet be compacted? Presumably so that the blows of sun and rain do not beat it to fragments. Why this complicated business of rolling up and rolling down?

Well, it is not for us to criticise the processes of nature; so I sat on top of the jutting rock, and watched the beetles rolling the ball towards it. In a few minutes of work they had reached it, and had hurled themselves and the dung ball at its foot. Their momentum took them a few inches up the slope, then they slipped, and ball and beetles rolled back to the flat again.

I got down off the rock, and sat in the grass behind them to view the ascent through their eyes.

The rock was about four feet long and three feet high. It was a jutting slab of granite, weeded and lichened, its edges blunted by rain and by wind. The beetles, hugging their ball between legs and bellies, looked up to a savage mountain, whose first slopes were an easy foot-assisting invitation. They rolled their ball, which was now crusted with dirt, to a small ridge under the foothills, and began, this time with slow care, to hitch it up from ridge to ridge, from one crust of lichen to the next. One beetle above, one below, they cherished their ball upwards. Soon they met the obstruction that had defeated them before: a sudden upswelling in the mountain wall. This time, one remained below the ball, holding its weight on its back legs, while the other scouted off sideways to find an easier path. It returned, gripped the ball with its legs, and the two beetles resumed their difficult, sideways scrambling progress, up around the swell in the rock into a small valley which led, or so it seemed, into the second great stage of the ascent. But this valley was a snare, for there was a crevasse across it. The mountain was riven. Heat and cold had split it to its base, and the narrow crack sloped down to a mountain lake full of warm fresh water over a bed of wind-gathered leaves and grass. The dung ball slipped over the edge of the crevasse into the gulf, and rolled gently into the lake where it was supported at its edge by a small fringe of lichen. The beetles flung themselves after it. One, straddling desperate legs from a raft of reed to the shore, held the ball from plunging into the depths of the lake. The other, gripping fast with its front legs to a thick bed of weed on shore, grappled the ball with its back legs, and together they heaved and shoved that precious dung out of the water and back into the ravine. But now the mountain walls rose high on either side, and the ball lay between them. The beetles remained still a moment. The dirt had been washed from the dung, and it was smooth and slippery.

They consulted. Again one remained on guard while the other scouted, returning to report that if they rolled the ball clear along the bottom of the ravine, this would in due course narrow, and they could, by use of legs and shoulders and backs, lift the ball up the crack to a new height on the mountain and, by crossing another dangerous shoulder, attain a gentle weed-roughed slope that led to the summit. This they tried. But on the dangerous shoulder there was a disaster. The lake-slippery ball left their grasp and plunged down the mountainside to the ground, to the point they had started from half an hour before. The two beetles flung themselves after it, and again they began their slow difficult climb. Again their dung ball fell into the crevasse, rolled down into the lake, and again they rescued it, at the cost of infinite resource and patience, again they pushed and pulled it up the ravine, again they maneuvered it up the crack, again they tried to roll it around the mountain's sharp shoulder, and again it fell back to the foot of the mountain, and they plunged after it.

"The dung beetle, *Scarabaeus* or *Aleuchus sacer,* lays its eggs in a ball of dung, then chooses a gentle slope, and compacts the pellet by pushing it uphill backwards with its hind legs and allowing it to roll down, eventually reaching its place of deposit."

I continued to sit in the low hot grass, feeling the sun first on my back, then hard down on my shoulders, and then direct from above on my head. The air was dry now, all the moisture from the night had gone up into the air. Clouds were packing the lower skies. Even the small pool in the rock was evaporating. Above it the air quivered with steam. When, for the third time, the beetles lost their ball in the mountain lake, it was no lake, but a spongy marsh, and getting it out involved no danger or difficulty. Now the ball was sticky, had lost its shape, and was crusted with bits of leaf and grass.

At the fourth attempt, when the ball rolled down to the starting point and the beetles bundled after it, it was past midday, my head ached with heat, and I took a large leaf, slipped it under the ball of dung and the beetles, and lifted this unit away to one side, away from the impossible and destructive mountain.

But when I slid the leaf from under them, they rested a moment in the new patch of territory, scouted this way and that among the grass stems, found their position, and at once rolled their ball back to the foot of the mountain where they prepared another ascent.

Meanwhile, the cow pats on the grass had been dismantled by flies and other dung beetles. Nothing remained but small grassy fragments, or dusty brown stains on the lifting stems. The buzzing of the flies was silenced. The pigeons were stilled by the heat. Far away thunder rolled, and sometimes there was the shriek of a train at the station or the puffing and clanging of shunting engines.

The beetles again got the ball up into the ravine, and this time it rolled down, not into a marsh, but into a damp bed of leaves. There they rested a while in a steam of heat.

Sacred beetles, these, the sacred beetles of the Egyptians, holding the symbol of the sun between their busy stupid feet. Busy, silly beetles, mothering their ball of dung again and again up a mountain when a few minutes' march to one side would take them clear of it.

Again I lifted them, dung and beetles, away from the precipice, to a clear place where they had the choice of a dozen suitable gentle slopes, but they rolled their ball patiently back to the mountain's foot.

"The slope is chosen," says the book, "by a beautiful instinct, so that the ball of dung comes to rest in a spot suitable for the hatching of the new generation of sacred insect."

The sun had now rolled past midday position and was shining onto my face. Sweat scattered off me. The air snapped with heat. The sky where the sun would go down was banked high with darkening cloud. Those beetles would have to hurry not to get drowned.

They continued to roll the dung up the mountain, rescue it from the dried bed of the mountain lake, force it up to the exposed dry shoulder, where it rolled down and they plunged after it. Again and again and again, while the ball became a ragged drying structure of fragmented grass clotted with dung. The afternoon passed. The sun was low in my eyes. I could hardly see the beetles or the dung because of the glare from a black pack of clouds which were red-rimmed from the lowering sun behind. The red streaming rays came down and the black beetles and their dung ball on the mountainside seemed dissolved in sizzling light.

It was raining away on the far hills. The drumming of the rain and the drumming of the thunder came closer. I could see the skirmishing side lances of an army of rain pass half a mile away beyond the rocks. A few great shining drops fell here, and hissed on burning sand and on the burning mountainside. The beetles laboured on.

The sun dropped behind the piled boulders and now this glade rested in a cool spent light, the black trees and black boulders standing around it, waiting for the rain and for the night. The beetles were again on the mountain. They had the ball tight between their legs, they clung on to the lichens, they clung on to rock wall and their treasure with the desperation of stupidity.

Now the hard red glare was gone it was possible to see them clearly. It was difficult to imagine the perfect shining globe the ball had been—it was now nothing more than a bit of refuse. There was a clang of thunder. The grasses hissed and swung as a bolt of wind came fast from the sky. The wind hit the ball of dung, it fell apart into a small puff of dusty grass, and the beetles ran scurrying over the surface of the rock looking for it.

Now the rain came marching towards us, it reached the boulders in a grey envelopment of wet. The big shining drops, outrunners of the rain army, reached the beetles' mountain and one, two! the drops hit the beetles smack, and they fell off the rock into the already seething wet grasses at its foot.

I ran out of the glade with the rain sniping at my heels and my shoulders, thinking of the beetles lying under the precipice up which, tomorrow, after the rain had stopped, and the cattle had come grazing, and the sun had come out, they would again labour and heave a fresh ball of dung.

A Woman on a Roof

IT WAS during the week of hot sun, that June.

Three men were at work on the roof, where the leads got so hot they had the idea of throwing water on to cool them. But the water steamed, then sizzled; and they made jokes about getting an egg from some woman in the flats under them, to poach it for their dinner. By two it was not possible to touch the guttering they were replacing, and they speculated about what workmen did in regularly hot countries. Perhaps they should borrow kitchen gloves with the egg? They were all a bit dizzy, not used to the heat; and they shed their coats and stood side by side squeezing themselves into a foot-wide patch of shade against a chimney, careful to keep their feet in the thick socks and boots out of the sun. There was a fine view across several acres of roofs. Not far off a man sat in a deck chair reading the newspapers. Then they saw her, between chimneys, about fifty yards away. She lay face down on a brown blanket. They could see the top part of her: black hair, a flushed solid back, arms spread out.

"She's stark naked," said Stanley, sounding annoyed.

Harry, the oldest, a man of about forty-five, said: "Looks like it."

Young Tom, seventeen, said nothing, but he was excited and grinning.

Stanley said: "Someone'll report her if she doesn't watch out."

"She thinks no one can see," said Tom, craning his head all ways to see more.

At this point the woman, still lying prone, brought her

two hands up behind her shoulders with the ends of a scarf in them, tied it behind her back, and sat up. She wore a red scarf tied around her breasts and brief red bikini pants. This being the first day of the sun she was white, flushing red. She sat smoking, and did not look up when Stanley let out a wolf whistle. Harry said: "Small things amuse small minds," leading the way back to their part of the roof, but it was scorching. Harry said: "Wait, I'm going to rig up some shade," and disappeared down the skylight into the building. Now that he'd gone, Stanley and Tom went to the farthest point they could to peer at the woman. She had moved, and all they could see were two pink legs stretched on the blanket. They whistled and shouted but the legs did not move. Harry came back with a blanket and shouted: "Come on, then." He sounded irritated with them. They clambered back to him and he said to Stanley: "What about your missus?" Stanley was newly married, about three months. Stanley said, jeering: "What about my missus?" —preserving his independence. Tom said nothing, but his mind was full of the nearly naked woman. Harry slung the blanket, which he had borrowed from a friendly woman downstairs, from the stem of a television aerial to a row of chimney pots. This shade fell across the piece of gutter they had to replace. But the shade kept moving, they had to adjust the blanket, and not much progress was made. At last some of the heat left the roof, and they worked fast, making up for lost time. First Stanley, then Tom, made a trip to the end of the roof to see the woman. "She's on her back," Stanley said, adding a jest which made Tom snicker, and the older man smile tolerantly. Tom's report was that she hadn't moved, but it was a lie. He wanted to keep what he had seen to himself: he had caught her in the act of rolling down the little red pants over her hips, till they were no more than a small triangle. She was on her back, fully visible, glistening with oil.

Next morning, as soon as they came up, they went to look. She was already there, face down, arms spread out, naked except for the little red pants. She had turned brown in the night. Yesterday she was a scarlet and white woman, today she was a brown woman. Stanley let out a whistle. She lifted her head, startled, as if she'd been asleep, and looked straight over at them. The sun was in her eyes, she blinked and stared, then she dropped her head again. At this gesture of indifference, they all three, Stanley, Tom, and old Harry, let out whistles and yells. Harry was doing it in parody of the younger men, making fun of them, but he was also angry. They were all angry because of her utter indifference to the three men watching her.

"Bitch," said Stanley.

"She should ask us over," said Tom, snickering.

Harry recovered himself and reminded Stanley: "If she's married, her old man wouldn't like that."

"Christ," said Stanley virtuously, "if my wife lay about like that, for everyone to see, I'd soon stop her."

Harry said, smiling: "How do you know, perhaps she's sunning herself at this very moment?"

"Not a chance, not on our roof." The safety of his wife put Stanley into a good humour, and they went to work. But today it was hotter than yesterday; and several times one or the other suggested they should tell Matthew, the foreman, and ask to leave the roof until the heat wave was over. But they didn't. There was work to be done in the basement of the big block of flats, but up here they felt free, on a different level from ordinary humanity shut in the streets or the buildings. A lot more people came out onto the roofs that day, for an hour at midday. Some married couples sat side by side in deck chairs, the women's legs stockingless and scarlet, the men in vests with reddening shoulders.

The woman stayed on her blanket, turning herself over and over. She ignored them, no matter what they did. When Harry went off to fetch more screws, Stanley said: "Come on." Her roof belonged to a different system of roofs, separated from theirs at one point by about twenty feet. It meant a scrambling climb from one level to another, edging along parapets, clinging to chimneys, while their big boots slipped and slithered, but at last they stood on a small square projecting roof looking straight down at her, close. She sat smoking, reading a book. Tom thought she looked like a poster, or a magazine cover, with the blue sky behind her and her legs stretched out. Behind her a great crane at work on a new building in Oxford Street swung its black arm across the roofs in a great arc. Tom imagined him-

self at work on the crane, adjusting the arm to swing over
and pick her up and swing her back across the sky to
drop her near him.

They whistled. She looked up at them, cool and remote,
then went on reading. Again, they were furious. Or rather,
Stanley was. His sun-heated face was screwed into rage as
he whistled again and again, trying to make her look up.
Young Tom stopped whistling. He stood beside Stanley,
excited, grinning; but he felt as if he were saying to the
woman: "Don't associate me with *him*," for his grin was
apologetic. Last night he had thought of the unknown
woman before he slept, and she had been tender with him.
This tenderness he was remembering as he shifted his feet
by the jeering, whistling Stanley, and watched the indifferent,
healthy brown woman a few feet off, with the gap that
plunged to the street between them. Tom thought it was
romantic, it was like being high on two hilltops. But there
was a shout from Harry, and they clambered back. Stanley's
face was hard, really angry. The boy kept looking at him and
wondered why he hated the woman so much, for by now
he loved her.

They played their little games with the blanket, trying
to trap shade to work under; but again it was not until
nearly four that they could work seriously, and they were
exhausted, all three of them. They were grumbling about
the weather, by now. Stanley was in a thoroughly bad
humour. When they made their routine trip to see the woman
before they packed up for the day, she was apparently asleep,
face down, her back all naked save for the scarlet triangle
on her buttocks. "I've got a good mind to report her to
the police," said Stanley, and Harry said: "What's eating
you? What harm's she doing?"

"I tell you, if she was my wife!"

"But she isn't, is she?" Tom knew that Harry, like himself, was uneasy at Stanley's reaction. He was normally a
sharp young man, quick at his work, making a lot of jokes,
good company.

"Perhaps it will be cooler tomorrow," said Harry.

But it wasn't, it was hotter, if anything, and the weather
forecast said the good weather would last. As soon as they
were on the roof, Harry went over to see if the woman were

there, and Tom knew it was to prevent Stanley going, to put off his bad humour. Harry had grown-up children, a boy the same age as Tom, and the youth trusted and looked up to him.

Harry came back and said: "She's not there."

"I bet her old man has put his foot down," said Stanley, and Harry and Tom caught each other's eyes and smiled behind the young married man's back.

Harry suggested they should get permission to work in the basement, and they did, that day. But before packing up Stanley said: "Let's have a breath of fresh air." Again Harry and Tom smiled at each other as they followed Stanley up to the roof, Tom in the devout conviction that he was there to protect the woman from Stanley. It was about five-thirty, and a calm, full sunlight lay over the roofs. The great crane still swung its black arm from Oxford Street to above their heads. She was not there. Then there was a flutter of white from behind a parapet, and she stood up, in a belted, white dressing gown. She had been there all day, probably, but on a different patch of roof, to hide from them. Stanley did not whistle, he said nothing, but watched the woman bend to collect papers, books, cigarettes, then fold the blanket over her arm. Tom was thinking: If they weren't here, I'd go over and say . . . what? But he knew from his nightly dreams of her that she was kind and friendly. Perhaps she would ask him down to her flat? Perhaps. . . . He stood watching her disappear down the skylight. As she went, Stanley let out a shrill derisive yell; she started, and it seemed as if she nearly fell. She clutched to save herself, they could hear things falling. She looked straight at them, angry. Harry said, facetiously: "Better be careful on those slippery ladders, love." Tom knew he said it to save her from Stanley, but she could not know it. She vanished, frowning. Tom was full of a secret delight, because he knew her anger was for the others, not for him.

"Roll on some rain," said Stanley, bitter, looking at the blue evening sky.

Next day was cloudless, and they decided to finish the work in the basement. They felt excluded, shut in the grey cement basement fitting pipes, from the holiday atmosphere of London in a heat wave. At lunchtime they came up for some air, but while the married couples, and the men in shirt-sleeves or vests, were there, she was not there, either on her usual patch of roof or where she had been yesterday. They all, even Harry, clambered about, between chimney pots, over parapets, the hot leads stinging their fingers. There was not a sign of her. They took off their shirts and vests and exposed their chests, feeling their feet sweaty and hot. They did not mention the woman. But Tom felt alone again. Last night she had asked him into her flat: it was big and had fitted white carpets and a bed with a padded white leather headtop. She wore a black filmy negligée and her kindness to Tom thickened his throat as he remembered it. He felt she had betrayed him by not being there.

And again after work they climbed up, but still there was nothing to be seen of her. Stanley kept repeating that if it was as hot as this tomorrow he wasn't going to work and that's all there was to it. But they were all there next day. By ten the temperature was in the middle seventies, and it was eighty long before noon. Harry went to the foreman to say it was impossible to work on the leads in that heat; but the foreman said there was nothing else he could put them on, and they'd have to. At midday they stood, silent, watching the skylight on her roof open, and then she slowly emerged in her white gown, holding a bundle of blanket. She looked at them, gravely, then went to the part of the roof where she was hidden from them. Tom was pleased. He felt she was more his when the other men couldn't see her. They had taken off their shirts and vests, but now they put them back again, for they felt the sun bruising their flesh. "She must have the hide of a rhino," said Stanley, tugging at guttering and swearing. They stopped work, and sat in the shade, moving around behind chimney stacks. A woman came to water a yellow window box just opposite them. She was middle-aged, wearing a flowered summer dress. Stanley said to her: "We need a drink more than them." She smiled and said: "Better drop down to the pub quick, it'll be closing in a minute." They exchanged pleasantries, and she left them with a smile and a wave.

"Not like Lady Godiva," said Stanley. "She can give us a bit of a chat and a smile."

"You didn't whistle at *her*," said Tom, reproving.

"Listen to him," said Stanley, "you didn't whistle, then?"

But the boy felt as if he hadn't whistled, as if only Harry and Stanley had. He was making plans, when it was time to knock off work, to get left behind and somehow make his way over to the woman. The weather report said the hot spell was due to break, so he had to move quickly. But there was no chance of being left. The other two decided to knock off work at four, because they were exhausted. As they went down, Tom quickly climbed a parapet and hoisted himself higher by pulling his weight up a chimney. He caught a glimpse of her lying on her back, her knees up, eyes closed, a brown woman lolling in the sun. He slipped and clattered down, as Stanley looked for information: "She's gone down," he said. He felt as if he had protected her from Stanley, and that she must be grateful to him. He could feel the bond between the woman and himself.

Next day, they stood around on the landing below the roof, reluctant to climb up into the heat. The woman who had lent Harry the blanket came out and offered them a cup of tea. They accepted gratefully, and sat around Mrs. Pritchett's kitchen an hour or so, chatting. She was married to an airline pilot. A smart blonde, of about thirty, she had an eye for the handsome sharp-faced Stanley; and the two teased each other while Harry sat in a corner, watching, indulgent, though his expression reminded Stanley that he was married. And young Tom felt envious of Stanley's ease in badinage; felt, too, that Stanley's getting off with Mrs. Pritchett left his romance with the woman on the roof safe and intact.

"I thought they said the heat wave'd break," said Stanley, sullen, as the time approached when they really would have to climb up into the sunlight.

"You don't like it, then?" asked Mrs. Pritchett.

"All right for some," said Stanley. "Nothing to do but lie about as if it was a beach up there. Do you ever go up?"

"Went up once," said Mrs. Pritchett. "But it's a dirty place up there, and it's too hot."

"Quite right too," said Stanley.

Then they went up, leaving the cool neat little flat and the friendly Mrs. Pritchett.

As soon as they were up they saw her. The three men

looked at her, resentful at her ease in this punishing sun. Then Harry said, because of the expression on Stanley's face: "Come on, we've got to pretend to work, at least."

They had to wrench another length of guttering that ran beside a parapet out of its bed, so that they could replace it. Stanley took it in his two hands, tugged, swore, stood up. "Fuck it," he said, and sat down under a chimney. He lit a cigarette. "Fuck them," he said. "What do they think we are, lizards? I've got blisters all over my hands." Then he jumped up and climbed over the roofs and stood with his back to them. He put his fingers either side of his mouth and let out a shrill whistle. Tom and Harry squatted, not looking at each other, watching him. They could just see the woman's head, the beginnings of her brown shoulders. Stanley whistled again. Then he began stamping with his feet, and whistled and yelled and screamed at the woman, his face getting scarlet. He seemed quite mad, as he stamped and whistled, while the woman did not move, she did not move a muscle.

"Barmy," said Tom.

"Yes," said Harry, disapproving.

Suddenly the older man came to a decision. It was, Tom knew, to save some sort of scandal or real trouble over the woman. Harry stood up and began packing tools into a length of oily cloth. "Stanley," he said, commanding. At first Stanley took no notice, but Harry said: "Stanley, we're packing it in, I'll tell Matthew."

Stanley came back, cheeks mottled, eyes glaring.

"Can't go on like this," said Harry. "It'll break in a day or so. I'm going to tell Matthew we've got sunstroke, and if he doesn't like it, it's too bad." Even Harry sounded aggrieved, Tom noted. The small, competent man, the family man with his grey hair, who was never at a loss, sounded really off balance. "Come on," he said, angry. He fitted himself into the open square in the roof, and went down, watching his feet on the ladder. Then Stanley went, with not a glance at the woman. Then Tom who, his throat beating with excitement, silently promised her in a backward glance: Wait for me, wait, I'm coming.

On the pavement Stanley said: "I'm going home." He looked white now, so perhaps he really did have sunstroke.

Harry went off to find the foreman who was at work on the plumbing of some flats down the street. Tom slipped back, not into the building they had been working on, but the building on whose roof the woman lay. He went straight up, with an iron ladder leading up. He emerged onto the roof a couple of yards from her. She sat up, pushing back her black hair with both hands. The scarf across her breasts bound them tight, and brown flesh bulged around it. Her legs were brown and smooth. She stared at him in silence. The boy stood grinning, foolish, claiming the tenderness he expected from her.

"What do you want?" she asked.

"I . . . I came to . . . make your acquaintance," he stammered, grinning, pleading with her.

They looked at each other, the slight, scarlet-faced excited boy, and the serious, nearly naked woman. Then, without a word, she lay down on her brown blanket, ignoring him.

"You like the sun, do you?" he enquired of her glistening back.

Not a word. He felt panic, thinking of how she had held him in her arms, stroked his hair, brought him where he sat, lordly, in her bed, a glass of some exhilarating liquor he had never tasted in life. He felt that if he knelt down, stroked her shoulders, her hair, she would turn and clasp him in her arms.

He said: "The sun's all right for you, isn't it?"

She raised her head, set her chin on two small fists. "Go away," she said. He did not move. "Listen," she said, in a slow reasonable voice, where anger was kept in check, though with difficulty; looking at him, her face weary with anger: "If you get a kick out of seeing women in bikinis, why don't you take a sixpenny bus ride to the Lido? You'd see dozens of them, without all this mountaineering."

She hadn't understood him. He felt her unfairness pale him. He stammered: "But I like you, I've been watching you and . . ."

"Thanks," she said, and dropped her face again, turned away from him.

She lay there. He stood there. She said nothing. She had simply shut him out. He stood, saying nothing at all, for some minutes. He thought: She'll have to say something if I stay. But the minutes went past, with no sign of them in her, except in the tension of her back, her thighs, her arms—the tension of waiting for him to go.

He looked up at the sky, where the sun seemed to spin in heat; and over the roofs where he and his mates had been earlier. He could see the heat quivering where they had worked. "And they expect us to work in these conditions!" he thought, filled with righteous indignation. The woman hadn't moved. A bit of hot wind blew her black hair softly, it shone, and was iridescent. He remembered how he had stroked it last night.

Resentment of her at last moved him off and away down the ladder, through the building, into the street. He got drunk then, in hatred of her.

Next day when he woke the sky was grey. He looked at the wet grey and thought, vicious: "Well, that's fixed you, hasn't it now? That's fixed you good and proper."

The three men were at work early on the cool leads, surrounded by damp drizzling roofs where no one came to sun themselves, black roofs, slimy with rain. Because it was cool now, they would finish the job that day, if they hurried.

How I Finally Lost My Heart

It would be easy to say that I picked up a knife, slit open my side, took my heart out, and threw it away; but unfortunately it wasn't as easy as that. Not that I, like everyone else, had not often wanted to do it. No, it happened differently, and not as I expected.

It was just after I had had a lunch and a tea with two different men. My lunch partner I had lived with for (more or less) four and seven-twelfths years. When he left me for new pastures, I spent two years, or was it three, half dead, and my heart was a stone, impossible to carry about, considering all the other things weighing on one. Then I slowly, and with difficulty, got free, because my heart cherished a thousand adhesions to my first love—though from another point of view he could be legitimately described as either my second *real* love (my father being the first) or my third (my brother intervening).

As the folk song has it:

> *I have loved but three men in my life,*
> *My father, my brother, and the man that*
> *took my life.*

But if one were going to look at the thing from outside, without insight, he could be seen as (perhaps, I forget) the thirteenth, but to do that means disregarding the inner emotional truth. For we all know that those affairs or entanglements one has between *serious* loves, though they may number dozens and stretch over years, *don't really count.*

77

This way of looking at things creates a number of unhappy people, for it is well known that what doesn't really count for me might very well count for you. But there is no way of getting over this difficulty, for a *serious* love is the most important business in life, or nearly so. At any rate, most of us are engaged in looking for it. Even when we are in fact being very serious indeed with one person we still have an eighth of an eye cocked in case some stranger unexpectedly encountered might turn out to be even more serious. We are all entirely in agreement that we are in the right to taste, test, sip and sample a thousand people on our way to the *real* one. It is not too much to say that in our circles tasting and sampling is probably the second most important activity, the first being earning money. Or to put it another way, "If you are serious about this thing, you go on laying everybody that offers until something clicks and you're all set to go."

I have digressed from an earlier point: that I regarded this man I had lunch with (we will call him A) as my first love; and still do, despite the Freudians, who insist on seeing my father as A and possibly my brother as B, making my (real) first love C. And despite, also, those who might ask: What about your two husbands and all those affairs?

What about them? I did not *really* love them, the way I loved A.

I had lunch with him. Then, quite by chance, I had tea with B. When I say B, here, I mean my *second* serious love, not my brother, or the little boys I was in love with between the ages of five and fifteen, if we are going to take fifteen (arbitrarily) as the point of no return . . . which last phrase is in itself a pretty brave defiance of the secular arbiters.

In between A and B (my count) there were a good many affairs, or samples, but they didn't score. B and I *clicked*, we went off like a bomb, though not quite as simply as A and I had clicked, because my heart was bruised, sullen, and suspicious because of A's throwing me over. Also there were all those ligaments and adhesions binding me to A still to be loosened, one by one. However, for a time B and I got on like a house on fire, and then we came to grief. My heart was again a ton weight in my side.

If this were a stone in my side, a stone,
I could pluck it out and be free. . . .

Having lunch with A, then tea with B, two men who between them had consumed a decade of my precious years (I am not counting the test or trial affairs in between) and, it is fair to say, had balanced all the delight (plenty and intense) with misery (oh Lord, Lord)—moving from one to the other, in the course of an afternoon, conversing amiably about this and that, with meanwhile my heart giving no more than slight reminiscent tugs, the fish of memory at the end of a long slack line. . . .

To sum up, it was salutary.

Particularly as that evening I was expecting to meet C, or someone who might very well turn out to be C—though I don't want to give too much emphasis to C, the truth is I can hardly remember what he looked like, but one can't be expected to remember the unimportant ones one has sipped or tasted in between. But after all, he might have turned out to be C, we might have *clicked,* and I was in that state of mind (in which we all so often are) of thinking: He might turn out to be the one. (I use a woman's magazine phrase deliberately here, instead of saying, as I might: *Perhaps it will be serious.*)

So there I was (I want to get the details and atmosphere right) standing at a window looking into a street (Great Portland Street, as a matter of fact) and thinking that while I would not dream of regretting my affairs, or experiences, with A and B (it is better to have loved and lost than never to have loved at all), my anticipation of the heart because of spending an evening with a possible C had a certain unreality, because there was no doubt that both A and B had caused me unbelievable pain. Why, therefore, was I looking forward to C? I should rather be running away as fast as I could.

It suddenly occurred to me that I was looking at the whole phenomenon quite inaccurately. My (or perhaps I am permitted to say our?) way of looking at it is that one must search for an A, or a B, or a C or a D with a certain combination of desirable or sympathetic qualities so that one may click, or spontaneously combust: or to put it differently, one needs a person who, like a saucer of water, allows one to float off on him/her, like a transfer. But this wasn't so at all. Actually one carries with one a sort of burning spear stuck in one's side, that one waits for someone else to pull out; it is something painful, like a sore or a wound, that one cannot wait to share with someone else.

I saw myself quite plainly in a moment of truth: I was standing at a window (on the third floor) with A and B (to mention only the mountain peaks of my emotional experience) behind me, a rather attractive woman, if I may say so, with a mellowness that I would be the first to admit is the sad harbinger of age, but is attractive by definition, because it is a testament to the amount of sampling and sipping (I nearly wrote simpling and sapping) I have done in my time . . . there I stood, brushed, dressed, red-lipped, kohl-eyed, all waiting for an evening with a possible C. And at another window overlooking (I think I am right in saying) Margaret Street, stood C, brushed, washed, shaved, smiling: an attractive man (I think), and *he* was thinking: Perhaps she will turn out to be D (or A or 3 or ? or %, or whatever symbol he used). We stood, separated by space, certainly, in identical conditions of pleasant uncertainty and anticipation, and we both held our hearts in our hands, all pink and palpitating and ready for pleasure and pain, and we were about to throw these hearts in each other's face like snowballs, or cricket balls (How's that?) or more accurately, like great bleeding wounds: "Take my wound." Because the last thing one ever thinks at such moments is that he (or she) will say: Take *my* wound, please remove the spear from *my* side. No, not at all, one simply expects to get rid of one's own.

I decided I must go to the telephone and say C!—You know that joke about the joke-makers who don't trouble to tell each other jokes, but simply say Joke 1, or Joke 2, and everyone roars with laughter, or snickers, or giggles appropriately. . . . Actually one could reverse the game by guessing whether it was Joke C(b) or Joke A(d) according to what sort of laughter a person made to match the silent thought. . . . Well, C (I imagined myself saying), the analogy is for our instruction: Let's take the whole thing as read or said. Let's not lick each other's sores; let's keep our hearts to ourselves. Because just consider it, C, how utterly absurd—here we stand at our respective windows with our palpitating hearts in our hands. . . .

At this moment, dear reader, I was forced simply to put down the telephone with an apology. For I felt the fingers of my left hand push outwards around something rather large, light, and slippery—hard to describe this sensation, really. My hand is not large, and my heart was in a state of inflation after having had lunch with A, tea with B, and then looking forward to C. . . . Anyway, my fingers were stretching out rather desperately to encompass an unknown, largish, lightish object, and I said: Excuse me a minute, to C, looked down, and there was my heart, in my hand.

I had to end the conversation there.

For one thing, to find that one has achieved something so often longed for, so easily, is upsetting. It's not as if I had been trying. To get something one wants simply by accident—no, there's no pleasure in it, no feeling of achievement. So to find myself heart-whole, or, more accurately, heart-less, or at any rate, rid of the damned thing, and at such an awkward moment, in the middle of an imaginary telephone call with a man who might possibly turn out to be C, well, it was irritating rather than not.

For another thing, a heart, raw and bleeding and fresh from one's side, is not the prettiest sight. I'm not going into that at all. I was appalled, and indeed embarrassed that *that* was what had been loving and beating away all those years, because if I'd had any idea at all—well, enough of that.

My problem was how to get rid of it.

Simple, you'll say, drop it into the waste bucket.

Well, let me tell you, that's what I tried to do. I took a good look at this object, nearly died with embarrassment, and walked over to the rubbish can, where I tried to let it roll off my fingers. It wouldn't. It was stuck. There was my heart, a large red pulsing bleeding repulsive object, stuck to my fingers. What was I going to do? I sat down, lit a cigarette (with one hand, holding the matchbox between my knees), held my hand with the heart stuck on it over the side of the chair so that it could drip into a bucket, and considered.

If this were a stone in my hand, a stone,
I could throw it over a tree. . . .

When I had finished the cigarette, I carefully unwrapped some tin foil, of the kind used to wrap food in when cooking, and fitted a sort of cover around my heart. This was absolutely and urgently necessary. First, it was smarting badly. After all, it had spent some forty years protected by flesh and ribs and the air was too much for it. Secondly, I couldn't have any Tom, Dick and Harry walking in and looking at it. Thirdly, I could not look at it for too long myself, it filled me with shame. The tin foil was effective, and indeed rather striking. It is quite pliable and now it seemed as if there were a stylised heart balanced on my palm, like a globe, in glittering, silvery substance. I almost felt I needed a sceptre in the other hand to balance it. . . . But the thing was, there is no other word for it, in bad taste. I then wrapped a scarf around hand and tin-foiled heart, and felt safer. Now it was a question of pretending to have hurt my hand until I could think of a way of getting rid of my heart altogether, short of amputating my hand.

Meanwhile I telephoned (really, not in imagination) C, who now would never be C. I could feel my heart, which was stuck so close to my fingers that I could feel every beat or tremor, give a gulp of resigned grief at the idea of this beautiful experience now never to be. I told him some idiotic lie about having flu. Well, he was all stiff and indignant, but concealing it urbanely, as I would have done, making a joke but allowing a tiny barb of sarcasm to rankle in the last well-chosen phrase. Then I sat down again to think out my whole situation.

There I sat.

What was I going to do?

There I sat.

I am going to have to skip about four days here, vital enough in all conscience, because I simply cannot go heartbeat by heartbeat through my memories. A pity, since I suppose this is what this story is about; but in brief: I drew the curtains, I took the telephone off the hook, I turned on the lights, I took the scarf off the glittering shape, then the tin foil, then I examined the heart. There were two-fifths of a century's experience to work through, and before I had even got through the first night, I was in a state hard to describe. . . .

> *Or if I could pull the nerves from my skin*
> *A quick red net to drag through a sea for fish. . . .*

By the end of the fourth day I was worn out. By no act of will, or intention, or desire, could I move that heart by a fraction—on the contrary, it was not only stuck to my fingers, like a sucked boiled sweet, but was actually growing to the flesh of my fingers and my palm.

I wrapped it up again in tin foil and scarf, and turned out the lights and pulled up the blinds and opened the curtains. It was about ten in the morning, an ordinary London day, neither hot nor cold nor clear nor clouded nor wet nor fine. And while the street is interesting, it is not exactly beautiful, so I wasn't looking at it so much as waiting for something to catch my attention while thinking of something else.

Suddenly I heard a tap-tap-tapping that got louder, sharp and clear, and I knew before I saw her that this was the sound of high heels on a pavement though it might just as well have been a hammer against stone. She walked fast opposite my window and her heels hit the pavement so hard that all the noises of the street seemed absorbed into that single tap-tap-clang-clang. As she reached the corner at Great Portland Street two London pigeons swooped diagonally from the sky very fast, as if they were bullets aimed to kill her; and then as they saw her they swooped up and off at an angle. Meanwhile she had turned the corner. All this has taken time to write down, but the thing happening took a couple of seconds: the woman's body hitting the pavement bang-bang through her heels then sharply turning the corner in a right angle; and the pigeons making another acute angle across hers and intersecting it in a fast swoop of displaced air. Nothing to all that, of course, nothing— she had gone off down the street, her heels tip-tapping, and the pigeons landed on my windowsill and began cooing. All gone, all vanished, the marvellous exact coordination of sound and movement, but it had happened, it had made me happy and exhilarated, I had no problems in this world, and I realized that the heart stuck to my fingers was quite loose. I couldn't get it off altogether, though I was tugging at it under the scarf and the tin foil, but almost.

I understood that sitting and analysing each movement or pulse or beat of my heart through forty years was a mistake. I was on the wrong track altogether: this was the way to attach my red, bitter, delighted heart to my flesh forever and ever. . . .

> *Ha! So you think I'm done! You think. . . .*
> *Watch, I'll roll my heart in a mesh of rage*
> *And bounce it like a handball off*
> *Walls, faces, railings, umbrellas and pigeons' backs. . . .*

No, all that was no good at all, it just made things worse. What I must do is to take myself by surprise, as it were, the way I was taken by surprise over the woman and the pigeons and the sharp sounds of heels and silk wings.

I put on my coat, held my lumpy scarfed arm across my chest, so that if anyone said: What have you done with your hand? I could say: I've banged my finger in the door. Then I walked down into the street.

It wasn't easy to go among so many people, when I was worried that they were thinking: What has that woman done to her hand? because that made it hard to forget myself. And all the time it tingled and throbbed against my fingers, reminding me.

Now I was out I didn't know what to do. Should I go and have lunch with someone? Or wander in the park? Or buy myself a dress? I decided to go to the Round Pond, and walk around it by myself. I was tired after four days and nights without sleep. I went down into the Underground at Oxford Circus. Midday. Crowds of people. I felt self-conscious, but of course need not have worried. I swear you could walk naked down the street in London and no one would even turn round.

So I went down the escalator and looked at the faces coming up past me on the other side, as I always do; and wondered, as I always do, how strange it is that those people and I should meet by chance in such a way, and how odd that we would never see each other again, or, if we did, we wouldn't know it. And I went on to the crowded platform and looked at the faces as I always do, and got into the train, which was very full, and found a seat. It wasn't as bad as rush hour, but all the seats were filled. I leaned back and closed my eyes, deciding to sleep a little, being so tired. I was just beginning to doze off, when I heard a woman's voice muttering, or rather, declaiming:

> *"A gold cigarette case, well, that's a nice thing,*
> *isn't it, I must say, a gold case, yes. . . ."*

There was something about this voice which made me open my eyes: on the other side of the compartment, about eight persons away, sat a youngish woman, wearing a cheap green cloth coat, gloveless hands, flat brown shoes, and lisle stockings. She must be rather poor—a woman dressed like this is a rare sight, these days. But it was her posture that struck me. She was sitting half twisted in her seat, so that her head was turned over her left shoulder, and she was looking straight at the stomach of an elderly man next to her. But it was clear she was not seeing it: her young staring eyes were sightless, she was looking inwards.

She was so clearly alone, in the crowded compartment, that it was not as embarrassing as it might have been. I looked around, and people were smiling, or exchanging glances, or winking, or ignoring her, according to their natures, but she was oblivious of us all.

She suddenly aroused herself, turned so that she sat straight in her seat, and directed her voice and her gaze to the opposite seat:

> *"Well so that's what you think, you think that, you*
> *think that do you, well, you think I'm just going*
> *to wait at home for you, but you gave her a gold*
> *case and . . ."*

And with a clockwork movement of her whole thin person, she turned her narrow pale-haired head sideways over her left shoulder, and resumed her stiff empty stare at the man's stomach. He was grinning uncomfortably. I leaned forward to look along the line of people in the row of seats I sat in, and the man opposite her, a young man, had exactly the same look of discomfort which he was determined to keep amused. So we all looked at her, the young, thin, pale woman in her private drama of misery, who was so completely unconscious of us that she spoke and thought out loud. And again, without particular warning or reason, in between stops, so it wasn't that she was disturbed from her dream by the train stopping at Bond Street, and then jumping forward again, she twisted her body frontways, and addressed the seat opposite her (the young man had got off, and a smart grey-curled matron had got in):

*"Well I know about it now, don't I, and if you come
in all smiling and pleased well then I know, don't
I, you don't have to tell me, I know, and I've said
to her, I've said, I know he gave you a gold cigarette
case. . . ."*

At which point, with the same clockwork impulse, she stopped, or was checked, or simply ran out, and turned herself half around to stare at the stomach—the same stomach, for the middle-aged man was still there. But we stopped at Marble Arch and he got out, giving the compartment, rather than the people in it, a tolerant half-smile which said: I am sure I can trust you to realize that this unfortunate woman is stark staring mad. . . .

His seat remained empty. No people got in at Marble Arch, and the two people standing waiting for seats did not want to sit by her to receive her stare.

We all sat, looking gently in front of us, pretending to ourselves and to each other that we didn't know the poor woman was mad and that in fact we ought to be doing something about it. I even wondered what I should say: Madam, you're mad—shall I escort you to your home? Or: Poor thing, don't go on like that, it doesn't do any good, you know—just leave him, that'll bring him to his senses. . . .

And behold, after the interval that was regulated by her inner mechanism had elapsed, she turned back and said to the smart matron who received this statement of accusation with perfect self-command:

> *"Yes, I know! Oh yes! And what about my*
> *shoes, what about them, a golden cigarette*
> *case is what she got, the filthy bitch,*
> *a golden case. . . ."*

Stop. Twist. Stare. At the empty seat by her.

Extraordinary. Because it was a frozen misery, how shall I put it? A passionless passion—we were seeing unhappiness embodied, we were looking at the essence of some private tragedy—rather, Tragedy. There was no emotion in it. She was like an actress doing Accusation, or Betrayed Love, or Infidelity, when she has only just learned her lines and is not bothering to do more than get them right.

And whether she sat in her half-twisted position, her un-blinking eyes staring at the greenish, furry, ugly covering of the train seat, or sat straight, directing her accusation to the smart woman opposite, there was a frightening immobility about her—yes, that was why she frightened us. For it was clear that she might very well (if the inner machine ran down) stay silent, forever, in either twisted or straight position, or at any point between them—yes, we could all imagine her, frozen perpetually in some arbitrary pose. It was as if we watched the shell of some woman going through certain predetermined motions.

For *she* was simply not there. *What* was there, who she was, it was impossible to tell, though it was easy to imagine her thin, gentle little face breaking into a smile in total for-getfulness of what she was enacting now. She did not know she was in a train between Marble Arch and Queensway, nor that she was publicly accusing her husband or lover, nor that we were looking at her.

And we, looking at her, felt an embarrassment and shame that was not on her account at all. . . .

Suddenly I felt, under the scarf and the tin foil, a lighten-ing of my fingers, as my heart rolled loose.

I hastily took it off my palm, in case it decided to adhere there again, and I removed the scarf, leaving balanced on my knees a perfect stylised heart, like a silver heart on a Valentine card, though of course it was three-dimensional.

This heart was not so much harmless, no that isn't the word, as artistic, but in very bad taste, as I said. I could see that the people in the train, now looking at me and the heart, and not at the poor madwoman, were pleased with it.

I got up, took the four or so paces to where she was, and laid the tin-foiled heart down on the seat so that it received her stare.

For a moment she did not react, then with a groan or a mutter of relieved and entirely theatrical grief, she leaned forward, picked up the glittering heart, and clutched it in her arms, hugging it and rocking it back and forth, even laying her cheek against it, while staring over its top at her husband as if to say: Look what I've got, I don't care about you and your cigarette case, I've got a silver heart.

I got up, since we were at Notting Hill Gate, and, followed by the pleased congratulatory nods and smiles of the people left behind, I went out onto the platform, up the escalators, into the street, and along to the park.

No heart. No heart at all. What bliss. What freedom. . . .

Hear that sound? That's laughter, yes.
That's me laughing, yes, that's me.

A Man and Two Women

•

•   •

STELLA'S friends the Bradfords had taken a cheap cottage in Essex for the summer, and she was going down to visit them. She wanted to see them, but there was no doubt there was something of a letdown (and for them too) in the English cottage. Last summer Stella had been wandering with her husband around Italy; had seen the English couple at a café table, and found them sympathetic. They all liked each other, and the four went about for some weeks, sharing meals, hotels, trips. Back in London the friendship had not, as might have been expected, fallen off. Then Stella's husband departed abroad, as he often did, and Stella saw Jack and Dorothy by herself. There were a great many people she might have seen, but it was the Bradfords she saw most often, two or three times a week, at their flat or hers. They were at ease with each other. Why were they? Well, for one thing they were all artists—in different ways. Stella designed wallpapers and materials; she had a name for it.

The Bradfords were real artists. He painted, she drew. They had lived mostly out of England in cheap places around the Mediterranean. Both from the North of England, they had met at art school, married at twenty, had taken flight from England, then returned to it, needing it, then off again: and so on, for years, in the rhythm of so many of their kind, needing, hating, loving England. There had been seasons of real poverty, while they lived on *pasta* or bread or rice, and wine and fruit and sunshine, in Majorca, southern Spain, Italy, North Africa.

A French critic had seen Jack's work, and suddenly he was

successful. His show in Paris, then one in London, made money; and now he charged in the hundreds where a year or so ago he charged ten or twenty guineas. This had deepened his contempt for the values of the markets. For a while Stella thought that this was the bond between the Bradfords and herself. They were so very much, as she was, of the new generation of artists (and poets and playwrights and novelists) who had one thing in common, a cool derision about the racket. They were so very unlike (they felt) the older generation with their Societies and their Lunches and their salons and their cliques: their atmosphere of connivance with the snobberies of success. Stella, too, had been successful by a fluke. Not that she did not consider herself talented; it was that others as talented were unfêted, and unbought. When she was with the Bradfords and other fellow spirits, they would talk about the racket, using each other as yardsticks or fellow consciences about how much to give in, what to give, how to use without being used, how to enjoy without becoming dependent on enjoyment.

Of course Dorothy Bradford was not able to talk in quite the same way, since she had not yet been "discovered"; she had not "broken through." A few people with discrimination bought her unusual delicate drawings, which had a strength that was hard to understand unless one knew Dorothy herself. But she was not at all, as Jack was, a great success. There was a strain here, in the marriage, nothing much; it was kept in check by their scorn for their arbitrary rewards of "the racket." But it was there, nevertheless.

Stella's husband had said: "Well, I can understand that, it's like me and you—you're creative, whatever that may mean, I'm just a bloody TV journalist." There was no bitterness in this. He was a good journalist, and besides he sometimes got the chance to make a good small film. All the same, there was that between him and Stella, just as there was between Jack and his wife.

After a time Stella saw something else in her kinship with the couple. It was that the Bradfords had a close bond, bred of having spent so many years together in foreign places, dependent on each other because of their poverty. It had been a real love marriage, one could see it by looking at them. It was now. And Stella's marriage was a real marriage.

She understood she enjoyed being with the Bradfords because the two couples were equal in this. Both marriages were those of strong, passionate, talented individuals; they shared a battling quality that strengthened them, not weakened them.

The reason why it had taken Stella so long to understand this was that the Bradfords had made her think about her own marriage, which she was beginning to take for granted, sometimes even found exhausting. She had understood, through them, how lucky she was in her husband; how lucky they all were. No marital miseries; nothing of (what they saw so often in friends) one partner in a marriage victim to the other, resenting the other; no claiming of outsiders as sympathisers or allies in an unequal battle.

There had been a plan for these four people to go off again to Italy or Spain, but then Stella's husband departed, and Dorothy got pregnant. So there was the cottage in Essex instead, a bad second choice, but better, they all felt, to deal with a new baby on home ground, at least for the first year. Stella, telephoned by Jack (on Dorothy's particular insistence, he said), offered and received commiserations on its being only Essex and not Majorca or Italy. She also received sympathy because her husband had been expected back this weekend, but had wired to say he wouldn't be back for another month, probably—there was trouble in Venezuela. Stella wasn't really forlorn; she didn't mind living alone, since she was always supported by knowing her man would be back. Besides, if she herself were offered the chance of a month's "trouble" in Venezuela, she wouldn't hesitate, so it wasn't fair . . . fairness characterised their relationship. All the same, it was nice that she could drop down (or up) to the Bradfords, people with whom she could always be herself, neither more nor less.

She left London at midday by train, armed with food unobtainable in Essex: salamis, cheeses, spices, wine. The sun shone, but it wasn't particularly warm. She hoped there would be heating in the cottage, July or not.

The train was empty. The little station seemed stranded in a green nowhere. She got out, cumbered by bags full of food. A porter and a stationmaster examined, then came to succour her. She was a tallish, fair woman, rather ample;

her soft hair, drawn back, escaped in tendrils, and she had great helpless-looking blue eyes. She wore a dress made in one of the materials she had designed. Enormous green leaves laid hands all over her body, and fluttered about her knees. She stood smiling, accustomed to men running to wait on her, enjoying them enjoying her. She walked with them to the barrier where Jack waited, appreciating the scene. He was a smallish man, compact, dark. He wore a blue-green summer shirt, and smoked a pipe and smiled, watching. The two men delivered her into the hands of the third, and departed, whistling, to their duties.

Jack and Stella kissed, then pressed their cheeks together.

"Food," he said, "food," relieving her of the parcels.

"What's it like here, shopping?"

"Vegetables all right, I suppose."

Jack was still Northern in this: he seemed brusque, to strangers; he wasn't shy, he simply hadn't been brought up to enjoy words. Now he put his arm briefly around Stella's waist, and said: "Marvellous, Stell, marvellous." They walked on, pleased with each other. Stella had with Jack, her husband had with Dorothy, these moments, when they said to each other wordlessly: If I were not married to my husband, if you were not married to your wife, how delightful it would be to be married to you. These moments were not the least of the pleasures of this four-sided friendship.

"Are you liking it down here?"

"It's what we bargained for."

There was more than his usual shortness in this, and she glanced at him to find him frowning. They were walking to the car, parked under a tree.

"How's the baby?"

"Little bleeder never sleeps, he's wearing us out, but he's fine."

The baby was six weeks old. Having the baby was a definite achievement: getting it safely conceived and born had taken a couple of years. Dorothy, like most independent women, had had divided thoughts about a baby. Besides, she was over thirty and complained she was set in her ways. All this—the difficulties, Dorothy's hesitations—had added up to an atmosphere which Dorothy herself described as "like wondering if some damned horse is going to take the fence."

Dorothy would talk, while she was pregnant, in a soft staccato voice: "Perhaps I don't really want a baby at all? Perhaps I'm not fitted to be a mother? Perhaps . . . and if so . . . and how . . . ?"

She said: "Until recently Jack and I were always with people who took it for granted that getting pregnant was a disaster, and now suddenly all the people we know have young children and baby-sitters and . . . perhaps . . . if . . ."

Jack said: "You'll feel better when it's born."

Once Stella had heard him say, after one of Dorothy's long troubled dialogues with herself: "Now that's enough, that's enough, Dorothy." He had silenced her, taking the responsibility.

They reached the car, got in. It was a second-hand job recently bought. "They" (being the press, the enemy generally) "wait for us" (being artists or writers who have made money) "to buy flashy cars." They had discussed it, decided that *not* to buy an expensive car if they felt like it would be allowing themselves to be bullied; but bought a second-hand one after all. Jack wasn't going to give *them* so much satisfaction, apparently.

"Actually we could have walked," he said, as they shot down a narrow lane, "but with these groceries, it's just as well."

"If the baby's giving you a tough time, there can't be much time for cooking." Dorothy was a wonderful cook. But now again there was something in the air as he said: "Food's definitely not too good just now. You can cook supper, Stell, we could do with a good feed."

Now Dorothy hated anyone in her kitchen, except, for certain specified jobs, her husband; and this was surprising.

"The truth is, Dorothy's worn out," he went on, and now Stella understood he was warning her.

"Well, it is tiring," said Stella soothingly.

"You were like that?"

Like that was saying a good deal more than just worn out, or tired, and Stella understood that Jack was really uneasy. She said, plaintively humorous: "You two always expect me to remember things that happened a hundred years ago. Let me think. . . ."

She had been married when she was eighteen, got pregnant at once. Her husband had left her. Soon she had married Philip, who also had a small child from a former marriage. These two children, her daughter, seventeen, his son, twenty, had grown up together.

She remembered herself at nineteen, alone, with a small baby. "Well, I was alone," she said. "That makes a difference. I remember I was exhausted. Yes, I was definitely irritable and unreasonable."

"Yes," said Jack, with a brief reluctant look at her.

"All right, don't worry," she said, replying aloud as she often did to things that Jack had not said aloud.

"Good," he said.

Stella thought of how she had seen Dorothy, in the hospital room, with the new baby. She had sat up in bed, in a pretty bed jacket, the baby beside her in a basket. He was restless. Jack stood between basket and bed, one large hand on his son's stomach. "Now, you just shut up, little bleeder," he had said, as he grumbled. Then he had picked him up, as if he'd been doing it always, held him against his shoulder, and, as Dorothy held her arms out, had put the baby into them. "Want your mother, then? Don't blame you."

That scene, the ease of it, the way the two parents were together, had, for Stella, made nonsense of all the months of Dorothy's self-questioning. As for Dorothy, she had said, parodying the expected words but meaning them: "He's the most beautiful baby ever born. I can't imagine why I didn't have him before."

"There's the cottage," said Jack. Ahead of them was a small labourer's cottage, among full green trees, surrounded by green grass. It was painted white, had four sparkling windows. Next to it a long shed or structure that turned out to be a greenhouse.

"The man grew tomatoes," said Jack. "Fine studio now."

The car came to rest under another tree.

"Can I just drop in to the studio?"

"Help yourself." Stella walked into the long, glass-roofed shed. In London Jack and Dorothy shared a studio. They had shared huts, sheds, any suitable building, all around the Mediterranean. They always worked side by side. Dorothy's end was tidy, exquisite, Jack's lumbered with great canvases, and he worked in a clutter. Now Stella looked to see if this friendly arrangement continued, but as Jack came in behind her he said: "Dorothy's not set herself up yet. I miss her, I can tell you."

The greenhouse was still partly one: trestles with plants stood along the ends. It was lush and warm.

"As hot as hell when the sun's really going, it makes up. And Dorothy brings Paul in sometimes, so he can get used to a decent climate young."

Dorothy came in, at the far end, without the baby. She had recovered her figure. She was a small dark woman, with neat, delicate limbs. Her face was white, with scarlet rather irregular lips, and black glossy brows, a little crooked. So while she was not pretty, she was lively and dramatic-looking. She and Stella had their moments together, when they got pleasure from contrasting their differences, one woman so big and soft and blond, the other so dark and vivacious.

Dorothy came forward through shafts of sunlight, stopped, and said: "Stella, I'm glad you've come." Then forward again, to a few steps off, where she stood looking at them. "You two look good together," she said, frowning. There was something heavy and overemphasised about both statements, and Stella said: "I was wondering what Jack had been up to."

"Very good, I think," said Dorothy, coming to look at the new canvas on the easel. It was of sunlit rocks, brown and smooth, with blue sky, blue water, and people swimming in spangles of light. When Jack was in the South he painted pictures that his wife described as "dirt and grime and misery"—which was how they both described their joint childhood background. When he was in England he painted scenes like these.

"Like it? It's good, isn't it?" said Dorothy.

"Very much," said Stella. She always took pleasure from the contrast between Jack's outward self—the small, self-contained little man who could have vanished in a moment into a crowd of factory workers in, perhaps Manchester, and the sensuous bright pictures like these.

"And you?" asked Stella.

"Having a baby's killed everything creative in me—quite different from being pregnant," said Dorothy, but not complaining of it. She had worked like a demon while she was pregnant.

"Have a heart," said Jack, "he's only just got himself born."

"Well, I don't care," said Dorothy. "That's the funny thing, I *don't* care." She said this flat, indifferent. She seemed to be looking at them both again from a small troubled distance. "You two look good together," she said, and again there was the small jar.

"Well, how about some tea?" said Jack, and Dorothy said at once: "I made it when I heard the car. I thought better inside, it's not really hot in the sun." She led the way out of the greenhouse, her white linen dress dissolving in lozenges of yellow light from the glass panes above, so that Stella was reminded of the white limbs of Jack's swimmers disintegrating under sunlight in his new picture. The work of these two people was always reminding one of each other, or each other's work, and in all kinds of ways: they were so much married, so close.

The time it took to cross the space of rough grass to the door of the little house was enough to show Dorothy was right: it was really chilly in the sun. Inside two electric heaters made up for it. There had been two little rooms downstairs, but they had been knocked into one fine low-ceilinged room, stone-floored, whitewashed. A tea table, covered with a purple checked cloth, stood waiting near a window where flowering bushes and trees showed through clean panes. Charming. They adjusted the heaters and arranged themselves so they could admire the English countryside through glass. Stella looked for the baby; Dorothy said: "In the pram at the back." Then she asked: "Did yours cry a lot?"

Stella laughed and said again: "I'll try to remember."

"We expect you to guide and direct, with all your experience," said Jack.

"As far as I can remember, she was a little demon for about three months, for no reason I could see, then suddenly she became civilised."

"Roll on the three months," said Jack.

"Six weeks to go," said Dorothy, handling teacups in a languid indifferent manner Stella found new in her.

"Finding it tough going?"

"I've never felt better in my life," said Dorothy at once, as if being accused.

"You look fine."

She looked a bit tired, nothing much; Stella couldn't see what reason there was for Jack to warn her. Unless he meant the languor, a look of self-absorption? Her vivacity, a friendly aggressiveness that was the expression of her lively intelligence, was dimmed. She sat leaning back in a deep airchair, letting Jack manage things, smiling vaguely.

"I'll bring him in in a minute," she remarked, listening to the silence from the sunlit garden at the back.

"Leave him," said Jack. "He's quiet seldom enough. Relax, woman, and have a cigarette."

He lit a cigarette for her, and she took it in the same vague way, and sat breathing out smoke, her eyes half closed.

"Have you heard from Philip?" she asked, not from politeness, but with sudden insistence.

"Of course she has, she got a wire," said Jack.

"I want to know how she feels," said Dorothy. "How do you feel, Stell?" She was listening for the baby all the time.

"Feel about what?"

"About his not coming back."

"But he is coming back, it's only a month," said Stella, and heard, with surprise, that her voice sounded edgy.

"You see?" said Dorothy to Jack, meaning the words, not the edge on them.

At this evidence that she and Philip had been discussed, Stella felt, first, pleasure: because it was pleasurable to be understood by two such good friends; then she felt discomfort, remembering Jack's warning.

"See what?" she asked Dorothy, smiling.

"That's enough now," said Jack to his wife in a flash of stubborn anger, which continued the conversation that had taken place.

Dorothy took direction from her husband, and kept quiet a moment, then seemed impelled to continue: "I've been thinking it must be nice, having your husband go off, then come back. Do you realise Jack and I haven't been separated since we married? That's over ten years. Don't you think there's something awful in two grown people stuck together all the time like Siamese twins?" This ended in a wail of genuine appeal to Stella.

"No, I think it's marvellous."

"But you don't mind being alone so much?"

"It's not *so* much, it's two or three months in a year. Well of course I mind. But I enjoy being alone, really. But I'd enjoy it too if we were together all the time. I envy you two." Stella was surprised to find her eyes wet with self-pity because she had to be without her husband another month.

"And what does he think?" demanded Dorothy. "What does Philip think?"

Stella said: "Well, I think he likes getting away from time to time—yes. He likes intimacy, he enjoys it, but it doesn't come as easily to him as it does to me." She had never said this before because she had never thought about it. She was annoyed with herself that she had had to wait for Dorothy to prompt her. Yet she knew that getting annoyed was what she must not do, with the state Dorothy was in, whatever it was. She glanced at Jack for guidance, but he was determinedly busy on his pipe.

"Well, I'm like Philip," announced Dorothy. "Yes, I'd love it if Jack went off sometimes. I think I'm being stifled being shut up with Jack day and night, year in year out."

"Thanks," said Jack, short but good-humoured.

"No, but I mean it. There's something humiliating about two adult people never for one second out of each other's sight."

"Well," said Jack, "when Paul's a bit bigger, you buzz off for a month or so and you'll appreciate me when you get back."

"It's not that I don't appeciate you, it's not that at all," said Dorothy, insistent, almost strident, apparently fevered with restlessness. Her languor had quite gone, and her limbs jerked and moved. And now the baby, as if he had been prompted by his father's mentioning him, let out a cry. Jack got up, forestalling his wife, saying: "I'll get him."

Dorothy sat, listening for her husband's movements with the baby, until he came back, which he did, supporting the infant sprawled against his shoulder with a competent hand. He sat down, let his son slide onto his chest, and said:

"There now, you shut up and leave us in peace a bit longer." The baby was looking up into his face with the astonished expression of the newly born, and Dorothy sat smiling at both of them. Stella understood that her restlessness, her repeated curtailed movements, meant that she longed—more, needed—to have the child in her arms, have its body against hers. And Jack seemed to feel this, because Stella could have sworn it was not a conscious decision that made him rise and slide the infant into his wife's arms. Her flesh, her needs, had spoken direct to him without words, and he had risen at once to give her what she wanted. This silent instinctive conversation between husband and wife made Stella miss her own husband violently, and with resentment against fate that kept them apart so often. She ached for Philip.

Meanwhile Dorothy, now the baby was sprawled softly against her chest, the small feet in her hand, seemed to have lapsed into good humour. And Stella, watching, remembered something she really had forgotten: the close, fierce physical tie between herself and her daughter when she had been a tiny baby. She saw this bond in the way Dorothy stroked the small head that trembled on its neck as the baby looked up into his mother's face. Why, she remembered it was like being in love, having a new baby. All kinds of forgotten or unused instincts woke in Stella. She lit a cigarette, took herself in hand; set herself to enjoy the other woman's love affair with her baby instead of envying her.

The sun, dropping into the trees, struck the windowpanes; and there was a dazzle and a flashing of yellow and white light into the room, particularly over Dorothy in her white dress and the baby. Again Stella was reminded of Jack's picture of the white-limbed swimmers in sun-dissolving water. Dorothy shielded the baby's eyes with her hand and remarked dreamily: "This is better than any man, isn't it, Stell? Isn't it better than any man?"

"Well—no," said Stella laughing. "No, not for long."

"If you say so, you should know . . . but I can't imagine ever . . . tell me, Stell, does your Philip have affairs when he's away?"

"For God's sake!" said Jack, angry. But he checked himself.

"Yes, I am sure he does."

"Do you mind?" asked Dorothy, loving the baby's feet with her enclosing palm.

And now Stella was forced to remember, to think about having minded, minding, coming to terms, and the ways in which she now did not mind.

"I don't think about it," she said.

"Well, I don't think I'd mind," said Dorothy.

"Thanks for letting me know," said Jack, short despite himself. Then he made himself laugh.

"And you, do you have affairs while Philip's away?"

"Sometimes. Not really."

"Do you know, Jack was unfaithful to me this week," remarked Dorothy, smiling at the baby.

"That's *enough*," said Jack, really angry.

"No it isn't enough, it isn't. Because what's awful is, I don't care."

"Well why should you care, in the circumstances?" Jack turned to Stella. "There's a silly bitch Lady Edith lives across that field. She got all excited, real live artists living down her lane. Well Dorothy was lucky, she had an excuse in the baby, but I had to go to her silly party. Booze flowing in rivers, and the most incredible people—you know. If you read about them in a novel you'd never believe . . . but I can't remember much after about twelve."

"Do you know what happened?" said Dorothy. "I was feeding the baby, it was terribly early. Jack sat straight up in bed and said: 'Jesus, Dorothy, I've just remembered, I screwed that silly bitch Lady Edith on her brocade sofa.' "

Stella laughed. Jack let out a snort of laughter. Dorothy laughed, an unscrupulous chuckle of appreciation. Then she said seriously: "But that's the point, Stella—the thing is, I don't care a tuppenny damn."

"But why should you?" asked Stella.

"But it's the first time he ever has, and surely I should have minded?"

"Don't you be too sure of that," said Jack, energetically puffing his pipe. "Don't be too sure." But it was only for form's sake, and Dorothy knew it, and said: "Surely I should have cared, Stell?"

"No. You'd have cared if you and Jack weren't so marvellous together. Just as I'd care if Philip and I weren't. . . ."

Tears came running down her face. She let them. These were her good friends; and besides, instinct told her tears weren't a bad thing, with Dorothy in this mood. She said, sniffing: "When Philip gets home, we always have a flaming bloody row in the first day or two, about something unimportant, but what it's really about, and we know it, is that I'm jealous of any affair he's had and vice versa. Then we go to bed and make up." She wept, bitterly, thinking of this happiness, postponed for a month, to be succeeded by the delightful battle of their day to day living.

"Oh Stella," said Jack. "Stell . . ." He got up, fished out a handkerchief, dabbed her eyes for her. "There, love, he'll be back soon."

"Yes, I know. It's just that you two are so good together and whenever I'm with you I miss Philip."

"Well, I suppose we're good together?" said Dorothy, sounding surprised. Jack, bending over Stella with his back to his wife, made a warning grimace, then stood up and turned, commanding the situation. "It's nearly six. You'd better feed Paul. Stella's going to cook supper."

"Is she? How nice," said Dorothy. "There's everything in the kitchen, Stella. How lovely to be looked after."

"I'll show you our mansion," said Jack.

Upstairs were two small white rooms. One was the bedroom, with their things and the baby's in it. The other was an overflow room, jammed with stuff. Jack picked up a large leather folder off the spare bed and said: "Look at these, Stell." He stood at the window, back to her, his thumb at work in his pipe bowl, looking into the garden. Stella sat on the bed, opened the folder and at once exclaimed: "When did she do these?"

"The last three months she was pregnant. Never seen anything like it, she just turned them out one after the other."

There were a couple of hundred pencil drawings, all of two bodies in every kind of balance, tension, relationship. The two bodies were Jack's and Dorothy's, mostly unclothed, but not all. The drawings startled, not only because they marked a real jump forward in Dorothy's achievement, but because of their bold sensuousness. They were a kind of chant, or exaltation about the marriage. The instinctive closeness, the harmony of Jack and Dorothy, visible in every movement they made towards or away from each other, visible even when they were not together, was celebrated here with a frank, calm triumph.

"Some of them are pretty strong," said Jack, the Northern working-class boy reviving in him for a moment's puritanism.

But Stella laughed, because the prudishness masked pride: some of the drawings were indecent.

In the last few of the series the woman's body was swollen in pregnancy. They showed her trust in her husband, whose body, commanding hers, stood or lay in positions of strength and confidence. In the very last Dorothy stood turned away from her husband, her two hands supporting her big belly, and Jack's hands were protective on her shoulders.

"They are marvellous," said Stella.

"They are, aren't they."

Stella looked, laughing, and with love, towards Jack; for she saw that his showing her the drawings was not only pride in his wife's talent; but that he was using this way of telling Stella not to take Dorothy's mood too seriously. And to cheer himself up. She said, impulsively: "Well that's all right then, isn't it?"

"What? Oh yes, I see what you mean, yes, I think it's all right."

"Do you know what?" said Stella, lowering her voice. "I think Dorothy's guilty because she feels unfaithful to you."

"*What?*"

"No, I mean, with the baby, and that's what it's all about."

He turned to face her, troubled, then slowly smiling. There was the same rich unscrupulous quality of appreciation in that smile as there had been in Dorothy's laugh over her husband and Lady Edith. "You think so?" They laughed together, irrepressibly and loudly.

"What's the joke?" shouted Dorothy.

"I'm laughing because your drawings are so good," shouted Stella.

"Yes, they are, aren't they?" But Dorothy's voice changed to flat incredulity: "The trouble is, I can't imagine how I ever did them, I can't imagine ever being able to do it again."

"Downstairs," said Jack to Stella, and they went down to

find Dorothy nursing the baby. He nursed with his whole being, all of him in movement. He was wrestling with the
breast, thumping Dorothy's plump pretty breast with his
fists. Jack stood looking down at the two of them, grinning.
Dorothy reminded Stella of a cat, half closing her yellow
eyes to stare over her kittens at work on her side, while
she stretched out a paw where claws sheathed and unsheathed
themselves, making a small rip-rip-rip on the carpet she lay
on.

"You're a savage creature," said Stella, laughing.

Dorothy raised her small vivid face and smiled. "Yes, I
am," she said, and looked at the two of them calm, and
from a distance, over the head of her energetic baby.

Stella cooked supper in a stone kitchen, with a heater
brought by Jack to make it tolerable. She used the good food
she had brought with her, taking trouble. It took some time,
then the three ate slowly over a big wooden table. The baby
was not asleep. He grumbled for some minutes on a cushion
on the floor, then his father held him briefly, before passing
him over, as he had done earlier, in response to his mother's
need to have him close.

"I'm supposed to let him cry," remarked Dorothy. "But
why should he? If he were an Arab or an African baby
he'd be plastered to my back."

"And very nice too," said Jack. "I think they come out
too soon into the light of day, they should just stay inside
for about eighteen months, much better all around."

"Have a heart," said Dorothy and Stella together, and
they all laughed; but Dorothy added, quite serious: "Yes,
I've been thinking so too."

This good nature lasted through the long meal. The light
went cool and thin outside; and inside they let the summer
dusk deepen, without lamps.

"I've got to go quite soon," said Stella, with regret.

"Oh, no, you've got to stay!" said Dorothy, strident. It
was sudden, the return of the woman who made Jack and
Dorothy tense themselves to take strain.

"We all thought Philip was coming. The children will be
back tomorrow night, they've been on holiday."

"Then stay till tomorrow, I *want* you," said Dorothy,
petulant.

"But I can't," said Stella.

"I never thought I'd want another woman around, cooking in my kitchen, looking after me, but I do," said Dorothy, apparently about to cry.

"Well, love, you'll have to put up with me," said Jack.

"Would you mind, Stell?"

"Mind *what?*" asked Stella, cautious.

"Do you find Jack attractive?"

"Very."

"Well I know you do. Jack, do you find Stella attractive?"

"Try me," said Jack, grinning; but at the same time signalling warnings to Stella.

"Well, then!" said Dorothy.

"A *ménage à trois?*" asked Stella laughing. "And how about my Philip? Where does he fit in?"

"Well, if it comes to that, I wouldn't mind Philip myself," said Dorothy, knitting her sharp black brows and frowning.

"I don't blame you," said Stella, thinking of her handsome husband.

"Just for a month, till he comes back," said Dorothy. "I tell you what, we'll abandon this silly cottage, we must have been mad to stick ourselves away in England in the first place. The three of us'll just pack up and go off to Spain or Italy with the baby."

"And what else?" enquired Jack, good-natured at all costs, using his pipe as a safety valve.

"Yes, I've decided I approve of polygamy," announced Dorothy. She had opened her dress and the baby was nursing again, quietly this time, relaxed against her. She stroked his head, softly, softly, while her voice rose and insisted at the other two people: "I never understood it before, but I do now. I'll be the senior wife, and you two can look after me."

"Any other plans?" enquired Jack, angry now. "You just drop in from time to time to watch Stella and me have a go, is that it? Or are you going to tell us when we can go off and do it, give us your gracious permission?"

"Oh I don't care what you do, that's the point," said Dorothy, sighing, sounding forlorn, however.

Jack and Stella, careful not to look at each other, sat waiting.

"I read something in the newspaper yesterday, it struck me," said Dorothy, conversational. "A man and two women living together—here, in England. They are both his wives, they consider themselves his wives. The senior wife has a baby, and the younger wife sleeps with him—well, that's what it looked like, reading between the lines."

"You'd better stop reading between lines," said Jack. "It's not doing you any good."

"No, I'd like it," insisted Dorothy. "I think our marriages are silly. Africans and people like that, they know better, they've got some sense."

"I can just see you if I did make love to Stella," said Jack.

"Yes!" said Stella, with a short laugh which, against her will, was resentful.

"But I wouldn't mind," said Dorothy, and burst into tears.

"Now, Dorothy, that's enough," said Jack. He got up, took the baby, whose sucking was mechanical now, and said: "Now listen, you're going right upstairs and you're going to sleep. This little stinker's full as a tick, he'll be asleep for hours, that's my bet."

"I don't feel sleepy," said Dorothy, sobbing.

"I'll give you a sleeping pill, then."

Then started a search for sleeping pills. None to be found.

"That's just like us," wailed Dorothy, "we don't even have a sleeping pill in the place. . . . Stella, I wish you'd stay, I really do. Why can't you?"

"Stella's going in just a minute, I'm taking her to the station," said Jack. He poured some Scotch into a glass, handed it to his wife and said: "Now drink that, love, and let's have an end of it. I'm getting fed-up." He sounded fed-up.

Dorothy obediently drank the Scotch, got unsteadily from her chair and went slowly upstairs. "Don't let him cry," she demanded, as she disappeared.

"Oh you silly bitch," he shouted after her. "When have I let him cry? Here, you hold on a minute," he said to Stella, handing her the baby. He ran upstairs.

Stella held the baby. This was almost for the first time, since she sensed how much another woman's holding her child made Dorothy's fierce new possessiveness uneasy. She looked down at the small, sleepy, red face and said softly: "Well, you're causing a lot of trouble, aren't you?"

Jack shouted from upstairs: "Come up a minute, Stell." She went up, with the baby. Dorothy was tucked up in bed, drowsy from the Scotch, the bedside light turned away from her. She looked at the baby, but Jack took it from Stella.

"Jack says I'm a silly bitch," said Dorothy, apologetic, to Stella.

"Well, never mind, you'll feel different soon."

"I suppose so, if you say so. All right, I *am* going to sleep," said Dorothy, in a stubborn, sad little voice. She turned over, away from them. In the last flare of her hysteria she said: "Why don't you two walk to the station together? It's a lovely night."

"We're going to," said Jack, "don't worry."

She let out a weak giggle, but did not turn. Jack carefully deposited the now sleeping baby in the bed, about a foot from Dorothy. Who suddenly wriggled over until her small, defiant white back was in contact with the blanketed bundle that was her son.

Jack raised his eyebrows at Stella: but Stella was looking at mother and baby, the nerves of her memory filling her with sweet warmth. What right had this woman, who was in possession of such delight, to torment her husband, to torment her friend, as she had been doing—what right had she to rely on their decency as she did?

Surprised by these thoughts, she walked away downstairs, and stood at the door into the garden, her eyes shut, holding herself rigid against tears.

She felt a warmth on her bare arm—Jack's hand. She opened her eyes to see him bending towards her, concerned.

"It'd serve Dorothy right if I did drag you off into the bushes. . . ."

"Wouldn't have to drag me," she said; and while the words had the measure of facetiousness the situation demanded, she felt his seriousness envelop them both in danger.

The warmth of his hand slid across her back, and she turned towards him under its pressure. They stood together, cheeks touching, scents of skin and hair mixing with the smells of warmed grass and leaves.

She thought: What is going to happen now will blow

Dorothy and Jack and that baby sky-high; it's the end of my marriage; I'm going to blow everything to bits. There was almost uncontrollable pleasure in it.

She saw Dorothy, Jack, the baby, her husband, the two halfgrown children, all dispersed, all spinning downwards through the sky like bits of debris after an explosion.

Jack's mouth was moving along her cheek towards her mouth, dissolving her whole self in delight. She saw, against closed lids, the bundled baby upstairs, and pulled back from the situation, exclaiming energetically: "Damn Dorothy, damn her, damn her, I'd like to kill her. . . ."

And he, exploding into reaction, said in a low furious rage: "Damn you both! I'd like to wring both your bloody necks. . . ."

Their faces were at a foot's distance from each other, their eyes staring hostility. She thought that if she had not had the vision of the helpless baby they would now be in each other's arms—generating tenderness and desire like a couple of dynamos, she said to herself, trembling with dry anger.

"I'm going to miss my train if I don't go," she said.

"I'll get your coat," he said, and went in, leaving her defenceless against the emptiness of the garden.

When he came out, he slid the coat around her without touching her, and said: "Come on, I'll take you by car." He walked away in front of her to the car, and she followed meekly over rough lawn. It really was a lovely night.

A Room

•

•   •

WHEN I first came into this flat of four small boxlike rooms, the bedroom was painted pale pink, except for the fireplace wall, which had a fanciful pink and blue paper. The woodwork was a dark purple, almost black. This paint is sold by a big decorating shop in the West End and is called Bilberry.

Two girls had the flat before me. Very little money, obviously, because the carpeting was going into holes and the walls were decorated with travel posters. The woman upstairs told me they often had parties that lasted all night. "But I liked to hear them, I enjoy the sounds of life." She was reproachful. I don't have parties often enough for her. The girls left no forwarding address, following the tradition for this flat. Over the years it has often happened that the bell rings and people ask for "Angus Ferguson—I thought he lived here?" And the Maitlands? And Mrs. Dowland? And the young Caitsbys? All these people, and probably many others, have lived in this flat, and departed leaving nothing behind. I know nothing about them, nor does anyone else in the building, though some of them have lived here for years.

I found the pink too assertive, and after several mistakes settled on white walls, leaving the plum-colour, or Bilberry, woodwork. First I had grey curtains, then blue ones. My bed is under the window. There is a desk, which I had meant to write on, but it is always too cluttered with papers. So I write in the living room or on the kitchen table. But I spend a lot of time in the bedroom. Bed is the best place for reading, thinking, or doing nothing. It is my room; it is where I feel I live, though the shape is bad and there are things about it that can never be anything but ugly. For instance, the fireplace was of iron—a bulging, knobbed, ornamented black. The girls had left it as it was, using a small gas heater in the opening. Its heavy ugliness kept drawing my eyes towards it; and I painted a panel from the ceiling downwards in the dark plum colour, so that the fireplace and the small thick shelf over it would be absorbed. On either side of the panel, since I could not have the whole wall in plum, which at night looks black, were left two panels of the absurd wallpaper which has bright people-like birds in pink and blue cages. The fireplace seemed less obtrusive, but my fire is a gas fire, a square solid shape of bronze, brought from an earlier flat where it did not look too bad. But it does not fit here at all. So the whole wall doesn't work, it fails to come off.

Another wall, the one beside my bed, is also deformed. Over the bed swells a grainy irregular lump two or more feet across. Someone—Angus Ferguson? The Maitlands? Mrs. Dowland?—attempted to replace falling plaster and made a hash of it. No professional plasterer could have got away with such a protuberance.

On the whole, this wall gives me pleasure: it reminds me of the irregular whitewashed walls of another house I lived in once. Probably I chose to paint this room white because I wanted to have the whitewashed lumpy walls of that early house repeated here in London?

The ceiling is a ceiling: flat, white, plain. It has a plaster border which is too heavy for the room and looks as if it might fall easily. The whole building has a look of solid ugliness, but it was built cheap and is not solid at all. For instance, walls, tapped, sound hollow; the plaster, when exposed, at once starts to trickle as if the walls were of loose sand held together by wallpaper. I can hear anything that goes on over my head, where the old woman who likes to hear a bit of life lives with her husband. She is Swedish, gives Swedish lessons. She dresses prettily, and looks a dear respectable old thing. Yet she is quite mad. Her door has four heavy, specially fitted locks inside, as well as bolts and bars. If I knock she opens the door on a chain four inches long and peers through to make sure that I (or they) will not attack her. Inside is a vision of neatness and order. She spends all day cleaning and arranging. When she can't find anything more to do in her flat she posts notices on the stairs saying: "Any person who drops rubbish on these stairs will be reported to the Authorities!" Then she visits every flat in turn (there are eight identical flats one above the other) and says confidingly: "Of course the notice isn't meant for you."

Her husband works for an export firm and is away a good deal. When she expects him back, she dresses as carefully as a bride and goes off to meet him, blushing. On the nights he comes back from his trips the bed creaks over my head, and I hear them giggling.

They are an orderly couple, bed at eleven every night, up every morning at nine. As for myself, my life has no outward order and I like having them up there. Sometimes, when I've worked late, I hear them getting up and I think through my sleep or half sleep: Good, the day's started, has it? And I drift back to a semiconsciousness blended with their footsteps and the rattling of cups.

Sometimes, when I sleep in the afternoons, which I do because afternoon sleep is more interesting than night sleep, she takes a nap too. I think of her and of myself lying horizontally above each other, as if we were on two shelves.

When I lie down after lunch there is nothing unplanned about it. First I must feel the inner disturbance or alertness that is due to overstimulation, or being a little sick or very tired. Then I darken the room, shut all the doors so the telephone won't wake me (though its distant ringing can be a welcome dream-progenitor) and I get into bed carefully, preserving the mood. It is these sleeps which help me with my work, telling me what to write or where I've gone wrong. And they save me from the fever of restlessness that comes from seeing too many people. I always drift off to sleep in the afternoons with the interest due to a long journey into the unknown, and the sleep is thin and extraordinary and takes me into regions hard to describe in a waking state.

But one afternoon there was no strange journey, nor was there useful information about my work. The sleep was so different from usual that for some time I thought I was awake.

I had been lying in the semidark, the curtains, of varying shades of dark blue, making a purply-moving shade. Outside it was a busy afternoon. I could hear sounds from the market underneath, and there was angry shouting, a quarrel of some kind, a man's voice and a woman's. I was looking at the fireplace and thinking how ugly it was, wondering what sort of person had deliberately chosen such a hideous shape of black iron. Though of course I had painted it over. Yes, whether I could afford it or not, I must get rid of the square bronze gas fire and find a prettier one. I saw the bronze shape had gone; there was a small black iron grate and a small fire in it, smoking. The smoke was coming into the room, and my eyes were sore.

The room was different; I felt chilled and estranged from myself as I looked. The walls had a paper whose general effect was a dingy brown, but looking closely at it I saw a small pattern of brownish-yellow leaves and brown stems. There were stains on it. The ceiling was yellowish and shiny from the smoke. There were some shreds of pinky-brown curtains at the windows with a tear in one so that the bottom edge hung down.

I was no longer lying on the bed, but sitting by the fire across the room, looking at the bed and at the window. Outside a shrill quarrel went on, the voices rising up from the street. I felt cold, I was shivering, and my eyes watered. In the little grate sat three small lumps of shiny coal, smoking dismally. Under me was a cushion or a folded coat, something like that. The room seemed much larger. Yes, it was a largish room. A chest of brown-varnished wood stood by the bed which was low, a good foot lower than mine. There was a red army blanket stretched across the bed's foot. The recesses on either side of the fireplace had shallow wooden shelves down them, holding folded clothes, old magazines, crockery, a brown teapot. These things conveyed an atmosphere of thin poverty.

I was alone in the room, though someone was next door. I could hear sounds that made me unhappy, apprehensive. From upstairs a laugh, hostile to me. Was the old Swedish lady laughing? With whom? Had her husband come back suddenly?

I was desolate with a loneliness that felt it would never

be assuaged, no one would ever come to comfort me. I sat and looked at the bed which had the cheap red blanket on it that suggested illness, and sniffed because the smoke was tearing at the back of my throat. I was a child, I knew that. And that there was a war, something to do with war, war had something to do with this dream or memory—*whose?* I came back to my own room, lying on my bed, with silence upstairs and next door. I was alone in the flat, watching my soft dark blue curtains softly moving. I was filled with misery.

I left my pretty bedroom and made myself tea; then returned to draw the curtains and let the light in. I switched on the gas heater which came up hot and red, driving the memory of cold away; and I looked behind its bronze efficiency into a grate that had not had coals in it, I knew, for years.

I have tried to dream myself back into that other room which is under this room, or beside it, or in it, or existing in someone's memory. Which war was it? Whose was the chilly poverty? And I would like to know more about the frightened little child. He (or she) must have been very small for the room to look so big. So far I have failed. Perhaps it was the quarrel outside in the street that . . . that *what?* And why?

England versus England

.

.   .

"I THINK I'll be off," said Charlie. "My things are packed." He had made sure of getting his holdall ready so that his mother wouldn't. "But it's early," she protested. Yet she was already knocking red hands together to rid them of water while she turned to say goodbye: she knew her son was leaving early to avoid the father. But the back door now opened and Mr. Thornton came in. Charlie and his father were alike: tall, overthin, big-boned. The old miner stooped, his hair had gone into grey wisps, and his hollow cheeks were coal-pitted. The young man was still fresh, with jaunty fair hair and alert eyes. But there were scoops of strain under his eyes.

"You're alone," said Charlie involuntarily, pleased, ready to sit down again. The old man was not alone. Three men came into view behind him in the light that fell into the yard from the door, and Charlie said quickly: "I'm off, Dad, it's goodbye till Christmas." They all came crowding into the little kitchen, bringing with them the spirit of facetiousness that seemed to Charlie his personal spiteful enemy, like a poltergeist always standing in wait somewhere behind his right shoulder. "So you're back to the dreaming spires," said one man, nodding goodbye. "Off to t'palaces of learning," said another. Both were smiling. There was no hostility in it, or even envy, but it shut Charlie out of his family, away from his people. The third man, adding his tribute to this, the most brilliant son of the village, said: "You'll be coming back to a right Christmas with us, then, or will you be frolicking with t'lords and t'earls you're the equal of now?"

"He'll be home for Christmas," said the mother sharply.

She turned her back on them, and dropped potatoes one by one from a paper bag into a bowl.

"For a day or so, any road," said Charlie, in obedience to the prompting spirit. "That's time enough to spend with t'hewers of wood and t'drawers of water." The third man nodded, as if to say: That's right! and put back his head to let out a relieved bellow. The father and the other two men guffawed with him. Young Lennie pushed and shoved Charlie encouragingly and Charlie jostled back, while the mother nodded and smiled because of the saving horseplay. All the same, he had not been home for nearly a year, and when they stopped laughing and stood waiting for him to go, their grave eyes said they were remembering this fact.

"Sorry I've not had more time with you, son," said Mr. Thornton, "but you know how 'tis."

The old miner had been union secretary, was now chairman, and had spent his working life as miners' representative in a dozen capacities. When he walked through the village, men at a back door, or a woman in an apron, called: "Just a minute, Bill," and came after him. Every evening Mr. Thornton sat in the kitchen, or in the parlour when the television was claimed by the children, giving advice about pensions, claims, work rules, allowances; filling in forms; listening to tales of trouble. Ever since Charlie could remember, Mr. Thornton had been less his father than the father of the village. Now the three miners went into the parlour, and Mr. Thornton laid his hand on his son's shoulder, and said: "It's been good seeing you," nodded, and followed them. As he shut the door he said to his wife: "Make us a cup of tea, will you, lass?"

"There's time for a cup, Charlie," said the mother, meaning there was no need for him to rush off now, when it was unlikely any more neighbours would come in. Charlie did not hear. He was watching her slosh dirty potatoes about under the running tap while with her free hand she reached for the kettle. He went to fetch his raincoat and his holdall listening to the nagging inner voice which he hated, but which he felt as his only protection against the spiteful enemy outside: "I can't stand it when my father apologises to me— he was apologising to me for not seeing more of me. If he wasn't as he is, better than anyone else in the village, and our home the only house with real books in it, I wouldn't be at Oxford, I wouldn't have done well at school, so it cuts both ways." The words, cuts both ways, echoed uncannily in his inner ear, and he felt queasy, as if the earth he stood on was shaking. His eyes cleared on the sight of his mother, standing in front of him, her shrewd, non-judging gaze on his face. "Eh, lad," she said, "you don't look any too good to me." "I'm all right," he said hastily, and kissed her, adding: "Say my piece to the girls when they come in." He went out, with Lennie behind him.

The two youths walked in silence past fifty crammed lively brightly lit kitchens whose doors kept opening as the miners came in from the pit for their tea. They walked in silence along the fronts of fifty more houses. The fronts were all dark. The life of the village, even now, was in the kitchens where great fires roared all day on the cheap coal. The village had been built in the thirties by the company, now nationalised. There were two thousand houses, exactly alike, with identical patches of carefully tended front garden, and busy back yards. Nearly every house had a television aerial. From every chimney poured black smoke.

At the bus stop Charlie turned to look back at the village, now a low hollow of black, streaked and spattered with sullen wet lights. He tried to isolate the gleam from his own home, while he thought how he loved his home and how he hated the village. Everything about it offended him, yet as soon as he stepped inside his kitchen he was received into warmth. That morning he had stood on the front step and looked out on lines of grey stucco houses on either side of grey tarmac; on grey ugly lampposts and greyish hedges, and beyond to the grey minetip and the neat black diagram of the minehead.

He had looked, listening while the painful inner voice lectured: "There's nothing in sight, not one object or building anywhere, that is beautiful. Everything is so ugly and mean and graceless that it should be bulldozed into the earth and out of the memory of man." There was not even a cinema. There was a post office, and attached to it a library that had romances and war stories. There were two miners' clubs for drinking. And there was television. These were the amenities for two thousand families.

When Mr. Thornton stood on his front step and looked forth he smiled with pride and called his children to say: "You've never seen what a miners' town can be like. You couldn't even imagine the conditions. Slums, that's what they used to be. Well, we've put an end to all that. . . . Yes, off you go to Doncaster, I suppose, dancing and the pictures—that's all you can think about. And you take it all for granted. Now, in our time . . ."

And so when Charlie visited his home he was careful that none of his bitter criticisms reached words, for above all, he could not bear to hurt his father.

A group of young miners came along for the bus. They wore smartly shouldered suits, their caps set at angles, and scarves flung back over their shoulders. They greeted Lennie, looked to see who the stranger was, and when Lennie said: "This is my brother," they nodded and turned quickly to board the bus. They went upstairs, and Lennie and Charlie went to the front downstairs. Lennie looked like them, with a strong cloth cap and a jaunty scarf. He was short, stocky, strong—"built for t'pit," Mr. Thornton said. But Lennie was in a foundry in Doncaster. No pit for him, he said. He had heard his father coughing through all the nights of his childhood, and the pit wasn't for him. But he had never said this to his father.

Lennie was twenty. He earned seventeen pounds a week, and wanted to marry a girl he had been courting for three years now. But he could not marry until the big brother was through college. The father was still on the coal face, when by rights of age he should have been on the surface, because he earned four pounds a week more on the face. The sister in the office had wanted to be a schoolteacher, but at the moment of decision all the extra money of the family had been needed for Charlie. It cost them two hundred pounds a year for his extras at Oxford. The only members of the family not making sacrifices for Charlie were the schoolgirl and the mother.

It was half an hour on the bus, and Charlie's muscles were set hard in readiness for what Lennie might say, which must be resisted. Yet he had come home thinking: Well, at least I can talk it out with Lennie, I can be honest with him.

Now Lennie said facetiously, but with an anxious loving

inspection of his brother's face: "And what for do we owe the pleasure of your company, Charlie boy? You could have knocked us all down with a feather when you said you were coming this weekend."

Charlie said angrily: "I got fed with t'earls and t'dukes."

"Eh," said Lennie quickly, "but you didn't need to mind *them,* they didn't mean to rile you."

"I know they didn't."

"Mum's right," said Lennie, with another anxious but carefully brief glance, "you're not looking too good. What's up?"

"What if I don't pass t'examinations," said Charlie in a rush.

"Eh, but what is this, then? You were always first in school. You were the best of everyone. Why shouldn't you pass, then?"

"Sometimes I think I won't," said Charlie lamely, but glad he had let the moment pass.

Lennie examined him again, this time frankly, and gave a movement like a shrug. But it was a hunching of the shoulders against a possible defeat. He sat hunched, his big hands on his knees. On his face was a small critical grin. Not critical of Charlie, not at all, but of life.

His heart beating painfully with guilt, Charlie said: "It's not as bad as that, I'll pass." The inner enemy remarked softly: "I'll pass, then I'll get a nice pansy job in a publisher's office with the other wet-nosed little boys, or I'll be a sort of clerk. Or I'll be a teacher—I've no talent for teaching, but what's that matter? Or I'll be on the management side of industry, pushing people like Lennie around. And the joke is, Lennie's earning more than I shall for years." The enemy behind his right shoulder began satirically tolling a bell and intoned: "Charlie Thornton, in his third year at Oxford, was found dead in a gas-filled bed-sitting-room this morning. He had been overworking. Death from natural causes." The enemy added a loud rude raspberry and fell silent. But he was waiting: Charlie could feel him there waiting.

Lennie said: "Seen a doctor, Charlie boy?"

"Yes. He said I should take it easy a bit. That's why I came home."

"No point killing yourself working."

"No, it's not serious, he just said I must take it easy."

Lennie's face remained grave. Charlie knew that when he got home he would say to the mother: "I think Charlie's got summat on his mind." And his mother would say (while she stood shaking chips of potato into boiling fat): "I expect sometimes he wonders is the grind worth it. And he sees you earning, when he isn't." She would say, after a silence during which they exchanged careful looks: "It must be hard for him, coming here, everything different, then off he goes, everything different again."

"Shouldn't worry, Mum."

"I'm not worrying. Charlie's all right."

The inner voice enquired anxiously: "If she's on the spot about the rest, I suppose she's right about the last bit too— *I suppose I am all right?*"

But the enemy behind his right shoulder said: "A man's best friend is his mother, she never lets a thing pass."

Last year he had brought Jenny down for a weekend, to satisfy the family's friendly curiosity about the posh people he knew these days. Jenny was a poor clergyman's daughter, bookish, a bit of a prig, but a nice girl. She had easily navigated the complicated currents of the weekend, while the family waited for her to put on "side." Afterwards Mrs. Thornton had said, putting her finger on the sore spot: "That's a right nice girl. She's a proper mother to you, and that's a fact." The last was not a criticism of the girl, but of Charlie. Now Charlie looked with envy at Lennie's responsible profile and said to himself: Yes, he's a man. He has been for years, since he left school. Me, I'm a proper baby, and I've got two years over him.

For above everything else, Charlie was made to feel, every time he came home, that these people, his people, were serious; while he and the people with whom he would now spend his life (if he passed the examination) were not serious. He did not believe this. The inner didactic voice made short work of any such idea. The outer enemy could, and did, parody it in a hundred ways. His family did not believe it, they were proud of him. Yet Charlie felt it in everything they said and did. They protected him. They sheltered him. And above all, they still paid for him. At his age, his father had been working in the pit for eight years.

Lennie would be married next year. He already talked of a family. He, Charlie (if he passed the examination), would be running around licking people's arses to get a job, Bachelor of Arts, Oxford, and a drug on the market.

They had reached Doncaster. It was raining. Soon they would pass where Doreen, Lennie's girl, worked. "You'd better get off here," Charlie said. "You'll have all that drag back through the wet." "No, s'all right, I'll come with you to the station."

There were another five minutes to go. "I don't think it's right, the way you get at Mum," Lennie said, at last coming to the point.

"But I haven't said a bloody word," said Charlie, switching without having intended it into his other voice, the middle-class voice which he was careful never to use with his family except in joke. Lennie gave him a glance of surprise and reproach and said: "All the same. She feels it."

"But it's bloody ridiculous." Charlie's voice was rising. "She stands in that kitchen all day, pandering to our every whim, when she's not doing housework or making a hundred trips a day with that bloody coal. . . ." In the Christmas holidays, when Charlie had visited home last, he had fixed up a bucket on the frame of an old pram to ease his mother's work. This morning he had seen the contrivance collapsed and full of rainwater in the back yard. After breakfast Lennie and Charlie had sat at the table in their shirt-sleeves watching their mother. The door was open into the back yard. Mrs. Thornton carried a shovel whose blade was nine inches by ten, and was walking back and forth from the coalhole in the yard, through the kitchen, into the parlour. On each inward journey, a small clump of coal balanced on the shovel. Charlie counted that his mother walked from the coalhole to the kitchen fire and the parlour fire thirty-six times. She walked steadily, the shovel in front, held like a spear in both hands, and her face frowned with purpose. Charlie had dropped his head onto his arms and laughed soundlessly until he felt Lennie's warning gaze and stopped the heave of his shoulders. After a moment he had sat up, straight-faced. Lennie said: "Why do you get at

Mum, then?" Charlie said: "But I haven't said owt." "No, but she's getting riled. You always show what you think, Charlie boy." As Charlie did not respond to this appeal— for far more than present charity—Lennie went on: "You can't teach an old dog new tricks." "Old! She's not fifty!"

Now Charlie said, continuing the early conversation: "She goes on as if she were an old woman. She wears herself out with nothing—she could get through all the work she has in a couple of hours if she organised herself. Or if just for once she told us where to get off."

"What'd she do with herself then?"

"Do? Well, she could do something for herself. Read. Or see friends. Or something."

"She feels it. Last time you went off she cried."

"She *what?*" Charlie's guilt almost overpowered him, but the inner didactic voice switched on in time and he spoke through it: "What right have we to treat her like a bloody servant? Betty likes her food this way and that way, and Dad won't eat this and that, and she stands there and humours the lot of us—like a servant."

"And who was it last night said he wouldn't have fat on his meat and changed it for hers?" said Lennie smiling, but full of reproach.

"Oh, I'm just as bad as the rest of you," said Charlie, sounding false. "It makes me wild to see it," he said, sounding sincere. Didactically he said: "All the women in the village—they take it for granted. If someone organised them so that they had half a day to themselves sometimes, they'd think they were being insulted—they can't stop working. Just look at Mum, then. She comes into Doncaster to wrap sweets two or three times a week—well, she actually loses money on it, by the time she's paid bus fares. I said to her, 'You're actually losing money on it,' and she said: 'I like to get out and see a bit of life.' A bit of life! Wrapping sweets in a bloody factory. Why can't she just come into town of an evening and have a bit of fun without feeling she has to pay for it by wrapping sweets, sweated bloody labour? And she actually loses on it. It doesn't make sense. They're human beings, aren't they? Not just . . ."

"Not just what?" asked Lennie angrily. He had listened

to Charlie's tirade, his mouth setting harder, his eyes narrowing. "Here's the station," he said in relief. They waited for the young miners to clatter down and off before going forward themselves. "I'll come with you to your stop," said Charlie; and they crossed the dark, shiny, grimy street to the opposite stop for the bus which would take Lennie back to Doreen.

"It's no good thinking we're going to change, Charlie boy."

"Who said change?" said Charlie excitedly; but the bus had come, and Lennie was already swinging onto the back. "If you're in trouble just write and say," said Lennie, and the bell pinged and his face vanished as the lit bus was absorbed by the light-streaked drizzling darkness.

There was half an hour before the London train. Charlie stood with the rain on his shoulders, his hands in his pockets, wondering whether to go after his brother and explain—what? He bolted across the street to the pub near the station. It was run by an Irishman who knew him and Lennie. The place was still empty, being just after opening time.

"It's you, then," said Mike, drawing him a pint of bitter without asking. "Yes, it's me," said Charlie, swinging himself up onto a stool.

"And what's in the great world of learning?"

"Oh, Jesus, *no!*" said Charlie. The Irishman blinked, and Charlie said quickly: "What have you gone and tarted this place up for?"

The pub had been panelled in dark wood. It was ugly and comforting. Now it had half a dozen bright wallpapers and areas of shining paint, and Charlie's stomach moved again, light filled his eyes, and he set his elbows hard down for support, and put his chin on his two fists.

"The youngsters like it," said the Irishman. "But we've left the bar next door as it was for the old ones."

"You should have a sign up: Age This Way," said Charlie. "I'd have known where to go." He carefully lifted his head off his fists, narrowing his eyes to exclude the battling colours of the wallpapers, the shine of the paint.

"You look bad," said the Irishman. He was a small, round, alcoholically cheerful man who, like Charlie, had two voices. For the enemy—that is, all the English whom he did not regard as a friend, which meant people who were not regulars—he put on an exaggerated brogue which was bound, if he persisted, to lead to the political arguments he delighted in. For friends like Charlie he didn't trouble himself. He now said: "All work and no play."

"That's right," said Charlie. "I went to the doctor. He gave me a tonic and said I am fundamentally sound in wind and limb. 'You are sound in wind and limb,' he said," said Charlie, parodying an upper-class English voice for the Irishman's pleasure.

Mike winked, acknowledging the jest, while his professionally humorous face remained serious. "You can't burn the candle at both ends," he said in earnest warning.

Charlie laughed out. "That's what the doctor said. You can't burn the candle at both ends, he said."

This time, when the stool he sat on, and the floor beneath the stool, moved away from him, and the glittering ceiling dipped and swung, his eyes went dark and stayed dark. He shut them and gripped the counter tight. With his eyes still shut he said facetiously: "It's the clash of cultures, that's what it is. It makes me light-headed." He opened his eyes and saw from the Irishman's face that he had not said these words aloud.

He said aloud: "Actually the doctor was all right, he meant well. But Mike, I'm not going to make it, I'm going to fail."

"Well, it won't be the end of the world."

"*Jesus*. That's what I like about you, Mike, you take a broad view of life."

"I'll be back," said Mike, going to serve a customer.

A week ago Charlie had gone to the doctor with a cyclostyled leaflet in his hand. It was called "A Report Into the Increased Incidence of Breakdown Among Undergraduates." He had underlined the words: "Young men from working-class and lower-middle-class families on scholarships are particularly vulnerable. For them, the gaining of a degree is obviously crucial. In addition they are under the continuous strain of adapting themselves to middle-class mores that are foreign to them. They are victims of a clash of standards, a clash of cultures, divided loyalties."

The doctor, a young man of about thirty, provided by

the college authorities as a sort of father figure to advise on work problems, personal problems and (as the satirical alter ego took pleasure in pointing out) on clash-of-culture problems, glanced once at the pamphlet and handed it back. He had written it. As, of course, Charlie had known. "When are your examinations?" he asked. *Getting to the root of the matter, just like Mum,* remarked the malevolent voice from behind Charlie's shoulder.

"I've got five months, doctor, and I can't work and I can't sleep."

"For how long?"

"It's been coming on gradually." *Ever since I was born,* said the enemy.

"I can give you sedatives and sleeping pills, of course, but that's not going to touch what's really wrong."

Which is, all this unnatural mixing of the classes. Doesn't do, you know. People should know their place and stick to it. "I'd like some sleep pills, all the same."

"Have you got a girl?"

"Two."

The doctor paid out an allowance of man-of-the-world sympathy, then shut off his smile and said: "Perhaps you'd be better with one?"

Which, my mum figure, or my lovely bit of sex? "Perhaps I would, at that."

"I could arrange for you to have some talks with a psychiatrist—well, not if you don't want," he said hastily, for the alter ego had exploded through Charlie's lips in a horse-laugh and: "What can the trick cyclist tell me I don't know?" He roared with laughter, flinging his legs up; and an ashtray went circling around the room on its rim. Charlie laughed, watched the ashtray, and thought: There, I knew all the time it was a poltergeist sitting there behind my shoulder. I swear I never touched that damned ashtray.

The doctor waited until it circled near him, stopped it with his foot, picked it up, laid it back on the desk. "It's no point your going to him if you feel like that."

All avenues explored, all roads charted.

"Well now, let's see, have you been to see your family recently?"

"Last Christmas. No, doctor, it's not because I don't want

to, it's because I can't work there." *You try working in an atmosphere of trade union meetings and the telly and the pictures in Doncaster. You try it, doc. And besides all my energies go into not upsetting them. Because I do upset them. My dear doc, when we scholarship boys jump our class, it's not we who suffer, it's our families. We are an expense, doc. And besides—write a thesis, I'd like to read it. . . . Call it: Long-term effects on working-class or lower-middle-class family of a scholarship child whose existence is a perpetual reminder that they are nothing but ignorant noncultured clods. How's that for a thesis, doc? Why, I do believe I could write it myself.*

"If I were you, I'd go home for a few days. Don't try to work at all. Go to the pictures. Sleep and eat and let them fuss over you. Get this prescription made up and come and see me when you get back."

"Thanks, doc, I will." *You mean well.*

The Irishman came back to find Charlie spinning a penny, so intent on this game that he did not see him. First he spun it with his right hand, anticlockwise, then with his left, clockwise. The right hand represented his jeering alter ego. The left hand was the didactic and rational voice. The left hand was able to keep the coin in a glittering spin for much longer than the right.

"You ambidextrous?"

"Yes, always was."

The Irishman watched the boy's frowning, teeth-clenched concentration for a while, then removed the untouched beer and poured him a double whisky. "You drink that and get on the train and sleep."

"Thanks, Mike. Thanks."

"That was a nice girl you had with you last time."

"I've quarrelled with her. Or rather, she's given me the boot. And quite right too."

After the visit to the doctor Charlie had gone straight to Jenny. He had guyed the interview while she sat, gravely listening. Then he had given her his favourite lecture on the crass and unalterable insensibility of anybody anywhere born middle-class. No one but Jenny ever heard this lecture. She said at last: "You *should* go and see a psychiatrist. No, don't you see, it's not fair."

"Who to, me?"

"No, me. What's the use of shouting at me all the time? You should be saying these things to him."

"What?"

"Well, surely you can see that. You spend all your time lecturing me. You make use of me, Charles." (She always called him Charles.)

What she was really saying was: "You should be making love to me, not lecturing me." Charlie did not really like making love to Jenny. He forced himself when her increasingly tart and accusing manner reminded him that he ought to. He had another girl, whom he disliked, a tall crisp middle-class girl called Sally. She called him, mocking: Charlie boy. When he had slammed out of Jenny's room, he had gone to Sally and fought his way into her bed. Every act of sex with Sally was a slow, cold subjugation of her by him. That night he had said, when she lay at last, submissive, beneath him: "Horny-handed son of toil wins by his unquenched virility beautiful daughter of the moneyed classes. And doesn't she love it."

"Oh yes I do, Charlie boy."

"I'm nothing but a bloody sex symbol."

"Well," she murmured, already self-possessed, freeing herself, "that's all I am to you." She added defiantly, showing that she did care, and that it was Charlie's fault: "And I couldn't care less."

"Dear Sally, what I like about you is your beautiful honesty."

"Is that what you like about me? I thought it was the thrill of beating me down."

Charlie said to the Irishman: "I've quarrelled with everyone I know in the last weeks."

"Quarrelled with your family too?"

"No," he said, appalled, while the room again swung around him. "Good Lord no," he said in a different tone—grateful. He added savagely: "How could I? I can never say anything to them I really think." He looked at Mike to see if he had actually said these words aloud. He had, because now Mike said: "So you know how I feel. I've lived thirty years in this mucking country, and if you arrogant sods knew what I'm thinking half the time."

"Liar. You say whatever you think, from Cromwell to the Black and Tans and Casement. You never let up. But it's not hurting yourself to say it."

"Yourself, is it?"

"Yes. But it's all insane. Do you realise how insane it all is, Mike? There's my father. Pillar of the working class. Labour party, trade union, the lot. But I've been watching my tongue not to say I spent last term campaigning about—he takes it for granted even *now* that the British should push the wogs around."

"You're a great nation," said the Irishman. "But it's not your personal fault, so drink up and have another."

Charlie drank his first Scotch, and drew the second glass towards him. "Don't you see what I mean?" he said, his voice rising excitedly. "Don't you see that it's all *insane?* There's my mother, her sister is ill and it looks as if she'll die. There are two kids and my mother'll take them both. They're nippers, three and four, it's like starting a family all over again. She thinks nothing of it. If someone's in trouble, she's the mug, every time. But there she sits and says: 'Those juvenile offenders ought to be flogged until they are senseless.' She read it in the papers and so she says it. She said it to me and I kept my mouth shut. And they're all alike."

"Yes, but you're not going to change it, Charlie, so drink up."

A man standing a few feet down the bar had a paper sticking out of his pocket. Mike said to him: "Mind if I borrow your paper for the winners, sir?"

"Help yourself."

Mike turned the paper over to the back page. "I had five quid on today," he said. "Lost it. Lovely bit of horseflesh, but I lost it."

"Wait," said Charlie excitedly, straightening the paper so he could see the front page. WARDROBE MURDERER GETS SECOND CHANCE, it said. "See that?" said Charlie. "The Home Secretary says he can have another chance, they can review the case, he says."

The Irishman read, cold-faced. "So he does," he said.

"Well, I mean to say, there's some decency left, then. I mean if the case can be reviewed it shows they do *care* about something at least."

"I don't see it your way at all. It's England versus England, that's all. Fair play all round, but they'll hang the poor sod on the day appointed as usual." He turned the newspaper and studied the race news.

Charlie waited for his eyes to clear, held himself steady with one hand flat on the counter, and drank his second double. He pushed over a pound note, remembering it had to last three days, and that now he had quarrelled with Jenny there was no place for him to stay in London.

"No, it's on me," said Mike. "I asked you. It's been a pleasure seeing you, Charlie. And don't take the sins of the world on your personal shoulders, lad, because that doesn't do anyone any good, does it, now?"

"See you at Christmas, Mike, and thanks."

He walked carefully out into the rain. There was no solitude to be had on the train that night, so he chose a compartment with one person in it, and settled himself in a corner before looking to see who it was he had with him. It was a girl. He saw then that she was pretty, and then that she was upper-class. Another Sally, he thought, sensing danger, seeing the cool, self-sufficient little face. Hey, there, Charlie, he said to himself, keep yourself in order, or you've had it. He carefully located himself: *he,* Charlie, was now a warm, whisky-comforted belly, already a little sick. Close above it, like a silent loudspeaker, was the source of the hectoring voice. Behind his shoulder waited his grinning familiar. *He must keep them all apart.* He tested the didactic voice: It's not her fault, poor bitch, victim of the class system, she can't help she sees everyone under her like dirt. . . . But the alcohol was working strongly and meanwhile his familiar was calculating: She's had a good look, but can't make me out. My clothes are right, my haircut's on the line, but there's something that makes her wonder. She's waiting for me to speak, then she'll make up her mind. Well, first I'll get her, and then I'll speak.

He caught her eyes and signalled an invitation, but it was an aggressive invitation, to make it as hard for her as he could. After a bit, she smiled at him. Then he roughened his speech to the point of unintelligibility and said: " 'Appen you'd like t'window up? What wi' t'rain and t'wind and all."

"What?" she said sharply, her face lengthening into such a comical frankness of shock that he laughed out, and afterwards enquired impeccably: "Actually it is rather cold, isn't it? Wouldn't you like to have the window up?" She picked up a magazine and shut him out, while he watched, grinning, the blood creep up from her neat suit collar to her hairline.

The door slid back; two people came in. They were a man and his wife, both small, crumpled in face and flesh, and dressed in their best for London. There was a fuss and a heaving of suitcases and murmured apologies because of the two superior young people. Then the woman, having settled herself in a corner, looked steadily at Charlie, while he thought: Deep calls to deep, *she* knows who I am all right, she's not foxed by the trimmings. He was right, because soon she said familiarly: "Would you put the window up for me, lad? It's a rare cold night and no mistake."

Charlie put up the window, not looking at the girl, who was hiding behind the magazine. Now the woman smiled, and the man smiled too, because of her ease with the youth.

"You comfortable like that, father?" she asked.

"Fair enough," said the husband on the stoical note of the confirmed grumbler.

"Put your feet up beside me, any road."

"But I'm all right, lass," he said bravely. Then, making a favour of it, he loosened his laces, eased his feet inside too-new shoes, and set them on the seat beside his wife.

She, for her part, was removing her hat. It was of shapeless grey felt, with a pink rose at the front. Charlie's mother owned just such a badge of respectability, renewed every year or so at the sales. Hers was always bluish felt, with a bit of ribbon or coarse net, and she would rather be seen dead than without it in public.

The woman sat fingering her hair, which was thin and greying. For some reason, the sight of her clean pinkish scalp shining through the grey wisps made Charlie wild with anger. He was taken by surprise, and again summoned himself to himself, making the didactic voice lecture: "The working woman of these islands enjoys a position in the family superior to that of the middle-class woman, etc., etc." This was an article he had read recently, and he continued to recite from it, until he realised the voice had become an open sneer, and was saying: "Not only is she the emotional bulwark of the family, but she is frequently the breadwinner as well, such as wrapping sweets at night, sweated labour for pleasure, anything to get out of the happy home for a few hours."

The fusion of the two voices, the nagging inside voice, and the jeer from the dangerous force outside, terrified Charlie, and he told himself hastily: "You're drunk, that's all, now keep your mouth shut, for God's sake."

The woman was asking him: "Are you feeling all right?"

"Yes, I'm all right," he said carefully.

"Going all the way to London?"

"Yes, I'm going all the way to London."

"It's a long drag."

"Yes, it's a long drag."

At this echoing dialogue, the girl lowered her magazine to give him a sharp contemptuous look, up and down. Her face was now smoothly pink, and her small pink mouth was judging.

"You have a mouth like a rosebud," said Charlie, listening horrified to these words emerging from him.

The girl jerked up the magazine. The man looked sharply at Charlie, to see if he had heard aright, and then at his wife, for guidance. The wife looked doubtfully at Charlie, who offered her a slow desperate wink. She accepted it, and nodded at her husband: boys will be boys. They both glanced warily at the shining face of the magazine.

"We're on our way to London too," said the woman.

"So you're on your way to London."

Stop it, he told himself. He felt a foolish slack grin on his face, and his tongue was thickening in his mouth. He shut his eyes, trying to summon Charlie to his aid, but his stomach was rolling, warm and sick. He lit a cigarette for support, watching his hands at work. "Lily-handed son of learning wants a manicure badly," commented a soft voice in his ear; and he saw the cigarette poised in a parody of a cad's gesture between displayed nicotined fingers. Charlie, smoking with poise, sat preserving a polite, sarcastic smile.

He was in the grip of terror. He was afraid he might slide off the seat. He could no longer help himself.

"London's a big place, for strangers," said the woman.

"But it makes a nice change," said Charlie, trying hard.

The woman, delighted that a real conversation was at last under way, settled her shabby old head against a leather bulge, and said: "Yes, it does make a nice change." The shine on the leather confused Charlie's eyes; he glanced over at the magazine, but its glitter, too, seemed to invade his pupils. He looked at the dirty floor for comfort, and said: "It's good for people to get a change now and then."

"Yes, that's what I tell my husband, don't I, father? It's good for us to get away now and then. We have a married daughter in Streatham."

"It's a great thing, family ties."

"Yes, but it's a drag," said the man. "Say what you like, but it is. After all, I mean, when all is said and done." He paused, his head on one side, with a debating look, waiting for Charlie to take it up.

Charlie said: "There's no denying it, say what you like, I mean, there's no doubt about *that*." And he looked interestedly at the man for his reply.

The woman said: "Yes, but the way I look at it, you've got to get *out* of yourself sometimes, look at it that way."

"It's all very well," said the husband, on a satisfied but grumbling note, "but if you're going to do that, well, for a start-off, it's an expense."

"If you don't throw a good penny after a bad one," said Charlie judiciously, "I mean, what's the point?"

"Yes, that's it," said the woman excitedly, her old face animated. "That's what I say to father, what's the point if you don't sometimes let yourself go?"

"I mean, life's bad enough as it is," said Charlie, watching the magazine slowly lower itself. It was laid precisely on the seat. The girl now sat, two small brown-gloved hands in a ginger-tweed lap, staring him out. Her blue eyes glinted into his, and he looked quickly away.

"Well, I can see that right enough," said the man, "but there again, you've got to know where to stop."

"That's right," said Charlie, "you're dead right."

"I know it's all right for some," said the man, "I know that, but if you're going to do that, you've got to consider. That's what I think."

"But father, you know you enjoy it, once you're there and Joyce has settled you in your own corner with your own chair and your cup to yourself."

"Ah," said the man, nodding heavily, "but it's not as easy as that, now, is it? Well, I mean, that stands to reason."

"Ah," said Charlie, shaking his head, feeling it roll heavily in the socket of his neck, "but if you're going to consider at all, then what's the point? I mean, what I think is, for a start-off, there's no doubt about it."

The woman hesitated, started to say something, but let her small bright eyes falter away. She was beginning to colour.

Charlie went on compulsively, his head turning like a clockwork man's: "It's what you're used to, that's what I say, well I mean. *Well,* and there's another thing, when all is said and done, and after all, if you're going to take one thing with another . . ."

"Stop it," said the girl, in a sharp high voice.

"It's a question of principle," said Charlie, but his head had stopped rolling and his eyes had focussed.

"If you don't stop I'm going to call the guard and have you put in another compartment," said the girl. To the old people she said in a righteous scandalised voice: "Can't you see he's laughing at you? Can't you see?" She lifted the magazine again.

The old people looked suspiciously at Charlie, dubiously at each other. The woman's face was very pink and her eyes bright and hot.

"I think I am going to get forty winks," said the man, with general hostility. He settled his feet, put his head back, and closed his eyes.

Charlie said. "Excuse me," and scrambled his way to the corridor over the legs of the man, then the legs of the woman, muttering: "Excuse me, excuse me, I'm sorry."

He stood in the corridor, his back jolting slightly against the shifting wood of the compartment's sides. His eyes were shut, his tears running. Words, no longer articulate, muttered and jumbled somewhere inside him, a stream of frightened protesting phrases.

Wood slid against wood close to his ear, and he heard

the softness of clothed flesh on wood.

"If it's that bloody little bint I'll kill her," said a voice, small and quiet, from his diaphragm.

He opened his murderous eyes on the woman. She looked concerned.

"I'm sorry," he said, stiff and sullen, "I'm sorry, I didn't mean . . ."

"It's all right," she said, and laid her two red hands on his crossed quivering forearms. She took his two wrists, and laid his arms gently down by his sides. "Don't take on," she said, "it's all right, it's all right, son."

The tense rejection of his flesh caused her to take a step back from him. But there she stood her ground and said: "Now look, son, there's no point taking on like that, well, is there? I mean to say, you've got to take the rough with the smooth, and there's no other way of looking at it."

She waited, facing him, troubled but sure of herself.

After a while Charlie said: "Yes, I suppose you're right."

She nodded and smiled, and went back into the compartment. After a moment, Charlie followed her.

Two Potters

•

•   •

I HAVE only known one potter in this country, Mary Taw-nish, and she lives out of London in a village where her husband is a schoolteacher. She seldom comes to town, and I seldom leave it, so we write.

The making of pots is not a thing I often think of, so when I dreamed about the old potter it was natural to think of Mary. But it was difficult to tell her: there are two kinds of humanity, those who dream and those who don't, and both tend to despise, or to tolerate, the other. Mary Tawnish says, when others relate their dreams: "I've never had a dream in my life." And adds, to soften or placate: "At least, I don't remember. They say it's a question of remembering?"

I would have guessed her to be a person who would dream a good deal, I don't know why.

A tall woman, and rather large, she has bright brown clustering hair, and brown eyes that give the impression of light, thought not from their surface: it is not a "bright" or "brilliant" glance. She looks at you, smiling or not, but always calm, and there is an impression of light, which seems caught in the structure of colour in the iris, so sometimes her eyes look yellow, set off by smooth brown eyebrows.

A large, slow-moving woman, with large white slow hands. And a silent one—she is a listener.

Her life has been a series of dramas: a childhood on the move with erratic parents, a bad first marriage, a child that died, lovers, but none lasting; then a second marriage to William Tawnish who teaches physics and biology. He is a quick, biting, bitter little man with whom she has three half-grown children.

More than once I have told her story, without comment, in order to observe the silent judgement: Another misfit, another unhappy soul, only to see the judger confounded on meeting her, for there was never a woman less fitted by nature for discord or miseries. Or so it would seem. So it seems she feels herself, for she disapproves of other people's collisions with themselves, just as if her own life had nothing to do with her.

The first dream about the potter was simple and short. Once upon a time . . . there was a village or a settlement, not in England, that was certain, for the scene was of a baked red-dust bareness. Low rectangular structures, of simple baked mud, also reddish-brown, were set evenly on the baked soil, yet because some were roofless and others in the process of crumbling, and others half built, there was nothing finished or formed about this place. And for leagues and leagues, in all directions, the great plain, of reddish earth, and in the middle of the plain, the settlement, that looked as if it were hastily moulded by a great hand out of wet clay, allowed to dry, and left there. It seemed uninhabited, but in an empty space among the huts, all by himself, working away on a primitive potter's wheel turned by foot, was an old man. He wore a garment of coarse sacking over yellowish and dusty limbs. One bare foot was set in the dust near me, the cracked toes spread and curled. He had a bit of yellow straw stuck in close grizzling hair.

When I woke from this dream I was rested and excited, in spite of the great dried-up plain and the empty settlement one precarious stage from the dust. In the end I sat down and wrote to Mary Tawnish, although I could hear her flat comment very clearly: Well, that's interesting. Our letters are usually of the kind known as "keeping in touch." First I enquired about her children, and about William, and then I told the dream: "For some reason I thought of you. I did know a man who made pots in Africa. The farmer he worked for discovered he had a talent for pot-making (it seemed his tribe were potters by tradition) because when they made bricks for the farm, this man, Elija, slipped little dishes and bowls into the kiln to bake with the bricks. The farmer used to pay him a couple of shillings a week extra, and sold the dishes to a dealer in the city. He made simple things, not like yours. He had no wheel, of course. He didn't use colour. His things were a darkish yellow, because of the kind of soil on that farm. A bit monotonous after a bit. And they broke easily. If you come up to London give me a ring. . . ."

She didn't come, but soon I had a letter with a postscript: What an interesting dream, thanks so much for telling me.

I dreamed about the old potter again. There was the great, flat, dust-beaten reddish plain, ringed by very distant blue-hazed mountains, so far away they were like mirages, or clouds, or low-lying smoke. There was the settlement. And there the old potter, sitting on one of his own upturned pots, one foot set firmly in the dust, and the other moving the wheel; one palm shaping the clay, the other shedding water which glittered in the low sullen glare in flashes of moving light on its way to the turning wet clay. He was extremely old, his eyes faded and of the same deceiving blue as the mountains. All around him, drying in rows on a thin scattering of yellow straw, were pots of different sizes. They were all round. The huts were rectangular, the pots round. I looked at these two different manifestations of the earth, separated by shape; and then through a gap in the huts to the plain. No one in sight. It seemed no one lived there. Yet there sat the old man, with the hundreds of pots and dishes drying in rows on the straw, dipping his hand into an enormous jar of water and scattering drops that smelled sweet as they hit the dust and pitted it.

Again I thought of Mary. But they had nothing in common, that poor old potter who had no one to buy his work, and Mary who sold her strange coloured bowls and jugs to the big shops in London. I wondered what the old potter would think of Mary's work—particularly what he'd think of a square flat dish I'd bought from her, coloured a greenish-yellow. The square had, as it were, slipped out of whack, and the surface is rough, with finger marks left showing. I serve cheese on it. The old man's jars were for millet, I knew that, or for soured milk.

I wrote and told Mary the second dream, thinking: Well,

if it bores or irritates her, it's too bad. This time she rang me up. She wanted me to go down to one of the shops which had been slow in making a new order. Weren't her things selling? she wanted to know. She added she was getting a fellow feeling for the old potter, he didn't have any customers either, from the size of his stock. But it turned out that the shop had sold all Mary's things, and had simply forgotten to order more.

I waited, with patient excitement, for the next instalment, or unfolding, of the dream.

The settlement was now populated, indeed, teeming, and it was much bigger. The low flat rooms of dull earth had spread over an area of some miles. They were not separated now, but linked. I walked through a system of these rooms. They were roughly the same size, but set at all angles to each other so that, standing in one, it might have one, two, three doors, leading to a corresponding number of mud rooms. I walked for something like half a mile through low dark rooms without once needing to cross a roofless space, and when I emerged in the daylight, there was the potter, and beyond him a marketplace. But a poor one. From out of his great jars, women, wearing the same sort of yellowish sacking as he, sold grain and milk to dusty, smallish, rather listless people. The potter worked on, under heavy sunlight, with his rows of clay vessels drying on the glinting yellow straw. A very small boy crouched by him, watching every movement he made. I saw how the water shaken from the old fingers on the whirling pot flew past it and spattered the small intent poverty-shaped faced with its narrowed watching eyes. But the face received the water unflinching, probably unnoticed.

Beyond the settlement stretched the plain. Beyond that, the thin, illusory mountains. Over the red flat plain drifted small shadows: they were from great birds wheeling and banking and turning.

I wrote to Mary and she wrote back that she was glad the old man had some customers at last, she had been worried about him. As for her, she thought it was time he used some colour, all that red dust was depressing. She said she could see the settlement was short of water, since I hadn't mentioned a well, let alone a river, only the potter's great brimming jar which reflected the blue sky, the sun, the great birds.

Wasn't a diet of milk and millet bad for people? Here she broke off to say she supposed I couldn't help all this, it was my nature, and "Apropos, isn't it time your poor village had a storyteller at least? How bored the poor things must be!"

I wrote back to say I was not responsible for this settlement, and whereas if I had my way, it would be set in groves of fruit trees and surrounded by whitening corn fields, with a river full of splashing brown children, I couldn't help it, that's how things were in this place, wherever it was.

One day in a shop I saw a shelf of her work and noticed that some of them were of smooth, dully shining brown, like polished skin—jars, and flat round plates. Our village potter would have known these, nothing to surprise him here. All the same, there was a difference between Mary's consciously simple vessels and the simplicity of the old potter. I looked at them and thought: Well, my dear, that's not going to get you very far. . . . But I would have found it hard to say exactly what I meant, and in fact I bought a plate and a jar, and they gave me great pleasure, thinking of Mary and the old potter linked in them, between my hands.

Quite a long time passed. When I dreamed again all the plain was populated. The mountains had come closer in, reaching up tall and blue into blue sky, circumscribing the plain. The settlements, looked at from the height of the mountaintops, seemed like patches of slightly raised surfaces on the plain. I understood their nature and substance: a slight raising of the dust here and there, like the frail patterning of raindrops hitting dry dust, pitting it, then the sun coming out swiftly to dry the dust. The resulting tiny fragile patterned crust of dried dust—that gives, as near as I can, the feeling the settlements gave me, viewed from the mountains. Except that the raised dried crusts were patterned in rectangles. I could see the tiny patternings all over the plain. I let myself down from the mountains, through the great birds that wheeled and floated, and descended to the settlement I knew. There sat the potter, the clay curving under his left hand as he flicked water over it from his right. It was all going on as usual—I was reassured by his being there, creating his pots. Nothing much had changed, though so much time had passed. The low flat monotonous dwellings were the same, though they had crumbled to dust and raised themselves from it a hundred times since I had been here last. No green yet, no river. A scum-covered creek had goats grazing beside it, and the millet grew in straggly patches, flattened and brown from drought. In the marketplace were pinkish fruits, lying in heaps by the soft piles of millet, on woven straw mats. I didn't know the fruit: it was small, about plum-size, smooth-skinned, and I felt it had a sharp pulpy taste. Pinky-yellow skins lay scattered in the dust. A man passed me, with a low slinking movement of the hips, holding his sacklike garment in position at his side with the pressure of an elbow, staring in front of him over the pink fruit which he pressed against sharp yellow teeth.

I wrote and told Mary the plain was more populated, but that things hadn't improved much, except for the fruit. But it was astringent, I wouldn't care for it myself.

She wrote back to say she was glad she slept so soundly, she would find such dreams depressing.

I said there was nothing depressing about it. I entered the dream with pleasure, as if listening to a storyteller say: Once upon a time . . .

But the next was discouraging, I woke depressed. I stood by the old potter in the marketplace, and for once his hands were still, the wheel at rest. His eyes followed the movements of the people buying and selling, and his mouth was bitter. Beside him, his vessels stood in rows on the warm glinting straw. From time to time a woman came picking her way along the rows, bending to narrow her eyes at the pots. Then she chose one, dropped a coin in the potter's hand, and bore it off over her shoulder.

I was inside the potter's mind and I knew what he was thinking. He said: "Just once, Lord, just once, just once!" He put his hand down into a patch of hot shade under the wheel and lifted on his palm a small clay rabbit which he held out to the ground. He sat motionless, looking at the sky, then at the rabbit, praying: "Please, Lord, just once." But nothing happened.

I wrote Mary the old man was tired with long centuries of making pots whose life was so short: the litter of broken pots under the settlement had raised its level twenty feet by now, and every pot had come off his wheel. He wanted God to breathe life into his clay rabbit. He had hoped to see it lift up its long red-veined ears, to feel its furry feet on his palm, and watch it hop down and off among the great earthenware pots, sniffing at them and twitching its ears—a live thing among the forms of clay.

Mary said the old man was getting above himself. She said further: "Why a *rabbit*? I simply don't *see* a rabbit. What use would a rabbit be? Do you realise that apart from goats (you say they have milk), and those vultures overhead, they have no animals at all? Wouldn't a cow be better than a rabbit?"

I wrote: "I can't do anything about that place when I'm dreaming it, but when I'm awake, why not? Right then, the rabbit hopped off the old man's hand into the dust. It sat twitching its nose and throbbing all over, the way rabbits do. Then it sprang slowly off and began nibbling at the straw, while the old man wept with happiness. Now what have you to say? If I say there was a rabbit, a rabbit there was. Besides, that poor old man deserves one, after so long. God could have done so much, it wouldn't have cost Him anything."

I had no reply to that letter, and I stopped dreaming about the settlement. I knew it was because of my effrontery in creating that rabbit, inserting myself into the story. Very well, then. . . . I wrote to Mary: "I've been thinking: suppose it had been you who'd dreamed about the potter—all right, all right, just suppose it. Now. Next morning you sat at the breakfast table, your William at one end, and the children between eating cornflakes and drinking milk. You were rather silent. (Of course you usually are.) You looked at your husband and you thought: What on earth would he say if I told him what I'm going to do? You said nothing, presiding at the table; then you sent the children off to school, and your husband to his classes. Then you were alone and when you'd washed the dishes and put them away, you went secretly into the stone-floored room where your wheel and the kiln are, and you took some clay and you made a small rabbit and you set it on a high shelf behind some finished vases to dry. You didn't want anyone to see that rabbit. One day, a week later, when it was dry, you waited until your family was of out the house, then you put your rabbit on your palm,

and you went into a field, and you knelt down and held the
rabbit out to the grass, and you waited. You didn't pray,
because you don't believe in God, but you wouldn't have
been in the least surprised if that rabbit's nose had started to
twitch and its long soft ears stood up. . . ."

Mary wrote: "There aren't any rabbits any more, had you
forgotten myxomatosis? Actually I did make some small rabbits recently, for the children, in blue and green glaze, because it occurred to me the two youngest haven't seen a
rabbit out of a picture book. Still, they're coming back in
some parts, I hear. The farmers will be angry."

I wrote: "Yes, I had forgotten. Well then . . . sometimes at
evening, when you walk in the fields, you think: How nice to
see a rabbit lift his paws and look at us. You remember the
rotting little corpses of a few years back. You think: *I'll try
again*. Meantime, you're nervous of what William will say,
he's such a rationalist. Well of course, so are we, but he
wouldn't even play a little. I may be wrong, but I think
you're afraid of William catching you out, and you are careful not to be caught. One sunny morning you take it out on
to the field and . . . all right then, it *doesn't* hop away. You
can't decide whether to lay your clay rabbit down among
the warm grasses (it's a sunny day) and let it crumble back
into the earth, or whether to bake it in your kiln. You
haven't baked it, it's even rather damp still: the old potter's
rabbit was wet, just before he held it out into the sun he
sprinkled water on it, I saw him.

"Later you decide to tell your husband. Out of curiosity?
The children are in the garden, you can hear their voices,
and William sits opposite you reading the newspaper. You
have a crazy impulse to say: I'm going to take my rabbit
into the field tonight and pray for God to breathe life into it,
a field without rabbits is empty. Instead you say: 'William,
I had a dream last night. . . .' First he frowns, a quick frown,
then he turns those small quick sandy-lashed intelligent eyes
on you, taking it all in. To your surprise, instead of saying:
'I don't remember your ever dreaming,' he says: 'Mary, I
didn't know you disapproved of the farmers killing off their
rabbits.' You say: 'I didn't disapprove. I'd have done the
same, I suppose.' The fact that he's not reacted with sarcasm
or impatience, as he might very well, makes you feel guilty

when you lift the clay rabbit down, take it out to a field and set it in a hedge, its nose pointing out towards some fresh grass. That night William says, casual, 'You'll be glad to hear the rabbits are back. Basil Smith shot one in his field—the first for eight years, he says. Well, I'm glad myself, I've missed the little beggars.' You are delighted. You slip secretly into a cold misty moonlight and you run to the hedge and of course the rabbit is gone. You stand, clutching your thick green stole around you, because it's cold, shivering, but delighted, delighted! Though you know quite well one of your children, or someone else's child, has slipped along this hedge, seen the rabbit, and taken it off to play with."

Mary wrote: "Oh all right, if you say so, so it is. But I must tell you, if you are interested in *facts,* that the only thing that has happened is that Dennis (the middle one) put his blue rabbit out in a hedge for a joke near the Smith's gate, and Basil Smith shot it to smithereens one dusk thinking it was real. He used to lose a small fortune every year to rabbits, he didn't think it was a funny joke at all. Anyway, why don't you come down for a weekend?"

The Tawnishes live in an old farmhouse on the edge of the village. There is a great garden, with fruit trees, roses— everything. The big house and the three boys mean a lot of work, but Mary spends all the time she can in the shed that used to be a dairy where she pots. I arrived to find them in the kitchen, having lunch. Mary nodded to me to sit down. William was in conflict with the middle boy, Dennis, who was, as the other two boys kept saying, "showing off." Or rather, he was in that torment of writhing self-consciousness that afflicts small boys sometimes, rolling his eyes while he stuttered and wriggled, his whole sandy freckled person scarlet and miserable.

"Well I did I did I did I did I did . . ." He paused for breath, his eyes popping, and his older brother chanted: "No you didn't, you didn't, you didn't."

"Yes I did I did I did I did . . ."

And the father said, brisk but irritated: "Now then, Dennis, use your loaf, you couldn't have, because it is obvious you have *not.*"

"But I did I did I did I did . . ."

"Well, then, you had better go out of the room until you come to your senses and are fit company for rational people," said his father, triumphantly in the right.

The child choked on his battling breath, and ran howling out into the garden. Where, after a minute, the older boy followed, ostensibly to control him.

"He did what?" I asked.

"Who knows?" said Mary. There she sat, at the head of the table, bright-eyed and smiling, serving apple pie and custard, a dark changeling in the middle of her gingery, freckled family.

Her husband said, brisk: "What do you mean, who knows? You know quite well."

"It's his battle with Basil Smith," said Mary to me. "Ever since Basil Smith shot at his blue rabbit and broke it, there's been evil feeling on both sides. Dennis claims that he set fire to the Smith farmhouse last night."

"What?"

Mary pointed through a low window, where the Smith's house showed, two fields away, like a picture in a frame.

William said: "He's hysterical and he's got to stop it."

"Well," said Mary "if Basil shot my blue rabbit I'd want to burn his house down too. It seems quite reasonable to me."

William let out an exclamation of rage; checked himself because of my presence, shot fiery glances all round, and went out, taking the youngest boy with him.

"Well," said Mary. "Well. . . ." She smiled. "Come into the pottery, I've got something to show you." She went ahead along a stone passage, a tall, lazy-moving woman, her bright brown hair catching the light. As we passed an open window, there was a fearful row of shrieks, yells, blows; and we saw the three boys rolling and tussling in the grass, while William danced futilely around them shouting: "Stop it, stop it at once." Their mother proceeded, apparently uninterested, into the potting room.

This held the potting apparatus, and a great many jars, plates and jugs of all colours and kinds, ranged on shelves. She lifted down a creature from a high shelf, and set it before me. Then she left it with me, while she bent to attend to the kiln.

It was yellowish-brown, a sort of rabbit or hare, but with ears like neither—narrower, sharp, short, like the pointed unfolding shoots of a plant. It had a muzzle more like a dog's than a rabbit's; it looked as if it did not eat grass—perhaps insects and beetles? Yellowish eyes were set on the front of its head. Its hind legs were less powerful than a rabbit's, or hare's; and I saw its talents were for concealment, not for escaping enemies in great pistoning leaps. It rested on short, stubby hind legs, with front paws held up in a queer, twisted, almost affected posture, head turned to one side, and ears furled around each other. It looked as if it had been wound up like a spring, and had half unwound. It looked like a strangely shaped rock, or like the harsh twisted plants that sometimes grow on rocks.

Mary came back and stood by me, her head slightly on one side, with her characteristic small patient smile that nevertheless held a sweet concealed exasperation.

"Well," she said, "there it is."

I hesitated, because it was not the creature I had seen on the old potter's palm.

"What was an English rabbit doing there at all?" she asked.

"I didn't say it was an English rabbit."

But of course, she was right: this animal was far more in keeping with the dried mud houses, the dusty plain, than the pretty furry rabbit I had dreamed.

I smiled at Mary, because she was humouring me, as she humoured her husband and her children. For some reason I thought of her first husband and her lovers, two of whom I had known. At moments of painful crisis, or at parting, had she stood thus—a calm, pretty woman, smiling her sweetly satirical smile, as if to say: "Well, make a fuss if you like, it's got nothing at all to do with me"? If so, I'm surprised that one of them didn't murder her.

"Well," I said at last, "thanks. Can I take this thing, whatever it is?"

"Of course. I made it for you. You must admit, it may not be pretty, but it's more likely to be *true*."

I accepted this, as I had to; and I said: "Well, thanks for coming down to our level long enough to play games with us."

At which there was a flash of yellow light from her luminous eyes, while her face remained grave, as if amusement, or acknowledgement of the *truth,* could only be focussed in her thus, through a change of light in her irises.

A few minutes later, the three boys and the father came round this part of the house in a whirlwind of quarrelling energy. The aggrieved Dennis was in tears, and the father almost beside himself. Mary, who until now had remained apart from it all, gave an exclamation, slipped on a coat, and said: "I can't stand this. I'm going to talk to Basil Smith."

She went out, and I watched her cross the fields to the other house.

Meanwhile Dennis, scarlet and suffering, came into the pottery in search of his mother. He whirled about, looking for her, then grabbed my creature, said: "Is that for me?", snatched it possessively to him when I said: "No, it's for me," set it down when I told him to, and stood breathing like a furnace, his freckles like tea leaves against his skin.

"Your mother's gone to see Mr. Smith," I said.

"He shot my rabbit," he said.

"It wasn't a real rabbit."

"But he thought it was a real rabbit."

"Yes, but you knew he would think so, and that he'd shoot at it."

"He killed it!"

"You wanted him to!"

At which he let out a scream and danced up and down like a mad boy, shouting: "I didn't I didn't I didn't I didn't . . ."

His father, entering on this scene, grabbed him by his flailing arms, fought the child into a position of tensed stillness, and held him there, saying, in a frenzy of incredulous common sense: "I've never—in—my—life—heard—such—lunacy!"

Now Mary came in, accompanied by Mr. Smith, a large, fair, youngish man, with a sweet open face, which was uncomfortable now, because of what he had agreed to do.

"Let that child go," said Mary to her husband. Dennis dropped to the floor, rolled over, and lay face down, heaving with sobs.

"Call the others!"

Resignation itself, William went to the window, and shouted: "Harry, John, Harry, John, come here at once, your mother wants you." He then stood, with folded arms, a defeated philosopher, grinning angrily while the two other children came in and stood waiting by the door.

"Now," said Mary. "Get up, Dennis."

Dennis got up, his face battered with suffering, and looked with hope towards his mother.

Mary looked at Basil Smith.

Who said, careful to get the words right: "I am very sorry that I killed your rabbit."

The father let out a sharp outraged breath, but kept quiet at a glance from his wife.

The chest of Dennis swelled and sang—in one moment there would be a storm of tears.

"Dennis," said Mary, "say after me: Mr. Smith, I'm very sorry I set fire to your house."

Dennis said in a rush, to get it out in time: "Mr. Smith I'm very sorry I set fire to your . . . to your . . . to your . . ." He sniffed and heaved, and Mary said firmly: *"House,* Dennis."

"House," said Dennis, in a wail. He then rushed at his mother, buried his head in her waist, and stood howling and wrestling, while she laid large hands on his ginger head and smiled over it at Mr. Basil Smith.

"Dear God," said her husband, letting his folded arms drop dramatically, now the ridiculous play was over. "Come and have a drink, Basil."

The men went off. The two other children stood silent and abashed, because of the force of Dennis's emotion, for which they clearly felt partly responsible. Then they slipped out to play. The house was tranquil again, save for Dennis's quietening sobs. Soon Mary took the boy up to his room to sleep it off. I stayed in the great, stone-floored pottery, looking at my strange twisted animal, and at the blues and greens of Mary's work all around the walls.

Supper was early and soon over. The boys were silent, Dennis too limp to eat. Bed was prescribed for everyone. William kept looking at his wife, his mouth set under his ginger moustache, and he could positively be heard thinking: Filling them full of this nonsense while I try to bring them up reasonable human beings! But she avoided his eyes, and sat calm and remote, serving mashed potatoes and brown stew. It was only when we had finished the washing up that she smiled at him—her sweet, amused smile. It was clear they needed to be alone. I said I wanted an early night and left them: he had gone to touch her before I was out of the room.

Next day, a warm summer Sunday, everyone was relaxed, the old house peaceful. I left that evening, with my clay creature, and Mary said smiling, humouring me: "Let me know how things go on with your place, wherever it is." But I had her beautiful animal in my suitcase, so I did not mind being humoured.

That night, at home, I went into the marketplace, and up to the old potter who stilled his wheel when he saw me coming. The small boy lifted his frowning attentive eyes from the potter's hands and smiled at me. I held out Mary's creature. The old man took it, screwed up his eyes to examine it, nodded. He held it in his left hand, scattered water on it with his right, held his palm down towards the littered dust, and the creature jumped off it and away, with quick, jerky movements, not stopping until it was through the huts, clear of the settlement, and against a small outcrop of jagged brown rocks where it raised its front paws and froze in the posture Mary had created for it. Overhead an eagle or a hawk floated by, looked down, but failed to see Mary's creature, and floated on, up and away into the great blue spaces over the flat dry plain to the mountains. I heard the wheel creak; the old man was back at work. The small boy crouched, watching, and the water flung by the potter's right hand sprayed the bowl he was making and the child's face, in a beautiful curving spray of glittering light.

Between Men

•

• •

THE chair facing the door was covered in coffee-brown satin. Maureen Jeffries wore dark brown silk tights and a white ruffled shirt. She would look a delectable morsel in the great winged chair. No sooner was she arranged in it, however, than she got out again (with a pathetic smile of which she was certainly unconscious) and sat less dramatically in the corner of a yellow settee. Here she remained some minutes, thinking that after all, her letter of invitation had said, jocularly (she was aware the phrase had an arch quality she did not altogether like): "Come and meet the new me!"

What was new was her hairstyle, that she was a stone lighter in weight, that she had been dowered afresh by nature (a word she was fond of) with delicacy of complexion. There was no doubt all this would be better displayed in the big brown chair: she made the change back again.

The second time she removed herself to the yellow settee was out of decency, a genuine calculation of kindness. To ask Peggy Bayley to visit her at all *was* brave of her, she had needed to swallow pride. But Peggy would not be able to compete with the ruffled lace shirt and all that it set off, and while this would be so precisely because of her advantages—that she was married, comfortably, to Professor Bayley (whose mistress she, Maureen, had been for four years)—nevertheless there was no need to rub in her, Maureen's, renewed and indeed incredible attractiveness, even though it had been announced by the words: *the new me*.

Besides, her attractiveness was all that she, Maureen, had to face the world with again, and why not display it to the wife of Professor Bayley, who had not married herself, but had married Peggy instead? Though (she whispered it to herself, fierce and bitter) if she had tricked Tom Bayley into it, put pressure on him, as Peggy had, no doubt she would be Mrs. Bayley. . . . She would go back to the brown chair.

But if *she* had tricked Tom into it, then it would have served her right, as it certainly served Peggy right, if from the start of this marriage Tom Bayley had insisted on a second bachelor flat into which she, Maureen, was never allowed to go, just as Peggy was not. She, Maureen, would have refused marriage on such terms, she must give herself credit for that; in fact, her insistence on fidelity from Tom, a natural philanderer, was doubtless the reason for his leaving her for Peggy. So on the whole she did not really envy Peggy, who had achieved marriage when she was already nearly forty with the eminent and attractive professor at the price of knowing from the start she would not be the only woman in his life; and knowing, moreover, she had achieved marriage by the oldest trick in the world. . . .

At this point Maureen left the brown chair for the third time, found the yellow settee obvious, and sat on the floor, in the grip of self-disgust. She was viewing the deterioration of her character, even while she was unable to stop the flow of her bitter thoughts about Peggy. Viewing herself clearsightedly had, in fact, been as much her occupation for the last six months of semiretreat as losing a stone and regaining her beauty.

Which she had: she was thirty-nine and she had never been more attractive. The tomboy who had left home in Iowa for the freedoms of New York had been lovely, as every fairly endowed young girl is lovely, but what she was now was the product of twenty years of work on herself. And other people's work too. . . . She was a small, round, white-skinned, big-brown-eyed black-haired beauty, but her sympathy, her softness, her magnetism were the creation of the loves of a dozen intelligent men. No, she did not envy her eighteen-year-old self at all. But she did envy, envied every day more bitterly, that young girl's genuine independence, largeness, scope, and courage.

It had been six months ago when her most recent—and, she had hoped, her final—lover, Jack Boles, had left her, and left her in pieces, that it had occurred to her that twenty—indeed, only ten—years ago *she* had discarded lovers, *she* had been the one to say, as Jack had said—embarrassed and guilty, but not more than he could easily come to terms with—"I'm sorry, forgive me, I'm off." And, and this was the point, she had never calculated the consequences to herself, had taken money from no man, save what she considered she had earned, had remained herself always. (In her time with Jack she had expressed opinions not her own to please him: he was a man who disliked women disagreeing with him.) Above all, she had never given a moment's thought to what people might say. But when Jack threw her over, after an affair which was publicised through the newspapers for months ("Famous film director shares flat in Cannes with the painter Maureen Jeffries") she had thought first of all: I'll be a laughingstock. She had told everyone, with reason, that he would marry her. Then she thought: But he stayed with me less than a year, no one has got tired of me before so quickly. Then: the woman he has thrown me over for is not a patch on me, and she can't even cook. Then back again to the beginning: People must be laughing at me.

Self-contempt poisoned her, particularly as she was unable to let Jack go, but pursued him with telephone calls, letters, reproaches, reminders that he had promised marriage. She spoke of what she had given him, did everything in fact that she despised most in women. Above all, she had not left this flat whose rent he had recently paid for five years. What it amounted to was, he was buying her off with the lease of this flat.

And instead of walking right out of it with her clothes (she was surely entitled to those?) she was still here, making herself beautiful and fighting down terror.

At eighteen, leaving her father's house (he was a post-office clerk), she had had her sex and her courage. Not beauty. For like many other professional beauties, women who spend their lives with men, she was not beautiful at all. What she had was a focussed sex, her whole being aware and sharpened by sex, that made her seem beautiful. Now, twenty years later, after being the mistress of eleven men, all of them eminent or at least potentially eminent, she had her sex, and her courage. *But*—since she had never put her own talent, painting, first; but always the career of whichever man she was living with, and out of an instinct of generosity which was probably the best thing in her—she now could not earn a living. At least, not in the style she had been used to.

Since she had left home she had devoted her talents, her warmth, her imagination to an art teacher (her first lover), two actors (then unknown, now world-famous), a choreographer; a writer; another writer; then, crossing the Atlantic to Europe, a film director (Italy), an actor (France), a writer (London), Professor Tom Bayley (London), Jack Boles, film director (London). Who could say how much of her offered self, her continually poured-forth devotion to their work, was responsible for their success? (As she demanded of herself fiercely, weeping, in the dark hours.)

She now had left her sympathy, her charm, her talents for dress and decor, a minor talent for painting (which did not mean she was not a discriminating critic of other people's work), the fact she was a perfect cook, and her abilities in bed, which she knew were outstanding.

And the moment she stepped out of this flat, she would step out, also, of the world of international money and prestige. To what? Her father, now living in a rooming house in Chicago? No, her only hope was to find another man as eminent and lustrous as the others; for she could no longer afford the unknown geniuses, the potential artists. This is what she was waiting for, and why she remained in the luxurious flat, which must serve as a base; and why she despised herself so painfully; and why she had invited Peggy Bayley to visit her. One: she needed to bolster herself up by seeing this woman, whose career (as the mistress of well-known men) had been similar to hers, and who was now well married. Second: she was going to ask her for help. She had gone carefully through the list of her ex-lovers, written to three, and drawn three friendly but unhelpful letters. She had remained, officially, a "friend" of Tom Bayley; but she knew better than to offend his wife by approaching him except with her approval. She would ask Peggy to ask Tom to use his influence to get her a job of the kind that would enable her to meet the right sort of man.

When the doorbell rang, and she had answered it, she went hastily to the big brown chair, this time out of bravado, even honesty. She was appealing to the wife of a man whose very publicised mistress she had been; and she did not wish to soften the difficulties of it by looking less attractive than she could; even though Peggy would enter with nothing left of her own beauty; for three years of marriage with Professor Bayley had turned her into a sensible, good-looking woman, the sleek feline quality gone that had led *her* from Cape Town to Europe as a minor actress, which career she had given up, quite rightly, for the one she was born for.

But Peggy Bayley entered, as it were, four years back: if Maureen was small, delicate, luscious, then Peggy's mode was to be a siren: Maureen jerked herself up, saw Peggy push pale hair off a brown cheek with a white ringed hand and slide her a green-eyed mocking smile. She involuntarily exclaimed: "Tom's ditched you!"

Peggy laughed—her voice, like Maureen's, was the husky voice of the sex-woman—and said: "How did you guess!" At which she turned, her hips angled in a mannequin's pose, letting her gold hair fall over her face, showing off a straight green linen dress that owed everything to a newly provocative body. Not a trace left of the sensible healthy housewife of the last three years: she, like Maureen, was once again focussed behind her sexuality, poised on it, vibrating with it.

She said: "We both of us *look* very much the better for being ditched!"

Now, with every consciousness of how she looked, she appropriated the yellow settee in a coil of femininity, and said: "Give me a drink and don't look so surprised. After all, I suppose I could have seen it coming?" This was a query addressed to—a fellow conspirator? No. Victim? No. Fellow artisan—yes. Maureen realised that the only-just-under-the-surface hostility that had characterised their meetings when Peggy was with Tom Bayley had vanished entirely. But she was not altogether happy yet about this flow of comradeship. Frowning, she got out of the brown satin chair, a cigarette clumsy between her lips. She remembered that the frown and the dangling cigarette belonged to the condition of *a woman sure of a man;* her instincts were, then, to lie to

Peggy, and precisely because she did not like to admit, even now, long after the fact, just how badly she was alone? She poured large brandies, and asked: "Who did he leave you for?"

Peggy said: "I left him," and kept her green eyes steady on Maureen's face to make her accept it, despite the incredulity she saw there.

"No, really, it's true—of course there were women all the time, that's why he insisted on the hidey-hole in Chelsea. . . ." Maureen definitely smiled now, to remind her of how often she had *not* acknowledged the reason for the hidey-hole. It had been "Tom's study, where he can get away from dreary domesticity." Peggy accepted the reminder with a small honest smile that nevertheless had impatience: "Well of course I told lies and played little games, don't we all?"— that's what the smile said; and Maureen's dislike of herself made her say aloud, so as to put an end to her silent rancorous criticism of Peggy: "Well, all right, then. But you did force him to marry you." She had taken three large gulps of brandy. Whereas she had drunk far too much in the months after Jack had left her, during the last weeks her diet had forbidden her alcohol, and she was out of practice. She felt herself already getting tight, and she said: "If I'm going to get tight, then you've got to too."

"I was drunk every day and night for two months," said Peggy, again with the level green look. "But you can't drink if you want to keep pretty."

Maureen went back to the brown chair, looked at Peggy through coiling blue smoke, and said: "I was drunk all the time for—it was ages. It was disgusting. I couldn't stop."

Peggy said: "Well all right, we've finished with that. But the point was, not the other women—we discussed his character thoroughly when we married and . . ." Here she stopped to acknowledge Maureen's rather sour smile, and said: "It's part of our role, isn't it, to thoroughly discuss their characters?" At this, both women's eyes filled with tears, which both blinked away. Another barrier had gone down.

Peggy said: "I came here to show myself off, because of your boasting little letter—I've been watching you patronise me since I married Tom, being dull and ordinary—I wanted *you* to see the new me! . . . God knows why one loses one's sex when one's settled with a man."

They both giggled suddenly, rolling over, Peggy on her yellow linen, Maureen on her glossy brown. Then at the same moment, they had to fight back tears.

"No," said Maureen, sitting up, "I'm not going to cry, oh no! I've stopped crying, there's not the slightest point."

"Then let's have some more to drink," and Peggy handed over her glass.

They were both tight, already; since both were in any case on the edge of themselves with fasting.

Maureen half filled both glasses with brandy, and asked: "Did you really leave him?"

"Yes."

"Then you've got better reason to like yourself than I have. I fought, and I made scenes, and when I think of it now . . ." She took a brandy gulp, looked around the expensive room, and said: "And I'm still living on him now and that's what's so horrible."

"Well, don't cry, dear," said Peggy. The brandy was slurring her, making her indolent. The *dear* made Maureen shrink. It was the meaningless word of the theatre and film people, which was all right, even enjoyable, with the theatre and film people, but it was only one step from . . .

"Don't," said Maureen, sharp. Peggy widened her long green eyes in a "charming" way, then let them narrow into the honesty of her real nature, and laughed.

"I see your point," she said. "Well, we'd better face it, hadn't we? We're not so far off, are we?"

"Yes," said Maureen. "I've been thinking it out. If we had married them, that marriage certificate, you know, well then, we'd have felt quite all right to take money, in return for everything, everything, everything!" She put her face down and sobbed.

"Shut up," said Peggy. But it sounded because of her tightness like "Shhrrrp."

"No," said Maureen, sitting up and sniffing. "It's true. I've never taken money—I mean I've never taken anything more than housekeeping money and presents of clothes—have you?" Peggy was not looking at her, so she went on: "All right, but I'll take a guess that Tom Bayley's the first man you've taken a settlement from, or alimony—isn't that so? And that's because you were married to him."

"I suppose so. I told myself I wouldn't, but I have."

"And you don't really feel bad about it, just because of that marriage certificate?"

Peggy turned her glass round and round between long soft fingers and at length nodded: I suppose so.

"Yes. Of course. And all the fun we've both made about that marriage certificate in our time. But the point is, taking money when you're married doesn't make you *feel* like a tart. With all the men I've been with, I've always had to argue with myself, I've said, Well, how much would he have to pay for what I do for him—the cooking and the housekeeping and the interior decoration and the advice? A fortune! So there's no need for me to feel badly about living in his flat and taking clothes. But I did feel bad, always. But if Jack had married me, living in this bloody flat of his wouldn't make me feel like a bloody tart." She burst into savage angry tears, stopped herself, breathed deeply, and sat silent, breathing deep. Then she got up, refilled her glass and Peggy's, and sat down. The two women sat in silence, until at last Maureen said: "Why did you leave him?"

"When he married me we both thought I was pregnant . . . no, it's true. I know what you and everyone else said, but it was true. I had no periods for three months, and then I was very ill, they said it was a miscarriage."

"He wants children?"

"Didn't he with you?"

"No."

"Then he's changed. He wants them badly."

"Jack wouldn't hear of children, wouldn't hear of them, but that little bitch he's ditched me for . . . I hear you're great friends with them?" She meant Jack and the girl for whom she was thrown over.

Peggy said: "Jack is a great friend of Tom's." This was very dry, and Maureen said: "Yes. Yes! All Jack's friends— I cooked for them, I entertained them, but do you know not one of them has even rung me up since he left me? They were *his* friends, not mine."

"Exactly. Since I left Tom I haven't seen either Jack or his new girl. They visit Tom."

"I suppose one of Tom's girls got pregnant?"

"Yes. He came to me and told me. I knew what I was supposed to do, and I did it. I said: Right, you can have your divorce."

"Then you've got your self-respect, at least."

Peggy turned her glass round, looking into it; it slopped over onto the yellow linen. Both women watched the orange stain spread, without moving, in an aesthetic interest.

"No, I haven't," said Peggy. "Because I said: 'You can have your divorce, but you've got to give me so much money, or else I'll sue you for infidelity—I've got the evidence a thousand times over.'"

"How much?"

Peggy coloured, took a gulp of brandy and said: "I'm going to get forty pounds a month alimony. It's a lot for him —he's a professor, not a film director."

"He can't afford it?"

"No. He told me he must give up his hidey-hole. I said: 'Too bad.'"

"What's she like?"

"Twenty-seven. An art student. She's pretty and sweet and dumb."

"But she's pregnant."

"Yes."

"You've never had a baby?"

"No. But I've had several abortions and miscarriages."

The two women looked frankly at each other, their faces bitter.

"Yes," said Maureen. "I've had five abortions and one of them was by one of those old women. I don't even use anything, and I don't get pregnant. . . . How did you like Jack's new girl?"

"I liked her," said Peggy, apologetically.

"She's an intellectual," said Maureen: it sounded like "intelleshual."

"Yes."

"Ever so bright and well-informed." Maureen battled a while with her better self, won the battle, and said: "But *why?* She's attractive, but she's such a schoolgirl, she's a nice bright clever little schoolgirl with nice bright clever little clothes."

Peggy said: "Stop it. Stop it at once."

"Yes," said Maureen. But she added, out of her agonised depths: "And she can't even cook!"

And now Peggy laughed, flinging herself back and spilling more brandy from her drunken hand. After a while, Maureen laughed too.

Peggy said: "I was thinking, how many times have wives and mistresses said about us: Peggy's such a bore, Maureen's so obvious."

"I can hear them: of course they're very pretty, and of course they can dress well, and they're marvellous cooks, and I suppose they're good in bed, but what have they *got?*"

"Stop it," said Peggy.

Both women were now drunk. It was getting late. The room was full of shadow, its white walls fading into blue heights; the glossy chairs, tables, rugs, sending out deep gleams of light.

"Shall I turn on the light?"

"Not yet." Peggy now got up herself to refill her glass. She said: "I hope she has the sense not to throw up her job."

"Who, Jack's redheaded bitch?"

"Who else? Tom's girl is all right, she's actually pregnant."

"You're right. But I bet she does, I bet Jack's trying to make her give it up."

"I know he is. Just before I left Tom—before he threw me over—your Jack and she were over to dinner. Jack was getting at her for her column, he was sniping at her all evening—he said it was a left-wing society hostess's view of politics. A left-wing bird's-eye view, he said."

"He hated me painting," said Maureen. "Every time I said I wanted a morning to paint, he made gibes about Sunday painters. I'd serve him breakfast, and go up to the studio —well, it's the spare room really. First he'd shout up funny cracks, then he'd come up and say he was hungry. He'd start being hungry at eleven in the morning. Then if I didn't come down and cook, he'd make love. Then we'd talk about his work. We'd talk about his bloody films all day and half the night. . . ." Maureen's voice broke into a wail: "It's all so unfair, so unfair . . . they were all like that. I'm not saying I'd have been a great painter, but I might have been something. Something of my own. . . . Not one of those men did anything but make fun, or patronise me . . . all of them, in one way or another. And of course, one always gives in, because one cares more for . . ."

Peggy who had been half asleep, drooping over her settee, sat up and said: "Stop it, Maureen. What's the good of it?"

"But it's true. I've spent twenty years of my life, eighteen hours a day, bolstering up some man's ambition. Well, isn't it true?"

"It's true, but stop it. We chose it."

"Yes. And if that silly red-haired bitch gives up her job, she'll get what she deserves."

"She'll be where we are."

"But Jack says he's going to marry her."

"Tom married me."

"He was intrigued by that clever little redheaded mind of hers. All those bright remarks about politics. But now he's doing everything he can to stop her column. Not that it would be any loss to the nation, but she'd better watch out, oh yes, she had. . . ." Maureen waved her brandy glass back and forth in front of hypnotised eyes.

"Which is the other reason I came to see you."

"You didn't come to see the new me?"

"It's the same thing."

"Well?"

"How much money have you got?"

"Nothing."

"How long is the lease for this flat?" Maureen held up the fingers of one hand. "Five years? Then sell the lease."

"Oh I couldn't."

"Oh yes you could. It would bring you in about two thousand, I reckon. We could take a flat somewhere less expensive."

"*We* could?"

"And I've got forty pounds a month. Well, then."

"Well then what?" Maureen was lying practically flat in the big chair, her white lace shirt ruffled up around her breasts, so that a slim brown waist and diaphragm showed above the tight brown trousers. She held her brandy glass in front of her eyes and moved it back and forth, watching the amber liquid slopping in the glass. From time to time the brandy fell on her brown stomach flesh and she giggled.

Peggy said: "If we don't do something, I've got to go back to my parents in Outshoorn—they're ostrich farmers. I was the bright girl that escaped. Well, I'll never make an actress. So I'll be back living out my life among the sugar-bushes and the ostriches. And where will you be?"

"Ditto, ditto." Maureen now wriggled her soft brown head sideways and let brandy drip into her open mouth.

"We're going to open a dress shop. If there's one thing we both really understand, it's how to dress."

"Good idea."

"What city would you fancy?"

"I fancy Paris."

"We couldn't compete in Paris."

"No, can't compete in . . . how about Rome? I've got three ex-lovers in Rome."

"They're not much good when it comes to trouble."

"No good at all."

"Better stay in London."

"Better stay in London. Like another drink?"

"Yes. Yesssh."

"I'lll get-get-itit."

"Next time, we mustn't go to bed without the marriage shertificate."

"A likely shtory."

"But it's against my prinshiples, bargaining."

"Oh I know, I know."

"Yesh."

"Perhaps we'd better be leshbians, what do you think?"

Peggy got up, with difficulty, came to Maureen, and put her hand on Maureen's bare diaphragm. "Doesh that do anything for you?"

"Not a thing."

"I fanshy men myself," said Peggy, returning to her settee, where she sat with a bump, spilling liquor.

"Me too, and a fat lot of good it duz ush."

"Next time, we don't give up our jobs, we stick with the dress shop."

"Yessh. . . ."

A pause. Then Peggy sat up, and focussed. She was pervaded by an immense earnestness. "Listen," she said. "No, damn it, lishen, that's what I mean to shay all the time, I really mean it."

"I do too."

"No. No giving it up the firsht time a m-m-man appearsh. Damn it, I'm drunk, but I mean it. . . . No, Maureen, I'm not going to shtart a dresh shop unless that's undershtood from the shtart. We musht we *musht* agree to that, work firsht, or elshe, or *else* you know where we're going to end up." Peggy brought out the last in a rush, and lay back, satisfied.

Maureen now sat up, earnest, trying to control her tongue: "But . . . what . . . we are both *good* at, itsh, it's bolshtering up some damned genus, genius."

"Not any more. Oh no. You've got to *promish* me, Maureen, promish me, or *elshe*. . . ."

"All right, I promish."

"Good."

"Have another drink?"

"Lovely brandy, lovely lovely lovely blandy."

"Lovely brandy. . . ."

A Letter from Home

•

• •

. . . *Ja,* but that isn't why I'm writing this time. You asked about Dick. You're worrying about him?—man! But he's got a poetry scholarship from a Texas university and he's lecturing the Texans about letters and life too in Suid Afrika, South Africa to you (forgive the hostility), and his poems are read, so they tell me, wherever the English read poetry. He's fine, man, but I thought I'd tell you about Johannes Potgieter, remember him? Remember the young poet, The Young Poet? He was around that winter you were here. Don't tell me you've forgotten those big melting brown eyes and those dimples. About ten years ago (*ja,* time flies) he got a type of unofficial grace-gift of a job at St.——— University on the strength of those poems of his, and—God —they were good. Not that you or any other English-speaking *domkop* will ever know, because they don't translate out of Afrikaans. Remember me telling you and everyone else (give me credit for that at least; I give the devil his due, when he's a poet) what a poet he was, how blerry good he was—but several people tried to translate Hans's poems, including me, and failed. Right. *Goed.* Meanwhile a third of the world's population—or is it a fifth, or to put it another way, X5Y59 million people—speak English (and it's increasing by six births a minute) but one million people speak Afrikaans, and though I say it in a whisper, man, only a fraction of them can read it, I mean to read it. But Hans is still a great poet. Right.

He wasn't all that happy about being a sort of unofficial laureate at that university. It's no secret some poets don't make laureates. At the end of seven months he produced a book of poems which had the whole God-fearing place sweating and sniffing out heresy of all kinds, sin, sex, liberalism, brother love, and so forth and so on; but of course in a civilised country (I say this under my breath, or I'll get the sack from my university, and I've got four daughters these days, had you forgotten?) no one would see anything in them but good poetry. Which is how Hans saw them, poor innocent soul. He was surprised at what people saw in them, and he was all upset. He didn't like being called all those names, and the good country boys from their fine farms and the smart town boys from their big houses all started looking sideways, making remarks, and our Hans, he was reduced to pap, because he's not a fighter, Hans; he was never a taker of positions on the side of justice, freedom, and the rest, for tell you the truth, I don't think he ever got round to defining them. *Goed.* He resigned, in what might be called a dignified silence, but his friends knew it was just plain cowardice or, if you like, incomprehension about what the fuss was over, and he went to live in Blagspruit in the Orange Free, where his Tantie Gertrude had a house. He helped her in her store. *Ja,* that's what he did. What did we all say to this? Well, what do you think? The inner soul of the artist (et cetera) knows what is best, and he probably *needed* the Orange Free and his Auntie's store for his development. Well, something like that. To tell the truth, we didn't say much; he simply dropped out. And time passed. *Ja.* Then they made me editor of *Onwards,* and thinking about our indigenous poets, I remembered Johannes Potgieter, and wrote "What about a poem from you?"—feeling bad because when I counted up the years, it was eight since I'd even thought of him, even counting those times when one says drunk at dawn: Remember Hans? Now, there was a poet. . . .

No reply, so I let an editorial interval elapse and I wrote again, and I got a very correct letter back. Well phrased. Polite. But not just that, it took me an hour to work out the handwriting—it was in a sort of Gothic print, each letter a work of art, like a medieval manuscript. But all he said, in that beautiful black art-writing, was: he was very well, he hoped I was very well, the weather was good, except the rains were late, his Tantie Gertie was dead, and he was running the store. *"Jou vriend,* Johannes Potgieter."

Right. *Goed.* I was taking a trip up to Joburg, so I wrote and said I'd drop in at Blagspruit on my way back, and I got another Manu Script, or Missal, saying he hoped to see me, and he would prepare Esther for my coming. I thought, he's married, poor *kerel,* and it was the first time I'd thought of him as anything but a born bachelor, and I was right— because when I'd done with Joburg, not a moment too soon, and driven down to the Orange Free, and arrived on the doorstep, there was Hans, but not a sign of a wife, and Esther turned out to be—but first I take pleasure in telling you that the beautiful brown-eyed poet with his noble brow and pale dimpled skin was bald—he has a tonsure, I swear it —and he's fat, a sort of smooth pale fat. He's like a monk, lard-coloured and fat and smooth. Esther is the cook, or rather, his jailor. She's a Zulu, a great fat woman, and I swear she put the fear of God into me before I even got into the house. Tantie Gertie's house is a square brick four-roomed shack, you know the kind, with an iron roof and verandahs—well, what you'd expect in Blagspruit. And Esther stood about six feet high in a white apron and a white *doekie* and she held a lamp up in one great black fist and looked into my face and sighed and went off into her kitchen singing "Rock of Ages." *Ja,* I promise you. And I looked at Hans, and all he said was "It's O.K., man. She likes you. Come in."

She gave us a great supper of roast mutton and pumpkin fritters and samp, and then some preserved fruit. She stood over us, arms folded, as we ate, and when Johannes left some mutton fat, she said in her mellow hymn-singing voice: "Waste not, want not, Master Johannes." And he ate it all up. *Ja.* She told me I should have some more peaches for my health, but I defied her and I felt as guilty as a small kicker, and I could see Hans eyeing me down the table and wondering where I got the nerve. She lives in the *kia* at the back, one small room with four children by various fathers, but no man, because God is more than enough for her now, you can see, with all those kids and Hans to bring up the right away. Auntie's store is a Drapery and General Goods in the main street, called Gertie's Store, and Hans was running it with a coloured man. But I heard Esther with my own ears at supper saying to his bowed bald shamed head: "Master Johannes, I heard from the cook at the predikant's house today that the dried peaches have got worms in them." And Hans said: "O.K., Esther, I'll send them up some of the new stock tomorrow."

Right. We spent all that evening talking, and he was the same old Hans. You remember how he used to sit, saying not a blerry word, smiling that sweet dimpled smile of his, listening, listening, and then he'd ask a question, remember? Well, *do* you? Because it's only just now *I'm* beginning to remember. People'd be talking about I don't know what—the Nats or the weather or the grape crop, anything—and just as you'd start to get nervous because he never said anything, he'd lean forward and start questioning, terribly serious, earnest, about some detail, something not quite central, if you know what I mean. He'd lean forward, smiling, smiling, and he'd say: "You really mean that? It rained all morning? It rained all *morning?* Is that the truth?" That's right, you'd say, a bit uneasy, and he'd say, shaking his head: "God, man, it rained all morning, you say. . . ." And then there'd be a considerable silence till things picked up again. And half an hour later he'd say: "You really mean it? The hanepoort grapes are good this year?"

Right. We drank a good bit of brandewyn that night, but in a civilised way—you know: "Would you like another little drop, Martin?" *"Ja,* just a small tot Hans, thank you"—but we got pretty pickled, and when I woke Sunday morning, I felt like death, but Esther was setting down a tray of tea by my bed, all dressed up in her Sunday hat and her black silk saying: *"Goeie môre,* Master du Preez, it's nearly time for church," and I nearly said: "I'm not a churchgoer, Esther," but I thought better of it, because it came to me, can it be possible, has our Hans turned a God-fearing man in Blagspruit? So I said, *"Goed,* Esther. Thanks for telling me, and now just get out of here so that I can get dressed." Otherwise she'd have dressed me, I swear it. And she gave me a majestic nod, knowing that God had spoken through her to send me to church, sinner that I was and stinking of cheap *dop* from the night before.

Right. Johannes and I went to *kerk,* he in a black Sunday

suit, if you'd believe such a thing, and saying: "Good morning, Mr. Stein. *Goeie môre,* Mrs. Van Esslin," a solid and
respected member of the congregation, and I thought, poor
kerel, there but for the grace of God go I, if I had to live
in this godforsaken dorp stuck in the middle of the Orange
Free State. And he looked like death after the brandewyn,
and so did I, and we sat there swaying and sweating in that
blerry little church through a sermon an hour and a half
long, while all the faithful gave us nasty curious looks. Then
we had a cold lunch, Esther having been worshipping at the
Kaffir church down in the Location, and we slept it all off
and woke covered with flies and sweating, and it was as hot
as hell, which is what Blagspruit is, hell. And he'd been
there ten years, man, ten years. . . .

Right. It is Esther's afternoon off, and Johannes says he
will make us some tea, but I see he is quite lost without her,
so I say: "Give me a glass of water, and let's get out from
under this iron, that's all I ask." He looks surprised, because
his hide is hardened to it, but off we go, through the dusty
little garden full of marigolds and zinnias, you know those
sun-baked gardens with the barbed-wire fences and the gates
painted dried-blood colour in those little dorps stuck in the
middle of the veld, enough to make you get drunk even to
think of them, but Johannes is sniffing at the marigolds,
which stink like turps, and he sticks an orange zinnia in his
lapel, and says: "Esther likes gardening." And there we go
along the main street, saying good afternoon to the citizens,
for half a mile, then we're out in the veld again, just the
veld. And we wander about, kicking up the dust and watching the sun sink, because both of us have just one idea,
which is: how soon can we decently start sundowning?

Then there was a nasty stink on the air, and it came from
a small bird impaled on a thorn on a thorn tree, which was
a butcher-bird's cache, have you ever seen one? Every blerry
thorn had a beetle or a worm or something stuck on it, and
it made me feel pretty sick, coming on top of everything,
and I was just picking up a stone to throw at the damned
thorn tree, to spite the butcher-bird, when I saw Hans staring at a lower part of this tree. On a long black thorn was
a great big brown beetle, and it was waving all its six legs
and its two feelers in rhythm, trying to claw the thorn out

of its middle, or so it looked, and it was writhing and wriggling, so that at last it fell off the thorn, which was at right angles, so to speak, from the soil, and it landed on its back, still waving its legs, trying to up itself. At which Hans bent down to look at it for some time, his two monk's hands on his upper thighs, his bald head sweating and glowing red in the last sunlight. *Then he bent down, picked up the beetle and stuck it back on the thorn.* Carefully, you understand, so that the thorn went back into the hole it had already made. You could see he was trying not to hurt the beetle. I just stood and gaped, like a *domkop,* and for some reason I remembered how one used to feel when he leaned forward and said, all earnest and involved: "You say the oranges are no good this year? Honestly, is that really true?" Anyway, I said: "Hans, man, for God's sake!" And then he looked at me, and he said, reproachfully: "The ants would have killed it, just look!" Well, the ground was swarming with ants of one kind or another, so there was logic in it, but I said: "Hans, let's drink, man, let's drink."

Well, it was Sunday, and no bars open. I took a last look at the beetle, the black thorn through its oozing middle, waving its black legs at the setting sun, and I said: "Back home, Hans, and to hell with Esther. We're going to get drunk."

Esther was in the kitchen, putting out cold meat and tomatoes, and I said: "Esther, you can take the evening off."

She said: "Master Hans, I have had all the Sunday afternoon off talking to Sister Mary." Hans looked helpless at me, and I said: "Esther, I'm giving you the evening off. Good night."

And Hans said, stuttering and stammering: "That's right, Esther, I'll give you the evening off. Good night, Esther."

She looked at him. Then at me. Hey, what a woman. Hey, what a queen, man! She said, with dignity: "Good night, Mr. Johannes. Good night, Mr. du Preez." Then she wiped her hands free of evil on her white apron, and she strode off, singing "All things bright and beautiful," and I tell you we felt as if we weren't good enough to wash Esther's *broekies,* and that's the truth.

Goed. We got out the brandy, never mind about the cold meat and the tomatoes, and about an hour later I reached my point at last, which was, what about the poems, and the reason I'd taken so long was I was scared he'd say: "Take a look at Blagspruit, man. Take a look. Is this the place for poems, Martin?" But when I asked, he leaned forward and stared at me, all earnest and intent, then he turned his head carefully to the right, to see if the door into the kitchen was shut, but it wasn't; and then left at the window, and that was open too, and then past me at the door to the verandah. Then he got up on tiptoes and very carefully shut all three, and then he drew the curtains. It gave me the *skriks*, man, I can tell you. Then he went to a great old black chest and took out a Manu Script, because it was all in the beautiful black difficult writing, and gave it to me to read. And I sat and slowly worked it out, letter by letter, while he sat opposite, sweating and totting, and giving fearful looks over his shoulders.

What was it? Well, I was drunk, for one thing, and Hans sitting there all frightened scared me, but it was good, it was good, I promise you. A kind of chronicle of Blagspruit it was, the lives of the citizens—well, need I elaborate, since the lives of citizens are the same everywhere in the world, but worse in Suid Afrika, and worse a million times in Blagspruit. The Manu Script gave off a stink of church and right-doing, with the sin and the evil underneath. It had a medieval stink to it, naturally enough, for what is worse than the kerk in this our land? But I'm saying this to you, remember, and I never said it, but what is worse than the stink of the kerk and the God-fearing in this our feudal land?

But the poem. As far as I can remember, because I was full as a tick, it was a sort of prose chronicle that led up to and worked into the poems; you couldn't tell where they began or ended. The prose was stiff and old-fashioned, and formal, monk's language, and the poems too. But I knew when I read it it was the best I'd read in years—since I read those poems of his ten years before, man, not since then. And don't forget, God help me, I'm an editor now, and I read poems day and night, and when I come on something like Hans's poems that night I have nothing to say but— *Goed*.

Right. I was working away there an hour or more because of that damned black ornamented script. Then I put it down and I said: "Hans, can I ask you a question?" And he looked this way and that over his shoulder first, then leaned forward, the lamplight shining on his pate, and he asked in a low trembling sinner's voice: "What do you want to ask me, Martin?"

I said, "Why this complicated handwriting? What for? It's beautiful, but why this monkey's puzzle?"

And he lowered his voice and said: "It's so that Esther can't read it."

I said: "And what of it, Hans? Why not? Give me some more brandewyn and tell me."

He said: "She's a friend of the predikant's cook, and her sister Mary works in the Mayor's kitchen."

I saw it all. I was drunk, so I saw it. I got up, and I said: "Hans, you're right. You're right a thousand times. If you're going to write stuff like this, as true and as beautiful as God and all his angels, then Esther mustn't read it. But why don't you let me take this back with me and print it in *Onwards?*"

He went white and looked as if I might knife him there and then like a *totsti*. He grabbed the manuscript from me and held it against his fat chest, and he said: "They mustn't see it."

"You're right," I said, understanding him completely.

"It's dangerous keeping it here," he said, darting fearful looks all around.

"Yes, you're right," I said, and I sat down with a bump in my *rimpie* chair, and I said: *"Ja,* if they found that, Hans . . ."

"They'd kill me," he said.

I saw it, completely.

I was drunk. He was drunk. We put the manuscript *boekie* on the table and we put our arms around each other and we wept for the citizens of Blagspruit. Then we lit the hurricane lamp in the kitchen, and he took his *boekie* under his arm, and we tiptoed out into the moonlight that stank of marigolds, and out we went down the main street, all dark as the pit now because it was after twelve and the citizens were asleep, and we went staggering down the tarmacked street that shone in the moonlight between low dark houses, and out into the veld. There we looked sorrowfully at each other and wept some sad brandy tears, and right in front of us, the devil aiding us, was a thorn tree. All virgin it was, its big black spikes lifted up and shining in the devil's moon. And we wept a long time more, and we tore out the pages from his manuscript and we made them into little screws of paper and we stuck them all over the thorns, and when there were none left, we sat under the thorn tree in the moonlight, the black spiky thorns making thin purplish shadows all over us and over the white sand. Then we wept for the state of our country and the state of poetry. We drank a lot more brandy, and the ants came after it and us, so we staggered back down the gleaming sleeping main street of Blagspruit, and that's all I remember until Esther was standing over me with a tin tray that had a teapot, teacup, sugar and some condensed milk, and she was saying: "Master du Preez, where is Master Hans?"

I saw the seven o'clock sun outside the window, and I remembered everything, and I sat up and I said: "My God!"

And Esther said: "God has not been in this house since half past five on Saturday last." And went out.

Right. I got dressed, and went down the main street, drawing looks from the Monday morning citizens, all of whom had probably been watching us staggering along last night from behind their black drawn curtains. I reached the veld and there was Hans. A wind had got up, a hot dust-devilish wind, and it blew about red dust and bits of grit, and leaves, and dead grass into the blue sky, and those pale dry bushes that leave their roots and go bouncing and twirling all over the empty sand, like dervishes, round and around, and then up and around, and there was Hans, letting out yelps and cries and shouts, and he was chasing about after screws of paper that were whirling around among all the dust and stuff.

I helped him. The thorn tree had three squirls of paper tugging and blowing from spikes of black thorn, so I collected those, and we ran after the blowing white bits that had the black beautiful script on them, and we got perhaps a third back. Then we sat under the thorn tree, the hard sharp black shadows over us and the sand, and we watched a dust devil whirling columns of yellow sand and his poems up and off into the sky.

I said: "But Hans, you could write them down again, couldn't you? You couldn't have forgotten them, surely?"

And he said: "But Martin, anyone can read them now. Don't you see that, man? Esther could come out here next afternoon off, and pick any one of those poems up off the earth and read it. Or suppose the predikant or the Mayor got their hands on them?"

Then I understood. I promise you, it had never crossed my *domkop* mind until that moment. I swear it. I simply sat there, sweating out guilt and brandy, and I looked at that poor madman, and then I remembered back ten years and I thought: You idiot. You fool.

Then at last I got intelligent and I said: "But Hans, even if Esther and the predikant and the Mayor did come out here and pick up your poems, like leaves, off the bushes? They couldn't understand one word, because they are written in that *slim* back script you worked out for yourself."

I saw his poor crazy face get more happy, and he said: "You think so, Martin? Really? You really think so?"

I said: "*Ja,* it's the truth." And he got all happy and safe, while I thought of those poems whirling around forever, or until the next rainstorm, around the blue sky with the dust and the bits of shining grass.

And I said: "Anyway, at the best only perhaps a thousand, or perhaps two thousand, people would understand that beautiful *boekie*. Try to look at it that way, Hans, it might make you feel better."

By this time he looked fine; he was smiling and cheered up.

Right.

We got up and dusted each other off, and I took him home to Esther. I asked him to let me take the poems we'd rescued back to publish in *Onwards,* but he got desperate again and said: "No, no. Do you want to kill me? Do you want them to kill me? You're my friend, Martin, you can't do that."

So I told Esther that she had a great man in her charge, through whom Heaven Itself spoke, and she was right to take such care of him. But she merely nodded her queenly white-doeked head and said: "Goodbye, Master du Preez, and may God be with you."

So I came home to Kapstaad.

A week ago I got a letter from Hans, but I didn't see at once it was from him; it was in ordinary writing, like yours or mine, but rather unformed and wild, and it said: "I am leaving this place. They know me now. They look at me. I'm going north to the river. Don't tell Esther. *Jou vriend*, Johannes Potgieter."

Right.

Jou vriend,
Martin du Preez.

Our Friend Judith

I STOPPED inviting Judith to meet people when a Canadian woman remarked, with the satisfied fervour of one who has at last pinned a label on a rare specimen: "She is, of course, one of your typical English spinsters."

This was a few weeks after an American sociologist, having elicited from Judith the facts that she was fortyish, unmarried, and living alone, had enquired of me: "I suppose she has given up?" "Given up what?" I asked; and the subsequent discussion was unrewarding.

Judith did not easily come to parties. She would come after pressure, not so much—one felt—to do one a favour, but in order to correct what she believed to be a defect in her character. "I really ought to enjoy meeting new people more than I do," she said once. We reverted to an earlier pattern of our friendship: odd evenings together, an occasional visit to the cinema, or she would telephone to say: "I'm on my way past you to the British Museum. Would you care for a cup of coffee with me? I have twenty minutes to spare."

It is characteristic of Judith that the word spinster, used of her, provoked fascinated speculation about other people. There are my aunts, for instance: aged seventy-odd, both unmarried, one an ex-missionary from China, one a retired matron of a famous London hospital. These two old ladies live together under the shadow of the cathedral in a country town. They devote much time to the Church, to good causes, to letter writing with friends all over the world, to the grandchildren and the great-grandchildren of relatives. It would be a mistake, however, on entering a house in which nothing has been moved for fifty years, to diagnose a condition of fossilized late-Victorian integrity. They read every book reviewed in the *Observer* or the *Times,* so that I recently got a letter from Aunt Rose enquiring whether I did not think that the author of *On the Road* was not—perhaps?—exaggerating his difficulties. They know a good deal about music, and write letters of encouragement to young composers they feel are being neglected—"You must understand that anything new and original takes time to be understood." Well-informed and critical Tories, they are as likely to dispatch telegrams of protest to the Home Secretary as letters of support. These ladies, my aunts Emily and Rose, are surely what is meant by the phrase *English spinster.* And yet, once the connection has been pointed out, there is no doubt that Judith and they are spiritual cousins, if not sisters. Therefore it follows that one's pitying admiration for women who have supported manless and uncomforted lives needs a certain modification?

One will, of course, never know; and I feel now that it is entirely my fault that I shall never know. I had been Judith's friend for upwards of five years before the incident occurred which I involuntarily thought of—stupidly enough—as "the first time Judith's mask slipped."

A mutual friend, Betty, had been given a cast-off Dior dress. She was too short for it. Also she said: "It's not a dress for a married woman with three children and a talent for cooking. I don't know why not, but it isn't." Judith was the right build. Therefore one evening the three of us met by appointment in Judith's bedroom, with the dress. Neither Betty nor I were surprised at the renewed discovery that Judith was beautiful. We had both too often caught each other, and ourselves, in moments of envy when Judith's calm and severe face, her undemonstratively perfect body, succeeded in making everyone else in a room or a street look cheap.

Judith is tall, small-breasted, slender. Her light brown hair is parted in the centre and cut straight around her neck. A high straight forehead, straight nose, a full grave mouth are setting for her eyes, which are green, large and prominent. Her lids are very white, fringed with gold, and moulded close over the eyeball, so that in profile she has the look of a staring gilded mask. The dress was of dark green glistening stuff, cut straight, with a sort of loose tunic. It opened simply at the throat. In it Judith could of course evoke nothing but classical images. Diana, perhaps, back from the hunt, in a relaxed moment? A rather intellectual wood nymph who had opted for an afternoon in the British Museum reading room? Something like that. Neither Betty nor I said a word, since Judith was examining herself in a long mirror, and must know she looked magnificent.

Slowly she drew off the dress and laid it aside. Slowly she put on the old cord skirt and woollen blouse she had taken off. She must have surprised a resigned glance between us, for she then remarked, with the smallest of mocking smiles: "One surely ought to stay in character, wouldn't you say so?" She added, reading the words out of some invisible book, written not by her, since it was a very vulgar book, but perhaps by one of us: "It does everything *for* me, I must admit."

"After seeing you in it," Betty cried out, defying her, "I can't bear for anyone else to have it. I shall simply put it away." Judith shrugged, rather irritated. In the shapeless skirt and blouse, and without makeup, she stood smiling at us, a woman at whom forty-nine of fifty people would not look twice.

A second revelatory incident occurred soon after. Betty telephoned me to say that Judith had a kitten. Did I know that Judith adored cats? "No, but of course she would," I said.

Betty lived in the same street as Judith and saw more of her than I did. I was kept posted about the growth and habits of the cat and its effect on Judith's life. She remarked for instance that she felt it was good for her to have a tie and some responsibility. But no sooner was the cat out of kittenhood than all the neighbours complained. It was a tomcat, ungelded, and making every night hideous. Finally the landlord said that either the cat or Judith must go, unless she was prepared to have the cat "fixed." Judith wore herself out trying to find some person, anywhere in Britain, who would be prepared to take the cat. This person would, however, have to sign a written statement not to have the cat "fixed." When Judith took the cat to the vet to be killed, Betty told me she cried for twenty-four hours.

"She didn't think of compromising? After all, perhaps the cat might have preferred to live, if given the choice?"

"Is it likely I'd have the nerve to say anything so sloppy to Judith? It's the nature of a male cat to rampage lustfully about, and therefore it would be morally wrong for Judith to have the cat fixed, simply to suit her own convenience."

"She said that?"

"She wouldn't have to *say* it, surely?"

A third incident was when she allowed a visiting young American, living in Paris, the friend of a friend and scarcely known to her, to use her flat while she visited her parents over Christmas. The young man and his friends lived it up for ten days of alcohol and sex and marijuana, and when Judith came back it took a week to get the place clean again and the furniture mended. She telephoned twice to Paris, the first time to say that he was a disgusting young thug and if he knew what was good for him he would keep out of her way in the future; the second time to apologise for losing her temper. "I had a choice either to let someone use my flat, or to leave it empty. But having chosen that you should have it, it was clearly an unwarrantable infringement of your liberty to make any conditions at all. I do most sincerely ask your pardon." The moral aspects of the matter having been made clear, she was irritated rather than not to receive letters of apology from him—fulsome, embarrassed, but above all, baffled.

It was the note of curiosity in the letters—he even suggested coming over to get to know her better—that irritated her most. "What do you suppose he means?" she said to me. "He lived in my flat for ten days. One would have thought that should be enough, wouldn't you?"

The facts about Judith, then, are all in the open, unconcealed, and plain to anyone who cares to study them; or, as it became plain she feels, to anyone with the intelligence to interpret them.

She has lived for the last twenty years in a small tworoomed flat high over a busy West London street. The flat is shabby and badly heated. The furniture is old, was never anything but ugly, is now frankly rickety and fraying. She has an income of £200 a year from a dead uncle. She lives on this and what she earns from her poetry, and from lecturing on poetry to night classes and extramural university classes.

She does not smoke or drink, and eats very little, from preference, not self-discipline.

She studied poetry and biology at Oxford, with distinction.

She is a Castlewell. That is, she is a member of one of the academic upper-middle-class families, which have been producing for centuries a steady supply of brilliant but sound men and women who are the backbone of the arts and sciences in Britain. She is on cool good terms with her family who respect her and leave her alone.

She goes on long walking tours, by herself, in such places as Exmoor or West Scotland.

Every three or four years she publishes a volume of poems.

The walls of her flat are completely lined with books. They are scientific, classical and historical; there is a great deal of poetry and some drama. There is not one novel. When Judith says: "Of course I don't read novels," this does not mean that novels have no place, or a small place, in literature; or that people should not read novels; but that it must be obvious she can't be expected to read novels.

I had been visiting her flat for years before I noticed two long shelves of books, under a window, each shelf filled with the works of a single writer. The two writers are not, to put it at the mildest, the kind one would associate with Judith. They are mild, reminiscent, vague and whimsical. Typical English belles-lettres, in fact, and by definition abhorrent to her. Not one of the books in the two shelves has been read; some of the pages are still uncut. Yet each book is inscribed or dedicated to her: gratefully, admiringly, sentimentally and, more than once, amorously. In short, it is open to anyone who cares to examine these two shelves, and to work out dates, to conclude that Judith from the age of fifteen to twenty-five had been the beloved young companion of one elderly literary gentleman, and from twenty-five to thirty-five the inspiration of another.

During all that time she had produced her own poetry, and the sort of poetry, it is quite safe to deduce, not at all likely to be admired by her two admirers. Her poems are al-

ways cool and intellectual; that is their form, which is contradicted or supported by a gravely sensuous texture. They
are poems to read often; one has to, to understand them.

I did not ask Judith a direct question about these two
eminent but rather fusty lovers. Not because she would
not have answered, or because she would have found the
question impertinent, but because such questions are clearly
unnecessary. Having those two shelves of books where they
are, and books she could not conceivably care for, for their
own sake, is publicly giving credit where credit is due. I
can imagine her thinking the thing over, and deciding it was
only fair, or perhaps honest, to place the books there; and
this despite the fact that she would not care at all for the
same attention to be paid to her. There is something almost
contemptuous in it. For she certainly despises people who
feel they need attention.

For instance, more than once a new emerging wave of
"modern" young poets have discovered her as the only
"modern" poet among their despised and well-credited elders.
This is because, since she began writing at fifteen, her poems
have been full of scientific, mechanical and chemical im-
agery. This is how she thinks, or feels.

More than once has a young poet hastened to her flat,
to claim her as an ally, only to find her totally and by instinct unmoved by words like modern, new, contemporary.
He has been outraged and wounded by her principle, so
deeply rooted as to be unconscious, and to need no expression but a contemptuous shrug of the shoulders, that
publicity seeking or to want critical attention is despicable.
It goes without saying that there is perhaps one critic in the
world she has any time for. He has sulked off, leaving her
on her shelf, which she takes it for granted is her proper
place, to be read by an appreciative minority.

Meanwhile she gives her lectures, walks alone through
London, writes her poems, and is seen sometimes at a concert
or a play with a middle-aged professor of Greek who has a
wife and two children.

Betty and I had speculated about this professor, with such
remarks as: Surely she must sometimes be lonely? Hasn't she
ever wanted to marry? What about that awful moment when
one comes in from somewhere at night to an empty flat?

It happened recently that Betty's husband was on a business trip, her children visiting, and she was unable to stand the empty house. She asked Judith for a refuge until her own home filled again.

Afterwards Betty rang up to report:

"Four of the five nights Professor Adams came in about ten or so."

"Was Judith embarrassed?"

"Would you expect her to be?"

"Well, if not embarrassed, at least conscious there was a situation?"

"No, not at all. But I must say I don't think he's good enough for her. He can't possibly understand her. He calls her Judy."

"Good God."

"Yes. But I was wondering. Suppose the other two called her Judy—'little Judy'—imagine it! Isn't it awful? But it does rather throw a light on Judith?"

"It's rather touching."

"I suppose it's touching. But *I* was embarrassed—oh, not because of the situation. Because of how she was, with him. 'Judy, is there another cup of tea in that pot?' And she, rather daughterly and demure, pouring him one."

"Well yes, I can see how you felt."

"Three of the nights he went to her bedroom with her—very casual about it, because she was being. But he was not there in the mornings. So I asked her. You know how it is when you ask her a question. As if you've been having long conversations on that very subject for year and years, and she is merely continuing where you left off last. So when she says something surprising, one feels such a fool to be surprised?"

"Yes. And then?"

"I asked her if she was sorry not to have children. She said yes, but one couldn't have everything."

"One can't have everything, she said?"

"Quite clearly feeling she *has* nearly everything. She said she thought it was a pity, because she would have brought up children very well."

"When you come to think of it, she would, too."

"I asked about marriage, but she said on the whole the role of a mistress suited her better."

"She used the word mistress?"

"You must admit it's the accurate word."

"I suppose so."

"And then she said that while she liked intimacy and sex and everything, she enjoyed waking up in the morning alone and *her own person.*"

"Yes, *of course.*"

"Of course. But now she's bothered because the professor would like to marry her. Or he feels he ought. At least, he's getting all guilty and obsessive about it. She says she doesn't see the point of divorce, and anyway, surely it would be very hard on his poor old wife after all these years particularly after bringing up two children so satisfactorily. She talks about his wife as if she's a kind of nice old charwoman, and it wouldn't be *fair* to sack her, you know. Anyway. What with one thing and another, Judith's going off to Italy soon in order *to collect herself.*"

"But how's she going to pay for it?"

"Luckily the Third Programme's commissioning her to do some arty programmes. They offered her a choice of The Cid—El Thid, you know—and the Borgias. Well, the Borghese, then. And Judith settled for the Borgias."

"The Borgias," I said, *"Judith?"*

"Yes, quite. I said that too, in that tone of voice. She saw my point. She says the epic is right up her street, whereas the Renaissance has never been on her wave length. Obviously it couldn't be, all the magnificence and cruelty and *dirt.* But of course chivalry and a high moral code and all those idiotically noble goings-on are right on her wave length."

"Is the money the same?"

"Yes. But is it likely Judith would let money decide? No, she said that one should always choose something new, that isn't up one's street. Well, because it's better for her character, and so on, to get herself unsettled by the Renaissance. She didn't say *that,* of course."

"Of course not."

Judith went to Florence; and for some months postcards informed us tersely of her doings. Then Betty decided she must go by herself for a holiday. She had been appalled by the discovery that if her husband was away for a night she couldn't sleep; and when he went to Australia for three weeks, she stopped living until he came back. She had discussed this with him, and he had agreed that, if she really felt the situation to be serious, he would dispatch her by air, to Italy, in order to recover her self-respect. As she put it.

I got this letter from her: "It's no use, I'm coming home. I might have known. Better face it, once you're really married you're not fit for man nor beast. And if you remember what I used to be like! *Well!* I moped around Milan. I sunbathed in Venice, then I thought my tan was surely worth something, so I was on the point of starting an affair with another lonely soul, but I lost heart, and went to Florence to see Judith. She wasn't there. She'd gone to the Italian Riviera. I had nothing better to do, so I followed her. When I saw the place I wanted to laugh, it's so much not Judith, you know, all those palms and umbrellas and gaiety at all costs and ever such an ornamental blue sea. Judith is in an enormous stone room up on the hillside above the sea, with grape vines all over the place. You should see her, she's got beautiful. It seems for the last fifteen years she's been going to Soho every Saturday morning to buy food at an Italian shop. I must have looked surprised, because she explained she liked Soho. I suppose because all that dreary vice and nudes and prostitutes and everything prove how right she is to be as she is? She told the people in the shop she was going to Italy, and the *signora* said, what a coincidence, she was going back to Italy too, and she did hope an old friend like Miss Castlewell would visit her there. Judith said to me: 'I felt lacking, when she used the word friend. Our relations have have always been formal. Can you understand it?' she said to me. 'For fifteen years,' I said to her. She said: 'I think I must feel it's a kind of imposition, don't you know, expecting people to feel friendship for one.' *Well.* I said: 'You ought to understand it, because you're like that yourself.' 'Am I?' she said. 'Well, think about it,' I said. But I could see she didn't want to think about it. Anyway, she's here, and I've spent a week with her. The widow Maria Rineiri inherited her mother's house, so she came home, from Soho. On the ground floor is a tatty little *rosticcerìa* patronised by the neighbours. They are all working people. This isn't tourist country, up on the hill. The widow lives above the shop with her little boy, a nasty little brat of about ten. Say what you like, the English are the only people who know how to bring up children, I don't care if that's insular. Judith's room is at the back, with a balcony. Underneath her room is the barber's shop, and the barber is Luigi Rineiri, the widow's younger brother. Yes, I was keeping him until the last. He is about forty, tall dark handsome, a great *bull,* but rather a sweet fatherly bull. He has cut Judith's hair and made it lighter. Now it looks like a sort of gold helmet. Judith is all brown. The widow Rineiri has made her a white dress and a green dress. They fit, for a change. When Judith walks down the street to the lower town, all the Italian males take one look at the golden girl and melt in their own oil like ice cream. Judith takes all this in her stride. She sort of acknowledges the homage. Then she strolls into the sea and vanishes into the foam. She swims five miles every day. *Naturally.* I haven't asked Judith whether she has collected herself, because you can see she hasn't. The widow Rineiri is matchmaking. When I noticed this I wanted to laugh, but luckily I didn't because Judith asked me, really wanting to know: 'Can you see me married to an Italian barber?' (Not being snobbish, but stating the position, so to speak.) 'Well yes,' I said, 'you're the only woman I know who I can see married to an Italian barber.' Because it wouldn't matter who she married, she'd always be her *own person.* 'At any rate, for a time,' I said. At which she said, asperously: 'You can use phrases like for a time in England but not in Italy.' Did you ever see England, at least London, as the home of licence, liberty and free love? No, neither did I, but of course she's right. Married to Luigi it would be the family, the neighbours, the church and the *bambini.* All the same she's thinking about it, believe it or not. Here she's quite different, all relaxed and free. She's melting in the attention she gets. The widow mothers her and makes her coffee all the time, and listens to a lot of good advice about how to bring up that nasty brat of hers. Unluckily she doesn't take it. Luigi is crazy for her. At mealtimes she goes to the *trattoria* in the upper square and all the workmen treat her like a goddess. Well, a film star then. I said to her, you're mad to come home. For one thing her rent is ten bob a week, and you eat *pasta* and drink red wine till you bust for about one and sixpence. No, she said, it would be nothing but self-indulgence to stay. Why? I said. She said, she's got nothing to stay for. (ho ho.) And besides, she's done her research on the Borghese, though so far she can't see her way to an honest presentation of the facts. What made these people tick? she wants to know. And so she's only staying because of the cat. I forgot to mention the cat. This is a town of cats. The Italians here love their cats. I wanted to feed a stray cat at the table, but the waiter said no, and after lunch, all the waiters came with trays crammed with leftover food and stray cats came from everywhere to eat. And at dark when the tourists go in to feed and the beach is empty—you know how empty and forlorn a beach is at dusk?—well cats appear from everywhere. The beach seems to move, then you see it's cats. They go stalking along the thin inch of grey water at the edge of the sea, shaking their paws crossly at each step, snatching at the dead little fish, and throwing them with their mouths up on to the dry sand. Then they scamper after them. You've never seen such a snarling and fighting. At dawn when the fishing boats come in to the empty beach, the cats are there in dozens. The fishermen throw them bits of fish. The cats snarl and fight over it. Judith gets up early and goes down to watch. Sometimes Luigi goes too, being tolerant. Because what he really likes is to join the evening promenade with Judith on his arm around the square of the upper town. Showing her off. Can you *see* Judith? But she does it. Being tolerant. But she smiles and enjoys the attention she gets, there's no doubt of it.

"She has a cat in her room. It's a kitten really, but it's pregnant. Judith says she can't leave until the kittens are born. The cat is too young to have kittens. Imagine Judith. She sits on her bed in that great stone room, with her bare feet on the stone floor and watches the cat, and tries to work out why a healthy uninhibited Italian cat always fed on the best from the *rosticceria* should be neurotic. Because it is. When it sees Judith watching it gets nervous and starts licking at the roots of its tail. But Judith goes on watching, and says about Italy that the reason why the English love the Italians is because the Italians make the English feel superior. They have no discipline. And that's a despicable reason for one nation to love another. Then she talks about Luigi and says he has no sense of guilt, but a sense of sin; whereas she has no sense of sin but she has guilt. I haven't asked her if this has been an insuperable barrier, because judging from how she looks, it hasn't. She says she would rather have a sense of sin, because sin can be atoned for, and if she understood sin, perhaps she would be more at home with the Renaissance. Luigi is very healthy, she says, and not neurotic. He is a Catholic of course. He doesn't mind that she's an atheist. His mother has explained to him that the English are all pagans, but good people at heart. I suppose he thinks a few smart sessions with the local priest would set Judith on the right path for good and all. Meanwhile the cat walks nervously around the room, stopping to lick, and when it can't stand Judith watching it another second, it rolls over on the floor, with its paws tucked up, and rolls up its eyes, and Judith scratches its lumpy pregnant stomach and tells it to relax. It makes *me* nervous to see her, it's not like her, I don't know why. Then Luigi shouts up from the barber's shop, then he comes up and stands at the door laughing, and Judith laughs, and the widow says: Children, enjoy yourselves. And off they go, walking down to the town eating ice cream. The cat follows them. It won't let Judith out of its sight, like a dog. When she swims miles out to sea, the cat hides under a beach hut until she comes back. Then she carries it back up the hill, because that nasty little boy chases it. *Well.* I'm coming home tomorrow thank God, to my dear old Billy, I was mad ever to leave him. There is something about Judith and Italy that has upset me, I don't know what. The point is, what on earth can Judith and Luigi *talk* about? Nothing. How can they? And of course it doesn't matter. So I turn out to be a prude as well. See you next week."

It was my turn for a dose of the sun, so I didn't see Betty. On my way back from Rome I stopped off in Judith's resort and walked up through narrow streets to the upper town, where, in the square with the vine-covered *trattoria* at the corner, was a house with ROSTICCERIA written in black paint on a cracked wooden board over a low door. There was a door curtain of red beads, and flies settled on the beads. I opened the beads with my hands and looked in to a small dark room with a stone counter. Loops of salami hung from metal hooks. A glass bell covered some plates of cooked meats. There were flies on the salami and on the glass bell. A few tins on the wooden shelves, a couple of pale loaves, some wine casks and an open case of sticky pale green grapes covered with fruit flies seemed to be the only stock. A single wooden table with two chairs stood in a corner, and two workmen sat there, eating lumps of sausage and bread. Through another bead curtain at the back came a short, smoothly fat, slender-limbed woman with greying hair. I asked for Miss Castlewell, and her face changed. She said in an offended, offhand way: "Miss Castlewell left last week." She took a white cloth from under the counter, and flicked at the flies on the glass bell. "I'm a friend of hers," I said, and she said: *"Si,"* and put her hands palm down on the counter and looked at me, expressionless. The workmen got up, gulped down the last of their wine, nodded and went. She *ciao'd* them; and looked back at me. Then, since I didn't go, she called: "Luigi!" A shout came from the back room, there was a rattle of beads, and in came first a wiry sharp-faced boy, and then Luigi. He was tall, heavy-shouldered, and his black rough hair was like a cap, pulled low over his brows. He looked good-natured, but at the moment uneasy. His sister said something, and he stood beside her, an ally, and confirmed: "Miss Castlewell went away." I was on the point of giving up, when through the bead curtain that screened off a dazzling light eased a thin tabby cat. It was ugly and it walked uncomfortably, with its back quarters bunched up. The child suddenly let out a "Sssssss" through his teeth, and the cat froze. Luigi said something sharp to the child, and something encouraging to the cat, which sat down, looked straight in front of it, then began frantically licking at its flanks. "Miss Castlewell was offended with us," said Mrs. Rineiri suddenly, and with dignity. "She left early one morning. We did not expect her to go." I said. "Perhaps she had to go home and finish some work."

Mrs. Rineiri shrugged, then sighed. Then she exchanged a hard look with her brother. Clearly the subject had been discussed, and closed forever.

"I've known Judith a long time," I said, trying to find the right note. "She's a remarkable woman. She's a poet." But there was no response to this at all. Meanwhile the child, with a fixed bared-teeth grin, was staring at the cat, narrowing his eyes. Suddenly he let out another "Sssssss" and added a short high yelp. The cat shot backwards, hit the wall, tried desperately to claw its way up the wall, came to its senses and again sat down and began its urgent, undirected licking at its fur. This time Luigi cuffed the child, who yelped in earnest, and then ran out into the street past the cat. Now that the way was clear the cat shot across the floor, up onto the counter, and bounded past Luigi's shoulder and straight through the bead curtain into the barber's shop, where it landed with a thud.

"Judith was sorry when she left us," said Mrs. Rineiri uncertainly. "She was crying."

"I'm sure she was."

"And so," said Mrs. Rineiri, with finality, laying her hands down again, and looking past me at the bead curtain. That was the end. Luigi nodded brusquely at me, and went into the back. I said goodbye to Mrs. Rineiri and walked back to the lower town. In the square I saw the child, sitting on the running board of a lorry parked outside the *trattoria,* drawing in the dust with his bare toes, and directing in front of him a blank, unhappy stare.

I had to go through Florence, so I went to the address Judith had been at. No, Miss Castlewell had not been back. Her papers and books were still here. Would I take them back with me to England? I made a great parcel and brought them back to England.

I telephoned Judith and she said she had already written for the papers to be sent, but it was kind of me to bring them. There had seemed to be no point, she said, in returning to Florence.

"Shall I bring them over?"

"I would be very grateful, of course."

Judith's flat was chilly, and she wore a bunchy sage-green woollen dress. Her hair was still a soft gold helmet, but she looked pale and rather pinched. She stood with her back to a single bar of electric fire—lit because I demanded it—with her legs apart and her arms folded. She contemplated me.

"I went to the Rineiris' house."

"Oh. Did you?"

"They seemed to miss you."

She said nothing.

"I saw the cat too."

"Oh. Oh, I suppose you and Betty discussed it?" This was with a small unfriendly smile.

"Well, Judith, you must see we were likely to?"

She gave this her consideration and said: "I don't understand why people discuss other people. Oh—I'm not criticising you. But I don't see why you are so interested. I don't understand human behaviour and I'm not particularly interested."

"I think you should write to the Rineiris."

"I wrote and thanked them, of course."

"I don't mean that."

"You and Betty have worked it out?"

"Yes, we talked about it. We thought we should talk to you, so you should write to the Rineiris."

"Why?"

"For one thing, they are both very fond of you."

"Fond," she said smiling.

"Judith, I've never in my life felt such an atmosphere of being let down."

Judith considered this. "When something happens that shows one there is really a complete gulf in understanding, what is there to say?"

"It could scarcely have been a complete gulf in understanding. I suppose you are going to say we are being interfering?"

Judith showed distaste. "That is a very stupid word. And it's a stupid idea. No one can interfere with me if I don't let them. No, it's that I don't understand people. I don't understand why you or Betty should care. Or why the Rineiris should, for that matter," she added with the small tight smile.

"Judith!"

"If you've behaved stupidly, there's no point in going on. You put an end to it."

"What happened? Was it the cat?"

"Yes, I suppose so. But it's not important." She looked at me, saw my ironical face, and said: "The cat was too young to have kittens. That is all there was to it."

"Have it your way. But that is obviously not all there is to it."

"What upsets me is that I don't understand at all why I was so upset then."

"What happened? Or don't you want to talk about it?"

"I don't give a damn whether I talk about it or not. You really do say the most extraordinary things, you and Betty. If you want to know, I'll tell you. What does it matter?"

"I would like to know, of course."

"Of course!" she said. "In your place I wouldn't care. Well, I think the essence of the thing was that I must have had the wrong attitude to that cat. Cats are supposed to be independent. They are supposed to go off by themselves to have their kittens. This one didn't. It was climbing up onto my bed all one night and crying for attention. I don't like cats on my bed. In the morning I saw she was in pain. I stayed with her all that day. Then Luigi—he's the brother, you know."

"Yes."

"Did Betty mention him? Luigi came up to say it was time I went for a swim. He said the cat should look after itself. I blame myself very much. That's what happens when you submerge yourself in somebody else."

Her look at me was now defiant; and her body showed both defensiveness and aggression. "Yes. It's true. I've always been afraid of it. And in the last few weeks I've behaved badly. It's because I let it happen."

"Well, go on."

"I left the cat and swam. It was late, so it was only for a few minutes. When I came out of the sea the cat had followed me and had had a kitten on the beach. The little beast Michele—the son, you know?—well, he always teased the poor thing, and now he had frightened her off the kitten. It was dead, though. He held it up by the tail and waved it at me as I came out of the sea. I told him to bury it. He scooped two inches of sand away and pushed the kitten in—on the beach, where people are all day. So I buried it properly. He had run off. He was chasing the poor cat. She was terrified and running up the town. I ran too. I caught Michele and I was so angry I hit him. I don't believe in hitting children. I've been feeling beastly about it ever since."

"You were angry."

"It's no excuse. I would never have believed myself capable of hitting a child. I hit him very hard. He went off, crying. The poor cat had got under a big lorry parked in the square. Then she screamed. And then a most remarkable thing happened. She screamed just once, and all at once cats just materialised. One minute there was just one cat, lying under a lorry, and the next, dozens of cats. They sat in a big circle around the lorry, all quite still, and watched my poor cat."

"Rather moving," I said.

"Why?"

"There is no evidence one way or the other," I said in inverted commas, "that the cats were there out of concern for a friend in trouble."

"No," she said energetically. "There isn't. It might have been curiosity. Or anything. How do we know? However, I crawled under the lorry. There were two paws sticking out of the cat's back end. The kitten was the wrong way round. It was stuck. I held the cat down with one hand and I pulled the kitten out with the other." She held out her long white hands. They were still covered with fading scars and scratches. "She bit and yelled, but the kitten was alive. She left the kitten and crawled across the square into the house. Then all the cats got up and walked away. It was the most extraordinary thing I've ever seen. They vanished again. One minute they were all there, and then they had vanished. I went after the cat, with the kitten. Poor little thing, it was covered with dust—being wet, don't you know. The cat was on my bed. There was another kitten coming, but it got stuck too. So when she screamed and screamed I just pulled it out. The kittens began to suck. One kitten was very big. It was a nice fat black kitten. It must have hurt her. But she suddenly bit out—snapped, don't you know, like a reflex action, at the back of the kitten's head. It died, just like that. Extraordinary, isn't it?" she said, blinking hard, her lips quivering. "She was its mother, but she killed it. Then she ran off the bed and went downstairs into the shop under the counter. I called to Luigi. You know, he's Mrs. Rineiri's brother."

"Yes, I know."

"He said she was too young, and she was badly frightened and very hurt. He took the alive kitten to her but she got up and walked away. She didn't want it. Then Luigi told me not to look. But I followed him. He held the kitten by the tail and he banged it against the wall twice. Then he dropped it into the rubbish heap. He moved aside some rubbish with his toe, and put the kitten there and pushed rubbish over it. Then Luigi said the cat should be destroyed. He said she was badly hurt and it would always hurt her to have kittens."

"He hasn't destroyed her. She's still alive. But it looks to me as if he were right."

"Yes, I expect he was."

"What upset you—that he killed the kitten?"

"Oh, no, I expect the cat would if he hadn't. But that isn't the point, is it?"

"What is the point?"

"I don't think I really know." She had been speaking breathlessly, and fast. Now she said slowly: "It's not a question of right or wrong, is it? Why should it be? It's a question of what one is. That night Luigi wanted to go promenading with me. For him, that was *that*. Something had to be done, and he'd done it. But I felt ill. He was very nice to me. He's a very good person," she said, defiantly.

"Yes, he looks it."

"That night I couldn't sleep. I was blaming myself. I should never have left the cat to go swimming. Well, and then I decided to leave the next day. And I did. And that's all. The whole thing was a mistake, from start to finish."

"Going to Italy at all?"

"Oh, to go for a holiday would have been all right."

"You've done all that work for nothing? You mean you aren't going to make use of all that research?"

"No. It was a mistake."

"Why don't you leave it a few weeks and see how things are then?"

"Why?"

"You might feel differently about it."

"What an extraordinary thing to say. Why should I? Oh, you mean, time passing, healing wounds—that sort of thing?

What an extraordinary idea. It's always seemed to me an extraordinary idea. No, right from the beginning I've felt ill at ease with the whole business, not myself at all."

"Rather irrationally, I should have said."

Judith considered this, very seriously. She frowned while she thought it over. Then she said: "But if one cannot rely on what one feels, what can one rely on?"

"On what one thinks, I should have expected you to say."

"Should you? Why? Really, you people are all very strange. I don't understand you." She turned off the electric fire, and her face closed up. She smiled, friendly and distant, and said: "I don't really see any point at all in discussing it."

Each Other

.

. .

"I suppose your brother's coming again?"

"He might."

He kept his back bravely turned while he adjusted tie, collar, and jerked his jaw this way and that to check his shave. Then, with all pretexts used, he remained rigid, his hand on his tie knot, looking into the mirror past his left cheek at the body of his wife, which was disposed prettily on the bed, weight on its right elbow, its two white forearms engaged in the movements obligatory for filing one's nails. He let his hand drop and demanded: "What do you mean, he *might?*" She did not answer, but held up a studied hand to inspect five pink arrows. She was a thin, very thin, dark girl of about eighteen. Her pose, her way of inspecting her nails, her pink-striped nightshirt which showed long, thin, white legs—all her magazine attitudes were an attempt to hide an anxiety as deep as his; for her breathing, like his, was loud and shallow.

He was not taken in. The lonely fever in her black eyes, the muscles showing rodlike in the flesh of her upper arm, made him feel how much she wanted him to go; and he thought, sharp because of the sharpness of his need for her: There's something unhealthy about her, yes. . . . The word caused him guilt. He accepted it, and allowed his mind, which was overalert, trying to pin down the cause of his misery, to add: Yes, not clean, dirty. But this fresh criticism surprised him, and he remembered her obsessive care of her flesh, hair, nails, and the long hours spent in the bath. *Yes, dirty,* his rising aversion insisted.

Armed by it, he was able to turn, slowly, to look at her direct, instead of through the cold glass. He was a solid, well-set-up, brushed, washed young man who had stood several inches shorter than she at the wedding a month ago; but with confidence in the manhood which had mastered her freakish adolescence. He now kept on her the pressure of a blue stare both appealing (of which he was not aware) and aggressive—which he meant as a warning. Meanwhile he controlled a revulsion which he knew would vanish if she merely lifted her arms towards him.

"What do you mean, he *might?*" he said again.

After some moments of not-answering, she said, languid, turning her thin hand this way and that: "I said, he might."

This dialogue echoed, for both of them, not only from five minutes before; but from other mornings, when it had been as often as not unspoken. They were on the edge of disaster. But the young husband was late. He looked at his watch, a gesture which said, but unconvincingly, bravado merely: I go out to work while you lie there. . . . Then he about-turned, and went to the door, slowing on his way to it. Stopped. Said: "Well in that case I shan't be back to supper."

"Suit yourself," she said, languid. She now lay flat on her back, and waved both hands in front of her eyes to dry nail varnish which, however, was three days old.

He said loudly: "Freda! I mean it. I'm not going to . . ." He looked both trapped and defiant; but intended to do everything, obviously, to maintain his self-respect, his masculinity, in the face of—but what? Her slow smile across at him was something (unlike everything else she had done since waking that morning) she was quite unaware of. She surely could not be aware of the sheer brutality of her slow, considering, contemptuous smile? For it had invitation in it; and it was this, the unconscious triumph there, that caused him to pale, to begin a stammering: "Fre-Fre-Fred-Freda . . ." but give up, and leave the room. Abruptly though quietly, considering the force of his horror.

She lay still, listening to his footsteps go down, and the front door closing. Then, without hurrying, she lifted her long thin white legs that ended in ten small pink shields, over the edge of the bed, and stood on them by the window, to watch her husband's well-brushed head jerking away along the pavement. This was a suburb of London, and he had to get to the City, where he was a clerk-with-prospects: and most of the other people down there were on their way to work. She watched him and them, until at the corner he turned, his face lengthened with anxiety. She indolently waved, without smiling. He stared back, as if at a memory of nightmare; so she shrugged and removed herself from the window, and did not see his frantically too-late wave and smile.

She now stood, frowning, in front of the long glass in the new wardrobe: a very tall girl, stooped by her height, all elbows and knees, and even more ridiculous because of the short nightshirt. She stripped this off over her head, taking assurance in a side-glance from full-swinging breasts and a rounded waist; then slipped on a white negligee that had frills all down it and around the neck, from which her head emerged, poised. She now looked much better, like a model, in fact. She brushed her short gleaming black hair, stared at length into the deep anxious eyes, and got back into bed.

Soon she tensed, hearing the front door open, softly; and close, softly again. She listened, as the unseen person also listened and watched; for this was a two-roomed flatlet, converted in a semi-detached house. The landlady lived in the flatlet below this one on the ground floor; and the young husband had taken to asking her, casually, every evening, or listening, casually, to easily given information, about the comings and goings in the house and the movements of his wife. But the steps came steadily up towards her, the door opened, very gently, and she looked up, her face bursting into flower as in came a very tall, lank, dark young man. He sat on the bed beside his sister, took her thin hand in his thin hand, kissed it, bit it lovingly, then bent to kiss her on the lips. Their mouths held while two pairs of deep black eyes held each other. Then she shut her eyes, took his lower lip between her teeth, and slid her tongue along it. He began to undress before she let him go; and she asked, without any of the pertness she used for her husband: "Are you in a hurry this morning?"

"Got to get over to a job in Exeter Street."

An electrician, he was not tied to desk or office.

He slid naked into bed beside his sister, murmuring: "Olive Oyl."

Her long body was pressed against his in a fervor of gratitude for the love name, for it had never received absolution from her husband as it did from this man; and she returned, in as loving a murmur: "Popeye." Again the two pairs of eyes stared into each other at an inch or so's distance. His, though deep in bony sockets like hers, were prominent there, the eyeballs rounded under thin, already crinkling, bruised-looking flesh. Hers, however, were delicately outlined by clear white skin, and he kissed the perfected copies of his own ugly eyes, and said, as she pressed towards him: "Now, now, Olive Oyl, don't be in such a hurry, you'll spoil it."

"No, we won't."

"Wait, I tell you."

"All right then . . ."

The two bodies, deeply breathing, remained still a long while. Her hand, on the small of his back, made a soft, circular pressing motion, bringing him inwards. He had his two hands on her hip-bones, holding her still. But she succeeded, and they joined, and he said again: "Wait now. Lie still." They lay absolutely still, eyes closed.

After a while he asked suddenly: "Well, did he last night?"

"Yes."

His teeth bared against her forehead and he said: "I suppose you made him."

"Why *made* him?"

"You're a pig."

"All right then, how about Alice?"

"Oh her. Well, she screamed and said: 'Stop. Stop.'"

"Who's a pig, then?"

She wriggled circularly, and he held her hips still, tenderly murmuring: "No, no, no, no."

Stillness again. In the small bright bedroom, with the suburban sunlight outside, new green curtains blew in, flicking the too-large, too-new furniture, while the long white bodies remained still, mouth to mouth, eyes closed, united by deep soft breaths.

But his breathing deepened; his nails dug into the bones of her hips, he slid his mouth free and said: "How about Charlie, then?"

"He made me scream too," she murmured, licking his throat, eyes closed. This time it was she who held his loins steady, saying: "No, no, no, you'll spoil it."

They lay together, still. A long silence, a long quiet. Then the fluttering curtains roused her, her foot tensed, and she rubbed it delicately up and down his leg. He said, angry: "Why did you spoil it then? It was just beginning."

"It's much better afterwards if it's really difficult." She slid and pressed her internal muscles to make it more difficult, grinning at him in challenge, and he put his hands around her throat in a half-mocking, half-serious pressure to stop her, simultaneously moving in and out of her with exactly the same emulous, taunting but solicitous need she was showing—to see how far they both could go. In a moment they were pulling each other's hair, biting, sinking fingers between thin bones, and then, just before the explosion, they pulled apart at the same moment, and lay separate, trembling.

"We only just made it," he said, fond, uxorious, stroking her hair.

"Yes. Careful now, Fred."

They slid together again.

"Now it will be just perfect," she said, content, mouth against his throat.

The two bodies, quivering with strain, lay together, jerking involuntarily from time to time. But slowly they quietened. Their breathing, jagged at first, smoothed. They breathed together. They had become one person, abandoned against and in each other, silent and gone.

A long time, a long time, a long . . .

A car went past below in the usually silent street, very loud, and the young man opened his eyes and looked into the relaxed gentle face of his sister.

"Freda."

"Ohhh."

"Yes, I've got to go, it must be nearly dinnertime."

"Wait a minute."

"No, or we'll get excited again, we'll spoil everything."

They separated gently, but the movements both used, the two hands gentle on each other's hips, easing their bodies apart, were more like a fitting together. Separate, they lay

still, smiling at each other, touching each other's face with
fingertips, licking each other's eyelids with small cat licks.

"It gets better and better."

"Yes."

"Where did you go this time?"

"You know."

"Yes."

"Where did you go?"

"You know. Where you were."

"Yes. Tell me."

"Can't."

"I know. Tell me."

"With you."

"Yes."

"Are we one person, then?"

"Yes."

"Yes."

Silence again. Again he roused himself.

"Where are you working this afternoon?"

"I told you. It's a baker's shop in Exeter Street."

"And afterwards?"

"I'm taking Alice to the pictures."

She bit her lips, punishing them and him, then sunk her
nails into his shoulder.

"Well my darling, I just make her, that's all, I make her
come, she wouldn't understand anything better."

He sat up, began dressing. In a moment he was a tall sober
youth in a dark blue sweater. He slicked down his hair with
the young husband's hairbrushes, as if he lived here, while
she lay naked, watching.

He turned and smiled, affectionate and possessive, like a
husband. There was something in her face, a lost desperation, that made his harden. He crouched beside her, scowl-
ing, baring his teeth, gently fitting his thumb on her wind-
pipe, looking straight into her dark eyes. She breathed
hoarsely, and coughed. He let his thumb drop.

"What's that for, Fred?"

"You swear you don't do that with Charlie?"

"How could I?"

"What do you mean? You could show him."

"But why? Why do you think I want to? Fred!"

The two pairs of deep eyes, in bruised flesh, looked lonely with uncertainty into each other.

"How should I know what you want?"

"You're stupid," she said suddenly, with a small maternal smile.

He dropped his head, with a breath like a groan, onto her breasts, and she stroked his head gently, looking over it at the wall, blinking tears out of her eyes. She said: "He's not coming home to supper tonight, he's angry."

"Is he?"

"He keeps talking about you. He asked today if you were coming."

"Why, does he guess?" He jerked his head up off the soft support of her bosom, and stared, his face bitter, into hers. "Why? You haven't been stupid now, have you?"

"No, but Fred . . . but after you've been with me I suppose I'm different. . . ."

"Oh Christ!" He jumped up, desperate, beginning movements of flight, anger, hate, escape—checking each one. "What do you want, then? You want me to make you come, then? Well, that's easy enough, isn't it, if that's all you want. All right then, lie down and I'll do it, and I'll make you come till you cry, if that's all . . ." He was about to strip off his clothes; but she shot up from the bed, first hastily draping herself in her white frills, out of an instinct to protect what they had. She stood by him, as tall as he, holding his arms down by his sides. "Fred, Fred, Fred, darling, my sweetheart, don't spoil it, don't spoil it now when . . ."

"When what?"

She met his fierce look with courage, saying steadily: "Well, what do you expect, Fred? He's not stupid, is he? I'm not a . . . he makes love to me, well, he is my husband, isn't he? And . . . well, what about you and Alice, you do the same, it's normal, isn't it? Perhaps if you and I didn't have Charlie and Alice for coming, we wouldn't be able to do it our way, have you thought of that?"

"Have I thought of that! Well, what do you think?"

"Well, it's normal, isn't it?"

"Normal," he said, with horror, gazing into her loving face for reassurance against the word. "Normal, is it? Well, if you're going to use words like that . . ." Tears ran down his face, and she kissed them away in a passion of protective love.

"Well, why did you say I must marry him? I didn't want to, you said I should."

"I didn't think it would spoil us."

"But it hasn't, has it, Fred? Nothing could be like us. How could it? You know that from Alice, don't you, Fred?" Now she was anxiously seeking for his reassurance. They stared at each other, then their eyes closed, and they laid their cheeks together and wept, holding down each other's amorous hands, for fear that what they were might be cheapened by her husband, his girl.

He said: "What were you beginning to say?"

"When?"

"Just now. You said, don't spoil it now *when.*"

"I get scared."

"Why?"

"Suppose I get pregnant? Well, one day I must, it's only fair, he wants kids. Suppose he leaves me—he gets in the mood to leave me, like today. Well, he feels something . . . it stands to reason. It doesn't matter how much I try with him, you know he feels it. . . . Fred?"

"What?"

"There isn't any law against it, is there?"

"Against what?"

"I mean, a brother and sister can share a place, no one would say anything."

He stiffened away from her: "You're crazy."

"Why am I? Why, Fred?"

"You're just not thinking, that's all."

"What are we going to do, then?"

He didn't answer, and she sighed, letting her head lie on his shoulder beside his head, so that he felt her open eyes and their wet lashes on his neck.

"We can't do anything but go on like this, you've got to see that."

"Then I've got to be nice to him, otherwise he's going to leave me, and I don't blame him."

She wept, silently; and he held her, silent.

"It's so hard—I just wait for when you come, Fred, and I have to pretend all the time."

They stood silent, their tears drying, their hands linked. Slowly they quieted, in love and in pity, in the same way that they quieted in their long silences when the hungers of the flesh were held by love on the edge of fruition so long that they burned out and up and away into a flame of identity.

At last they kissed, brother-and-sister kisses, gentle and warm.

"You're going to be late, Fred. You'll get the sack."

"I can always get another job."

"I can always get another husband. . . ."

"Olive Oyl . . . but you look really good in that white naygleejay."

"Yes, I'm just the type that's no good naked, I need clothes."

"That's right—I must go."

"Coming tomorrow?"

"Yes. About ten?"

"Yes."

"Keep him happy, then. Ta-ta."

"Look after yourself—look after yourself, my darling, look after yourself. . . ."

Homage for Isaac Babel

THE day I had promised to take Catherine down to visit my young friend Philip at his school in the country, we were to leave at eleven, but she arrived at nine. Her blue dress was new, and so were her fashionable shoes. Her hair had just been done. She looked more than ever like a pink and gold Renoir girl who expects everything from life.

Catherine lives in a white house overlooking the sweeping brown tides of the river. She helped me clean up my flat with a devotion which said that she felt small flats were altogether more romantic than large houses. We drank tea, and talked mainly about Philip, who, being fifteen, has pure stern tastes in everything from food to music. Catherine looked at the books lying around his room, and asked if she might borrow the stories of Isaac Babel to read on the train. Catherine is thirteen. I suggested she might find them difficult, but she said: "Philip reads them, doesn't he?"

During the journey I read newspapers and watched her pretty frowning face as she turned the pages of Babel, for she was determined to let nothing get between her and her ambition to be worthy of Philip.

At the school, which is charming, civilised, and expensive, the two children walked together across green fields, and I followed, seeing how the sun gilded their bright friendly heads turned towards each other as they talked. In Catherine's left hand she carried the stories of Isaac Babel.

After lunch we went to the pictures. Philip allowed it to be seen that he thought going to the pictures just for the fun of it was not worthy of intelligent people, but he made the concession, for our sakes. For his sake we chose the more

serious of the two films that were showing in the little town.
It was about a good priest who helped criminals in New
York. His goodness, however, was not enough to prevent
one of them from being sent to the gas chamber; and Philip
and I waited with Catherine in the dark until she had
stopped crying and could face the light of a golden evening.

At the entrance of the cinema the doorman was lying in
wait for anyone who had red eyes. Grasping Catherine by
her suffering arm, he said bitterly: "Yes, why are you crying? He had to be punished for his crime, didn't he?" Catherine stared at him, incredulous. Philip rescued her by saying
with disdain: "Some people don't know right from wrong
even when it's *demonstrated* to them." The doorman turned
his attention to the next red-eyed emerger from the dark;
and we went on together to the station, the children silent
because of the cruelty of the world.

Finally Catherine said, her eyes wet again: "I think it's
all absolutely beastly, and I can't bear to think about it."
And Philip said: "But we've got to think about it, don't you
see, because if we don't it'll just go on and *on,* don't you
see?"

In the train going back to London I sat beside Catherine.
She had the stories open in front of her, but she said:
"Philip's awfully lucky. I wish I went to that school. Did
you notice that girl who said hullo to him in the garden?
They must be great friends. I wish my mother would let me
have a dress like that, it's *not* fair."

"I thought it was too old for her."

"Oh, *did* you?"

Soon she bent her head again over the book, but almost at
once lifted it to say: "Is he a very famous writer?"

"He's a marvellous writer, brilliant, one of the very best."

"Why?"

"Well, for one thing he's so simple. Look how few words
he uses, and how strong his stories are."

"I see. Do you know him? Does he live in London?"

"Oh no, he's dead."

"Oh. Then why did you—I thought he was alive, the way
you talked."

"I'm sorry, I suppose I wasn't thinking of him as dead."

"When did he die?"

"He was murdered. About twenty years ago, I suppose."

"Twenty years." Her hands began the movement of pushing the book over to me, but then relaxed. "I'll be fourteen in November," she stated, sounding threatened, while her eyes challenged me.

I found it hard to express my need to apologise, but before I could speak, she said, patiently attentive again: "You said he was murdered?"

"Yes."

"I expect the person who murdered him felt sorry when he discovered he had murdered a famous writer."

"Yes, I expect so."

"Was he old when he was murdered?"

"No, quite young really."

"Well, that was bad luck, wasn't it?"

"Yes, I suppose it was bad luck."

"Which do you think is the very best story here? I mean, in your honest opinion, the very very best one."

I chose the story about killing the goose. She read it slowly, while I sat waiting, wishing to take it from her, wishing to protect this charming little person from Isaac Babel.

When she had finished she said: "Well, some of it I don't understand. He's got a funny way of looking at things. Why should a man's legs in boots look like *girls?*" She finally pushed the book over at me, and said: "I think it's all morbid."

"But you have to understand the kind of life he had. First, he was a Jew in Russia. That was bad enough. Then his experience was all revolution and civil war and . . ."

But I could see these words bouncing off the clear glass of her fiercely denying gaze; and I said: "Look, Catherine, why don't you try again when you're older? Perhaps you'll like him better then?"

She said gratefully: "Yes, perhaps that would be best. After all, Philip is two years older than me, isn't he?"

A week later I got a letter from Catherine.

Thank you very much for being kind enough to take me to visit Philip at his school. It was the most lovely day in my whole life. I am extremely grateful to you for taking me. I have been thinking about the Hoodlum Priest. That was a film which demonstrated to me beyond any shadow of doubt that Capital Punishment is a Wicked Thing, and I shall never forget what I learned that afternoon, and the lessons of it will be with me all my life. I have been meditating about what you said about Isaac Babel, the famed Russian short story writer, and I now see that the conscious simplicity of his style is what makes him, beyond the shadow of a doubt, the great writer that he is, and now in my school compositions I am endeavouring to emulate him so as to learn a conscious simplicity which is the only basis for a really brilliant writing style. Love, Catherine. P.S. Has Philip said anything about my party? I wrote but he hasn't answered. Please find out if he is coming or if he just forgot to answer my letter. I hope he comes, because sometimes I feel I shall die if he doesn't. P.P.S. Please don't tell him I said anything, because I should die if he knew. Love, Catherine.

Outside the Ministry

As Big Ben struck ten, a young man arrived outside the portals of the Ministry, and looked sternly up and down the street. He brought his wrist up to eye level and frowned at it, the very picture of a man kept waiting, a man who had expected no less. His arm dropped, elbow flexed stiff, hand at mid-thigh level, palm downwards, fingers splayed. There the hand made a light movement, balanced from the wrist, as if sketching an arpeggio, or saying goodbye to the pavement—or greeting it? An elegant little gesture, full of charm, given out of an abundant sense of style to the watching world. Now he changed his stance, and became a man kept waiting, but maintaining his dignity. He was well dressed in a dark suit which, with a white shirt and a small grey silk bow tie that seemed positively to wish to fly away altogether, because of the energy imparted to it by his person, made a conventional enough pattern of colour—dark grey, light grey, white. But his black glossy skin, setting off this soberness, made him sparkle, a dandy—he might just as well have been wearing a rainbow.

Before he could frown up and down the street again, another young African crossed the road to join him. They greeted each other, laying their palms together, then shaking hands; but there was a conscious restraint in this which the first seemed to relish, out of his innate sense of drama, but made the second uneasy.

"Good morning, Mr. Chikwe."

"Mr. Mafente! Good morning!"

Mr. Mafente was a large smooth young man, well dressed

too, but his clothes on him were conventional European clothes, remained suit, striped shirt, tie; and his gestures had none of the inbuilt, delighting self-parody of the other man's. He was suave, he was dignified, he was calm; and this in spite of a situation which Mr. Chikwe's attitude (magisterial, accusing) said clearly was fraught with the possibilities of evil.

Yet these two had known each other for many years; had worked side by side, as the political situation shifted, in various phases of the Nationalist movement; had served prison sentences together; had only recently become enemies. They now (Mr. Chikwe dropped the accusation from his manner for this purpose) exchanged news from home, gossip, information. Then Mr. Chikwe marked the end of the truce by a change of pose, and said, soft and threatening: "And where is your great leader? Surely he is very late?"

"Five minutes only," said the other smiling.

"Surely when at last we have achieved this great honour, an interview with Her Majesty's Minister, the least we can expect is punctuality from the great man?"

"I agree, but it is more than likely that Her Majesty's Minister will at the last moment be too occupied to see us, as has happened before."

The faces of both men blazed with shared anger for a moment: Mr. Chikwe even showed a snarl of white teeth.

They recovered themselves together and Mr. Mafente said: "And where is your leader? Surely what applies to mine applies to yours also?"

"Perhaps the reasons for their being late are different? Mine is finishing his breakfast just over the road there and yours is—I hear that the night before last your Mr. Devuli was observed very drunk in the home of our hospitable Mrs. James?"

"Possibly, I was not there."

"I hear that the night before that he passed out in the hotel before some unsympathetic journalists and had to be excused."

"It is possible, I was not there."

Mr. Chikwe kept the full force of his frowning stare on Mr. Mafente's bland face as he said softly: "Mr. Mafente!"

"Mr. Chikwe?"

"Is it not a shame and a disgrace that your movement, which, though it is not mine, nevertheless represents several thousand people (not millions, I am afraid, as your publicity men claim)—is it not a pity that this movement is led by a man who is never sober?"

Mr. Mafente smiled, applauding this short speech which had been delivered with a grace and an attack wasted, surely, on a pavement full of London office workers and some fat pigeons. He then observed, merely: "Yet it is Mr. Devuli who is recognised by Her Britannic Majesty's Minister?"

Mr. Chikwe frowned.

"And it is Mr. Devuli who is recognised by those honourable British philanthropic movements—the Anti-Imperialist Society, the Movement for Pan African Freedom, and Freedom for British Colonies?"

Here Mr. Chikwe bowed, slightly, acknowledging the truth of what he said, but suggesting at the same time its irrelevance.

"I hear, for instance," went on Mr. Mafente, "that the Honourable Member of Parliament for Sutton North-West refused to have your leader on his platform on the grounds that he was a dangerous agitator with left-wing persuasions?"

Here both men exchanged a delighted irrepressible smile—that smile due to political absurdity. (It is not too much to say that it is for the sake of this smile that a good many people stay in politics.) Mr. Chikwe even lifted a shining face to the grey sky, shut his eyes, and while offering his smile to the wet heavens lifted both shoulders in a shrug of scorn.

Then he lowered his eyes, his body sprang into a shape of accusation and he said: "Yet you have to agree with me, Mr. Mafente—it is unfortunate that such a man as Mr. Devuli should be so widely accepted as a national representative, while the virtues of Mr. Kwenzi go unacknowledged."

"We all know the virtues of Mr. Kwenzi," said Mr. Mafente, and his accent on the word *we,* accompanied by a deliberately cool glance into the eyes of his old friend, made Mr. Chikwe stand silent a moment, thinking. Then he said softly, testing it: "Yes, yes, yes. And—*well,* Mr. Mafente?"

Mr. Mafente looked into Mr. Chikwe's face, with intent,

while he continued the other conversation: "Nevertheless, Mr. Chikwe, the situation is as I've said."

Mr. Chikwe, responding to the look, not the words, came closer and said: "Yet situations do not have to remain unchanged?" They looked deeply into each other's face as Mr. Mafente enquired, almost mechanically: "Is that a threat, perhaps?"

"It is a political observation. . . . Mr. Mafente?"

"Mr. Chikwe?"

"This particular situation could be changed very easily."

"Is that so?"

"You know it is so."

The two men were standing with their faces a few inches from each other, frowning with the concentration necessary for the swift mental balancing of a dozen factors: so absorbed were they, that clerks and typists glanced uneasily at them, and then, not wishing to be made uneasy, looked away again.

But here they felt approaching a third, and Mr. Mafente repeated quickly: "Is that a threat, perhaps?" in a loud voice, and both young men turned to greet Devuli, a man ten or more years older than they, large, authoritative, impressive. Yet even at this early hour he had a look of dissipation, for his eyes were red and wandering, and he stood upright only with difficulty.

Mr. Mafente now fell back a step to take his place half a pace behind his leader's right elbow; and Mr. Chikwe faced them both, unsmiling.

"Good morning to you, Mr. Chikwe," said Mr. Devuli.

"Good morning to you, Mr. Devuli. Mr. Kwenzi is just finishing his breakfast, and will join us in good time. Mr. Kwenzi was working all through the night on the proposals for the new constitution."

As Mr. Devuli did not answer this challenge, but stood, vague, almost swaying, his red eyes blinking at the passersby, Mr. Mafente said for him: "We all admire the conscientiousness of Mr. Kwenzi." The *we* was definitely emphasised, the two young men exchanged a look like a nod, while Mr. Mafente tactfully held out his right forearm to receive the hand of Mr. Devuli. After a moment the leader steadied himself, and said in a threatening way that managed also to sound like a grumble: "I, too, know all the implications of the proposed constitution, Mr. Chikwe."

"I am surprised to hear it, Mr. Devuli, for Mr. Kwenzi, who has been locked up in his hotel room for the last week, studying it, says that seven men working for seventy-seven years couldn't make sense of the constitution proposed by Her Majesty's Honourable Minister."

Now they all three laughed together, relishing absurdity, until Mr. Chikwe reimposed a frown and said: "And since these proposals are so complicated, and since Mr. Kwenzi understands them as well as any man with mere human powers could, it is our contention that it is Mr. Kwenzi who should speak for our people before the Minister."

Mr. Devuli held himself upright with five fingers splayed out on the forearm of his lieutenant. His red eyes moved sombrely over the ugly façade of the Ministry, over the faces of passing people, then, with an effort, came to rest on the face of Mr. Chikwe. "But I am the leader, I am the leader acknowledged by all, and therefore I shall speak for our country."

"You are not feeling well, Mr. Devuli?"

"No, I am not feeling well, Mr. Chikwe."

"It would perhaps be better to have a man in full possession of himself speaking for our people to the Minister?" (Mr. Devuli remained silent, preserving a fixed smile of general benevolence.) "Unless, of course, you expect to feel more in command of yourself by the time of"—he brought his wrist smartly up to his eyes, frowned, dropped his wrist—"ten-thirty A.M., which hour is nearly upon us?"

"No, Mr. Chikwe, I do not expect to feel better by then. Did you not know, I have severe stomach trouble?"

"You have stomach trouble, Mr. Devuli?"

"You did not hear of the attempt made upon my life when I was lying helpless with malaria in the Lady Wilberforce Hospital in Nkalolele?"

"Really, Mr. Devuli, is that so?"

"Yes, it is so, Mr. Chikwe. Some person bribed by my enemies introduced poison into my food while I was lying helpless in hospital. I nearly died that time, and my stomach is still unrecovered."

"I am extremely sorry to hear it."

"I hope that you are. For it is a terrible thing that political rivalry can lower men to such methods."

Mr. Chikwe stood slightly turned away, apparently delighting in the flight of some pigeons. He smiled, and enquired: "Perhaps not so much political rivalry as the sincerest patriotism, Mr. Devuli? It is possible that some misguided people thought the country would be better off without you."

"It must be a matter of opinion, Mr. Chikwe."

The three men stood silent: Mr. Devuli supported himself unobtrusively on Mr. Mafente's arm; Mr. Mafente stood waiting; Mr. Chikwe smiled at pigeons.

"Mr. Devuli?"

"Mr. Chikwe?"

"You are of course aware that if you agree to the Minister's proposals for this constitution civil war may follow?"

"My agreement to this constitution is because I wish to avert bloodshed."

"Yet when it was announced that you intended to agree, serious rioting started in twelve different places in our unfortunate country."

"Misguided people—misguided by your party, Mr. Chikwe."

"I remember, not twelve months ago, that when you were accused by the newspapers of inciting to riot, your reply was that the people had minds of their own. But of course that was when you refused to consider the constitution."

"The situation has changed, perhaps?"

The strain of this dialogue was telling on Mr. Devuli: there were great beads of crystal sweat falling off his broad face, and he mopped it with the hand not steadying him, while he shifted his weight from foot to foot.

"It is your attitude that has changed, Mr. Devuli. You stood for one man, one vote. Then overnight you became a supporter of the weighted vote. That cannot be described as a situation changing, but as a political leader changing—*selling out*." Mr. Chikwe whipped about like an adder and spat these two last words at the befogged man.

Mr. Mafente, seeing that his leader stood silent, blinking, remarked quietly for him: "Mr. Devuli is not accustomed to replying to vulgar abuse, he prefers to remain silent." The two young men's eyes consulted; and Mr. Chikwe said, his face not four inches from Mr. Devuli's: "It is not the first time a leader of our people has taken the pay of the whites and has been disowned by our people."

Mr. Devuli looked to his lieutenant, who said: "Yet it is Mr. Devuli who has been summoned by the Minister, and you should be careful, Mr. Chikwe—as a barrister you should know the law: a difference of political opinion is one thing, slander is another."

"As, for instance, an accusation of poisoning?"

Here they all turned, a fourth figure had joined them. Mr. Kwenzi, a tall, rather stooped, remote man, stood a few paces off, smiling. Mr. Chikwe took his place a foot behind him, and there were two couples, facing each other.

"Good morning, Mr. Devuli."

"Good morning, Mr. Kwenzi."

"It must be nearly time for us to go in to the Minister," said Mr. Kwenzi.

"I do not think that Mr. Devuli is in any condition to represent us to the Minister," said Mr. Chikwe, hot and threatening. Mr. Kwenzi nodded. He had rather small direct eyes, deeply inset under his brows, which gave him an earnest focussed gaze which he was now directing at the sweat-beaded brow of his rival.

Mr. Devuli blurted, his voice rising: "And who is responsible? Who? The whole world knows of the saintly Mr. Kwenzi, the hardworking Mr. Kwenzi, but who is responsible for my state of health?"

Mr. Chikwe cut in: "No one is responsible for your state of health but yourself, Mr. Devuli. If you drink two bottles of hard liquor a day, then you can expect your health to suffer for it."

"The present health of Mr. Devuli," said Mr. Mafente, since his chief was silent, biting his lips, his eyes red with tears as well as with liquor, "is due to the poison which nearly killed him some weeks ago in the Lady Wilberforce Hospital in Nkalolele."

"I am sorry to hear that," said Mr. Kwenzi mildly. "I trust the worst is over?"

Mr. Devuli was beside himself, his face knitting with emotion, sweat drops starting everywhere, his eyes roving, his fists clenching and unclenching.

"I hope," said Mr. Kwenzi, "that you are not suggesting I or my party had anything to do with it?"

"Suggest!" said Mr. Devuli. *"Suggest?* What shall I tell the Minister? That my political opponents are not ashamed to poison a helpless man in hospital? Shall I tell him that I have to have my food tasted, like an Eastern potentate? No, I cannot tell him such things—I am helpless there too, for he would say—black savages, stooping to poison, what else can you expect?"

"I doubt whether he would say that," remarked Mr. Kwenzi. "His own ancestors considered poison an acceptable political weapon, and not so very long ago either."

But Mr. Devuli was not listening. His chest was heaving, and he sobbed out loud. Mr. Mafente let his ignored forearm drop by his side, and stood away a couple of paces, gazing sombrely at his leader. After this sorrowful inspection, which Mr. Kwenzi and Mr. Chikwe did nothing to shorten, he looked long at Mr. Chikwe, and then at Mr. Kwenzi. During this three-sided silent conversation, Mr. Devuli, like a dethroned king in Shakespeare, stood to one side, his chest heaving, tears flowing, his head bent to receive the rods and lashes of betrayal.

Mr. Chikwe at last remarked: "Perhaps you should tell the Minister that you have ordered a bulletproof vest like an American gangster? It would impress him no doubt with your standing among our people?" Mr. Devuli sobbed again, and Mr. Chikwe continued: "Not that I do not agree with you—the vest is advisable, yes. The food tasters are not enough. I have heard our young hotheads talking among themselves and you would be wise to take every possible precaution."

Mr. Kwenzi, frowning, now raised his hand to check his lieutenant: "I think you are going too far, Mr. Chikwe, there is surely no need . . ."

At which Mr. Devuli let out a great groan of bitter laughter, uncrowned king reeling under the wet London sky, and said: "Listen to the good man, he knows nothing, no—he remains upright while his seconds do his dirty work, listen to the saint!"

Swaying, he looked for Mr. Mafente's forearm, but it was not there. He stood by himself, facing three men.

Mr. Kwenzi said: "It is a very simple matter, my friends. Who is going to speak for our people to the Minister? That is all we have to decide now. I must tell you that I have made a very detailed study of the proposed constitution and I am quite sure that no honest leader of our people could accept it. Mr. Devuli, I am sure you must agree with me— it is a very complicated set of proposals, and it. is more than possible there may be implications you have overlooked?"

Mr. Devuli laughed bitterly: "Yes, it is possible."

"Then we are agreed?"

Mr. Devuli was silent.

"I think we are all agreed," said Mr. Chikwe, smiling, looking at Mr. Mafente who after a moment gave a small nod, and then turned to face his leader's look of bitter accusation.

"It is nearly half past ten," said Mr. Chikwe. "In a few minutes we must present ourselves to Her Majesty's Minister."

The two lieutenants, one threatening, one sorrowful, looked at Mr. Devuli, who still hesitated, grieving, on the pavement's edge. Mr. Kwenzi remained aloof, smiling gently.

Mr. Kwenzi at last said: "After all, Mr. Devuli, you will certainly be elected, certainly we can expect that, and with your long experience the country will need you as Minister. A minister's salary, even for our poor country, will be enough to recompense you for your generous agreement to stand down now."

Mr. Devuli laughed—bitter, resentful, scornful.

He walked away.

Mr. Mafente said: "But Mr. Devuli, Mr. Devuli, where are you going?"

Mr. Devuli threw back over his shoulder: "Mr. Kwenzi will speak to the Minister."

Mr. Mafente nodded at the other two, and ran after his former leader, grabbed his arm, turned him around. "Mr. Devuli, you must come in with us, it is quite essential to preserve a united front before the Minister."

"I bow to superior force, gentlemen," said Mr. Devuli,

with a short sarcastic bow, which, however, he was forced to curtail: his stagger was checked by Mr. Mafente's tactful arm.

"Shall we go in?" said Mr. Chikwe.

Without looking again at Mr. Devuli, Mr. Kwenzi walked aloofly into the Ministry, followed by Mr. Devuli, whose left hand lay on Mr. Mafente's arm. Mr. Chikwe came last, smiling, springing off the balls of his feet, watching Mr. Devuli.

"And it is just half past ten," he observed, as a flunkey came forward to intercept them. "Half past ten to the second. I think I can hear Big Ben itself. Punctuality, as we all know, gentlemen, is the cornerstone of that efficiency without which it is impossible to govern a modern state. Is it not so, Mr. Kwenzi? Is it not so, Mr. Mafente? Is it not so, Mr. Devuli?"

Dialogue

•

•   •

THE building she was headed for, no matter how long she
delayed among the shops, stalls, older houses on the pavements, stood narrow and glass-eyed, six or eight stories
higher than this small shallow litter of buildings which
would probably be pulled down soon, as uneconomical. The
new building, economical, whose base occupied the space,
on a corner lot, of three small houses, two laundries and a
grocer's, held the lives of 160 people at forty families of
four each, one family to a flat. Inside this building was an
atmosphere both secretive and impersonal, for each time the
lift stopped, there were four identical black doors, in the
same positions exactly as the four doors on the nine other
floors, and each door insisted on privacy.

But meanwhile she was standing on a corner watching an
old woman in a print dress buy potatoes off a stall. The
man selling vegetables said: "And how's the rheumatism
today, Ada?" and Ada replied (so it was not *her* rheumatism): "Not so bad, Fred, but it's got him flat on his back,
all the same." Fred said: "It attacks my old woman between
the shoulders if she doesn't watch out." They went on talking about the rheumatism as if it were a wild beast that sunk
claws and teeth into their bodies but which could be coaxed
or bribed with heat or bits of the right food, until at last
she could positively see it, a jaguarlike animal crouched to
spring behind the brussels sprouts. Opposite was a music
shop which flooded the whole street with selections from
opera, but the street wasn't listening. Just outside the shop
a couple of youngsters in jerseys and jeans, both with thin

213

vulnerable necks and untidy shocks of hair, one dark, one fair, were in earnest conversation.

A bus nosed to a standstill; half a dozen people got off; a man passed and said: "What's the joke?" He winked, and she realised she had been smiling.

Well-being, created because of the small familiar busyness of the street, filled her. Which was of course why she had spent so long, an hour now, loitering around the foot of the tall building. This irrepressible good nature of the flesh, felt in the movement of her blood like a greeting to pavements, people, a thin drift of cloud across pale blue sky, she checked, or rather tested, by a deliberate use of the other vision on the scene: the man behind the neat arrangements of coloured vegetables had a stupid face, he looked brutal; the future of the adolescents holding their position outside the music-shop door against the current of pressing people could only too easily be guessed at by the sharply aggressive yet forlorn postures of shoulders and loins; Ada, whichever way you looked at her, was hideous, repulsive, with her loose yellowing flesh and her sour-sweat smell. Etc., etc. Oh yes, et cetera, on these lines, indefinitely, if she chose to look. Squalid, ugly, pathetic. . . . *And what of it?* insisted her blood, for now she was smiling, while she kept the other vision sharp as knowledge. She could feel the smile on her face. Because of it, people going past would offer jokes, comments, stop to talk, invite her for drinks or coffee, flirt, tell her the stories of their lives. She was forty this year, and her serenity was a fairly recent achievement. Wrong word: it had not been tried for; but it seemed as if years of pretty violent emotion, one way or another, had jelled or shaken into a joy which welled up from inside her independent of the temporary reactions—pain, disappointment, loss—for it was stronger than they. Well, would it continue? Why should it? It might very well vanish again, without explanation, as it had come. Possibly this was a room in her life, she had walked into it, found it furnished with joy and well-being, and would walk through and out again into another room, still unknown and unimagined. She had certainly never imagined this one, which was a gift from Nature? Chance? Excess? . . . A bookshop had a tray of dingy books outside it, and she rested her hand on their limp backs and loved them. Instantly she looked at the word *love*, which her palm, feeling delight at the contact, had chosen, and said to herself: Now it's enough, it's time for me to go in.

She looked at the vegetable stall, and entered the building, holding the colours of growth firm in her *heart* (word at once censored, though that was where she felt it). The lift was a brown cubicle brightly lit and glistening, and it went up fast. Instead of combatting the sink and sway of her stomach, she submitted to nausea; and arrived at the top landing giddy; and because of this willed discoordination of her nerves the enclosed cream-and-black glossiness of the little space attacked her with claustrophobia. She rang quickly at door 39. Bill stood aside as she went in, receiving her kiss on his cheekbone, which felt damp against her lips. He immediately closed the door behind her so that he could lean on it, using the handle for a support. Still queasy from the lift, she achieved, and immediately, a moment's oneness with him who stood giddily by the door.

But she was herself again (*herself* examined and discarded) at once; and while he still supported himself by the door, she went to sit in her usual place on a long benchlike settee that had a red blanket over it. The flat had two rooms, one very small and always darkened by permanently drawn midnight blue curtains, so that the narrow bed with the books stacked up the wall beside it was in a suffocating shadow emphasised by a small yellow glow from the bed lamp. This bedroom would have caused her to feel (he spent most of his time in it) at first panic of claustrophobia, and then a necessity to break out or let in light, open the walls to the sky. How long would her amiability of the blood survive in that? Not long, she thought, but she would never know, since nothing would make her try the experiment. As for him, this second room in which they both sat in their usual positions, she watchful on the red blanket, he in his expensive chair which looked surgical, being all black leather and chromium and tilting all ways with his weight, was the room that challenged him, because of its openness—he needed the enclosed dark of the bedroom. It was large, high, had airy white walls, a clear black carpet, the dark red settee, his machinelike chair, more books. But one wall was virtually all window: it was window from knee height to ceiling, and the squalors of this part of London showed as if from an aeroplane, the flat was so high, or seemed so, because what was beneath was so uniformly low. Here, around this room (in which, if she were alone, her spirits always spread into delight) winds clutched and shook and tore. To stand at those windows, staring straight back at sky, at wind, at cloud, at sun, was to her a release. To him, a terror. Therefore she had not gone at once to the windows; it would have destroyed the moment of equality over their shared giddiness—hers from the lift, his from illness. Though not-going had another danger, that he might know why she had refrained from enjoying what he knew she enjoyed, and think her too careful of him?

He was turned away from the light. Now, perhaps conscious that she was looking at him, he swivelled the chair so he could face the sky. No, this was not one of his good days, though at first she had thought his paleness was due to his dark blue sweater, whose tight high neck isolated and presented his head. It was a big head, made bigger because of the close-cut reddish hair that fitted the back of the skull like fur, exposing a large pale brow, strong cheekbones, chin, a face where every feature strove to dominate, where large calm green eyes just held the balance with a mouth designed, apparently, only to express the varieties of torment. A single glance from a stranger (or from herself before she had known better) would have earned him: big, strong, healthy, confident man. Now, however, she knew the signs, could, after glancing around a room, say: Yes, you and you and you. . . . Because of the times she had been him, achieved his being. But *they*, looking at her, would never claim her as one of them, because being him in split seconds and intervals had not marked her, could not, her nerves were too firmly grounded in normality. (*Normality?*) But she was another creature from them, another species, almost. To be envied? She thought so. But if she did not think them enviable, why had she come here, why did she always come? Why had she deliberately left behind the happiness (word defiantly held on to, despite them) she felt in the streets? Was it that she believed the pain in this room was more real than the happiness? Because of the courage behind it? She might herself not be able to endure the small dark-curtained room which would force her most secret terrors; but she respected this man who lived on the exposed platform swaying in the clouds (which is how his nerves felt it)—and from choice?

Doctors, friends, herself—everyone who knew enough to say—pronounced: the warmth of a family, marriage if possible, comfort, other people. Never isolation, never loneliness, not the tall wind-battered room where the sky showed through two walls. But he refused common sense. "It's no good skirting around what I am, I've got to crash right through it, and if I can't, whose loss is it?"

Well, she did not think she was strong enough to crash right through what she most feared, even though she had been born healthy, her nerves under her own command.

"Yes, but you have a choice, I haven't, unless I want to become a little animal living in the fur of other people's warmth."

(So went the dialogue.)

But he had a choice too: there were a hundred ways in which *they,* the people whom she could now recognise from their eyes in a crowd, could hide themselves. Not everyone recognised them, she would say; how many people do we know (men and women, but more men than women) enclosed in marriages, which are for safety only, or attached to other people's families, stealing (if you like) security? But theft means not giving back in exchange or kind, and these men and women, the solitary ones, do give back, otherwise they wouldn't be so welcome, so needed—so there's no need to talk about hanging on to the warmth of belly fur, like a baby kangaroo, it's a question of taking one thing, and giving back another.

"Yes, but I'm not going to pretend, I will not, it's not what I am—I can't and it's your fault that I can't."

This meant that he had been the other, through her, just as she had, through him.

"My dear, I don't understand the emotions, except through my intelligence, *normality* never meant anything to me until I knew you. Now all right, I give in. . . ."

This was sullen. With precisely the same note of sullenness she used to censor the words her healthy nerves supplied like love, happiness, myself, health. All right, this sullenness meant: I'll pay you your due, I have to, my intelligence tells me I must. I'll even be you, but briefly, for so long as I can stand it.

Meanwhile they were—not talking—but exchanging information. She had seen X and Y and Z, been to this place, read that book.

He had read so-and-so, seen X and Y, spent a good deal of his time listening to music.

"Do you want me to go away?"

"No, stay."

This very small gift made her happy; refusing to examine the emotion, she sat back, curled up her legs, let herself be comfortable. She smoked. He put on some jazz. He listened to it inert, his body not flowing into it, there was a light sweat on his big straining forehead. (This meant he had wanted her to stay not out of warmth, but for need of somebody there. She sat up straight again, pushed away the moment's delight.) She saw his eyes were closed. His face, mouth tight in an impersonal determination to endure, looked asleep, or—

"Bill," she said quick, in appeal.

Without opening his eyes, he smiled, giving her sweetness, friendship, and the irony, without bitterness, due from one kind of creature to another.

"It's all right," he said.

The piano notes pattered like rain before a gust of wind that swept around the corner of the building. White breaths of cloud were blown across the thin blue air. The drum shook, hissed, steadily, like her blood pumping the beat, and a wild flute danced a sky sign in the rippling smoke of a jet climbing perpendicular from sill to ceiling. But what did he hear, see, feel, sitting eyes closed, palm hard on the armrest for support? The record stopped. He opened his eyes, they resolved themselves out of a knot of inward difficulty, and rested on the wall opposite him, while he put out his hand to stop the machine. Silence now.

He closed his eyes again. She discarded the cross talk in her flesh of music, wind, cloud, raindrops patterning grass and earth, and tried to see—first the room, an insecure platform in height, tenacious against storm and rocking foundations; then a certain discordance of substance that belonged to his vision; then herself, as he saw her—at once she felt a weariness of the spirit, like a cool sarcastic wink from a third eye, seeing them both, two little people, him and herself, as she had seen the vegetable seller, the adolescents, the woman whose husband had rheumatism. Without charity she saw them, sitting there together in silence on either side of the tall room, and the eye seemed to expand till it filled the universe with disbelief and negation.

Now, she admitted the prohibited words love, joy (et cetera), and gave them leave to warm her, for not only could she not bear the world without them, she needed them to disperse her anger against him: Yes, yes, it's all very well, but how could the play go on, how could it, if it wasn't for me, the people like me? We create you in order that you may use us, and consume us; and with our willing connivance; but it doesn't do to despise . . .

He said, not surprising her that he did, since their minds so often moved together: "You are more split than I am, do you know that?"

She thought: If I were not split, if one-half (if that is the division) were not able to move in your world, even if only for short periods, then I would not be sitting here, you would not want me.

He said: "I wasn't criticising. Not at all. Because you have the contact. What more do you want?"

"Contact," she said, looking at the cold word.

"Yes. Well, it's everything."

"How can you sit there, insisting on the things you insist on, and say it's everything?"

"If that's what you are, then *be* it."

"Just one thing or the other?"

"Yes."

"Why? It's true that what I think contradicts what I feel, but . . ."

"But?"

"All right, it's all meaningless, with my mind I know it, it's an accident, it's a freak, but all the same, everything gives me pleasure all the time. Why should it be a contradiction, why should it?"

"You don't see it as a contradiction?"

"No."

"You're living on the fat of your ancestors, the fat of their belief, that's all."

"Possibly, but why should I care?"

"A fly buzzing in the sun," he said. His smile was first wry and tender, then full of critical dislike. The criticism, the coldness of it, hurt her, and she felt tears rise. So today she could not stay long, because tears were not allowed, they were part of the other argument, or fight, a personal one, played out (or fought out), finished.

She was blinking her eyes dry, without touching them, so that he would not see she wanted to cry, when he said: "Suppose that *I* am the future?"

A long silence, and she thought: Possibly, possibly.

"It seems to me that I am. Suppose the world fills more and more with people like me, then—"

"The little flies will have to buzz louder."

He laughed, short but genuine. She thought, I don't care what you say, that laugh is stronger than anything. She sat in silence for the thousandth time, *willing* it to be stronger, feeling herself to be a centre of life, or warmth, with which she would fill this room.

He sat, smiling, but in an inert, heavy way, his limbs seeming, even from where she sat across the room, cold and confused. She went to him, squatted on her knees by his chair, lifted his hand off the black leather arm-piece, and felt it heavy with cold. It gave her hand a squeeze more polite than warm, and she gripped it firmly, willing life to move down her arm through her hand into his. Closing her eyes, she now made herself remember, with her flesh, what she had discarded (almost contemptuous) on the pavement— the pleasure from the touch of faded books, pleasure from the sight of ranked fruit and vegetables. Discoloured print, shut between limp damp cotton, small voices to be bought for sixpence or ninepence, became a pulse of muttering sound, a pulse of vitality, like the beating colours of oranges, lemons and cabbages, gold and green, a dazzle, a vibration in the eyes—she held her breath, willed, and made life move down into his hand. It lay warmer and more companionable in hers. After a while he opened his eyes and smiled at her: sadness came into the smile, then a grimness, and she kissed his cheek and went back to her place on the rough blanket. "Flies," she said.

He was not looking at her. She thought: Why do I do it? These girls who come through here for a night, or two nights, because he needs their generous naïveté, give him no less. I, or one of them, it makes no difference. "I'd like a drink," she said.

He hesitated, hating her drinking at all, but he poured her one, while she said silently (feeling adrift, without resources, and cold through every particle of herself): All right, but in the days when our two bodies together created warmth (flies, if you like, but I don't feel it) I wouldn't have asked for a drink. She was thinking: And suppose it is yours that is the intoxication and not mine? when he remarked: "Sometimes when I've been alone here a couple of days I wonder if I'm not tipsy on sheer . . ." He laughed, in an intellectual pleasure at an order of ideas she was choosing not to see.

"The delight of nihilism?"

"Which of course you don't feel, ever!"

She saw that this new aggressiveness, this thrust of power and criticism (he was now moving about the room, full of energy) was in fact her gift to him; and she said, suddenly bitter: "Flies don't feel, they buzz."

The bitterness, being the note of the exchange they could not allow themselves, made her finish her few drops of liquor, making a new warmth in her stomach where she had needed a spark of warmth.

He said: "For all that, it seems to me I'm nearer the truth than you are."

The word *truth* did not explode into meaning: it sounded hard and self-defined, like a stone; she let it lie between them, setting against it the pulse that throbbed in the soft place by the ankle bone—her feet being stretched in front of her, so she could see them.

He said: "It seems to me that the disconnected like me must see more clearly than you people. Does that sound ridiculous to you? I've thought about it a great deal, and it seems to me you are satisfied with too little."

She thought: I wish he would come over here, sit by me on this blanket, and put his arm around me—that's all. That's

all and that's all. She was very tired. Of course I'm tired—
it's all the buzzing I have to do. . . .

Without warning, without even trying, she slipped into
being him, his body, his mind. She looked at herself and
thought: This little bundle of flesh, this creature who will
respond and warm, lay its head on my shoulder, feel happiness—how unreal, how vulgar, and how meaningless!

She shook herself away from him, up and away from the
settee. She went to the window.

"What are you doing?"

"Enjoying your view."

The sky was clear, it was evening, and far below in the
streets the lights had come on, making small yellow pools
and gleams on pavements where the tiny movement of people
seemed exciting and full of promise. Now he got himself
out of his machinelike chair and came to stand by her.
He did not touch her; but he would not have come at all
if she had not been there. He supported himself with one big
hand on the sill and looked out. She felt him take in a deep
breath. She stood silent, feeling the life ebbing and coiling
along the pavements and hoping he felt it. He let out his
breath. She did not look at him. He took it in again. The
hand trembled, then tensed, then set solid, a big, firmly
made hand, with slightly freckled knuckles—its steadiness
comforted her. It would be all right. Still without looking
at his face, she kissed his cheek and turned away. He went
back to his chair, she resumed her place on the blanket.
The room was filling with dusk, the sky was greying, enormous, distant.

"You should get curtains, at least."

"I should be tempted to keep them drawn all the time."

"Why not, then, why not?" she insisted, feeling her eyes
wet again. "All right, I won't cry," she said reasonably.

"Why not? If you feel like crying."

She no longer wept. But once, and not so long ago, she
had wept herself almost to pieces over him, her, their closeness which nevertheless the cold third, like a cruel king,
refused to sanction. She noted that the pulse moving in her
ankle had the desperate look of something fighting death;
her foot in the dusk was a long way off; she felt divided, not
in possession of herself. But she remained where she was,

containing her fragmentation. And he held out his fist, steady, into the glimmer of grey light from the sky, watching it exactly as she looked at her own pulse, the stranger.

"For God's sake turn the light on," she said, giving in. He put out his hand, pressed down the switch, a harsh saving light filled the room.

He smiled. But he looked white again, and his forehead gleamed wet. Her heart ached for him, and for herself, who would now get up deliberately and go away from him. The ache was the hurt of exile, and she was choosing it. She sat smiling, chafing her two ankles with her hands, feeling the warmth of her breathing flesh. Their smiles met and exchanged, and now she said: "Right, it's time to go."

She kissed him again, he kissed her, and she went out, saying: "I'll ring you."

Always, when she left his door shut behind her, the black door which was exactly the same as all the others in the building except for the number, she felt in every particle of herself how loneliness hit him when she (or anybody) left.

The street she went out into was unfamiliar to her, she felt she did not know it. The hazy purple sky that encloses London at night was savage, bitter, and the impulse behind its shifting lights was a form of pain. The roughness of the pavement, which she knew to be warm, struck cold through the soles of her sandals, as if the shadows were black ice. The people passing were hostile, stupid animals from whom she wished to hide herself. But worse than this, there was a flat, black-and-white two-dimensional jagged look to things, and (it was this that made it terrifying) the scene she walked through was a projection of her own mind, there was no life in it that belonged there save what she could breathe into it. And she herself was dead and empty, a cardboard figure in a flat painted set of streets.

She thought: Why should it not all come to an end, why not? She saw again the potato face of Fred the vegetable seller whose interest in Ada's husband's illness was only because she was a customer at his stall; she looked at Ada whose ugly life (she was like a heave of dirty earth or some unnameable urban substance) showed in her face and movements like a visible record of thick physical living. The pathos of the adolescents did not move her, she felt disgust.

She walked on. The tall building, like a black tower, stood over her, kept pace with her. It was not possible to escape from it.

Her hand, swinging by her thigh, on its own life, suddenly lifted itself and took a leaf off a hedge. The leaf trembled: she saw it was her fingers which shook, with exhaustion. She stilled her fingers, and the leaf became a thin hard slippery object, like a coin. It was small, round, shining, a blackish-green. A faint pungent smell came to her nostrils. She understood it was the smell of the leaf which, as she lifted it to her nostrils, seemed to explode with a vivid odour into the senses of her brain so that she understood the essence of the leaf and through it the scene she stood in.

She stood fingering the leaf, while life came back. The pulses were beating again. A warmth came up through her soles. The sky's purplish orange was for effect, for the sake of self-consciously exuberant theatricality, a gift to the people living under it. An elderly woman passed, mysterious and extraordinary in the half-light, and smiled at her. So. She was saved from deadness, she was herself again. She walked slowly on, well-being moving in her, making a silent greeting to the people passing her. Meanwhile the dark tower kept pace with her, she felt it rising somewhere just behind her right shoulder. It was immensely high, narrow, terrible, all in darkness save for a light flashing at its top where a man, held upright by the force of his will, sat alone staring at a cold sky in vertiginous movement.

She moved steadily on, on the rhythm of her own pleasantly coursing blood. With one hand, however, she secretly touched the base of the tower whose shadow would always follow her now, challenging her, until she dared to climb it. With the other hand she held fast to the leaf.

Notes for a Case History

•

• •

Maureen Watson was born at 93 Nelson's Way, N.1., in 1942. She did not remember the war, or rather, when people said "The War," she thought of Austerity: couponed curtains, traded clothes, the half pound of butter swapped for the quarter of tea. (Maureen's parents preferred tea to butter.) Further back, at the roots of her life, she *felt* a movement of fire and shadow, a leaping and a subsidence of light. She did not know whether this was a memory or a picture she had formed, perhaps from what her parents had told her of the night the bomb fell two streets from Nelson's Way and they had all stood among piles of smoking rubble for a day and night, watching firemen hose the flames. This feeling was not only of danger, but of fatality, of being helpless before great impersonal forces; and was how she most deeply felt, saw, or thought an early childhood which the social viewer would describe perhaps like this: "Maureen Watson, conceived by chance on an unexpected granted-at-the-last-minute leave, at the height of the worst war in history, infant support of a mother only occasionally upheld (the chances of war deciding) by a husband she had met in a bomb shelter during an air raid: poor baby, born into a historical upheaval which destroyed forty million and might very well have destroyed her."

As for Maureen, her memories and the reminiscences of her parents made her dismiss the whole business as boring, and nothing to do with her.

It was at her seventh birthday party she first made this clear. She wore a mauve organdy frock with a pink sash, and her golden hair was in ringlets. One of the mothers said: "This is the first unrationed party dress my Shirley has had. It's a shame, isn't it?" And her own mother said: "Well of course these war children don't know what they've missed." At which Maureen said: "*I* am not a war child." "What are you then, love?" said her mother, fondly exchanging glances.

"I'm Maureen," said Maureen.

"And I'm Shirley," said Shirley, joining cause.

Shirley Banner was Maureen's best friend. The Watsons and the Banners were better than the rest of the street. The Watsons lived in an end house, at higher weekly payments. The Banners had a sweets-paper-and-tobacco shop.

Maureen and Shirley remembered (or had they been told?) that once Nelson's Way was a curved terrace of houses. Then the ground-floor level had broken into shops: a grocer's, a laundry, a hardware, a baker, a dairy. It seemed as if every second family in the street ran a shop to supply certain defined needs of the other families. What other needs were there? Apparently none; for Maureen's parents applied for permission to the Council, and the ground floor of their house became a second grocery shop, by way of broken-down walls, new shelves, a deepfreeze. Maureen remembered two small rooms, each with flowered curtains where deep shadows moved and flickered from the two small fires that burned back to back in the centre wall that divided them. These two rooms disappeared in clouds of dust from which sweet-smelling planks of wood stuck out. Strange but friendly men paid her compliments on her golden corkscrews and asked her for kisses, which they did not get. They gave her sips of sweet tea from their canteens (filled twice a day by her mother) and made her bracelets of the spiralling fringes of yellow wood. Then they disappeared. There was the new shop. Maureen's Shop. Maureen went with her mother to the sign shop to arrange for these two words to be written in yellow paint on a blue ground.

Even without the name, Maureen would have known that the shop was connected with hopes for her future; and that her future was what her mother lived for.

She was pretty. She had always known it. Even where the shadows of fire and dark were, they had played over a pretty baby. "You were such a pretty baby, Maureen." And at the birthday parties: "Maureen's growing really pretty, Mrs. Watson." But all babies and little girls are pretty, she knew that well enough . . . no, it was something more. For Shirley was plump, dark—pretty. Yet their parents'—or rather, their mothers'—talk had made it clear from the start that Shirley was not in the same class as Maureen.

When Maureen was ten there was an episode of importance. The two mothers were in the room above Maureen's Shop and they were brushing their little girls' hair out. Shirley's mother said: "Maureen could do really well for herself, Mrs. Watson." And Mrs. Watson nodded, but sighed deeply. The sigh annoyed Maureen, because it contradicted the absolute certainty that she felt (it had been bred into her) about her future. Also because it had to do with the *boring* era which she remembered, or thought she did, as a tiger-striped movement of fire. *Chance:* Mrs. Watson's sigh was like a prayer to the gods of Luck: it was the sigh of a small helpless thing being tossed about by big seas and gales. Maureen made a decision, there and then, that she had nothing in common with the little people who were prepared to be helpless and tossed about. For she was going to be quite different. She was already different. Not only The War but the shadows of war had long gone, except for talk in the newspapers which had nothing to do with her. The shops were full of everything. The Banners' sweets-tobacco-paper shop had just been done up; and Maureen's was short of nothing. Maureen and Shirley, two pretty little girls in smart mother-made dresses, were children of plenty, and knew it, because their parents kept saying (apparently they did not care how tedious they were): "These kids don't lack for anything, do they? They don't know what it can be like, do they?" This, with the suggestion that they ought to be grateful for not lacking anything, always made the children sulky, and they went off to flirt their full many-petticoated skirts where the neighbours could see them and pay them compliments.

Eleven years. Twelve years. Already Shirley had subsided into her role of pretty girl's plainer girl friend, although of course she was not plain at all. Fair girl, dark girl, and Maureen by mysterious birthright was the "pretty one," and there was no doubt in either of their minds which girl the boys would try first for a date. Yet this balance was by no means as unfair as it seemed. Maureen, parrying and jesting on street corners, at bus stops, knew she was doing battle for two, because the boys she discarded Shirley got: Shirley got far more boys than she would have done without Maureen who, for her part, needed—more, *had* to have—a foil. Her role demanded one.

They both left school at fifteen, Maureen to work in the shop. She was keeping her eyes open: her mother's phrase. She wore a slim white overall, pinned her fair curls up, was neat and pretty in her movements. She smiled calmly when customers said: "My word, Mrs. Watson, your Maureen's turned out, hasn't she?"

About that time there was a second moment of consciousness. Mrs. Watson was finishing a new dress for Maureen, and the fitting was taking rather long. Maureen fidgeted and her mother said: "Well, it's your capital, isn't it? You've got to see that, love." And she added the deep unconscious sigh. Maureen said: "Well don't go on about it, it's not very nice, is it?" And what she meant was, not that the idea was not very nice, but that she had gone beyond needing to be reminded about it; she was feeling the irritated embarrassment of a child when it is reminded to clean its teeth after this habit has become second nature. Mrs. Watson saw and understood this, and sighed again; and this time it was the maternal sigh which means: Oh dear, you are growing up fast! "Oh *Mum*," said Maureen, "sometimes you just make me tired, you do really."

Sixteen. She was managing her capital perfectly. Her assets were a slight delicate prettiness, and a dress sense that must have been a gift from God, or more probably because she had been reading the fashion magazines since practically before consciousness. Shirley had put in six months of beehive hair, pouting scarlet lips, and an air of sullen disdain; but Maureen's sense of herself was much finer. She modelled herself on film stars, but with an understanding of how far she could go—of what was allowable to Maureen. So the experience of being Bardot, Monroe, or whoever it was, refined her: she took from it an essence, which was learning to be a vehicle for other people's fantasies. So while Shirley had been a dozen stars, but really *been* them, in violent temporary transmogrifications, from which she emerged (often enough with a laugh) Shirley—plump, good-natured, and herself—Maureen remained herself through every role, but creating her appearance, like an alter ego, to meet the expression in people's eyes.

Round about sixteen, another incident: prophetic. Mrs. Watson had a cousin who worked in the dress trade, and this man, unthought-of for many years, was met at a wedding. He commented on Maureen, a vision in white gauze. Mrs. Watson worked secretly on this slender material for some weeks; then wrote to him: Could Maureen be a model? He had only remote connections with the world of expensive clothes and girls, but he dropped into the shop with frankly personal aims. Maureen in a white wrapper was still pretty, very; but her remote air told this shrewd man that she would certainly not go out with him. She was saving herself; he knew that air of self-esteem very well from other exemplars. Such girls do not go out with middle-aged cousins, except as a favour or to get something. However, he told Mrs. Watson that Maureen was definitely model material, but that she would have to do something about her voice. (He meant her accent of course; and so Mrs. Watson understood him.) He left addresses and advice, and Mrs. Watson was in a state of quivering ambition. She said so to Maureen: "This is your chance, girl. Take it." What Maureen heard was: "This is *my* chance."

Maureen, nothing if not alert for her Big Chance, for which her whole life had prepared her, accepted her mother's gift of a hundred pounds (she did not thank her, no thanks were due) and actually wrote to the school where she would be taught voice training.

Then she fell into sullen withdrawal, which she understood so little that a week had gone by before she said she must be sick—or something. She was rude to her mother: very rare, this. Her father chided her for it: even rarer. But he spoke in such a way that Maureen understood for the first time that this drive, this push, this family effort to gain her a glamorous future, came from her mother, her father was not implicated. For him, she was a pretty-enough girl, spoiled by a silly woman.

Maureen slowly understood she was not sick, she was

growing up. For one thing: if she changed her "voice" so as to be good enough to mix with new people, she would no longer be part of this street, she would no longer be *Our Maureen*. What would she be then? Her mother knew: she would marry a duke and be whisked off to Hollywood. Maureen examined her mother's ideas for her and shrank with humiliation. She was above all no fool, but she had been very foolish. For one thing: when she used her eyes, with the scales of illusion off them, she saw that the million streets of London blossomed with girls as pretty as she. What, then, had fed the illusion in herself and in other people? What accounted for the special tone, the special looks that always greeted her? Why, nothing more than that she, Maureen, because of her mother's will behind her, had carried herself from childhood as something special, apart, destined for a great future.

Meanwhile (as she clearly saw) she was in 93 Nelson's Way, serving behind the counter of Maureen's Shop. (She now wondered what the neighbours had thought—before they got used to it—about her mother's fondness so terribly displayed.) She was dependent on nothing less than that a duke or a film producer would walk in to buy a quarter of tea and some sliced bread.

Maureen sulked. So her father said. So her mother complained. Maureen was—thinking? Yes. But more, a wrong had been done her, she knew it, and the sulking was more of a protective silence while she grew a scab over a wound.

She emerged demanding that the hundred pounds should be spent on sending her to secretarial school. Her parents complained that she could have learned how to be a secretary for nothing if she had stayed on at school another year. She said: "Yes, but you didn't have the sense to make me, did you? What did you think—I was going to sell butter like you all my life?" Unfair, on the face of it; but deeply fair, in view of what they had done to her. In their different ways they knew it. (Mr. Watson knew in his heart, for instance, that he should never have allowed his wife to call the shop "Maureen's.") Maureen went, then, to secretarial school for a year. Shirley went with her: she had been selling cosmetics in the local branch of a big chain store. To raise the hundred pounds was difficult for Shirley's parents: the shop had done badly, had been bought by a big firm; her father was an assistant in it. For that matter, it wasn't all that easy for the Watsons: the hundred pounds was the result of small savings and pinchings over years.

This was the first time Maureen had thought of the word capital in connection with money, rather than her own natural assets: it was comparatively easy for the Watsons to raise money, because they had capital: the Banners had no capital. (Mrs. Watson said the Banners had had *bad luck*.) Maureen strengthened her will; and as a result the two families behaved even more as if the girls would have different futures—or, to put it another way, that while the two sums of a hundred pounds were the same, the Watsons could be expected to earn more on theirs than the Banners.

This was reflected directly in the two girls' discussions about boys. Shirley would say: "I'm more easygoing than you."

Maureen would reply: *"I* only let them go so far."

Their first decisions on this almighty subject had taken place years before, when they were thirteen. Even then Shirley went further ("let them go further") than Maureen. It was put down, between them, to Shirley's warmer temperament—charitably; for both knew it was because of Maureen's higher value in the market.

At the secretarial school they met boys they had not met before. Previously boys had been from the street or the neighbourhood, known from birth, and for this reason not often gone out with—that would have been boring (serious, with possibilities of marriage). Or boys picked up after dances or at the pictures. But now there were new boys met day after day in the school. Shirley went out with one for weeks, thought of getting engaged, changed her mind, went out with another. Maureen went out with a dozen, chosen carefully. She knew what she was doing—and scolded Shirley for being so *soft*. "You're just stupid, Shirl—I mean, you've got to get on. Why don't you do like me?"

What Maureen did was to allow herself to be courted, until she agreed at last, as a favour, to be taken out. First, lunch—a word she began to use now. She would agree to to go out to lunch two or three times with one boy, while she was taken out to supper (dinner) by another. The dinner partner, having been rewarded by a closed-mouth kiss for eight, ten, twelve nights, got angry or sulky or reproachful, according to his nature. He dropped her, and the lunch partner was promoted to dinner partner.

Maureen ate free for the year of her training. It wasn't that she planned it like this: but when she heard other girls say they paid their way or liked to be independent, it seemed to Maureen wrongheaded. To pay for herself would be to let herself be undervalued: even the idea of it made her nervous and sulky.

At the end of the training Maureen got a job in a big architect's office. She was a junior typist. She stuck out for a professional office because the whole point of the training was to enable her to meet a better class of people. Of course she had already learned not to use the phrase, and when her mother did snubbed her with: "I don't know what you mean, better *class*, but it's not much point my going into that hardware stuck upstairs in an office by myself if I can get a job where there's some life about."

Shirley went into a draper's shop where there was one typist (female) and five male assistants.

In Maureen's place there were six architects, out most of the time, or invisible in large offices visited only by the real secretaries; a lower stratum of young men in training, designers, draftsmen, managers, etc., and a pool of typists.

The young men were mostly of her own class. For some months she ate and was entertained at their expense; and at each week's end there was a solemn ceremony, the high point of the week, certainly the most exciting moment in it, when she divided her wage. It was seven pounds (rising to ten in three years) and she allocated two pounds for clothes, four for the post office, and one pound for the week's odd expenses.

At the end of a year she understood two things. That she had saved something like two hundred pounds. That there was not a young man in the office who would take her out again. They regarded her, according to their natures, with resentment or with admiration for her cool management of them. But there was nothing doing *there*—so they all knew.

Maureen thought this over. If she were not taken out

to meals and entertainment, she must pay for herself and save no money, or she must never go out at all. If she was going to be taken out, then she must give something in return. What she gave was an open mouth, and freedom to the waist. She calculated that because of her prettiness she could give much less than other girls.

She was using her *capital* with even more intelligence than before. A good part of her time—all not spent in the office or being taken out—went in front of her looking glass, or with the better-class fashion magazines. She studied them with formidable concentration. By now she knew she could have gone anywhere in these islands, except for her voice. Whereas, months before, she had sulked in a sort of fright at the idea of cutting herself off from her street and the neighbours, now she softened and shaped her voice, listening to the clients and the senior architects in the office. She knew her voice had changed when Shirley said: "You're talking nice, Maureen, much nicer than me."

There was a boy in the office who teased her about it. His name was Tony Head. He was in training to be an accountant for the firm, and was very much from her own background. After having taken her out twice to lunch, he had never asked her again. She knew why: he had told her. "Can't afford you, Maureen," he said. He earned not much more than she did. He was nineteen, ambitious, serious, and she liked him.

Then she was nineteen. Shirley was engaged to one of the assistants in her shop, and would be married next Christmas.

Maureen took forty pounds out of her savings and went on a tour to Italy. It was her first time out of England. She hated it: not Italy, but the fact that half the sixty people on the tour were girls, like herself, looking for a good time, and the other half elderly couples. In Rome, Pisa, Florence, Venice, the Italians mooned over Maureen, courted her with melting eyes, while she walked past them, distant as a starlet. They probably thought she was one. The courier, a sharp young man, took Maureen out to supper one night after he had finished his duties, and made it clear that her mouth, even if opened, and her breasts, were not enough. Maureen smiled at him sweetly through the rest of the trip. No one paid for her odd coffees, ices and drinks. On the last night of the trip, in a panic because the forty-pound investment had yielded so little, she went out with an Italian boy who spoke seven words of English. She thought him crude, and left him after an hour.

But she had learned a good deal for her forty pounds. Quietly, in her lunch hour, she went off to the National Gallery and to the Tate. There she looked, critical and respectful, at pictures, memorising their subjects, or main colours, learning names. When invited out, she asked to be taken to "foreign" films, and when she got back home wrote down the names of the director and the stars. She looked at the book page of the *Express* (she made her parents buy it instead of the *Mirror*) and sometimes bought a recommended book, if it was a best seller.

Twenty. Shirley was married and had a baby. Maureen saw little of her—both girls felt they had a new world of knowledge the other couldn't appreciate.

Maureen was earning ten pounds a week, and saved six.

There came to the office, as an apprentice architect, Stanley Hunt, from grammar school and technical college. Tallish, well-dressed, fair, with a small moustache. They took each other's measure, knowing they were the same kind. It was some weeks before he asked her out. She knew, by putting herself in his place, that he was looking for a wife with a little money or a house of her own, if he couldn't get a lady. (She smiled when she heard him using this word about one of the clients.) He tried to know clients socially, to be accepted by them as they accepted the senior architects. All this Maureen watched, her cool little face saying nothing.

One day, after he had invited a Miss Plast (Chelsea, well-off, investing money in houses) to coffee, and been turned down, he asked Maureen to join him in a sandwich lunch. Maureen thanked him delightfully, but said she already had an engagement. She went off to the National Gallery, sat on the steps, froze off wolves and pickups, and ate a sandwich by herself.

A week later, invited to lunch by Stanley, she suggested the Trattoria Siciliana which was more expensive, as she knew quite well, than he had expected. But this meal was

. success. He was impressed with her, though he knew
how could he not, when his was similar?) her background.

She was careful to be engaged for two weeks. Then
he agreed to go to the pictures—"a foreign film, if you
don't mind, I think the American films are just boring."
She did not offer to pay, but remarked casually that she
had nearly six hundred pounds in the post office. "I'm thinking of buying a little business, sometime. A dress shop.
I've got a cousin in the trade."

Stanley agreed that "with your taste" it would be a sure
thing.

Maureen no longer went to the Palais, or similar places
though she certainly did not conceal from Stanley that
he had "once"), but she loved to dance. Twice they went
to the West End together and danced at a Club which was
"a nice place." They danced well together. On the second
occasion she offered to pay her share, for the first time
in her life. He refused, as she had known he would, but she
could see he liked her for offering: more, was relieved;
in the office they said she was mean, and he must have
heard them. On that night, taken home lingeringly, she
opened her mouth for him and let his hands go down to
her thighs. She felt a sharp sexuality which made her con-
gratulate herself that she had never, like Shirley, gone
"halfway" before. Well of course, girls were going to get
married to just anybody if they let themselves be all worked
up every time they were taken out!

But Stanley was not at all caught. He was too cool a customer, as she was. He was still looking for something
better.

He would be an architect in a couple of years; he would
be in a profession; he was putting down money for a house;
he was good-looking, attractive to women, and with these
assets he ought to do better than marry Maureen. Maureen
agreed with him.

But meanwhile he took her out. She was careful often to
be engaged elsewhere. She was careful always to be worth
taking somewhere expensive. When he took her home, while
he did not go so far as "nearly the whole way," she went
everything but"; and she was glad she did not like him
better, because otherwise she would have been lost. She

knew quite well she did not really like him, although her mind was clouded by her response to his hands, his moustache, his clothes and his new car.

She knew, because meanwhile a relationship she understood very well, and regretted, had grown up with Tony. He, watching this duel between the well-matched pair, would grin and drop remarks at which Maureen coloured and turned coldly away. He often asked her out—but only for a "Dutch treat"—expecting her to refuse. "How's your savings account, Maureen? I can't save, you girls get it all spent on you." Tony took out a good many girls: Maureen kept a count of them. She hated him; yet she liked him, and knew she did. She relied on him above all for this grinning, honest understanding of her: he did not approve of her, but perhaps (she felt in her heart) he was right? During this period she several times burst into tears when alone, without apparent reason; afterwards she felt that life had no flavour. Her future was narrowing down to Stanley; and at these times she viewed it through Tony Head's eyes.

One night the firm had a party for the senior members of the staff. Stanley was senior, Maureen and Tony were not. Maureen knew that Stanley had previously asked another girl to go, and when he asked herself, was uncertain whether she could make it until the very last moment: particularly as his inviting her, a junior, meant that he was trying out on the senior members the idea of Maureen as a wife. But she acquitted herself very well. First, she was the best-looking woman in the room by far, and the best-dressed. Everyone looked at her and commented: they were used to her as a pretty typist; but tonight she was using all her will to make them look at her, to make her face and body reflect what they admired. She made no mistakes. When the party was over Stanley and two of the younger architects suggested they drive out to London airport for breakfast, and they did. The two other girls were middle-class. Maureen kept silent for the most part, smiling serenely. She had been to Italy, she remarked, when a plane rose to go to Italy. Yes, she had liked it, though she thought the Italians were too noisy; what she had enjoyed best was the Sistine Chapel and a boat trip on the Adriatic. She hadn't cared for Venice much, it was beautiful, but the canals smelled, and there were far too many people; perhaps it would be better to go in winter? She said all this, having a right to it, and it came off. As she spoke she remembered Tony, who had once met her on her way to the National Gallery. "Getting yourself an education, Maureen? That's right, it'll pay off well, that will."

She knew, thinking it all over afterwards, that the evening had been important for her with Stanley. Because of this, she did not go out with him for a week, she said she was busy talking to her cousin about the possibilities of a dress shop. She sat in her room thinking about Stanley, and when thoughts of Tony came into her mind, irritatedly pushed them away. If she could succeed with Stanley, why not with someone better? The two architects from that evening had eyed her all the following week: they did not, however, ask her out. She then found that both were engaged to marry the girls they had been with. It was bad luck: she was sure that otherwise they would have asked her out. How to meet more like them? Well, that was the trouble—the drive to the airport was a bit of a fluke; it was the first time she had actually met the seniors socially.

Meanwhile Stanley showed an impatience in his courtship —and for the first time. As for her, she was getting on for twenty-one, and all the girls she had grown up with were married and had had their first or even their second babies.

She went out with Stanley to a dinner in the West End at an Italian restaurant. Afterwards they were both very passionate. Maureen, afterwards, was furious with herself: some borderline had been crossed (she supposed she still could be called a virgin?) and now decisions would have to be made.

Stanley was in love with her. She was in love with Stanley. A week later he proposed to her. It was done with a violent moaning intensity that she knew was due to his conflicts over marrying her. She was not good enough. He was not good enough. They were second-best for each other. They writhed and moaned and bit in the car, and agreed to marry. Her eight hundred pounds would make it easier to buy the house in a good suburb. He would formally meet her parents next Sunday.

"So you're engaged to Stanley Hunt?" said Tony.

"Looks like it, doesn't it?"

"Caught him—good for you!"

"He's caught me, more like it!"

"Have it your way."

She was red and angry. He was serious.

"Come and have a bite?" he said. She went.

It was a small restaurant, full of office workers eating on luncheon vouchers. She ate fried plaice ("No chips, please") and he ate steak-and-kidney pudding. He joked, watched her, watched her intently, said finally: "Can't you do better than that?" He meant, and she knew it, better in the sense she would use herself, in her heart: he meant *nice*. Like himself. But did that mean that Tony thought *she* was nice? Unlike Stanley? She did not think she was, she was moved to tears (concealed) that he did. "What's wrong with him then?" she demanded, casual. "What's wrong with *you?* You need your head examined." He said it seriously, and they exchanged a long look. The two of them sat looking goodbye at each other: the extremely pretty girl at whom everyone in the room kept glancing and remarking on, and the good-looking, dark, rather fat young accountant who was brusque and solemn with disappointment in her. With love for her? Very likely.

She went home silent, thinking of Tony. When she thought of him she needed to cry. She also needed to hurt him.

But she told her parents she was engaged to Stanley, who would be an architect. They would have their own house, in (they thought) Hemel Hampstead. He owned a car. He was coming to tea on Sunday. Her mother forgot the dukes and the film producers before the announcement ended: her father listened judiciously, then congratulated her. He had been going to a football match on Sunday, but agreed, after persuasion, that this was a good-enough reason to stay home.

Her mother then began discussing, with deference to Maureen's superior knowledge, how to manage next Sunday to best advantage. For four days she went on about it. But she was talking to herself. Her husband listened, said nothing. And Maureen listened, critically, like her father. Mrs. Watson began clamouring for a definite opinion on what sort of cake to serve on Sunday. But Maureen had no opinion. She sat, quiet, looking at her mother, a largish ageing woman, her ex-fair hair dyed yellow, her flesh guttering. She was like an excited child, and it was not attractive. *Stupid, stupid, stupid*—that's all you are, thought Maureen.

As for Maureen, if anyone had made the comparison, she was "sulking" as she had before over being a model and having to be drilled out of her "voice." She said nothing but: "It'll be all right, Mum, don't get so worked up." Which was true, because Stanley knew what to expect; he knew why he had not been invited to meet her parents until properly hooked. He would have done the same in her place. He *was* doing the same: she was going to meet his parents the week after. What Mrs. Watson, Mr. Watson, wore on Sunday; whether sandwiches or cake were served; whether there were fresh or artificial flowers—none of it mattered. The Watsons were part of the bargain; what he was paying in return for publicly owning the most covetable woman anywhere they were likely to be; and for the right to sleep with her after the public display.

Meanwhile Maureen said not a word. She sat on her bed looking at nothing in particular. Once or twice she examined her face in the mirror, and even put cream on it. And she cut out a dress, but put it aside.

On Sunday Mrs. Watson laid tea for four, using her own judgement since Maureen was too deeply in love (so she told everyone) to notice such trifles. At four Stanley was expected, and at 3:55 Maureen descended to the living room. She wore: a faded pink dress from three summers before; her mother's cretonne overall used for housework; and a piece of cloth tied round her hair that might very well have been a duster. At any rate, it was a faded grey. She had put on a pair of her mother's old shoes. She could not be called plain; but she looked like her own faded elder sister, dressed for a hard day's spring cleaning.

Her father, knowledgeable, said nothing: he lowered the paper, examined her, let out a short laugh, and lifted it again. Mrs. Watson, understanding at last that this was a real crisis, burst into tears. Stanley arrived before Mrs. Watson could stop herself crying. He nearly said to Mrs. Watson: "I didn't know Maureen had an older sister." Maureen sat listless at one end of the table; Mr. Watson sat grinning at the other, and Mrs. Watson sniffed and wiped her eyes between the two.

Maureen said: "Hello, Stanley, meet my father and mother." He shook their hands and stared at her. She did not meet his eyes: rather, the surface of her blue gaze met the furious, incredulous, hurt pounce of his glares at her. Maureen poured tea, offered him sandwiches and cake, and made conversation about the weather, and the prices of food, and the dangers of giving even good customers credit in the shop. He sat there, a well-set-up young man, with his brushed hair, his brushed moustache, his checked brown cloth jacket, and a face flaming with anger and affront. He said nothing but Maureen talked on, her voice trailing and cool. At five o'clock, Mrs. Watson again burst into tears, her whole body shaking, and Stanley brusquely left.

Mr. Watson said: "Well, why did you lead him on, then?" and turned on the television. Mrs. Watson went to lie down. Maureen, in her own room, took off the various items of her disguise, and returned them to her mother's room. "Don't cry, Mum. What are you carrying on like that for? What's the matter?" Then she dressed extremely carefully in a new white linen suit, brown shoes, beige blouse. She did her hair and her face, and sat looking at herself. The last two hours (or week) hit her, and her stomach hurt so that she doubled up. She cried; but the tears smeared her makeup, and she stopped herself with the side of a fist against her mouth.

It now seemed to her that for the last week she had simply not been Maureen; she had been someone else. What had she done it for? Why? Then she knew it was for Tony: during all that ridiculous scene at the table, she had imagined Tony looking on, grinning, but understanding her.

She now wiped her face quite clear of tears, and went quietly out of the house so as not to disturb her father and mother. There was a telephone booth at the corner. She stepped calm and aloof along the street, her mouth held (as it always was) in an almost smile. Bert from the grocer's shop said: "Hey, Maureen, that's a smasher. Who's it for?" And she gave him the smile and the toss of the head that went with the street and said: "You, Bert, it's all for you." She went to the telephone booth thinking of Tony. She felt as if he already knew what had happened. She would say: "Let's go and dance, Tony." He would say "Where shall I meet you?" She dialled his number, and it rang and it rang and it rang. She stood holding the receiver, waiting. About ten minutes—more. Slowly she replaced it. *He had let her down.* He had been telling her, in words and without, to be something, to stay something, and now he did not care, he had let her down.

Maureen quietened herself and telephoned Stanley.

All right then, if that's how you want it, she said to Tony. Stanley answered, and she said amiably: "Hello."

Silence. She could hear him breathing, fast. She could see his affronted face.

"Well, aren't you going to say anything?" She tried to make this casual, but she could hear the fear in her voice. Oh yes, she could lose him and probably had. To hide the fear she said: "Can't you take a joke, Stanley?" and laughed.

"A joke!"

She laughed. Not bad, it sounded all right.

"I thought you'd gone off your nut, clean off your rocker. . . ." He was breathing in and out, a rasping noise. She was reminded of his hot breathing down her neck and her arms. Her own breath quickened, even while she thought: I don't like him, I really don't like him at all . . . and she said softly: "Oh Stan, I was having a bit of a giggle, that's all."

Silence. Now, this was the crucial moment.

"Oh Stan, can't you see—I thought it was all just boring, that's all it was." She laughed again.

He said: "Nice for your parents, I don't think."

"Oh they don't mind—they laughed after you'd left, though first they were cross." She added hastily, afraid he might think they were laughing at him: "They're used to me, that's all it is."

Another long silence. With all her willpower she insisted that he should soften. But he said nothing, merely breathed in and out, into the receiver.

"Stanley, it was only a joke, you aren't really angry, are you, Stanley?" The tears sounded in her voice now, and she judged it better that they should.

He said, after hesitation. "Well, Maureen, I just didn't like it, I don't like that kind of thing, that's all." She allowed herself to go on crying, and after a while he said, forgiving her in a voice that was condescending and irritated: "Well, all right, all right, there's no point in crying, is there?"

He was annoyed with himself for giving in, she knew that, because she would have been. He had given her up, thrown her over, during the last couple of hours: he was pleased, really, that something from outside had forced him to give her up. Now he could be free for the something better that would turn up—someone who would not strike terror into him by an extraordinary performance like this afternoon's.

"Let's go off to the pictures, Stan. . . ."

Even now, he hesitated. Then he said, quick and reluctant: "I'll meet you at Leicester Square, outside the Odeon, at seven o'clock." He put down the receiver.

Usually he came to pick her up in the car from the corner of the street.

She stood smiling, the tears running down her face. She knew she was crying because of the loss of Tony, who had let her down. She walked back to her house to make up again, thinking that she was in Stanley's power now: there was no balance between them, the advantage was all his.

The New Man

.

.   .

ABOUT three miles on the track to the station a smaller over-grown road branched to the Manager's House. This house had been built by the Rich Mitchells for their manager. Then they decided to sell a third of their farm, with the house ready for its owner. It stood empty a couple of years, with sacks of grain and oxhides in it. The case had been discussed and adjudicated on the verandahs of the district: no, Rich Mitchell was not right to sell that part of his farm, which was badly watered and poorish soil, except for 100 acres or so. At the very least he should have thrown in a couple of miles of his long vlei with the lands adjacent to it. No wonder Rich Mitchell was rich (they said); and when they met him their voices had a calculated distance: "Sold your new farm yet, Mitch?" No, he hadn't sold it, nor did he, for one year, then another. But the rich can afford to wait. (As they said on the verandahs.)

The farm was bought by a Mr. Rooyen who had already gone broke farming down Que Que way. The Grants went to visit, Mrs. Grant in her new silk, Mr. Grant grumbling because it was the busy season. The small girl did not go, she refused, she wanted to stay in the kitchen with old Tom the cookboy, where she was happy, watching him make butter.

That evening, listening with half an ear to the parents' talk, it was evident things weren't too good. Mr. Rooyen hadn't a penny of his own; he had bought the farm through the Land Bank, and was working on an £800 loan. What it amounted to was, it was a gamble on the first season. "It's all very well," said Mr. Grant, summing up with the reluctant

243

critical note in his voice that meant he knew he would have to help Mr. Rooyen, would do so, but found it all too much. And sure enough, in the dry season the Rooyen cattle were running on Grant land and using the Grant well. But Mr. Rooyen had become "the new man in the Manager's House."

The first season wasn't too bad, so the small girl gathered from the talk on the verandahs, and Mr. Rooyen might make out after all. But he was very poor. Mrs. Grant, when they had too much cheese or butter or baked, sent supplies over by the cook. In the second year Mr. Grant lent Mr. Rooyen £200 to tide him over. The small girl knew that the new neighbour belonged forever to that category of people who, when parting from the Grants, would wring their hands and say in a low, half-ashamed voice: "You've been very good to me and I'll never forget it."

The first time she saw the new farmer, who never went anywhere, was when the Grants went into the station and gave Mr. Rooyen a lift. He could not afford a car yet. He stood on the track waiting for the Grants, and behind him the road to his house was even more overgrown with bushes and grass, like a dry riverbed between the trees. He sat in the back, answering Mr. Grant's questions about how things were going. She did not notice him much, or rather refused to notice him, because she definitely did not like him, although he was nothing she had not known all her life. A tallish man, dressed in bush khaki, blue eyes inflamed by the sun, he was burned—not a healthy reddish brown, but a mahogany colour—because he was never out of the sun, never stopped working. This colour in a white man, the small girl already knew, meant a desperate struggling poverty and it usually preceded going broke or getting very ill. But the reason she did not like him, or that he scared her, was the violence of his grievance. The hand which lay on the back of the car seat behind Mr. Grant trembled slightly; his voice trembled as he spoke of Rich Mitchell, his neighbour, who had a vlei seven miles long and would neither sell nor rent him any of it. "It isn't right," he kept saying. "He doesn't make use of my end. Perhaps his cattle graze there a couple of weeks in the dry season, but that's all." All this meant that his cattle would be running with the Grants' again when the grass was low. More: that he was appealing, through Mr. Grant, for justice, to the unconstituted council of farmers who settled these matters on their verandahs.

That night Mr. Grant said: "It's all very well!" a good many times. Then he rang up Mr. Matthews (Glasgow Bob) from the Glenisle Farm; and Mr. Paynter (Tobacco Paynter) from Bellevue; and Mr. Van Doren (the Dutchman) from Blue Hills. Their farms adjoined Rich Mitchell's.

Soon after, the Grants went into the station again. At the last minute they had remembered to ring up and ask Mr. Rooyen if he wanted a lift. He did. It wasn't altogether convenient, particularly for the small girl, because two-thirds of the back seat was packed to the roof with plough parts being sent into town for repair. And beside Mrs. Grant on the front seat was a great parcel full of dead chickens ready for sale to the hotel. "It's no bother," said Mrs. Grant to Mr. Rooyen, "the child can sit on your knee."

The trouble was that the small girl was definitely not a child. She was pretty certain she was no longer a small girl either. For one thing, her breasts had begun to sprout, and while this caused her more embarrassment than pleasure, she handled her body in a proud, gingerly way that made it impossible, as she would have done even a season before, to snuggle in onto the grownup's lap. She got out of the car in a mood of fine proud withdrawal, not looking at Mr. Rooyen as he fitted himself into the narrow space on the back seat. Then, with a clumsy fastidiousness, she perched on the very edge of his bare bony knees and supported herself with two hands on the back of the front seat. Mr. Rooyen's arms were about her waist, as if she were indeed a child, and they trembled, as she had known they would—as his voice still trembled, talking about Rich Mitchell. But soon he stopped talking.

The car sped forward through the heavy, red-dust-laden trees, rocking and bouncing over the dry ruts, and she was jerked back to fit against the body of Mr. Rooyen, whose fierceness was that of lonely tenderness, as she knew already, though never before in her life had she met it. She longed for the ride to be over, while she sat squeezed, pressed, suffering, in the embrace of Mr. Rooyen, a couple of feet behind the Grants. She ignored, so far as was possible, with politeness; was stiff with resistance; looked at the backs of her parents' heads and marvelled at their blindness. "If you only knew what your precious Mr. Rooyen was doing to your precious daughter . . ."

When it was time to come home from the station, she shed five years and became petulant and wilful: she would sit on her mother's knee, not on Mr. Rooyen's. Because now the car was stacked with groceries, and it was a choice of one knee or the other. "Why, my dear child," said the fond Mrs. Grant, pleased at this rebirth of the charming child in her daughter. But the girl sat as stiffly on her mother's knee as she had on the man's, for she felt his eyes continually returning to her, over her mother's shoulder, in need or in fear or in guilt.

When the car stopped at the turning to the Manager's House, she got off her mother's knee and would not look at Mr. Rooyen. Who then did something really not allowable, not in the code, for he bent, squeezed her in his great near-black hairy arms and kissed her. Her mother laughed, gay and encouraging. Mr. Grant said merely: "Goodbye, Rooyen," as the tall forlorn fierce man walked off to his house along the grass-river road.

The girl got into the back seat, silent. Her mother had let her down, had let her new breasts down by that gay social laugh. As for her father, she looked at his profile, absorbed in the business of starting the car and setting it in motion, but the profile said nothing. She said, resentful: "Who does he think he *is*, kissing me?" And Mrs. Grant said briskly: "My dear child, why ever not?" At which Mr. Grant gave his wife a quick grave look, but remained silent. And this comforted the girl, supported her.

She thought about Mr. Rooyen. Or rather she felt him—felt the trembling of his arms, felt as if he were calling to her. One hot morning, saying she was going for a walk, she set off to his house. When she got there she was overheated and tired and needed a drink. Of course there was no one there. The house was two small rooms, side by side under corrugated iron, with a lean-to kitchen behind. In front was a narrow brick verandah with pillars. Plants stood in painted paraffin tins, and they were dry and limp. She went into the first room. It had two older leather armchairs, a sideboard with a mirror that reflected trees and blue sky and long grass from the low window, and an eating table. The second room had an iron bed and a chest of drawers. She looked, long and thoughtful, at the narrow bed, and her heart was full of pity because of the lonely trembling of Mr. Rooyen's arms. She went into the tiny kitchen. It had an iron Carron Dover stove, where the fire was out. A wooden table had some cold meat on it with a piece of gauze over it. The meat smelled sourish. Flies buzzed. Up the legs of the table small black ants trickled. There was no servant visible. After getting herself a glass of tepid-tasting water from the filter, she walked very slowly through the house again, taking in everything, then went home.

At supper she said, casual: "I went to see Mr. Rooyen today."

Her father looked quickly at her mother, who dropped her eyes and crumbled bread. That meant they had discussed the incident of the kiss. "How is he?" asked Mrs. Grant, casual and bright.

"He wasn't there." Her father said nothing.

Next day she lapsed back into her private listening world. In the afternoon she read, but the book seemed childish. She wept enjoyably, alone. At supper she looked at her parents from a long way off, and knew it was a different place, where she had never been before. They were smaller, definitely. She saw them clear: the rather handsome phlegmatic man at one end of the table, brown in his khaki (but not mahogany, he could afford not to spend every second of his waking hours in the sun). And at the other end a brisk, airy, efficient woman in a tailored striped dress. The girl thought: "I came out of them," and shrank away in dislike from knowing how she had. She looked at these two strange people and felt Mr. Rooyen's arms call to her across three miles of veld. Before she went to bed she stood for a long time gazing at the small light from his house.

Next morning she went to his house again. She wore a new dress, which her mother had made. It was a childish dress that ignored her breasts, which is why she chose it. Not that she expected to see Mr. Rooyen. She wanted to see the small, brick, ant-and-fly-ridden house, walk through it and come home again.

When she got there, there was not a sign of anyone. She

fetched water in a half-paraffin tin from the kitchen and soaked the half-dead plants. Then she sat on the edge of the brick verandah with her feet in the hot dust. Quite soon Mr. Rooyen came walking up through the trees from the lands. He saw her, but she could not make out what he thought. She said, girlish: "I've watered your plants for you."

"The boy's supposed to water them," he said, sounding angry. He strode onto the verandah, into the room behind, and out at the back in three great paces shouting: "Boy! Boy!" A shouting went on, because the cook had gone to sleep under a tree. The girl watched the man run himself a glass of water from the filter, gulp it down, run another, gulp that. He came back to the verandah. Standing like a great black hot tower over her, he demanded: "Does your father know you're here?"

She shook her head, primly. But she felt he was unfair. He would not have liked her father to know how his arms had trembled and pressed her in the car.

He returned to the room, and sat, knees sprawling apart, his arms limp, in one of the big ugly leather chairs. He looked at her steadily, his mouth tight. He had a thin mouth. The lips were burned and black from the sun, and the cracks in them showed white and unhealthy.

"Come here," he said, softly. It was tentative and she chose not to hear it, remained sitting with her back to him.

Over her shoulder she asked, one neighbour to another: "Have you fixed up your vlei with Mr. Mitchell yet?" He sat looking at her, his head lowered. His eyes were really ugly, she thought, red with sun glare. He was an ugly man, she thought. For now she was wishing—not that she had not come, but that he had not come. Then she could have walked, secretly and delightfully, through the house and gone secretly. And tomorrow she could have come and watered his plants again. She imagined saying to him, meeting him by chance somewhere: "Guess who was watering your plants all that time?"

"You're a pretty little girl," he said. He was grinning. The grin had no relation to the lonely hunger of his touch on her in the car. Nor was it a grin addressed to a pretty little girl— far from it. She looked at the grin, repudiating it for her future and was glad that she wore this full, childish dress.

"Come and sit on my knee," he tried again, in the way people had been saying through her childhood: Come and sit on my knee. She obligingly went, like a small girl, and balanced herself on a knee that felt all bone under her. His hands came out and gripped her thin arms. His face changed from the ugly grin to the look of lonely hunger. She was sitting upright, using her feet as braces on the floor to prevent herself being pulled into the trembling man's body. Unable to pull her, he leaned his face against her neck, so that she felt his eyelashes and eyebrows hairy on her skin, and he muttered: "Maureen, Maureen, Maureen, my love."

She stood up, smoothing down her silly dress. He opened his eyes, sat still, hands on his knees. His mouth was half open, he breathed irregularly, and his eyes stared, not at her, but at the brick floor where tiny black ants trickled.

She sat herself on the chair opposite, tucking her dress well in around her legs. In the silence the roof cracked suddenly overhead from the heat. There was the sound of a car on the main road half a mile off. The car came nearer. Neither the girl nor the man moved. Their eyes met from time to time, frowning, serious, then moved away to the ants, to the window, anywhere. He still breathed fast. She was full of revulsion against his body, yet she remembered the heat of his face, the touch of his lashes on her neck, and his loneliness spoke to her through her dislike of him, so that she longed to assuage him. The car stopped outside the house. She saw, without surprise, that it was her father. She remained where she was as Mr. Grant stepped out of the car and came in, his eyes narrowed because of the glare and the heat under the iron roof. He nodded at his daughter, and said. "How do you do, Rooyen?" There being only two chairs, the men were standing; but the girl knew what she had to do, so she went out onto the verandah, and sat on the hot rough brick, spreading her blue skirts wide so that air could come under them and cool her thighs.

Now the two men were sitting in the chairs.

"Like some tea, Mr. Grant?"

"I could do with a cup."

Mr. Rooyen shouted: "Tea, boy!" and a shout came back from the kitchen. The girl could hear the iron stove being banged and blown into heat. It was nearly midday and she wondered what Mr. Rooyen would have for lunch. That rancid beef? She thought: If I were Maureen I wouldn't leave him alone, I'd look after him. I suppose she's some silly woman in an office in town. . . . But since he loved Maureen, she became her and heard his voice saying: Maureen, Maureen, my love. Simultaneously she held her thin brown arms into the sun and felt how they were dark dry brown and she felt the flesh melting off hard lank bones.

"I spoke to Tobacco Paynter last night on the telephone, and he said he thinks Rich Mitchell might very well be in a different frame of mind by now, he's had a couple of good seasons."

"If a couple of good seasons could make any difference to Mr. Mitchell," came Mr. Rooyen's hot resentful voice. "But thank you, Mr. Grant. Thank you."

"He's close," said her father. "Near. Canny. Careful. Those North Country people are, you know." He laughed. Mr. Rooyen laughed too, after a pause—he was a Dutchman and had to work out the unfamiliar phrase "North Country."

"If I were you," said Mr. Grant, "I'd get the whole of the lands on either side of the vlei under mealies the first season. Rich has never had it under cultivation, and the soil'd go sixteen bags to the acre for the first couple of seasons."

"Yes, I've been thinking that's what I should do."

She heard the sounds of tea being brought in.

Mr. Rooyen said to her through the door: "Like a cup?" but she shook her head. She was thinking that if she were Maureen she'd fix up the house for him. Her father's next remark was therefore no surprise to her.

"Thought of getting married, Rooyen?"

He said bitterly: "Take a look at this house, Mr. Grant."

"Well you could build on a couple of rooms for about thirty pounds, I reckon; I'll lend you my building boy. And a wife'd get it all spick and span in no time."

Soon the two men came out, and Mr. Rooyen stood on the verandah as she and her father got into the car and drove off. She waved to him, politely, with a polite smile.

She waited for her father to say something, but although he gave her several doubtful looks, he did not. She said: "Mr. Rooyen's in love with a girl called Maureen."

"Did he say so?"

"Yes, he did."

"Well," he said, talking to her, as was his habit, one grown person to another, "I'd say it was time he got married."

"Yes."

"Everything all right?" he inquired, having worked out exactly the right words to use.

"Yes, thank you."

"Good."

That season Rich Mitchell leased a couple of miles of his big vlei to Mr. Rooyen, with a promise of sale later. Tobacco Paynter's wife got a governess from England, called Miss Betty Blunt, and almost at once Mr. Rooyen and she were engaged. Mrs. Paynter complained that she could never keep a governess longer than a couple of months, they always got married; but she couldn't have been too angry about it, because she laid on a big wedding for them, and all the district was there. The girl was asked if she would be a bridesmaid, but she very politely refused. On the track to the station there was a new signpost pointing along a well-used road which said: THE BIG VLEI FARM. C. ROOYEN.

To Room Nineteen

•

•   •

THIS is a story, I suppose, about a failure in intelligence: the Rawlings' marriage was grounded in intelligence.

They were older when they married than most of their married friends: in their well-seasoned late twenties. Both had had a number of affairs, sweet rather than bitter; and when they fell in love—for they did fall in love—had known each other for some time. They joked that they had saved each other "for the real thing." That they had waited so long (but not too long) for this real thing was to them a proof of their sensible discrimination. A good many of their friends had married young, and now (they felt) probably regretted lost opportunities; while others, still unmarried, seemed to them arid, self-doubting, and likely to make desperate or romantic marriages.

Not only they, but others, felt they were well matched: their friends' delight was an additional proof of their happiness. They had played the same roles, male and female, in this group or set, if such a wide, loosely connected, constantly changing constellation of people could be called a set. They had both become, by virtue of their moderation, their humour, and their abstinence from painful experience people to whom others came for advice. They could be, and were, relied on. It was one of those cases of a man and a woman linking themselves whom no one else had ever thought of linking, probably because of their similarities. But then everyone exclaimed: Of course! How right! How was it we never thought of it before!

And so they married amid general rejoicing, and because

of their foresight and their sense for what was probable, nothing was a surprise to them.

Both had well-paid jobs. Matthew was a subeditor on a large London newspaper, and Susan worked in an advertising firm. He was not the stuff of which editors or publicised journalists are made, but he was much more than "a subeditor," being one of the essential background people who in fact steady, inspire and make possible the people in the limelight. He was content with this position. Susan had a talent for commercial drawing. She was humorous about the advertisements she was responsible for, but she did not feel strongly about them one way or the other.

Both, before they married, had had pleasant flats, but they felt it unwise to base a marriage on either flat, because it might seem like a submission of personality on the part of the one whose flat it was not. They moved into a new flat in South Kensington on the clear understanding that when their marriage had settled down (a process they knew would not take long, and was in fact more a humorous concession to popular wisdom than what was due to themselves) they would buy a house and start a family.

And this is what happened. They lived in their charming flat for two years, giving parties and going to them, being a popular young married couple, and then Susan became pregnant, she gave up her job, and they bought a house in Richmond. It was typical of this couple that they had a son first, then a daughter, then twins, son and daughter. Everything right, appropriate, and what everyone would wish for, if they could choose. But people did feel these two had chosen; this balanced and sensible family was no more than what was due to them because of their infallible sense for *choosing* right.

And so they lived with their four children in their gardened house in Richmond and were happy. They had everything they had wanted and had planned for.

And yet . . .

Well, even this was expected, that there must be a certain flatness. . . .

Yes, yes, of course, it was natural they sometimes felt like this. Like what?

Their life seemed to be like a snake biting its tail. Matthew's job for the sake of Susan, children, house, and garden—which caravanserai needed a well-paid job to maintain it. And Susan's practical intelligence for the sake of Matthew, the children, the house and the garden—which unit would have collapsed in a week without her.

But there was no point about which either could say: "For the sake of *this* is all the rest." Children? But children can't be a centre of life and a reason for being. They can be a thousand things that are delightful, interesting, satisfying, but they can't be a wellspring to live from. Or they shouldn't be. Susan and Matthew knew that well enough.

Matthew's job? Ridiculous. It was an interesting job, but scarcely a reason for living. Matthew took pride in doing it well; but he could hardly be expected to be proud of the newspaper: the newspaper he read, *his* newspaper, was not the one he worked for.

Their love for each other? Well, that was nearest it. If this wasn't a centre, what was? Yes, it was around this point, their love, that the whole extraordinary structure revolved. For extraordinary it certainly was. Both Susan and Matthew had moments of thinking so, of looking in secret disbelief at this thing they had created: marriage, four children, big house, garden, charwomen, friends, cars . . . and this *thing*, this entity, all of it had come into existence, been blown into being out of nowhere, because Susan loved Matthew and Matthew loved Susan. Extraordinary. So that was the central point, the wellspring.

And if one felt that it simply was not strong enough, important enough, to support it all, well whose fault was that? Certainly neither Susan's nor Matthew's. It was in the nature of things. And they sensibly blamed neither themselves nor each other.

On the contrary, they used their intelligence to preserve what they had created from a painful and explosive world: they looked around them, and took lessons. All around them, marriages collapsing, or breaking, or rubbing along (even worse, they felt). They must not make the same mistakes, they must not.

They had avoided the pitfall so many of their friends had fallen into—of buying a house in the country *for the sake of the children;* so that the husband became a weekend husband, a weekend father, and the wife always careful not to ask what went on in the town flat which they called (in joke) a bachelor flat. No, Matthew was a full-time husband, a full-time father, and at nights, in the big married bed in the big married bedroom (which had an attractive view of the river) they lay beside each other talking and he told her about his day, and what he had done, and whom he had met; and she told him about her day (not as interesting, but that was not her fault) for both knew of the hidden resentments and deprivations of the woman who has lived her own life—and above all, has earned her own living—and is now dependent on a husband for outside interests and money.

Nor did Susan make the mistake of taking a job for the sake of her independence, which she might very well have done, since her old firm, missing her qualities of humour, balance, and sense, invited her often to go back. Children needed their mother to a certain age, that both parents knew and agreed on; and when these four healthy wisely brought-up children were of the right age, Susan would work again, because she knew, and so did he, what happened to women of fifty at the height of their energy and ability, with grown-up children who no longer needed their full devotion.

So there was this couple, testing their marriage, looking after it, treating it like a small boat full of helpless people in a very stormy sea. Well, of course, so it was. . . . The storms of the world were bad, but not too close—which is not to say they were selfishly felt: Susan and Matthew were both well-informed and responsible people. And the inner storms and quicksands were understood and charted. So everything was all right. Everything was in order. Yes, things were under control.

So what did it matter if they felt dry, flat? People like themselves, fed on a hundred books (psychological, anthropological, sociological) could scarcely be unprepared for the dry, controlled wistfulness which is the distinguishing mark of the intelligent marriage. Two people, endowed with education, with discrimination, with judgement, linked together voluntarily from their will to be happy together and to be of use to others—one sees them everywhere, one knows them, one even is that thing oneself: sadness because so much is after all so little. These two, unsurprised, turned towards each other with even more courtesy and gentle love: this was life, that two people, no matter how carefully chosen, could not be everything to each other. In fact, even to say so, to think in such a way, was banal, they were ashamed to do it.

It was banal, too, when one night Matthew came home late and confessed he had been to a party, taken a girl home and slept with her. Susan forgave him, of course. Except that forgiveness is hardly the word. Understanding, yes. But if you understand something, you don't forgive it, you are the thing itself: forgiveness is for what you *don't* understand. Nor had he *confessed*—what sort of word is that?

The whole thing was not important. After all, years ago they had joked: Of course I'm not going to be faithful to you, no one can be faithful to one other person for a whole lifetime. (And there was the word *faithful*—stupid, all these words, stupid, belonging to a savage old world.) But the incident left both of them irritable. Strange, but they were both bad-tempered, annoyed. There was something unassimilable about it.

Making love splendidly after he had come home that night, both had felt that the idea that Myra Jenkins, a pretty girl met at a party, could be even relevant was ridiculous. They had loved each other for over a decade, would love each other for years more. Who, then, was Myra Jenkins?

Except, thought Susan, unaccountably bad-tempered, she was (is) the first. In ten years. So either the ten years' fidelity was not important, or she isn't. (No, no, there is something wrong with this way of thinking, there must be.) But if she isn't important, presumably it wasn't important either when Matthew and I first went to bed with each other that afternoon whose delight even now (like a very long shadow at sundown) lays a long, wandlike finger over us. (Why did I say sundown?) Well, if what we felt that afternoon was not important, nothing is important, because if it hadn't been for what we felt, we wouldn't be Mr. and Mrs. Rawlings with four children, etc., etc. The whole thing is *absurd*—for him to have come home and told me was absurd. For him not to have told me was absurd. For me to care, or for that matter not to care, is absurd . . . and who is Myra Jenkins? Why, no one at all.

There was only one thing to do, and of course these sensible people did it: they put the thing behind them, and consciously, knowing what they were doing, moved forward into a different phase of their marriage, giving thanks for past good fortune as they did so.

For it was inevitable that the handsome, blond, attractive, manly man, Matthew Rawlings, should be at times tempted (oh, what a word!) by the attractive girls at parties she could not attend because of the four children; and that sometimes he would succumb (a word even more repulsive, if possible) and that she, a good-looking woman in the big well-tended garden at Richmond, would sometimes be pierced as by an arrow from the sky with bitterness. Except that bitterness was not in order, it was out of court. Did the casual girls touch the marriage? They did not. Rather it was they who knew defeat because of the handsome Matthew Rawlings' marriage body and soul to Susan Rawlings.

In that case why did Susan feel (though luckily not for longer than a few seconds at a time) as if life had become a desert, and that nothing mattered, and that her children were not her own?

Meanwhile her intelligence continued to assert that all was well. What if her Matthew did have an occasional sweet afternoon, the odd affair? For she knew quite well, except in her moments of aridity, that they were very happy, that the affairs were not important.

Perhaps that was the trouble? It was in the nature of things that the adventures and delights could no longer be hers, because of the four children and the big house that needed so much attention. But perhaps she was secretly wishing, and even knowing that she did, that the wildness and the beauty could be his. But he was married to her. She was married to him. They were married inextricably. And therefore the gods could not strike him with the real magic, not really. Well, was it Susan's fault that after he came home from an adventure he looked harassed rather than fulfilled? (In fact, that was how she knew he had been *unfaithful,* because of his sullen air, and his glances at her, similar to hers at him: What is it that I share with this person that shields all delight from me?) But none of it by anybody's fault. (But what did they feel ought to be somebody's fault?) Nobody's fault, nothing to be at fault, no one to blame, no one to offer or to take it . . . and nothing wrong, either, except that Matthew never was really struck, as he wanted to be, by joy; and that Susan was more and more often threatened by emptiness. (It was usually in the garden that she was invaded by this feeling: she was coming to avoid the garden, unless the children or Matthew were with her.) There was no need to use the dramatic words, unfaithful, forgive, and the rest: intelligence forbade them. Intelligence barred, too, quarrelling, sulking, anger, silences of withdrawal, accusations and tears. Above all, intelligence forbids tears.

A high price has to be paid for the happy marriage with the four healthy children in the large white gardened house.

And they were paying it, willingly, knowing what they were doing. When they lay side by side or breast to breast in the big civilised bedroom overlooking the wild sullied river, they laughed, often, for no particular reason; but they knew it was really because of these two small people, Susan and Matthew, supporting such an edifice on their intelligent love. The laugh comforted them; it saved them both, though from what, they did not know.

They were now both fortyish. The older children, boy and girl, were ten and eight, at school. The twins, six, were still at home. Susan did not have nurses or girls to help her: childhood is short; and she did not regret the hard work. Often enough she was bored, since small children can be boring; she was often very tired; but she regretted nothing. In another decade, she would turn herself back into being a woman with a life of her own.

Soon the twins would go to school, and they would be away from home from nine until four. These hours, so Susan saw it, would be the preparation for her own slow emancipation away from the role of hub-of-the-family into woman-with-her-own-life. She was already planning for the hours of freedom when all the children would be "off her hands." That was the phrase used by Matthew and by Susan and by their friends, for the moment when the youngest child went off to school. "They'll be off your hands, darling Susan, and you'll have time to yourself." So said Matthew, the intelligent husband, who had often enough commended and consoled Susan, standing by her in spirit during the years when her soul was not her own, as she said, but her children's.

What it amounted to was that Susan saw herself as she had been at twenty-eight, unmarried; and then again somewhere about fifty, blossoming from the root of what she had been twenty years before. As if the essential Susan were in abeyance, as if she were in cold storage. Matthew said something like this to Susan one night: and she agreed that it was true—she did feel something like that. What, then, was this essential Susan? She did not know. Put like that it sounded ridiculous, and she did not really feel it. Anyway, they had a long discussion about the whole thing before going off to sleep in each other's arms.

So the twins went off to their school, two bright affectionate children who had no problems about it, since their older brother and sister had trodden this path so successfully before them. And now Susan was going to be alone in the big house, every day of the school term, except for the daily woman who came in to clean.

It was now, for the first time in this marriage, that something happened which neither of them had foreseen.

This is what happened. She returned, at nine-thirty, from taking the twins to the school by car, looking forward to seven blissful hours of freedom. On the first morning she was simply restless, worrying about the twins "naturally enough" since this was their first day away at school. She was hardly able to contain herself until they came back. Which they did happily, excited by the world of school, looking forward to the next day. And the next day Susan took them, dropped them, came back, and found herself reluctant to enter her big and beautiful home because it was as if something was waiting for her there that she did not wish to confront. Sensibly, however, she parked the car in the garage, entered the house, spoke to Mrs. Parkes the daily woman about her duties, and went up to her bedroom. She was possessed by a fever which drove her out again, downstairs, into the kitchen, where Mrs. Parkes was making cake and did not need her, and into the garden. There she sat on a bench and tried to calm herself, looking at trees, at a brown glimpse of the river. But she was filled with tension, like a panic: as if an enemy was in the garden with her. She spoke to herself severely, thus: All this is quite natural. First, I spent twelve years of my adult life working, *living my own life*. Then I married, and from the moment I became pregnant for the first time I signed myself over, so to speak, to other people. To the children. Not for one moment in twelve years have I been alone, had time to myself. So now I have to learn to be myself again. That's all.

And she went indoors to help Mrs. Parkes cook and clean, and found some sewing to do for the children. She kept herself occupied every day. At the end of the first term she understood she felt two contrary emotions. First: secret astonishment and dismay that during those weeks when the house was empty of children she had in fact been more occupied (had been careful to keep herself occupied) than ever she had been when the children were around her needing her continual attention. Second: that now she knew the house would be full of them, and for five weeks, she resented the fact she would never be alone. She was already looking back at those hours of sewing, cooking (but by herself), as at a lost freedom which would not be hers for five long weeks. And the two months of term which would succeed the five weeks stretched alluringly open to her—freedom. But what freedom—when in fact she had been so careful *not* to be free of small duties during the last weeks? She looked at herself, Susan Rawlings, sitting in a big chair by the window in the bedroom, sewing shirts or dresses, which she might just as well have bought. She saw herself making cakes for hours at a time in the big family kitchen: yet usually she bought cakes. What she saw was a woman alone, that was true, but she had not felt alone. For instance, Mrs. Parkes was always somewhere in the house. And she did not like being in the garden at all, because of the closeness there of the enemy—irritation, restlessness, emptiness, whatever it was, which keeping her hands occupied made less dangerous for some reason.

Susan did not tell Matthew of these thoughts. They were not sensible. She did not recognize herself in them. What should she say to her dear friend and husband Matthew? "When I go into the garden, that is, if the children are not there, I feel as if there is an enemy there waiting to invade me." "What enemy, Susan darling?" "Well I don't know, really. . . ." "Perhaps you should see a doctor?"

No, clearly this conversation should not take place. The holidays began and Susan welcomed them. Four children, lively, energetic, intelligent, demanding: she was never, not for a moment of her day, alone. If she was in a room, they would be in the next room, or waiting for her to do something for them; or it would soon be time for lunch or tea, or to take one of them to the dentist. Something to do: five weeks of it, thank goodness.

On the fourth day of these so welcome holidays, she found she was storming with anger at the twins, two shrinking beautiful children who (and this is what checked her) stood hand in hand looking at her with sheer dismayed disbelief. This was their calm mother, shouting at them. And for what? They had come to her with some game, some bit of nonsense. They looked at each other, moved closer for support, and went off hand in hand, leaving Susan holding on to the windowsill of the living room, breathing deep, feeling sick. She went to lie down, telling the older children she had a headache. She heard the boy Harry telling the little ones: "It's all right, Mother's got a headache." She heard that *It's all right* with pain.

That night she said to her husband: "Today I shouted at the twins, quite unfairly." She sounded miserable, and he said gently: "Well, what of it?"

"It's more of an adjustment than I thought, their going to school."

"But Susie, Susie darling. . . ." For she was crouched weeping on the bed. He comforted her: "Susan, what is all this about? You shouted at them? What of it? If you shouted at them fifty times a day it wouldn't be more than the little devils deserve." But she wouldn't laugh. She wept. Soon he comforted her with his body. She became calm. Calm, she wondered what was wrong with her, and why she should mind so much that she might, just once, have behaved unjustly with the children. What did it matter? They had forgotten it all long ago: Mother had a headache and everything was all right.

It was a long time later that Susan understood that that night, when she had wept and Matthew had driven the misery out of her with his big solid body, was the last time, ever in their married life, that they had been—to use their mutual language—with each other. And even that was a lie, because she had not told him of her real fears at all.

The five weeks passed, and Susan was in control of herself, and good and kind, and she looked forward to the holidays with a mixture of fear and longing. She did not know what to expect. She took the twins off to school (the elder children took themselves to school) and she returned to the house determined to face the enemy wherever he was, in the house, or the garden or—where?

She was again restless, she was possessed by restlessness. She cooked and sewed and worked as before, day after day, while Mrs. Parkes remonstrated: "Mrs. Rawlings, what's the need for it? I can do that, it's what you pay me for."

And it was so irrational that she checked herself. She would put the car into the garage, go up to her bedroom, and sit, hands in her lap, forcing herself to be quiet. She listened to Mrs. Parkes moving around the house. She looked out into the garden and saw the branches shake the trees. She sat defeating the enemy, restlessness. Emptiness. She ought to be thinking about her life, about herself. But she did not. Or perhaps she could not. As soon as she forced her mind to think about Susan (for what else did she want to be alone for?) it skipped off to thoughts of butter or school clothes. Or it thought of Mrs. Parkes. She realised that she sat listening for the movements of the cleaning woman, following her every turn, bend, thought. She followed her in her mind from kitchen to bathroom, from table to oven, and it was as if the duster, the cleaning cloth, the saucepan, were in her own hand. She would hear herself saying: No, not like that, don't put that there. . . . Yet she did not give a damn what Mrs. Parkes did, or if she did it at all. Yet she could not prevent herself from being conscious of her, every minute. Yes, this was what was wrong with her: she needed, when she was alone, to be really alone, with no one near. She could not endure the knowledge that in ten minutes or in half an hour Mrs. Parkes would call up the stairs: "Mrs. Rawlings, there's no silver polish. Madam, we're out of flour."

So she left the house and went to sit in the garden where

she was screened from the house by trees. She waited for the demon to appear and claim her, but he did not.

She was keeping him off, because she had not, after all, come to an end of arranging herself.

She was planning how to be somewhere where Mrs. Parkes would not come after her with a cup of tea, or a demand to be allowed to telephone (always irritating since Susan did not care who she telephoned or how often), or just a nice talk about something. Yes, she needed a place, or a state of affairs, where it would not be necessary to keep reminding herself: In ten minutes I must telephone Matthew about . . . and at half past three I must leave early for the children because the car needs cleaning. And at ten o'clock tomorrow I must remember. . . . She was possessed with resentment that the seven hours of freedom in every day (during weekdays in the school term) were not free, that never, not for one second, ever, was she free from the pressure of time, from having to remember this or that. She could never forget herself; never really let herself go into forgetfulness.

Resentment. It was poisoning her. (She looked at this emotion and thought it was absurd. Yet she felt it.) She was a prisoner. (She looked at this thought too, and it was no good telling herself it was a ridiculous one.) She must tell Matthew—but what? She was filled with emotions that were utterly ridiculous, that she despised, yet that nevertheless she was feeling so strongly she could not shake them off.

The school holidays came round, and this time they were for nearly two months, and she behaved with a conscious controlled decency that nearly drove her crazy. She would lock herself in the bathroom, and sit on the edge of the bath, breathing deep, trying to let go into some kind of calm. Or she went up into the spare room, usually empty, where no one would expect her to be. She heard the children calling "Mother, Mother," and kept silent, feeling guilty. Or she went to the very end of the garden, by herself, and looked at the slow-moving brown river; she looked at the river and closed her eyes and breathed slow and deep, taking it into her being, into her veins.

Then she returned to the family, wife and mother, smiling and responsible, feeling as if the pressure of these people— four lively children and her husband—were a painful pressure on the surface of her skin, a hand pressing on her brain. She did not once break down into irritation during these holidays, but it was like living out a prison sentence, and when the children went back to school, she sat on a white stone seat near the flowing river, and she thought: It is not even a year since the twins went to school, since *they were off my hands* (What on earth did I think I meant when I used that stupid phrase?) and yet I'm a different person. I'm simply not myself. I don't understand it.

Yet she had to understand it. For she knew that this structure—big white house, on which the mortgage still cost four hundred a year, a husband, so good and kind and insightful, four children, all doing so nicely, and the garden where she sat, and Mrs. Parkes the cleaning woman—all this depended on her, and yet she could not understand why, or even what it was she contributed to it.

She said to Matthew in their bedroom: "I think there must be something wrong with me."

And he said: "Surely not, Susan? You look marvellous—you're as lovely as ever."

She looked at the handsome blond man, with his clear, intelligent, blue-eyed face, and thought: Why is it I can't tell him? Why not? And she said: "I need to be alone more than I am."

At which he swung his slow blue gaze at her, and she saw what she had been dreading: Incredulity. Disbelief. And fear. An incredulous blue stare from a stranger who was her husband, as close to her as her own breath.

He said: "But the children are at school and off your hands."

She said to herself: I've got to force myself to say: Yes, but do you realize that I never feel free? There's never a moment I can say to myself: There's nothing I have to remind myself about, nothing I have to do in half an hour, or an hour, or two hours. . . .

But she said: "I don't feel well."

He said: "Perhaps you need a holiday."

She said, appalled: "But not without you, surely?" For she could not imagine herself going off without him. Yet that was what he meant. Seeing her face, he laughed, and opened his arms, and she went into them, thinking: Yes, yes, but why can't I say it? And what is it I have to say?

She tried to tell him, about never being free. And he listened and said: "But Susan, what sort of freedom can you possibly want—short of being dead! Am I ever free? I go to the office, and I have to be there at ten—all right, half past ten, sometimes. And I have to do this or that, don't I? Then I've got to come home at a certain time—I don't mean it, you know I don't—but if I'm not going to be back home at six I telephone you. When can I ever say to myself: I have nothing to be responsible for in the next six hours?"

Susan, hearing this, was remorseful. Because it was true. The good marriage, the house, the children, depended just as much on his voluntary bondage as it did on hers. But why did he not feel bound? Why didn't he chafe and become restless? No, there was something really wrong with her and this proved it.

And that word *bondage*—why had she used it? She had never felt marriage, or the children, as bondage. Neither had he, or surely they wouldn't be together lying in each other's arms content after twelve years of marriage.

No, her state (whatever it was) was irrelevant, nothing to do with her real good life with her family. She had to accept the fact that after all, she was an irrational person and to live with it. Some people had to live with crippled arms, or stammers, or being deaf. She would have to live knowing she was subject to a state of mind she could not own.

Nevertheless, as a result of this conversation with her husband, there was a new regime next holidays.

The spare room at the top of the house now had a cardboard sign saying: PRIVATE! DO NOT DISTURB! on it. (This sign had been drawn in coloured chalks by the children, after a discussion between the parents in which it was decided this was psychologically the right thing.) The family and Mrs. Parkes knew this was "Mother's Room" and that she was entitled to her privacy. Many serious conversations took place between Matthew and the children about not taking Mother for granted. Susan overheard the first, between father and Harry, the older boy, and was surprised at her irritation over it. Surely she could have a room somewhere in that big house and retire into it without such a fuss being made? Without it being so solemnly discussed? Why couldn't she simply have announced: "I'm going to fit out the little top room for myself, and when I'm in it I'm not to be disturbed for anything short of fire"? Just that, and finished; instead of long earnest discussions. When she heard Harry and Matthew explaining it to the twins with Mrs. Parkes coming in—"Yes, well, a family sometimes gets on top of a woman"—she had to go right away to the bottom of the garden until the devils of exasperation had finished their dance in her blood.

But now there was a room, and she could go there when she liked, she used it seldom: she felt even more caged there than in her bedroom. One day she had gone up there after a lunch for ten children she had cooked and served because Mrs. Parkes was not there, and had sat alone for a while looking into the garden. She saw the children stream out from the kitchen and stand looking up at the window where she sat behind the curtains. They were all—her children and their friends—discussing Mother's Room. A few minutes later, the chase of children in some game came pounding up the stairs, but ended as abruptly as if they had fallen over a ravine, so sudden was the silence. They had remembered she was there, and had gone silent in a great gale of "Hush! Shhhhhh! Quiet, you'll disturb her. . . ." And they went tiptoeing downstairs like criminal conspirators. When she came down to make tea for them, they all apologised. The twins put their arms around her, from front and back, making a human cage of loving limbs, and promised it would never occur again. "We forgot, Mummy, we forgot all about it!"

What it amounted to was that Mother's Room, and her need for privacy, had become a valuable lesson in respect for other people's rights. Quite soon Susan was going up to the room only because it was a lesson it was a pity to drop. Then she took sewing up there, and the children and Mrs. Parkes came in and out: it had become another family room.

She sighed, and smiled, and resigned herself—she made jokes at her own expense with Matthew over the room. That is, she did from the self she liked, she respected. But at the same time, something inside her howled with impatience, with rage. . . . And she was frightened. One day she found herself kneeling by her bed and praying: "Dear God, keep it away from me, keep him away from me." She meant the devil, for she now thought of it, not caring if she were irrational, as some sort of demon. She imagined him, or it, as a youngish man, or perhaps a middle-aged man pretending to be young. Or a man young-looking from immaturity? At any rate, she saw the young-looking face which, when she drew closer, had dry lines about mouth and eyes. He was thinnish, meagre in build. And he had a reddish complexion, and ginger hair. That was he—a gingery, energetic man, and he wore a reddish hairy jacket, unpleasant to the touch.

Well, one day she saw him. She was standing at the bottom of the garden, watching the river ebb past, when she raised her eyes and saw this person, or being, sitting on the white stone bench. He was looking at her, and grinning. In his hand was a long crooked stick, which he had picked off the ground, or broken off the tree above him. He was absent-mindedly, out of an absent-minded or freakish impulse of spite, using the stick to stir around in the coils of a blindworm or a grass snake (or some kind of snakelike creature: it was whitish and unhealthy to look at, unpleasant). The snake was twisting about, flinging its coils from side to side in a kind of dance of protest against the teasing prodding stick.

Susan looked at him thinking: Who is the stranger? What is he doing in our garden? Then she recognised the man around whom her terrors had crystallised. As she did so, he vanished. She made herself walk over to the bench. A shadow from a branch lay across thin emerald grass, moving jerkily over its roughness, and she could see why she had taken it for a snake, lashing and twisting. She went back to the house thinking: Right, then, so I've seen him with my own eyes, so I'm not crazy after all—there *is* a danger because I've seen him. He is lurking in the garden and sometimes even in the house, and he wants *to get into me and to take me over.*

She dreamed of having a room or a place, anywhere, where she could go and sit, by herself, no one knowing where she was.

Once, near Victoria, she found herself outside a news

agent that had Rooms to Let advertised. She decided to rent a room, telling no one. Sometimes she could take the train in to Richmond and sit alone in it for an hour or two. Yet how could she? A room would cost three or four pounds a week, and she earned no money, and how could she explain to Matthew that she needed such a sum? What for? It did not occur to her that she was taking it for granted she wasn't going to tell him about the room.

Well, it was out of the question, having a room; yet she knew she must.

One day, when a school term was well established, and none of the children had measles or other ailments, and everything seemed in order, she did the shopping early, explained to Mrs. Parkes she was meeting an old school friend, took the train to Victoria, searched until she found a small quiet hotel, and asked for a room for the day. They did not let rooms by the day, the manageress said, looking doubtful, since Susan so obviously was not the kind of woman who needed a room for unrespectable reasons. Susan made a long explanation about not being well, being unable to shop without frequent rests for lying down. At last she was allowed to rent the room provided she paid a full night's price for it. She was taken up by the manageress and a maid, both concerned over the state of her health . . . which must be pretty bad if, living at Richmond (she had signed her name and address in the register), she needed a shelter at Victoria.

The room was ordinary and anonymous, and was just what Susan needed. She put a shilling in the gas fire, and sat, eyes shut, in a dingy armchair with her back to a dingy window. She was alone. She was alone. She was alone. She could feel pressures lifting off her. First the sounds of traffic came very loud; then they seemed to vanish; she might even have slept a little. A knock on the door: it was Miss Townsend the manageress, bringing her a cup of tea with her own hands, so concerned was she over Susan's long silence and possible illness.

Miss Townsend was a lonely woman of fifty, running this hotel with all the rectitude expected of her, and she sensed in Susan the possibility of understanding companionship. She stayed to talk. Susan found herself in the middle of a fantastic story about her illness, which got more and more improbable as she tried to make it tally with the large house at Richmond, well-off husband, and four children. Suppose she said instead: Miss Townsend, I'm here in your hotel because I need to be alone for a few hours, above all *alone and with no one knowing where I am*. She said it mentally, and saw, mentally, the look that would inevitably come on Miss Townsend's elderly maiden's face. "Miss Townsend, my four children and my husband are driving me insane, do you understand that? Yes, I can see from the gleam of hysteria in your eyes that comes from loneliness controlled but only just contained that I've got everything in the world you've ever longed for. Well, Miss Townsend, I don't want any of it. You can have it, Miss Townsend. I wish I was absolutely alone in the world, like you. Miss Townsend, I'm besieged by seven devils, Miss Townsend, Miss Townsend, let me stay here in your hotel where the devils can't get me. . . ." Instead of saying all this, she described her anaemia, agreed to try Miss Townsend's remedy for it, which was raw liver, minced, between whole-meal bread, and said yes, perhaps it would be better if she stayed at home and let a friend do shopping for her. She paid her bill and left the hotel, defeated.

At home Mrs. Parkes said she didn't really like it, no, not really, when Mrs. Rawlings was away from nine in the morning until five. The teacher had telephoned from school to say Joan's teeth were paining her, and she hadn't known what to say; and what was she to make for the children's tea, Mrs. Rawlings hadn't said.

All this was nonsense, of course. Mrs. Parkes's complaint was that Susan had withdrawn herself spiritually, leaving the burden of the big house on her.

Susan looked back at her day of "freedom" which had resulted in her becoming a friend to the lonely Miss Townsend, and in Mrs. Parkes's remonstrances. Yet she remembered the short blissful hour of being alone, really alone. She was determined to arrange her life, no matter what it cost, so that she could have that solitude more often. An absolute solitude, where no one knew her or cared about her.

But how? She thought of saying to her old employer: I want to back you up in a story with Matthew that I am doing part-time work for you. The truth is that . . . but she would have to tell him a lie too, and which lie? She could not say: I want to sit by myself three or four times a week in a rented room. And besides, he knew Matthew, and she could not really ask him to tell lies on her behalf, apart from his being bound to think it meant a lover.

Suppose she really took a part-time job, which she could get through fast and efficiently, leaving time for herself. What job? Addressing envelopes? Canvassing?

And there was Mrs. Parkes, working widow, who knew exactly what she was prepared to give to the house, who knew by instinct when her mistress withdrew in spirit from her responsibilities. Mrs. Parkes was one of the servers of this world, but she needed someone to serve. She had to have Mrs. Rawlings, her madam, at the top of the house or in the garden, so that she could come and get support from her: "Yes, the bread's not what it was when I was a girl. . . . Yes, Harry's got a wonderful appetite, I wonder where he puts it all. . . . Yes, it's lucky the twins are so much of a size, they can wear each other's shoes, that's a saving in these hard times. . . . Yes, the cherry jam from Switzerland is not a patch on the jam from Poland, and three times the price. . . ." And so on. That sort of talk Mrs. Parkes must have, every day, or she would leave, not knowing herself why she left.

Susan Rawlings, thinking these thoughts, found that she was prowling through the great thicketed garden like a wild cat: she was walking up the stairs, down the stairs, through the rooms, into the garden, along the brown running river, back, up through the house, down again. . . . It was a wonder Mrs. Parkes did not think it strange. But on the contrary, Mrs. Rawlings could do what she liked, she could stand on her head if she wanted, provided she was *there*. Susan Rawlings prowled and muttered through her house, hating Mrs. Parkes, hating poor Miss Townsend, dreaming of her hour of solitude in the dingy respectability of Miss Townsend's hotel bedroom, and she knew quite well she was mad. Yes, she was mad.

She said to Matthew that she must have a holiday. Matthew agreed with her. This was not as things had been once— how they had talked in each other's arms in the marriage bed. He had, she knew, diagnosed her finally as *unreasonable*.

She had become someone outside himself that he had to manage. They were living side by side in this house like two tolerably friendly strangers.

Having told Mrs. Parkes, or rather, asked for her permission, she went off on a walking holiday in Wales. She chose the remotest place she knew of. Every morning the children telephoned her before they went off to school, to encourage and support her, just as they had over Mother's Room. Every evening she telephoned them, spoke to each child in turn, and then to Matthew. Mrs. Parkes, given permission to telephone for instructions or advice, did so every day at lunchtime. When, as happened three times, Mrs. Rawlings was out on the mountainside, Mrs. Parkes asked that she should ring back at such and such a time, for she would not be happy in what she was doing without Mrs. Rawlings' blessing.

Susan prowled over wild country with the telephone wire holding her to her duty like a leash. The next time she must telephone, or wait to be telephoned, nailed her to her cross. The mountains themselves seemed trammelled by her unfreedom. Everywhere on the mountains, where she met no one at all, from breakfast time to dusk, excepting sheep, or a shepherd, she came face to face with her own craziness which might attack her in the broadest valleys, so that they seemed too small; or on a mountaintop from which she could see a hundred other mountains and valleys, so that they seemed too low, too small, with the sky pressing down too close. She would stand gazing at a hillside brilliant with ferns and bracken, jewelled with running water, and see nothing but her devil, who lifted inhuman eyes at her from where he leaned negligently on a rock, switching at his ugly yellow boots with a leafy twig.

She returned to her home and family, with the Welsh emptiness at the back of her mind like a promise of freedom.

She told her husband she wanted to have an *au pair* girl.

They were in their bedroom, it was late at night, the children slept. He sat, shirted and slippered, in a chair by the window, looking out. She sat brushing her hair and watching him in the mirror. A time-hallowed scene in the connubial bedroom. He said nothing, while she heard the arguments coming into his mind, only to be rejected because every one was *reasonable*.

"It seems strange to get one now, after all, the children are in school most of the day. Surely the time for you to have help was when you were stuck with them day and night. Why don't you ask Mrs. Parkes to cook for you? She's even offered to—I can understand if you are tired of cooking for six people. But you know that an *au pair* girl means all kinds of problems, it's not like having an ordinary char in during the day. . . ."

Finally he said carefully: "Are you thinking of going back to work?"

"No," she said, "no, not really." She made herself sound vague, rather stupid. She went on brushing her black hair and peering at herself so as to be oblivious of the short uneasy glances her Matthew kept giving her. "Do you think we can't afford it?" she went on vaguely, not at all the old efficient Susan who knew exactly what they could afford.

"It's not that," he said, looking out of the window at dark trees, so as not to look at her. Meanwhile she examined a round, candid, pleasant face with clear dark brows and clear grey eyes. A sensible face. She brushed thick healthy black hair and thought: Yet that's the reflection of a madwoman. How very strange! Much more to the point if what looked back at me was the gingery green-eyed demon with his dry meagre smile. . . . Why wasn't Matthew agreeing? After all, what else could he do? She was breaking her part of the bargain and there was no way of forcing her to keep it: that her spirit, her soul, should live in this house, so that the people in it could grow like plants in water, and Mrs. Parkes remain content in their service. In return for this, he would be a good loving husband, and responsible towards the children. Well, nothing like this had been true of either of them for a long time. He did his duty, perfunctorily; she did not even pretend to do hers. And he had become like other husbands, with his real life in his work and the people he met there, and very likely a serious affair. All this was her fault.

At last he drew heavy curtains, blotting out the trees, and turned to force her attention: "Susan, are you really sure we need a girl?" But she would not meet his appeal at all:

She was running the brush over her hair again and again, lifting fine black clouds in a small hiss of electricity. She was peering in and smiling as if she were amused at the clinging hissing hair that followed the brush.

"Yes, I think it would be a good idea on the whole," she said, with the cunning of a madwoman evading the real point.

In the mirror she could see her Matthew lying on his back, his hands behind his head, staring upwards, his face sad and hard. She felt her heart (the old heart of Susan Rawlings) soften and call out to him. But she set it to be indifferent.

He said: "Susan, the children?" It was an appeal that *almost* reached her. He opened his arms, lifting them from where they had lain by his sides, palms up, empty. She had only to run across and fling herself into them, onto his hard, warm chest, and melt into herself, into Susan. But she could not. She would not see his lifted arms. She said vaguely: "Well, surely it'll be even better for them? We'll get a French or a German girl and they'll learn the language."

In the dark she lay beside him, feeling frozen, a stranger. She felt as if Susan had been spirited away. She disliked very much this woman who lay here, cold and indifferent beside a suffering man, but she could not change her.

Next morning she set about getting a girl, and very soon came Sophie Traub from Hamburg, a girl of twenty, laughing, healthy, blue-eyed, intending to learn English. Indeed, she already spoke a good deal. In return for a room—"Mother's Room"—and her food, she undertook to do some light cooking, and to be with the children when Mrs. Rawlings asked. She was an intelligent girl and understood perfectly what was needed. Susan said "I go off sometimes, for the morning or for the day—well, sometimes the children run home from school, or they ring up, or a teacher rings up. I should be here, really. And there's the daily woman. . . ." And Sophie laughed her deep fruity *Fräulein's* laugh, showed her fine white teeth and her dimples, and said: "You want some person to play mistress of the house sometimes, not so?"

"Yes, that is just so," said Susan, a bit dry, despite herself, thinking in secret fear how easy it was, how much nearer to the end she was than she thought. Healthy *Fräulein* Traub's instant understanding of their position proved this to be true.

The *au pair* girl, because of her own common sense, or (as Susan said to herself with her new inward shudder) because she had been *chosen* so well by Susan, was a success with everyone, the children liking her, Mrs. Parkes forgetting almost at once that she was German, and Matthew finding her "nice to have around the house." For he was now taking things as they came, from the surface of life, withdrawn both as a husband and a father from the household.

One day Susan saw how Sophie and Mrs. Parkes were talking and laughing in the kitchen, and she announced that she would be away until teatime. She knew exactly where to go and what she must look for. She took the District Line to South Kensington, changed to the Circle, got off at Paddington, and walked around looking at the smaller hotels until she was satisfied with one which had FRED'S HOTEL painted on windowpanes that needed cleaning. The façade was a faded shiny yellow, like unhealthy skin. A door at the end of a passage said she must knock; she did, and Fred appeared. He was not at all attractive, not in any way, being fattish, and run-down, and wearing a tasteless striped suit. He had small sharp eyes in a white creased face, and was quite prepared to let Mrs. Jones (she chose the farcical name deliberately, staring him out) have a room three days a week from ten until six. Provided of course that she paid in advance each time she came? Susan produced fifteen shillings (no price had been set by him) and held it out, still fixing him with a bold unblinking challenge she had not known until then she could use at will. Looking at her still, he took up a ten-shilling note from her palm between thumb and forefinger, fingered it; then shuffled up two half crowns, held out his own palm with these bits of money displayed thereon, and let his gaze lower broodingly at them. They were standing in the passage, a red-shaded light above, bare boards beneath, and a strong smell of floor polish rising about them. He shot his gaze up at her over the still-extended palm, and smiled as if to say: What do you take me for? "I shan't," said Susan, "be using this room for the purposes of making money." He still waited. She added another five shillings, at which he nodded and said: "You pay, and I ask no questions." "Good," said Susan. He now went past her to the stairs, and there waited a moment: the light from the street door being in her eyes, she lost sight of him momentarily. Then she saw a sober-suited, white-faced, white-balding little man trotting up the stairs like a waiter, and she went after him. They proceeded in utter silence up the stairs of this house where no questions were asked—Fred's Hotel, which could afford the freedom for its visitors that poor Miss Townsend's hotel could not. The room was hideous. It had a single window, with thin green brocade curtains, a three-quarter bed that had a cheap green satin bedspread on it, a fireplace with a gas fire and a shilling meter by it, a chest of drawers, and a green wicker armchair.

"Thank you," said Susan, knowing that Fred (if this was Fred, and not George, or Herbert or Charlie) was looking at her, not so much with curiosity, an emotion he would not own to, for professional reasons, but with a philosophical sense of what was appropriate. Having taken her money and shown her up and agreed to everything, he was clearly disapproving of her for coming here. She did not belong here at all, so his look said. (But she knew, already, how very much she did belong: the room had been waiting for her to join it.) "Would you have me called at five o'clock, please?" and he nodded and went downstairs.

It was twelve in the morning. She was free. She sat in the armchair, she simply sat, she closed her eyes and sat and let herself be alone. She was alone and no one knew where she was. When a knock came on the door she was annoyed, and prepared to show it: but it was Fred himself, it was five o'clock and he was calling her as ordered. He flicked his sharp little eyes over the room—bed, first. It was undisturbed. She might never have been in the room at all. She thanked him, said she would be returning the day after tomorrow, and left. She was back home in time to cook supper, to put the children to bed, to cook a second supper for her husband and herself later. And to welcome Sophie back from the pictures where she had gone with a friend. All these things she did cheerfully, willingly. But she was thinking all the time of the hotel room, she was longing for it with her whole being.

Three times a week. She arrived promptly at ten, looked Fred in the eyes, gave him twenty shillings, followed him up the stairs, went into the room, and shut the door on him with gentle firmness. For Fred, disapproving of her being here at all, was quite ready to let friendship, or at least acquaintanceship, follow his disapproval, if only she would let him. But he was content to go off on her dismissing nod, with the twenty shillings in his hand.

She sat in the armchair and shut her eyes.

What did she *do* in the room? Why, nothing at all. From the chair, when it had rested her, she went to the window, stretching her arms, smiling, treasuring her anonymity, to look out. She was no longer Susan Rawlings, mother of four, wife of Matthew, employer of Mrs. Parkes and of Sophie Traub, with these and those relations with friends, schoolteachers, tradesmen. She no longer was mistress of the big white house and garden, owning clothes suitable for this and that activity or occasion. She was Mrs. Jones, and she was alone, and she had no past and no future. Here I am, she thought, after all these years of being married and having children and playing those roles of responsibility—and I'm just the same. Yet there have been times I thought that nothing existed of me except the roles that went with being Mrs. Matthew Rawlings. Yes, here I am, and if I never saw any of my family again, here I would still be . . . how very strange that is! And she leaned on the sill, and looked into the street, loving the men and women who passed, because she did not know them. She looked at the downtrodden buildings over the street, and at the sky, wet and dingy, or sometimes blue, and she felt she had never seen buildings or sky before. And then she went back to the chair, empty, her mind a blank. Sometimes she talked aloud, saying nothing— an exclamation, meaningless, followed by a comment about the floral pattern on the thin rug, or a stain on the green satin coverlet. For the most part, she woolgathered—what word is there for it?—brooded, wandered, simply went dark, feeling emptiness run deliciously through her veins like the movement of her blood.

This room had become more her own than the house she lived in. One morning she found Fred taking her a flight higher than usual. She stopped, refusing to go up, and demanded her usual room, Number 19. "Well, you'll have to wait half an hour then," he said. Willingly she descended to the dark disinfectant-smelling hall, and sat waiting until the two, man and woman, came down the stairs, giving her swift indifferent glances before they hurried out into the street, separating at the door. She went up to the room, *her* room, which they had just vacated. It was no less hers, though the windows were set wide open, and a maid was straightening the bed as she came in.

After these days of solitude, it was both easy to play her part as mother and wife, and difficult—because it was so easy: she felt an impostor. She felt as if her shell moved here, with her family, answering to Mummy, Mother, Susan, Mrs. Rawlings. She was surprised no one saw through her, that she wasn't turned out of doors, as a fake. On the contrary, it seemed the children loved her more; Matthew and she "got on" pleasantly, and Mrs. Parkes was happy in her work under (for the most part, it must be confessed) Sophie Traub. At night she lay beside her husband, and they made love again, apparently just as they used to, when they were really married. But she, Susan, or the being who answered so readily and improbably to the name of Susan, was not there: she was in Fred's Hotel, in Paddington, waiting for the easing hours of solitude to begin.

Soon she made a new arrangement with Fred and with Sophie. It was for five days a week. As for the money, five pounds, she simply asked Matthew for it. She saw that she was not even frightened he might ask what for: he would give it to her, she knew that, and yet it was terrifying it could be so, for this close couple, these partners, had once known the destination of every shilling they must spend. He agreed to give her five pounds a week. She asked for just so much, not a penny more. He sounded indifferent about it. It was as if he were paying her, she thought: *paying her off* —yes, that was it. Terror came back for a moment, when she understood this, but she stilled it: things had gone too far for that. Now, every week, on Sunday nights, he gave her five pounds, turning away from her before their eyes could meet on the transaction. As for Sophie Traub, she was to be somewhere in or near the house until six at night, after which she was free. She was not to cook, or to clean, she was simply to be there. So she gardened or sewed, and asked friends in, being a person who was bound to have a lot of friends. If the children were sick, she nursed them. If teachers telephoned, she answered them sensibly. For the five daytimes in the school week, she was altogether the mistress of the house.

One night in the bedroom, Matthew asked: "Susan, I don't want to interfere—don't think that, please—but are you sure you are well?"

She was brushing her hair at the mirror. She made two more strokes on either side of her head, before she replied: "Yes, dear, I am sure I am well."

He was again lying on his back, his big blond head on his hands, his elbows angled up and part-concealing his face. He said: "Then Susan, I have to ask you this question, though you must understand, I'm not putting any sort of pressure on you." (Susan heard the word pressure with dismay, because this was inevitable, of course she could not go on like this.) "Are things going to go on like this?"

"Well," she said, going vague and bright and idiotic again, so as to escape: "Well, I don't see why not."

He was jerking his elbows up and down, in annoyance or in pain, and, looking at him, she saw he had got thin, even gaunt; and restless angry movements were not what she remembered of him. He said: "Do you want a divorce, is that it?"

At this, Susan only with the greatest difficulty stopped herself from laughing: she could hear the bright bubbling laughter she *would* have emitted, had she let herself. He could only mean one thing: she had a lover, and that was why she spent her days in London, as lost to him as if she had vanished to another continent.

Then the small panic set in again: she understood that he hoped she did have a lover, he was begging her to say so, because otherwise it would be too terrifying.

She thought this out, as she brushed her hair, watching the fine black stuff fly up to make its little clouds of electricity, hiss, hiss, hiss. Behind her head, across the room, was a blue wall. She realised she was absorbed in watching the black hair making shapes against the blue. She should be answering him. "Do *you* want a divorce, Matthew?"

He said: "That surely isn't the point, is it?"

"You brought it up, I didn't," she said, brightly, suppressing meaningless tinkling laughter.

Next day she asked Fred: "Have enquiries been made for me?"

He hesitated, and she said: "I've been coming here a year now. I've made no trouble, and you've been paid every day. I have a right to be told."

"As a matter of fact, Mrs. Jones, a man did come asking."

"A man from a detective agency?"

"Well, he could have been, couldn't he?"

"I was asking you . . . well, what did you tell him?"

"I told him a Mrs. Jones came every weekday from ten until five or six and stayed in Number Nineteen by herself."

"Describing me?"

"Well Mrs. Jones, I had no alternative. Put yourself in my place."

"By rights I should deduct what that man gave you for the information."

He raised shocked eyes: she was not the sort of person to make jokes like this! Then he chose to laugh: a pinkish wet slit appeared across his white crinkled face: his eyes positively begged her to laugh, otherwise he might lose some money. She remained grave, looking at him.

He stopped laughing and said: "You want to go up now?" —returning to the familiarity, the comradeship, of the country where no questions are asked, on which (and he knew it) she depended completely.

She went up to sit in her wicker chair. But it was not the same. Her husband had searched her out. (The world had searched her out.) The pressures were on her. She was here with his connivance. He might walk in at any moment, here, into Room 19. She imagined the report from the detective agency: "A woman calling herself Mrs. Jones, fitting the description of your wife (etc., etc., etc.), stays alone all day in Room No. 19. She insists on this room, waits for it if it is engaged. As far as the proprietor knows, she receives no visitors there, male or female." A report something on these lines, Matthew must have received.

Well of course he was right: things couldn't go on like

this. He had put an end to it all simply by sending the detective after her.

She tried to shrink herself back into the shelter of the room, a snail pecked out of its shell and trying to squirm back. But the peace of the room had gone. She was trying consciously to revive it, trying to let go into the dark creative trance (or whatever it was) that she had found there. It was no use, yet she craved for it, she was as ill as a suddenly deprived addict.

Several times she returned to the room, to look for herself there, but instead she found the unnamed spirit of restlessness, a prickling fevered hunger for movement, an irritable self-consciousness that made her brain feel as if it had coloured lights going on and off inside it. Instead of the soft dark that had been the room's air, were now waiting for her demons that made her dash blindly about, muttering words of hate; she was impelling herself from point to point like a moth dashing itself against a windowpane, sliding to the bottom, fluttering off on broken wings, then crashing into the invisible barrier again. And again and again. Soon she was exhausted, and she told Fred that for a while she would not be needing the room, she was going on holiday. Home she went, to the big white house by the river. The middle of a weekday, and she felt guilty at returning to her own home when not expected. She stood unseen, looking in at the kitchen window. Mrs. Parkes, wearing a discarded floral overall of Susan's, was stooping to slide something into the oven. Sophie, arms folded, was leaning her back against a cupboard and laughing at some joke made by a girl not seen before by Susan—a dark foreign girl, Sophie's visitor. In an armchair Molly, one of the twins, lay curled, sucking her thumb and watching the grownups. She must have some sickness, to be kept from school. The child's listless face, the dark circles under her eyes, hurt Susan: Molly was looking at the three grownups working and talking in exactly the same way Susan looked at the four through the kitchen window: she was remote, shut off from them.

But then, just as Susan imagined herself going in, picking up the little girl, and sitting in an armchair with her, stroking her probably heated forehead, Sophie did just that: she had been standing on one leg, the other knee flexed, its foot set against the wall. Now she let her foot in its ribbon-tied red shoe slide down the wall, stood solid on two feet, clapping her hands before and behind her, and sang a couple of lines in German, so that the child lifted her heavy eyes at her and began to smile. Then she walked, or rather skipped, over to the child, swung her up, and let her fall into her lap at the same moment she sat herself. She said "Hopla! Hopla! Molly . . ." and began stroking the dark untidy young head that Molly laid on her shoulder for comfort.

Well. . . . Susan blinked the tears of farewell out of her eyes, and went quietly up the house to her bedroom. There she sat looking at the river through the trees. She felt at peace, but in a way that was new to her. She had no desire to move, to talk, to do anything at all. The devils that had haunted the house, the garden, were not there; but she knew it was because her soul was in Room 19 in Fred's Hotel; she was not really here at all. It was a sensation that should have been frightening: to sit at her own bedroom window, listening to Sophie's rich young voice sing German nursery songs to her child, listening to Mrs. Parkes clatter and move below, and to know that all this had nothing to do with her: she was already out of it.

Later, she made herself go down and say she was home: it was unfair to be here unannounced. She took lunch with Mrs. Parkes, Sophie, Sophie's Italian friend Maria, and her daughter Molly, and felt like a visitor.

A few days later, at bedtime, Matthew said: "Here's your five pounds," and pushed them over at her. Yet he must have known she had not been leaving the house at all.

She shook her head, gave it back to him, and said, in explanation, not in accusation: "As soon as you knew where I was, there was no point."

He nodded, not looking at her. He was turned away from her: thinking, she knew, how best to handle this wife who terrified him.

He said: "I wasn't trying to . . . it's just that I was worried."

"Yes, I know."

"I must confess that I was beginning to wonder . . ."

"You thought I had a lover?"

"Yes, I am afraid I did."

She knew that he wished she had. She sat wondering how to say: "For a year now I've been spending all my days in a very sordid hotel room. It's the place where I'm happy. In fact, without it I don't exist." She heard herself saying this, and understood how terrified he was that she might. So instead she said: "Well, perhaps you're not far wrong."

Probably Matthew would think the hotel proprietor lied: he would want to think so.

"Well," he said, and she could hear his voice spring up, so to speak, with relief: "in that case I must confess I've got a bit of an affair on myself."

She said, detached and interested: "Really? Who is she?" and saw Matthew's startled look because of this reaction.

"It's Phil. Phil Hunt."

She had known Phil Hunt well in the old unmarried days. She was thinking: No, she won't do, she's too neurotic and difficult. She's never been happy yet. Sophie's much better: Well Matthew will see that himself, as sensible as he is.

This line of thought went on in silence, while she said aloud: "It's no point telling you about mine, because you don't know him."

Quick, quick, invent, she thought. Remember how you invented all that nonsense for Miss Townsend.

She began slowly, careful not to contradict herself: "His name is Michael"—(*Michael What?*)—"Michael Plant." (What a silly name!) "He's rather like you—in looks, I mean." And indeed, she could imagine herself being touched by no one but Matthew himself. "He's a publisher." (Really? Why?) "He's got a wife already and two children."

She brought out this fantasy, proud of herself.

Matthew said: "Are you two thinking of marrying?"

She said, before she could stop herself: "Good God, *no!*"

She realised, if Matthew wanted to marry Phil Hunt, that this was too emphatic, but apparently it was all right, for his voice sounded relieved as he said: "It is a bit impossible to imagine oneself married to anyone else, isn't it?" With which he pulled her to him, so that her head lay on his shoulder. She turned her face into the dark of his flesh, and listened to the blood pounding through her ears saying: I am alone, I am alone, I am alone.

In the morning Susan lay in bed while he dressed.

He had been thinking things out in the night, because now he said: "Susan, why don't we make a foursome?"

Of course, she said to herself, of course he would be bound to say that. If one is sensible, if one is reasonable, if one never allows oneself a base thought or an envious emotion, naturally one says: Let's make a foursome!

"Why not?" she said.

"We could all meet for lunch. I mean, it's ridiculous, you sneaking off to filthy hotels, and me staying late at the office, and all the lies everyone has to tell."

What on earth did I say his name was?—she panicked, then said: "I think it's a good idea, but Michael is away at the moment. When he comes back though—and I'm sure you two would like each other."

"He's away, is he? So that's why you've been . . ." Her husband put his hand to the knot of his tie in a gesture of male coquetry she would not before have associated with him; and he bent to kiss her cheek with the expression that goes with the words: Oh you naughty little puss! And she felt its answering look, naughty and coy, come onto her face.

Inside she was dissolving in horror at them both, at how far they had both sunk from honesty of emotion.

So now she was saddled with a lover, and he had a mistress! How ordinary, how reassuring, how jolly! And now they would make a foursome of it, and go about to theatres and restaurants. After all, the Rawlings could well afford that sort of thing, and presumably the publisher Michael Plant could afford to do himself and his mistress quite well. No, there was nothing to stop the four of them developing the most intricate relationship of civilised tolerance, all enveloped in a charming afterglow of autumnal passion. Perhaps they would all go off on holidays together? She had known people who did. Or perhaps Matthew would draw the line there? Why should he, though, if he was capable of talking about "foursomes" at all?

She lay in the empty bedroom, listening to the car drive off with Matthew in it, off to work. Then she heard the children clattering off to school to the accompaniment of Sophie's cheerfully ringing voice. She slid down into the hollow of the bed, for shelter against her own irrelevance. And she stretched our her hand to the hollow where her husband's body had lain, but found no comfort there: he was not her husband. She curled herself up in a small tight ball under the clothes: she could stay here all day, all week, indeed, all her life.

But in a few days she must produce Michael Plant, and—but how? She must presumably find some agreeable man prepared to impersonate a publisher called Michael Plant. And in return for which she would—what? Well, for one thing they would make love. The idea made her want to cry with sheer exhaustion. Oh no, she had finished with all that—the proof of it was that the words "make love," or even imagining it, trying hard to revive no more than the pleasures of sensuality, let alone affection, or love, made her want to run away and hide from the sheer effort of the thing. . . . Good Lord, why make love at all? Why make love with anyone? Or if you are going to make love, what does it matter who with? Why shouldn't she simply walk into the street, pick up a man and have a roaring sexual affair with him? Why not? Or even with Fred? What difference did it make?

But she had let herself in for it—an interminable stretch of time with a lover, called Michael, as part of a gallant civilised foursome. Well, she could not, and she would not.

She got up, dressed, went down to find Mrs. Parkes, and asked her for the loan of a pound, since Matthew, she said, had forgotten to leave her money. She exchanged with Mrs. Parkes variations on the theme that husbands are all the same, they don't think, and without saying a word to Sophie, whose voice could be heard upstairs from the telephone, walked to the underground, travelled to South Kensington, changed to the Inner Circle, got out at Paddington, and walked to Fred's Hotel. There she told Fred that she wasn't going on holiday after all, she needed the room. She would have to wait an hour, Fred said. She went to a busy tea-room-cum-restaurant around the corner, and sat watching the people flow in and out the door that kept swinging open and shut, watched them mingle and merge and separate, felt her being flow into them, into their movement. When the hour was up she left a half crown for her pot of tea, and left the place without looking back at it, just as she had left her house, the big, beautiful white house, without another

look, but silently dedicating it to Sophie. She returned to
Fred, received the key of No. 19, now free, and ascended
the grimy stairs slowly, letting floor after floor fall away
below her, keeping her eyes lifted, so that floor after floor
descended jerkily to her level of vision, and fell away out
of sight.

No. 19 was the same. She saw everything with an acute,
narrow, checking glance: the cheap shine of the satin spread,
which had been replaced carelessly after the two bodies had
finished their convulsions under it; a trace of powder on the
glass that topped the chest of drawers; an intense green shade
in a fold of the curtain. She stood at the window, looking
down, watching people pass and pass and pass until her mind
went dark from the constant movement. Then she sat in the
wicker chair, letting herself go slack. But she had to be careful, because she did not want, today, to be surprised by
Fred's knock at five o'clock.

The demons were not here. They had gone forever, because she was buying her freedom from them. She was slip-
ping already into the dark fructifying dream that seemed to
caress her inwardly, like the movement of her blood . . .
but she had to think about Matthew first. Should she write a
letter for the coroner? But what should she say? She would
like to leave him with the look on his face she had seen this
morning—banal, admittedly, but at least confidently healthy.
Well, that was impossible, one did not look like that with
a wife dead from suicide. But how to leave him believing
she was dying because of a man—because of the fascinating
publisher Michael Plant? Oh, how ridiculous! How absurd!
How humiliating! But she decided not to trouble about it,
simply not to think about the living. If he wanted to believe
she had a lover, he would believe it. And he *did* want to believe it. Even when he had found out that there was no
publisher in London called Michael Plant, he would think:
Oh poor Susan, she was afraid to give me his real name.

And what did it matter whether he married Phil Hunt or
Sophie? Though it ought to be Sophie, who was already the
mother of those children . . . and what hypocrisy to sit
here worrying about the children, when she was going to
leave them because she had not got the energy to stay.

She had about four hours. She spent them delightfully,

darkly, sweetly, letting herself slide gently, gently, to the edge of the river. Then, with hardly a break in her consciousness, she got up, pushed the thin rug against the door, made sure the windows were tight shut, put two shillings in the meter, and turned on the gas. For the first time since she had been in the room she lay on the hard bed that smelled stale, that smelled of sweat and sex.

She lay on her back on the green satin cover, but her legs were chilly. She got up, found a blanket folded in the bottom of the chest of drawers, and carefully covered her legs with it. She was quite content lying there, listening to the faint soft hiss of the gas that poured into the room, into her lungs, into her brain, as she drifted off into the dark river.

RECENT FICTION TITLES BY IMPORTANT CONTEMPORARY AUTHORS FROM BALLANTINE BOOKS

NIKOS KAZANTZAKIS: "One of the great figures on the stage of world literature." (*New York Times Book Review*.) Now in print:

ZORBA THE GREEK	75¢
FREEDOM OR DEATH	95¢
THE GREEK PASSION	95¢

ANTHONY BURGESS: "The ablest satirist to appear since Evelyn Waugh." (Stanley Edgar Hyman in *The New Leader*.) Now in print:

THE WANTING SEED	60¢
HONEY FOR THE BEARS	60¢
A CLOCKWORK ORANGE	60¢
NOTHING LIKE THE SUN	60¢

DORIS LESSING: Author of *The Golden Notebook*. "One of the most powerfully equipped young novelists now writing." (C. P. Snow.) Now in print:

THE GRASS IS SINGING	60¢
THE HABIT OF LOVING	60¢
A MAN AND TWO WOMEN	75¢

ZOÉ OLDENBOURG: "The foremost living fictional interpreter of the Middle Ages." (Orville Prescott in *The New York Times*.) Now in print:

THE CORNERSTONE	95¢
DESTINY OF FIRE	95¢